M000266194

THIS IS MY BODY

August 2020

THIS IS MY BODY

ELENA GRAF

Purple Hand Press
www.purplehandpress.com

This is a work of fiction. Names, characters, places and incidents are the product of the author's imagination or used fictitiously, and any resemblance to actual persons, living or dead, businesses, institutions, companies, events, or locales is entirely coincidental.

Trade Paperback Edition
ISBN-13 978-1-7334492-3-6
Kindle Edition
ISBN-13 978-1-7334492-4-3
ePub Edition
ISBN-13 978-1-7334492-5-0

Editor: Laure Dherbécourt
Cover design: Castle Hill Media, LLC
Cover photo: Tursk Aleksandra

03.23.20

To Kathleen Adkins, my wingman

1

The woman walked at a brisk pace. Her red hair, tied in a loose ponytail, swayed with the rhythm of her steps. Her arms pumped up and down to the same beat. Obviously, this was a walk for exercise, not a morning stroll. Her legs were toned but deadly pale. Being a redhead, she probably needed to guard against too much sun.

Erika Bultmann, who had been reading on the porch of her summer cottage, stared. She stared not only because the woman was stunning, but because there was so much bare flesh. The last time Erika had seen the Reverend Lucille Bartlett, rector of St. Margaret's by the Sea Episcopal Church, she'd been modestly dressed in a black suit and wearing a clerical collar.

Although Erika had spent a lovely evening with Lucy Bartlett during the winter holidays and found her company stimulating in every sense of the word, she didn't immediately call out to get her attention. Erika was still on her first cup of coffee, hadn't showered, or brushed her teeth. The worn T-shirt and cotton shorts she wore to bed was not an outfit for greeting even the most casual acquaintance, and especially not one whom she very much wanted to impress. Instead, she watched Lucy head down Ocean Road toward the other end of the barrier island.

Erika checked the time on her phone. If she showered quickly, she could be dressed and looking presentable by the time Lucy passed the cottage on her return. Erika set aside her vintage copy of Habermas's *Erkenntnis und Interesse*. It dated back to her graduate school days. The binding had split, and the pages had begun to yellow, but it was full of invaluable notes, so she always handled it with care.

Stripping on the way to the bathroom, Erika headed straight for the shower. *Quick. I need to be quick.* She gave herself a fast scrub in all the important places. She blew dry her chin-length, blond hair, taking a little more time than usual to smooth it. She put on some makeup and lipstick and selected the least-wrinkled polo shirt and Bermuda shorts from her suitcase.

When she finished dressing, she checked the time, relieved to see that she had five minutes to spare. She brewed a fresh cup of coffee and returned to the porch, where she slouched in an Adirondack chair and resumed reading. Her aim was to appear relaxed and casual when Lucy returned. Erika checked the time on her phone with anxious glances while watching for Lucy out of the corner of her eye. Finally, there she was, right on time.

"Well, hello there!" Erika called when Lucy approached. Startled, the woman stopped in her tracks. She leaned on her knees to catch her breath, then looked all around her, up and down, trying to locate the speaker. Standing in the brilliant sunlight, she couldn't see into the porch. "Over here!" said Erika, rising. She was less careful of Habermas this time and needed to use her reflexes to rescue the book before it landed on the floor and spilled its pages.

Lucy's mouth curved up. She had the kind of smile that could light a darkened room. "Erika? Is that you?"

"It is," said Erika, opening the door. "I hardly recognized you without the collar."

Lucy blushed a little, which Erika found charming. As she came near, Erika could see the faint freckles on her face. Without makeup, Lucy looked wholesome and girlish.

"It's so nice to see you again," said Lucy, stepping into the porch and offering her hand.

"I see you're out for your morning constitutional." As she took the woman's hand, Erika looked directly into her green eyes because she so much wanted to gaze into the cleavage below. Glistening with a faint sheen of perspiration, it simply begged for attention. *Don't look*, Erika mentally ordered herself. *Don't!* Lucy turned, distracted by the footsteps of a runner passing by, and Erika stole a quick glance down her shirt. *Good God!* She managed to return her gaze to Lucy's face just in time.

"I try to get in a walk every day," Lucy explained. "I don't always succeed."

"You're looking quite fit, so it seems you do."

Lucy laughed softly. "Thank you. Good genes, I think."

"Would you like a cup of coffee?" Erika asked in her most casual voice.

Lucy pulled the phone out of her armband and checked the time. "A quick one. I need to be back by 9:30 for my bereavement group."

"I could drive you to the rectory."

"Which would defeat the purpose of the walk," said Lucy with one of her solar flare smiles.

"Well, come in. It takes only a minute to make a cup. Liz gave me one of those single-serve coffee makers for my birthday. Highly efficient."

"I understand that Germans value efficiency."

"Yes, we do."

Lucy followed Erika into the cottage. "This is so charming," she said, looking around. Erika wondered what she really thought. The furniture was all second hand, perfectly serviceable, if a bit shabby. The New England colonial style had always struck Erika as kitsch, but in Maine such furniture was cheap and abundant. The summer residents furnished their cottages from the second-hand stores masquerading as antique shops along Route 1. Erika drew the line at nautical knickknacks or clutter of any kind. Perhaps Lucy would think the local watercolor seascapes were a bit stark. Erika's mother had painted the few cheerful ones.

"Have a seat," said Erika gesturing to the small table in the kitchen.

Again, Lucy looked around, taking everything in. "When did you get back?" she asked, gazing at the pile of boxes in the corner.

"Last night. I was reading a bit before I tackled unpacking. It's a daunting task. I've brought more than usual. This time, I'm staying through the winter."

"You are?" asked Lucy, a hopeful note rising in her voice.

"I'm on sabbatical."

"That's great! We'll be neighbors now."

"Not exactly," replied Erika for no good reason. Obviously, Lucy wasn't trying to be precise, just making conversation.

"Do you have a project for your sabbatical?" Lucy pulled a Windsor chair away from the table. The legs made a little scraping sound on the linoleum.

"I've been writing a book for years. This summer, I hope to finish it. Now that I've resigned as chairman of the department, I have more space in my brain for scholarly pursuits." Erika tapped her temple with her fingertip for emphasis.

"What's the subject of your book?"

"Jürgen Habermas and his theories of political discourse. Apt, I think, given the current state of affairs."

Lucy nodded. Erika wondered if the woman had the least idea who Habermas was. No matter. She was intelligent, and certainly, there were other things to talk about besides philosophy. After thirty-five years of teaching the subject at Colby College, Erika had certainly had her fill.

"I like dark roast," said Erika, pointing to a coffee bag, "but I have a breakfast blend if that's too strong for you."

"No, it's fine. The darker the better!" said Lucy with another sunny smile.

Erika brewed Lucy's coffee and set the mug in front of her. She also made coffee for herself. The cup she'd abandoned on the porch would be cold by now, and she didn't want to waste a second with Lucy to retrieve it.

"I'm sorry I can't offer you breakfast," said Erika. "I haven't been to the market yet."

"Thank you. I've eaten." Again, Lucy looked around, studying the copper pots on the wall. When her gaze returned, her green eyes were mesmerizing.

Erika sat down in the chair opposite her. "Is this the usual route for your walk?"

"Unless I walk on the beach. Sometimes, I walk with Liz Stolz, but she walks too fast, and I'm out of breath by the end."

Erika nodded. "Liz. I must call and tell her that I've arrived, but I know what you mean about walking with her. I like to converse when I walk, and a brisk pace makes it rather difficult."

"Maybe you could walk with me," suggested Lucy brightly. "I'm always happy to slow down for good conversation."

Erika wanted to leap up and say, "Yes!" But she decided a more casual attitude might serve her better. "What a lovely idea," she said neutrally. "We must set a time."

"Unfortunately, it will have to wait. I'm pretty busy this week, so sunrise walks it is."

"That's a bit early for me." Erika became anxious. The opportunity to see Lucy again seemed to be slipping away. "Dinner perhaps?" She instantly scolded herself for being too forward.

Lucy looked momentarily surprised. "Sure. When?"

"Tonight?" Now, she really was being too forward.

But Lucy smiled and said, "All right. What time?"

"I'll pick you up at six."

Lucy nodded. "Fine."

Lucy stayed for another half hour, drawing out Erika with questions about teaching at Colby. She listened with the sort of open interest that makes people want to share their stories—a very good quality in a priest, Erika decided.

Her guest glanced at the clock over the sink. "Sorry, but I have to run. I need to get in a shower before my bereavement group." She got up and carefully rinsed her mug. "Thank you for the coffee."

"I'll see you soon."

"Yes," said Lucy with another radiant smile. "Soon."

Erika watched the red ponytail wag as Lucy resumed her power walk. She noted that the bare flesh was firm and barely jiggled despite the brisk pace.

***

"Here's Liz," said the receptionist as a door opened, and a tall woman with iron-gray hair stepped out. Liz Stolz was wearing her summer "uniform"—a polo shirt, cropped pants of some high-performance material, and sturdy hiking sandals. Only the stethoscope around her neck identified her as a doctor and not a tourist in need of medical care.

"Erika!" Liz called in a delighted voice. "*Wann bist du hier angekommen?*" She caught Erika in a hug.

"*Gestern Abend.*"

"Yesterday! And you didn't call? Bad girl! You could have come for dinner."

Erika shook her head. "I got in too late for dinner, and I had to unpack the car. Besides, I never know when you have guests."

"No one's visiting now. It's a little early. The kids are still in school."

"Of course," said Erika. "I'd forgotten. College schedules are so different."

"The good news is the beaches are still empty. More for us!" said Liz with a quick laugh.

Her friend laughed easily now, but at the end of her term as chief of surgery at Yale-New Haven, Liz had become angry and depressed. Being in her company was difficult, especially for Erika, who was naturally pessimistic and cynical. She'd always counted on Liz's heartiness to cheer her up. Since moving to Maine and buying Hobbs Family Practice, Liz was much more her old self—the wry, witty woman Erika remembered from forty years ago, when she was a graduate student at Yale and Liz, a first-year surgical resident.

"I stopped by to ask if you have time for lunch today," Erika explained.

Liz drummed her fingers on the counter of the receptionist station. "Ginny, can you look at my schedule to see if I have time for lunch with Erika?"

The office manager scanned her computer screen. "Mrs. Petersen canceled her one o'clock. After your 12:30, you're free for the rest of the day," she said in an efficient voice.

Liz turned back to Erika. "One o'clock okay? That will give me time to finish my notes and wind down here."

"Perfect. I'll pick up my groceries. Then I'll meet you back here."

After she left the office, Erika headed to the grocery store. She had deliberately planned to arrive in the middle of the week. Saturday was changeover day for the summer cottages. The weekend traffic was ridiculous, and the lines in the supermarket invariably stretched back into the aisles. Because Memorial Day was fast approaching, there were more visitors than usual. Erika made quick work of her purchases, mostly perishables she hadn't brought from her apartment in the faculty residence at Colby.

After she put away her groceries, she still had some time before meeting Liz, so she unpacked her clothing. As she did, she found a child's toy under the dresser. She puzzled over it for a moment until she realized it belonged to one of Maggie's granddaughters. When she saw Liz, she'd give it to her to return.

Her offer of the cottage to Maggie's daughter and her two young children had been impulsive. One reason she hated to rent the place was the possibility of a mess on her return, but she was pleased to see the place was orderly and spotless.

Erika met Liz in her office at the appointed hour. Liz was running late with a patient, as usual.

"She won't be much longer," Ginny assured her. "When did you get in, Dr. Bultmann?"

"Last night. I'm still unpacking. And please, call me Erika."

"You came at the right time. The spring has been so cold and rainy. That's how it is here in Maine. After a long winter, it's suddenly summer."

"It was a long, dreary winter in Waterville as well, and an equally dreary spring."

Liz came down the hall with her patient, an elderly man with a cane, and gave Ginny instructions for scheduling a future appointment. Then she turned to Erika with a smile. "Ready?"

"Absolutely!"

"Leave your car here," said Liz, as they headed out to the parking lot. "I'll drop you off on the way back. Down the Hatch okay?"

"Yes, it's not summer without a lobster roll and a cup of chowder."

"You sound like a tourist."

"I'm officially a resident. I qualify for a beach pass, even though I don't need one."

"That's true," said Liz, climbing into the cab of her truck. "Got mine already." She pointed to a brightly colored sticker on her windshield.

"You look good, Liz." Erika strapped herself into the passenger seat. "Married life agrees with you. You seem very content."

"I am. Maggie takes good care of me."

"And her health is good? No recurrence?"

"Not yet," said Liz, tapping her head with her knuckles because there was no wood in reach.

Erika sighed. "Liz, please don't become a pessimist. That's my job."

Liz laughed. "I wouldn't dare deprive you." When Liz looked at her for more than a moment, Erika had the sense that she was doing a quick, physician's assessment. "You look pretty good yourself. Are you in a better place with Jeannine's death?"

"Yes and no. Sometimes I think I'm fine about it. I go about my business as usual and feel relatively normal. Then, I find myself sobbing with grief."

Liz nodded thoughtfully. "Grief doesn't run in a straight path. You know, Lucy Bartlett runs a bereavement group at her church."

Erika shook her head. "Psychoanalysis is nonsense, and groups? Not for me." She sighed. "Sometimes, I wish Jeannine and I had made more of a commitment. I always thought we'd have more time." Erika shook her head. "You never know."

"No, you don't. But you never struck me as the commitment type."

"Well, we were together for almost twenty years. That's not insignificant."

"But you both had other partners."

"We did, and it worked for us."

Liz turned on Harbor Road. "Tide's in, I see. The marsh is so much prettier when it is."

Erika leaned forward to take in the full view of the salt marsh.

"Spectacular. This is why I love it here, all those myriad shades of green. I'm so glad you talked me into buying the cottage."

"It was a good investment. The house is small, but it has good bones."

"As long as I can count on you as my handy man, it's a good thing."

"Are you still thinking about adding on?"

Erika nodded. "I have all the plans and the planning board has approved them. Thank heavens, the previous owner raised the cottage to the level for the new flood map, or I could never afford it."

"So, what's preventing you from going ahead?"

"I'm not convinced I need all that space. After all, I'm only one person. And I'm still undecided about where to retire."

Liz found a parking space along the road. "Sorry we have to walk so far. I didn't expect it to be this busy."

They walked back to the restaurant, which was little more than an old shack. An enclosed porch had been added to create a dining room. There was a beached lobster boat sitting next to the completely filled parking area. Tourists took a while to find the place, but once they did, it was hard to keep them away.

The tables were arranged family style. Diners sat wherever they found vacant places at the long tables. A roll of paper towels, hanging overhead, provided napkins. Condiments were arranged in a small galvanized bucket. The salt and pepper came in beer bottles with holes in the caps. The rustic atmosphere was part of the appeal, but the food was excellent.

"I wish this place were open all year," Liz said as they sat down. She scrunched up her legs to her body to get them under the table without kicking her neighbor. "At times like this, it's no fun being tall."

"Agreed," said Erika, doing the same. She glanced at specials on the chalk board. "I already know what I want, and fortunately, it's on special."

"Lobster rolls and chowder are always on special when the summer people are here."

The waitress came and they ordered a local beer to accompany the special. A few minutes later, their beer arrived in frosted glasses. "To summer!" Liz proposed. They clicked glasses and drank. The brew was crisp and citrusy.

"Delicious," said Erika.

With the back of her hand, Liz wiped a bit of foam from her upper lip. "Was your place clean? Alina left it in good shape when she moved out, but I asked Ellie to give it a once over before you arrived."

"Your housekeeper is excellent. The place was spotless. But I did find this." Erika took the miniature horse out of her bag.

"That's Nicki's. I'll return it for you." Liz smiled and set the toy on the table. "I hope you know how grateful Alina is for letting them stay there this winter."

Erika shrugged. "No one else was using it. I was glad to have the cottage occupied." She took a sip of beer. "So, now you've bought her a condominium? In Scarborough?"

"I didn't *buy it* for her. I'm holding the mortgage because her credit was wrecked by her idiot husband."

"It's a shame. So many young women raising children alone. Men just aren't what they used to be."

Liz laughed. "Neither are women."

"Speaking of women. I saw her."

"Who?"

"The good Reverend Bartlett."

Liz raised her brows. "That didn't take long."

"Her morning constitutional takes her past my cottage."

"When she doesn't walk with me on the beach…"

"She said you walk too fast."

Liz made a face. "Really? She never told me."

"Maybe she's afraid of you. Most people are until they get to know you."

"Good to know. Thanks, Erika," said Liz, sounding mildly insulted.

"My pleasure." Erika knew Liz would be easily mollified with some sarcasm and a smile. "I invited her for dinner."

Liz sat up straight. "But I already told Maggie you were coming for dinner. She's making your favorite—tandoori chicken."

Erika frowned at the wrinkle in her plans, but she hadn't seen Liz and Maggie since spring and certainly owed them a visit. "Do you mind if I bring a friend?"

Liz grinned. "Lucy? Sure. Why not? Although I'm surprised she's still speaking to you."

"And why wouldn't she be?"

"She asked for your email address, but she said you never replied."

Erika sighed. "Oh, I meant to reply, but her email showed up in the middle of that ridiculous sexual harassment suit. What a mess! I ended up firing the bastard, but there was tenure involved, so it wasn't easy. Lawyers and board meetings ad nauseam. If I ever talk about taking on an administrative role again, shoot me."

"I wouldn't suggest that to me. You know I can." Liz patted her handbag, the special one in which she carried her pistol.

"If I ever find myself incapacitated, I may ask you to do me the favor."

"We have drugs for that, and it's the law now."

"That created quite a ruckus. Idiotic religious right." Erika rolled her eyes to convey her loathing for such people.

Liz put down her glass after a few gulps of beer. "Was she friendly?"

"Lucy? Very much so," said Erika. "What's her story? I wonder."

Liz raised her shoulders to her ears.

"Liz! You know something. Tell me!"

"She's my patient. I can't."

"That's not fair. I'm your oldest friend."

"Actually, Maggie is my oldest friend."

"Don't get technical on me. You know what I mean. If you can't say anything, just answer yes or no. If I made an advance, would she be repulsed?"

"I doubt it. She's a worldly woman, despite the collar, and very open minded."

"That's not what I meant!"

"I know what you meant."

Erika leaned forward and gave her a pleading look. "Liz, please. Just give me a tiny hint." She raised pinched fingers to indicate how small a hint she was willing to accept.

Liz shook her head. "Sorry. You'll just have to figure it out for yourself."

2

Lucy took off her clerical blouse and tentatively sniffed the armpit to see if she could get another day out of it. Keeping up with the laundry was one of her biggest challenges. Her parishioners always stared when she came into the laundromat as if they never imagined priests needing to wash their clothes. Lucy liked to fluff out her panties before she folded them to remind people that she was human like the rest of them.

She wished there was a washing machine and dryer at home so she wouldn't have to waste time dragging her laundry into town. Liz Stolz had looked over the plumbing in the rectory and said it would be easy to add appliances to the spare room off the office because it backed up to the kitchen. Liz was even willing to run the pipes and wiring to hook them up. "Just don't tell the code inspector I did the work. Say you did it yourself." Lucy hated to lie even more than she hated to take advantage of Liz. For one thing, she was the town doctor, not a plumber, and for another, Liz was far too generous for her own good.

But saving the time she spent in the laundromat made sense. When Lucy had applied to be rector of a parish in a resort town in Maine, she'd imagined leisurely walks by the ocean and time to read on the beach. Instead, her life was jammed from end to end with parish business, liturgies, chaplain duties, and a surprising amount of counseling. When Maggie Fitzgerald had said there was a lot going on in Hobbs, she wasn't exaggerating.

This was Lucy's first rectorate, and she was still shocked by the number of administrative duties that fell to her. The warden of St. Margaret's was elderly and failing. Fortunately, his term was almost done. Lucy hoped for the election of a younger, more vigorous member of the congregation, who could eventually shoulder some of the responsibility.

Lucy finished undressing and sponged off her makeup. She always associated this ritual with the end of a performance and her relief at having hit all the right notes. Before going on stage, there was that edge of anxiety pushing her to do her very best. The adrenalin rush was exciting. There were days when she missed the thrill, along with the bright lights and the swell of the orchestra at her feet. Since she was a girl, she had dreamed of singing at the Met. When she'd finally achieved it, the reality wasn't at all what she'd expected.

A part of her was glad she'd left that life behind: the travel, sleeping in a different city every night, her agent badgering her about the schedule and always pushing her to take on more engagements, arguments with conductors and directors. Being an opera star was about business, it seemed, not music.

Lucy loved music. One of the reasons she'd been drawn to the Episcopal Church was its long-standing music tradition. Although she'd left behind the operatic stage, she sang every day to keep her voice limber. The habit was so ingrained. Not exercising her voice would be like not brushing her teeth in the morning.

Lucy flipped through her closet to find something to wear for dinner. The closet was full of black, navy, gray, and black again. Sad and drab. It was summertime and she wanted to wear something bright. At the back of the closet, she found a red sleeveless dress, one of her favorites for stepping out on a special occasion. She hadn't worn it since she'd come to Hobbs, but until now, the weather hadn't been warm enough to go sleeveless. The dress had a modest neckline, but it was snug fitting, especially in the rear, and revealed every curve.

Lucy tried to picture Erika's face when she saw her in the red dress. Erika had obviously been a little shocked by Lucy's walking outfit. And did she really think she'd gotten away with checking out her cleavage?

The memory made Lucy smile. When they'd met last winter, Erika's interest came as a surprise. Lucy's appearance was so feminine no one ever guessed she preferred women. Men were always hitting on her, but never women.

Lucy loved listening to Erika talk. That English accent by way of German was charming. Lucy had only noticed because she had an ear for languages, which had been an enormous help when she was training to be an opera singer. Erika smiled when Lucy had asked about the slight German intonations. "I'm surprised anyone can hear it anymore. When I studied English in school, it was the Queen's proper English. But I really learned to speak the language in England, where we first landed after leaving the GDR." Erika explained that she and her parents had been refugees from East Germany in the 1970s. This strange twist in her story made her all the more intriguing.

Erika's wit was so dry, half of her quips went over Lucy's head, but at least, she explained things, unlike Liz, who sometimes left her hanging. Lucy also discovered that Erika was incredibly literate about music, well-traveled, and well-read. Her friendship would be very stimulating.

In the conversation, Lucy made the mistake of mentioning the theologian, Rudolf Bultmann. Erika made a face. "No relation, thank heavens!"

Wondering if she'd offended Erika, Lucy asked, "Are you an atheist?"

Erika frowned as she considered the question, which made Lucy anxious. "Atheism is far too strident for me," Erika said. "As a philosopher, I can no more disprove the existence of God than prove it. So, I confess ignorance. Much of philosophy is about admitting what we don't know."

Lucy admired the thoughtfulness and honesty of that response. This was no ordinary unbeliever. She could have real conversations about religion with this woman.

Afterwards, Lucy wondered if she'd conveyed her sexual interest that night. She was so bad at flirting because she never had to do it. Other people always took the initiative. Maybe if she'd responded more obviously, Erika would have answered her emails.

In the meanwhile, Lucy had kept up the conversation about Erika with Liz and Maggie. When she'd asked Liz how old her friend was, she'd bluntly said, "Sixty. Not bad for her age, don't you think?" Lucy certainly agreed. She found Erika more than attractive. She was almost as tall as her friend, Liz, shy maybe an inch, which meant she was a head taller than Lucy. She had a trim figure, obviously from looking after herself and exercise. Her blond hair was so pale Lucy realized only later that it was becoming white. And those stunning blue eyes, the palest eyes Lucy had ever seen.

Lucy glanced at the clock. She needed to get moving to be ready on time. She decided to take another shower, not because she needed one, but because the day had been so stressful. She wanted to wash it all away. The beat of the hot water always relaxed her. She lathered her hair and rinsed it. The red wasn't quite as vibrant as it had once been. Lately, she had begun to notice more grays. After all, she was fifty-five and should expect a few grays. She'd considered dyeing her hair, but so far, she'd decided to age gracefully.

She wrapped her hair in a towel while she put on her makeup, aiming for something dramatic rather than the standard conservative look she wore for priestly duties. As she applied the beige eye shadow and drew a crisp line across each lid, she realized her preparations were intended to tease out that look of admiration in Erika's eyes. Men looked at her like that every day, but there was something special about the way Erika looked at her.

Lucy decided to wear the red dress for the sheer pleasure of seeing Erika's reaction. As she laced up her wedge sandals, she hoped she wouldn't run into any parishioners. They might be a little surprised to see their priest in such a sexy outfit. Maybe she could talk Erika into going to dinner in Portland or Portsmouth to avoid them.

The doorbell rang. Lucy glanced at the clock by her bed. Five minutes early. Germans always seemed to think that being on time meant arriving early. When Lucy was a principal at the Stuttgart Opera, she'd arrived for her first rehearsal exactly on time and gotten a severe reprimand from the director. She was too young and inexperienced to even think of protesting. When she'd worked with the man many years later, and he tried to pull that stunt, she'd let him have it. Strange how those memories of the opera world kept returning, despite all those years away from the stage.

The bell rang again. Lucy grabbed her bag, hurried downstairs, and opened the door.

The expression on Erika's face was priceless. "My, but aren't you stunning!" Erika said, unabashedly looking her up and down. "What a lovely dress!" She frowned. "Perhaps I should have called to alert you to a slight change of plans."

Lucy held her breath and waited apprehensively for her to say more. *Please don't tell me we're going to eat in downtown Hobbs!* She breathed a sigh of relief when Erika said, "Maggie and Liz have invited us to dinner. I'm sorry, but I couldn't refuse. I haven't seen them for months, and Maggie is making a tandoori feast."

"Oh, I love her tandoori meals! But now, it seems I'm overdressed."

"Nonsense. You know Maggie. She'll dress up too. You actress types are always dressing the part." Erika gave her another frankly admiring look. "That wasn't an idle compliment I paid you. You are absolutely lovely!"

"Thank you. It's always nice to hear compliments."

"In that case, I shall make liberal use of them because they make you smile."

Lucy hooked her arm in Erika's as they walked to the car. "I like you. You can ask me out anytime."

Erika clicked open the doors of an Audi hatchback.

"This is just like Liz's car," said Lucy, climbing into the passenger seat.

"It is Liz's car, or it was." Erika clipped in her seat belt. "She sold it to me when she got a new one. You think I could afford such a vehicle on a professor's salary?"

Lucy shrugged. "I have no idea. Aren't professors paid well?"

"Professors at elite colleges like Colby are paid quite decently, but I've always been rather frugal. Comes of being so poor when we first left the GDR, and now, I'm saving like mad. I have a plan." She tapped her temple with her forefinger.

Lucy recognized she'd been set up to ask, "And what are you planning?"

"To retire early. After years of listening to freshmen rave about Nietzsche, I've hit my limit."

"Don't you like Nietzsche?"

Erika stared at her incredulously. "I adore Nietzsche. However, an eighteen-year-old can't possibly understand him. Most people can't."

"Try me."

"All right. What is the real meaning of the Eternal Return?"

"*Zarathustra*? Yes? It's a moral injunction to consider your actions as if you might have to live with the consequences over and over again into eternity."

"Very good," said Erika, looking at her with respect. "Is that what they teach now in seminary?"

Lucy laughed. "No. No. One of my friends was a philosophy major. She likes Nietzsche too."

"Let me guess. Liz Stolz. She likes to talk about Nietzsche when she has a few too many glasses of scotch." Erika navigated out of the parking lot.

"I've learned a lot from her."

"It sounds like you've become quite friendly with Liz."

"Maggie has taken me under her wing since she joined the choir and become active in the parish. She's helped ease me into the social network here. Liz is my friend too, but we're not as tight. You understand."

"Maggie is very warm and charming. Liz is...well, Liz." Erika chuckled.

"I spend a lot of time over there. It's my safe haven when things become overwhelming."

"We all need friends who can listen without judgment. Maggie and Liz are good people."

"They are," agreed Lucy.

There was a lull in the conversation as they drove to their destination. Lucy didn't mind. She'd done enough talking for one day, and the silence between them felt comfortable, not brittle as it often was on a first date. It was a date, wasn't it? The thought was both exciting and unsettling.

Lucy turned as she stifled a yawn. She was so tired. It had been impulsive to accept this invitation. She still had to put the finishing touches on her sermon for a funeral in the morning.

Hopefully, she'd have the energy for social conversation. The day had been overwhelming. One of her parishioners was going through a divorce from an abusive husband and needed so much attention. The woman was fast approaching the limit on pastoral counseling, and Lucy would soon have to take her on as a client in her practice or refer her to the mental health clinic. There was so much need in the community and so few resources.

"You're very quiet," Erika observed.

"Hard day." Lucy sighed.

"You mean priests don't sit around and pray all day? I suppose I should say kneel."

"My knees are pretty bad, which is why I don't run anymore. Kneeling a lot wouldn't be good for them."

"Indeed, not."

"As the rector, I have a lot of administrative duties—managing the finances, making sure all the parish buildings are maintained. I visit parishioners in the hospital and shut-ins and bring them communion. This morning I had a funeral after my bereavement group."

"Spiritual and corporal work of mercy. Visit the sick. Bury the dead."

"You know about that?"

"I've devoted quite a bit of study to religion. People of faith intrigue me."

"Is that why you're attracted to me?" Lucy asked, then held her breath.

"What makes you think I'm attracted to you?"

"Maybe you're not, but I think you might be."

"I hope I haven't made myself too obvious. Forgive me if I have. I meant no offense."

"None taken. I'm flattered that one of Liz's brainy friends enjoys my company."

"That, I most certainly do."

"Good. I enjoy yours too," said Lucy.

Erika turned into a long driveway and parked in front of the garage. She reached behind her seat and produced two bottles of wine. If she'd had some warning, Lucy would have brought something too. Now, she felt embarrassed arriving empty handed. As if Erika had read her mind, she handed her the bottle of white wine. "You take this one."

They went up the stairs to the porch, and Erika rang the ship's bell. Barefoot, Liz opened the screen door and came out. She gave Erika a pat on the shoulder and scooped Lucy into a hug, practically lifting her off the ground. Maggie came out and kissed them both. "Lucy, I'm so glad you found time for dinner with us. It's been too long."

"I'm sorry. It's been insane since the summer visitors started to arrive."

"Get used to it. It will only get worse. First, the Q-tips come, and then the deluge!"

"What's a Q-tip?" asked Lucy, looking puzzled.

Maggie pointed to her stunningly white, long hair. She'd confided to Lucy that she'd stopped dyeing her hair blond because the chemicals could cause breast cancer—one of the reasons Lucy wasn't eager to dye hers.

"The motels and cottages reduce their rates off season, so the seniors, who don't need to worry about kids in school, come up on vacation," Liz explained. "The town is suddenly overrun with old people. The merchants call them the Q-tips."

"Ah, I get it," said Lucy. "Clever."

"You haven't heard that before?" asked Liz. "Now that you're officially a resident of Hobbs, you need to learn our ways."

Lucy smiled. She loved the humor and warmth of these people.

"How are you?" Maggie asked, taking Lucy's arm to lead her inside. "You look exhausted."

"I am, but Erika really wanted to go out to dinner tonight, and I didn't want to disappoint her."

Maggie arched a curious brow.

"I'll tell you later," Lucy promised.

3

After dinner, Maggie and Lucy remained on the porch to listen to music and catch up, while Liz and Erika cleaned up the kitchen.

"Are you really going to retire?" Liz asked, adding detergent to the dishwasher. She turned it on and leaned against the counter.

"I think I must. I can't bear the thought of returning to the classroom after my sabbatical. It actually keeps me awake at night."

"That's not good," said Liz, shaking her head. "The same thing happened to me the last few years at Yale. I'd wake up in the middle of the night and have mental arguments with the administration. Jenny said she could hear my brain working. She finally threw me out of bed because I was keeping her awake."

"That was probably the beginning of the end."

Liz looked reflective. "Probably, but that relationship was long past its expiration date."

"But you seem quite content with Maggie."

"Maggie and I were always meant to be together. If she hadn't run home to mommy and daddy and come out to them, we would have been together long ago."

"Now, now, Liz, that's all in the past. Forty-five years in the past. Forget it. You can't make time run backwards."

"What about those experiments with the molecules coming out of the jar? Some of them go back in. That proves the second law of thermodynamics isn't absolute."

"You know what I mean. Sometimes, you're worse than I am."

"Impossible. You're a professional." Liz opened a cabinet and took out a bottle of single-malt scotch. "Want some?"

Erika shook her head. "Not tonight. I have to drive, and I've had some wine."

"Should we join the ladies on the porch?" asked Liz, pouring herself a glass of scotch.

"No, let them catch up. Sounds like they're having a good time. I hear laughter."

"But it's your date with the redhead, not Maggie's."

"It's not really a date. I have no idea what her story is, or whether she's interested. Maybe it's an elaborate tease on her part."

Liz nodded. "She's a hard one to read. She shares more with Maggie than she does with me."

"Female bonding."

"Whatever..." murmured Liz and took a sip of scotch. She smiled with pure pleasure. "Let's sit in the living room."

They settled themselves on the leather sofas. Liz put her feet up on the hassock. "So, when will you retire?"

"I am entitled to a double sabbatical because I declined one earlier. That buys me two years and gets me closer to sixty-two and Social Security. Enrollment in philosophy classes has declined. Majors are at an all-time low. The college is keen to cut the department."

"Maybe they'll offer to buy out your remaining contract."

"Yes, I think they might. I've put out some feelers to the dean. My pension will be decent. And you've given me excellent advice on my investments, thank you."

Liz nodded. "So, you don't need to work. What will you do after you retire?"

"I don't know exactly. Maybe I'll go home."

"Home? You mean, *nach Deutschland*?"

"Yes, the former GDR is now almost totally integrated into the West. Berlin is such a different city since the wall came down. Nothing like the dingy, cramped place I remember. It's full of energy and culture. I could probably find a teaching position there. Some of the professors at the Humboldt remember my father. I've been in touch."

"But I thought you were done with teaching."

"Only teaching American students. They're not interested in the liberal arts. They're so focused on preparing for a career."

"Can you blame them? College has become so expensive. How much does Colby cost these days?"

"With room and board, about $72,000 a year."

"Wowzer!" Liz whistled through her teeth. "That's more than it cost to put me through four years of med school!"

"That was ages ago. We're dinosaurs now. Remember?"

"But you can't leave, Erika," said Liz with a pout. "I'd miss you too much."

"You and Maggie are always welcome to visit."

"What about your new friend?" Liz wagged her head in the direction of the porch.

"Ah, yes, Mother Lucy. Why do you ask such a question after refusing to share any information?"

Liz threw up her hands. "Because I really don't know anything!"

"Don't you ask that question when you interview your patients?"

"You mean someone's sexual orientation? No. I only ask if they're sexually active...to determine whether they're at risk for STD's."

"Well? Is she?"

"Erika, you know I can't tell you that!"

Erika grunted dismissively. "You're useless."

"Thank you," replied Liz with a mock scowl.

"I admit I find her intriguing. I don't really understand the religious mindset, but it fascinates me. And the backstory. Singers work like demons to get to the Met. Why would anyone give it up?"

Liz shrugged. "I have no idea. But I'm sure you'll get it out of her with the Socratic method."

"No, I wouldn't do that. If we become close enough for her to tell me, I'll listen, but I won't pry it out of her."

Liz sat back and studied Erika. "That's new for you. Maybe you're developing feelings for her."

"No," said Erika emphatically.

"So, you're not really interested. You just want to get into her panties."

Lucy flew into the room. "Liz!" she exclaimed and flung her arms around Liz's neck, almost spilling her glass of scotch. "Thank you so much!"

"You seem to be popular tonight," observed Erika.

"Maggie must have told her we're donating a washer and dryer to the church. The tax man cometh, and we need deductions."

"Bollocks," replied Erika. "That's only an excuse. Maggie talked you into it."

"Maggie has suddenly gotten religion. It does worry me," said Liz, frowning. She glanced at Lucy. "No offense, Lucy."

"Everyone must think I'm very thin-skinned. They keep apologizing."

"It's your role and the thingy at your neck," Liz said, pointing to her own. "We're trying to mind our manners."

"Why start now?" Erika asked, laughing. "Your mouth could make a sailor blush."

"Ignore her, Lucy," said Liz. "I'm not that bad."

"I know." Lucy affectionately patted Liz's cheek. Erika frowned. She did not like the look of that.

"I'll come over next week to run the pipes and cables for the washer and dryer hook up. Okay?" Liz asked.

"As long as it's during business hours, Samantha will be there to let you in."

"Why are you all hiding in here?" asked Maggie, coming into the living room with a plate of cookies. "We were waiting for you to join us on the porch."

"We're discussing Erika's retirement," Liz explained.

"I see," said Maggie, glancing at Erika. "Planning your retirement with the doctor who never retires?"

"I'll retire...eventually," said Liz, and threw down the rest of her scotch.

Maggie set the cookies on the coffee table. "I'll believe it when I see it."

Liz frowned in Maggie's direction. "You're not retired either. You're busier than ever between your teaching, the Playhouse and The State Theater. Never mind coaching the drama club at the high school."

"I'm resigning from UNE. I want to focus on acting and directing. That's why I retired in the first place." Maggie offered the plate of cookies around. "Tea? Coffee, anyone?" Their guests shook their heads. Maggie sat down next to Liz and moved closer until they were hip to hip.

"Thank you, dear. You're such a good hostess," said Liz, kissing her forehead.

"A great hostess," said Lucy. "That was an amazing, dinner, Maggie. And as much as I'd like to stay, I have to polish a homily before I go to bed. I have a funeral tomorrow."

"Another one?" asked Erika skeptically.

"There are more people dying up here than being born," Liz said. "Maine is the grayest state in the Union."

"So, would you like to leave, Mother Bartlett?" asked Erika.

Lucy smiled in her direction. "If you don't mind, Professor Bultmann," she teased back. The warm, sweet smile remained. Erika felt herself melting into a pool of desire.

Their hosts walked them to the door. Maggie kissed Erika on the cheek. "We've missed you. Although, now that you're back, I'll have to keep a closer eye on Liz to make sure she doesn't get into mischief. You two are a bad influence on one another."

Liz feigned insult. "What a terrible thing to say about me."

"I'm afraid it's true," Erika admitted.

Liz walked her guests down to their car. "How's it running?" she asked, looking it over. "It's probably going to start burning a little oil now. Make sure to change it on time."

"Don't worry, Liz," said Erika, patting the steering wheel. "I'll take care of your baby."

Liz leaned down to speak through Erika's open window. "Keep an eye on her, Lucy. She has a heavy foot on the pedal, and as you know, our Hobbs police are always watching."

"Have you gotten a speeding ticket, Mother Bartlett?" Erika asked, looking in Lucy's direction.

Lucy visibly squirmed. "They let me off with a warning."

"They always let me off too," said Liz. "In my case, it's the MD plates. In yours, it's probably the collar, but don't tempt them. They can be tough."

Liz waited on the porch steps while Erika turned the car around. She waved as they headed down the driveway.

"That was lovely," Lucy said, touching Erika's thigh, which instantly sent a jolt through her. Her thigh actually twitched. She hoped Lucy hadn't noticed. "Thank you for including me."

"Well, I had asked you to dinner. When Liz invited me, I felt I had to go. Double duty."

"Very efficient," observed Lucy.

"Yes," said Erika slowly, glancing in her direction. "Do you have something against efficiency?"

"No, I think it's wonderful. But sometimes you're so stereotypically German. I think it's funny."

"Really? That amuses you?"

"I'm sorry. I didn't mean to offend you," Lucy said quickly in a worried voice.

"I took no offense. I am German. There are certain ethnic characteristics that are indelible no matter how long one lives abroad. Efficiency is not a bad thing."

Lucy was silent for a moment, evidently absorbing the information. "I wish I were more efficient about getting my sermons together. Then I wouldn't need to spend late nights in front of my computer."

"What does one preach at a funeral?" Erika asked.

"I don't call what I do preaching. I don't believe in preaching."

"I see." Erika nodded. "I stand corrected."

"I mean, I try to give people a different way to look at things, to consider another perspective."

"Then you and I are in the same business. But I wouldn't know what to say at a funeral."

Lucy sat back and stared ahead. "It's one of my hardest duties as a priest," she said after a long moment. "When there's a death, people often come back to the Church for solace and reassurance, but saying 'don't worry, you'll see your loved one in the afterlife' doesn't really cut it. I always elaborate on the scripture readings because they can be comforting. I try to find out as much as I can about the deceased, so I can relate stories that help people remember the good times. To be honest, I deliberately try to make them cry, because that's part of the purpose of a funeral. Public and communal grief."

Erika had listened carefully. "You sound like you have it well thought out."

"From a philosophy professor, that's a high compliment. I'll take it."

"Do. It was meant."

Lucy turned in her seat. "You're a very interesting lady, Erika Bultmann."

"I feel the same about you."

"Then we'll just have to find a way to spend more time together."

"There's always that walk we talked about."

"I'll check my schedule when I get back. I could walk at sunrise, but I'm sure that's too early for you."

Erika groaned aloud at the thought of getting up before dawn, but the idea of seeing Lucy the very next day was appealing. "What time?"

"Six too early? I'll check the tide schedule too. Maybe the island walk would be better."

"Whatever you like." Erika was surprised to find herself so accommodating. Generally, she was definite about her likes and dislikes and expressed them freely.

Erika pulled into the rectory parking lot and parked in front of the entrance. "Thank you for coming out with me tonight. I truly enjoyed it." Before she engaged the parking brake, her mind was already two steps ahead, considering a good night kiss—something friendly but without obligation.

"So, did I," said Lucy, unbuckling her seat belt, but she made no move to leave.

Erika reached out her hand and took Lucy's, but for some reason, she couldn't move. Lucy seemed to understand. She leaned forward and kissed Erika gently on the lips, barely a touch. "Good night, Erika. Until a few hours from now." Then to Erika's surprise, Lucy kissed her again. Her lips were soft and open, but Erika dared not take the invitation.

Finally, Lucy opened the door and got out. She bent to speak through the open door. "And you can't get into my panties because I'm not wearing any."

She laughed when Erika's mouth gaped open.

"Only kidding," said Lucy and blew a kiss before she closed the door.

As Lucy ran up the steps to the rectory, Erika admired her shapely backside encased in the red dress.

Lucy unlocked the door and blew another kiss before she went inside.

4

Lucy kissed the stole and put it on the coat rack while she took off the surplice. She unbuttoned the black cassock. The garment, specially sized for her because she was short, went to her feet. There were so many buttons. Always impatient to get to the bottom, her fingers became clumsy, and then it took even longer. She carefully put the cassock on a hanger and added it to the others in the closet. So much black! It brought back the sadness of the mourners at the funeral. When she had led the prayers at the grave, she could practically feel the palpable ache in their souls.

She always tried to be especially kind during funerals, a reaction to her own father's funeral over twenty years before. She remembered the Catholic priest railing against "fallen away Catholics" as she sat in a pew, stunned and paralyzed by grief. Her father had died suddenly and so young, struck down by a heart attack at sixty-two.

In the pulpit, the old priest went on and on about showing repentance for unfaithfulness through generosity to the church. By that, he meant an extravagant contribution. That's what Lucy associated with Catholicism now—money and pedophilia. She knew she shouldn't be so judgmental, but at the time, Lucy had wanted to jump up from her seat and scream, "How dare you!" Afterwards, her uncle, who'd been sitting behind her, said he had been ready to hold her down because he could see the tension in her shoulders and the twitch of the muscles in her neck. He said he didn't want her to embarrass the family.

Lucy slipped her arms into her black suit jacket. She rolled up the stole to bring back to her office. It was not to be shared. Susan had given it to Lucy on her ordination. Full of love and pride, she had presented it. "You are so worthy," she had said. "Never doubt it."

The memories were an odd juxtaposition of emotions—her feelings of love and longing for Susan, and her fury over her father's botched funeral.

While her father's polished coffin sat on the braces over the grave, the old priest had droned on about gifts to the church to atone for past sins until Lucy wanted to kick him into the grave. Evidently, the Catholic Church was still selling indulgences. After the burial, she had wanted to pound on the rectory door and shout at the old man: "Go to hell, you old drunk!" She had smelled the stench of whiskey on him as he passed. Her mother had talked her out of it. She said it would dishonor her father, and Lucy had finally let it go.

After that nightmare, Lucy had hated the Church and God, but now she was a priest, although not in the Roman rite in which she'd grown up. The Catholic Church still banned the ordination of women. Even in her own faith, there were traditionalists who hated the idea of women priests. Their websites were full of arguments refuting the validity of female ordination. *Stop. Don't give into mirroring their anger and hatred. Remember why you are a priest. Remember who brought you here.* Lucy thought of Susan, and her heart ached.

Lucy locked the robing room. Her footsteps echoed in the hall as she headed to the door. The flagstones shone. The women of the parish kept everything spotless. She'd offered to help with some of the housekeeping chores, but they would have none of it. She was their priest, they said. It was their way of serving God.

In her rectory office, Lucy opened a drawer in her desk and put the rolled stole into it. She gazed at it for a moment and saw Susan's face. She remembered the softness of her lips and lying in her arms, a sweetness beyond imagination. It was just a moment in time, gone now forever. Susan was in the Midwest somewhere. Lucy wasn't quite sure where. They no longer spoke.

Lucy sighed. She thought about her walk with Erika that morning. She'd looked so sleepy, but she'd put on makeup, although, with her coloring, she didn't need it. Her complexion was golden and contrasted nicely with her pale-yellow hair and glacially blue eyes. Her skin was beautiful, hardly a wrinkle except for a few around her eyes and mouth. Laugh lines, they called them. Lucy had them too. Lucy always felt women of a certain age had character lines, not wrinkles. The young ones were so smooth and perfect because life hadn't etched its lessons yet. It took time to develop character.

Erika had been quiet on their walk. Maybe she wasn't awake yet. She had listened while Lucy made elaborate apologies about the panties joke and explained why she didn't mind presiding at funerals. Lucy had left out the part about her father. She'd save that for another time.

She didn't know why she was surprised to find that Erika was a good listener. Usually, that was Lucy's job. She listened for hours during pastoral counseling sessions, in parish meetings, and while the dying told her their regrets. It was such a gift to have someone listen to her for a change.

She still didn't know yet what to make of Erika. From their first meeting, Lucy had gotten the impression that Erika was witty and sharp-tongued. Now that she was spending more time in her company, she found her surprisingly easy to be with. The look of pure attraction was still there, but Lucy could also see the kindness in those icy blue eyes.

Lucy glanced at the clock on her desk. Her appointment would be arriving in less than ten minutes. Lucy should really get some parish business done in the meanwhile. She opened her laptop and navigated to the parish accounts files. The numbers swam in front of her eyes as her mind drifted toward thoughts of Erika.

She hadn't been able to fall asleep after their dinner date. At first, she thought it was the tea she'd had to help stay awake while she'd finished her sermon. The truth was, she kept thinking of Erika.

Lucy had felt mortified after making the panty comment. It had just shot out of her mouth before she could stop herself. Yes, it was fresh, but it was also clever and funny. The look on Erika's face was unforgettable. Even more unforgettable was the sweet and gentle kiss, but Lucy had never expected she'd have to make the first move.

There was a knock at the door. "Mother Lucy, your twelve o'clock is here," said her admin.

"Thank you, Samantha."

Lucy's stomach growled. She realized she should have grabbed something for lunch before the counseling session. It would be hours before she'd have the chance to eat. She scheduled appointments during lunch time because so many of the parishioners she counseled were working, single mothers. Midday was often the only time they had available.

"Hello, Renee," said Lucy, rising and extending her hand to the dark-haired woman. Renee Langdon was in her forties and always looked a bit harried. She worked two jobs to support her family. In her day job, she was a manager at the local savings bank. At night, she worked at Home Depot in the paint department. Lucy had a hard time picturing someone so petite lugging around five-gallon pails of paint.

Renee reached into a brown paper bag and offered Lucy something wrapped in plastic wrap.

"I'm sorry, Mother Lucy, but I have to eat during our session. I won't have time when I get back to work. I hope you don't mind, but I brought you a sandwich too."

"That is so kind," said Lucy, although she knew she probably shouldn't accept the sandwich. "Thank you!"

The woman looked uneasy at the compliment. "If you've already eaten, you could save it for later."

"I haven't eaten, and I'm ravenous." Lucy caught herself. She often used big words with parishioners and had to remind herself that smaller words would do just as well. Not everyone had the education she'd enjoyed, and she wanted to speak to people in language they could understand. "I was just thinking how hungry I am," Lucy added. "You must have read my mind."

"My kids say I'm psychic."

"All kids think their mothers are psychic, and in some ways, they are."

Renee looked curious. "Do you have any children, Mother Lucy?"

Lucy debated what to say. One of the cardinal rules of counseling was to avoid personal conversation except to express sympathetic context, and then sparingly. "No, I don't have children," she said simply, but she couldn't meet Renee's curious gaze.

Renee nodded. "If I'd known what I was getting myself into, I might have made other choices myself."

"So would we all, but life is full of surprises." Lucy smiled to help her client relax. "Are things going better with Peter?"

"He went on a job interview the other day. I told him if he's not going to school, he has to get a job. I won't have him sitting around all day in the basement playing video games. It's not good for him."

"Getting a job interview is a good sign," said Lucy in an encouraging voice.

Renee sighed. "It's not much of a job. It's with the department of transportation as a flag man, but it pays well. It would be nice if he contributed something. He eats like a horse." She grinned. "My other son shovels it away too. Thank God, my youngest is a girl."

"But things are better?" Lucy asked to encourage more conversation.

"I'm still worried about the guns."

Lucy looked right into Renee's brown eyes. "Have you considered asking him to get rid of them?"

Renee shook her head. "He would never do that. He has a lot of money in those guns."

"You could call the police and ask them to talk to him."

"He would go nuts if the police were involved. Plus, they wouldn't do anything but talk."

"How many guns does he have?"

"I don't know exactly. A lot. I don't mind the hunting rifles or the shotguns. Everyone up here hunts deer or birds. It's the pistols and those assault guns. The ones with the big magazines. You can kill a lot of people with those things."

Lucy sighed. "Yes, you can."

"So, you know about guns?"

"Not much," Lucy admitted. "But I took Dr. Stolz's women's firearms class." Liz had insisted that her wife take the class, and Maggie had invited Lucy to come along. Lucy listened carefully while Liz had described the different types of guns. Afterwards, she'd taken them out to the range to experience firing them. Lucy thought the .45 pistol would wrench her arm out of the socket. The 12-gauge shotgun recoil into her shoulder had hurt for days. But it was the AR-15, spewing bullets at an amazing rate, that had scared the shit out of her. She'd said exactly that, to Maggie's surprise.

"Women should know about guns," said Renee, nodding in approval. "We have a lot of them here in Maine. Even if you don't shoot, you should know how to handle guns safely."

"That's why I agreed to take the class, but honestly, guns frighten me."

"Me too. I really wish Peter would get rid of them, but if I say anything, he gets all pissy on me. I'm worried one of the younger kids will find them and hurt themselves."

"Doesn't he have them locked up?"

"No, just lying around in his room. He locks the door when he goes out. That keeps the younger kids from getting their hands on them."

"I suppose that helps a little."

"The main thing is I'm afraid all the time. It was bad enough when I had to be afraid of my husband, and now my son has an arsenal in the basement."

"Surely, that's an exaggeration."

"No, it's not. There are a lot of guns down there, and those big military cannisters that hold a thousand rounds each. That's a lot of ammo."

Renee's fear was contagious. Lucy felt her body tense as she listened to her. "Does Peter drink or use drugs?"

"He was a stoner in high school. He still smokes pot. Not in the house, but I can smell it on his clothes. You won't report him, will you?"

"Marijuana is legal in Maine now," Lucy reminded her.

"I mean about the guns."

"Not unless you tell me he's threatened you or your children. I still think you should go to the police."

Renee shook her head. After that, she changed the subject. When she left, neither of them had eaten the sandwiches she'd brought.

Lucy was distracted by thoughts of Renee Langdon as she saw her other parishioners, an elderly widower who'd lost his wife after a long battle with cancer, and a young wife, pregnant with a third baby she wasn't sure she wanted to keep. She was overwhelmed with the two children she had, both preschoolers. Lucy found those cases really difficult and usually fell back on her training rather than her instincts to deal with them. So far, that had worked.

When the young woman left, Lucy finally ate the sandwich Renee had brought. The peanut butter and jelly on white bread made her feel like a little girl again. As she ate it, she realized that Renee had probably packed it while rushing around that morning. That she'd even thought of Lucy was touching. The kindness of the people of Hobbs sometimes brought tears to Lucy's eyes.

Lucy was wiping the sticky grape jelly off her fingers when she saw a text message flash on her phone.

It was from Erika. *Come to dinner tonight.*

Lucy blinked. They were seeing a lot of one another. Was that a good thing? She made sure her hands were clean before she texted, *Are you sure?*

Certainty is debatable, Erika texted. Lucy had to think about it. *Oh, it's a philosopher's joke. What a smartass!*

I'm going to wear out my welcome, Lucy texted back.

Not possible. Come when you're done there.

Okay.

Erika sent a purple heart emoticon. Lucy was tempted to send back a red one but stopped herself. Instead, she texted, *What can I bring?*

Yourself. Two purple heart emoticons and a smiley face.

Lucy smiled at the screen. She put the phone in her jacket pocket and closed her laptop before heading to her quarters.

She was almost too tired to get undressed, but she took off her black suit and clerical stock. The collar needed a wash. She'd do it tomorrow. She had extras in the drawer. She let down her hair and put it into a French braid, visualizing the plaits as she wove them.

She chose a nautical look: white capris and a striped knit shirt with long sleeves. The May nights were still cool and down at the beach, the wind off the water would make it even cooler. She didn't have the energy to walk to Ocean Road and back, so she went out to start her SUV.

Erika smiled when she came to the screen door. "Another outfit? The many faces of Mother Bartlett."

"I was always good at costume changes. Quick."

"I'll bet you were," said Erika, opening the door. "Come in."

Erika looked cool and relaxed in shorts, a T-shirt and bare feet. "Have a seat in the living room, and I'll deal with the alcohol. What's your poison? Wine? Gin and Tonic? Perhaps a martini? I always have beer in the fridge for Liz."

"Oh, I don't know," said Lucy, sinking down on the sofa. The idea of making a decision was exhausting. "What are you having?"

"Pinot grigio."

"Perfect."

Erika returned with a tray containing two glasses of white wine in stemless wine glasses and snacks: crackers and soft cheese, multicolored heirloom carrot sticks and dip.

"When I first saw those purple carrots, I wondered if they'd gone bad," Lucy admitted.

"Because you're a city girl."

"No, because I can't afford fancy food on a priest's salary, so I try not to have a roving eye."

"Regarding food, you mean," said Erika, handing her a glass of wine. Lucy liked her casual style of entertaining and that she was comfortable enough to sit there in bare feet. "Welcome to my humble abode, Mother Bartlett." They touched glasses.

"So formal. My congregation calls me 'Mother Lucy.'"

"You are not my mother, nor am I your congregant. I shall call you Lucy, if that suits."

"It does," said Lucy, realizing she could get lost in Erika's blue eyes. She blinked to break the spell. "What are you cooking?" she asked, sitting up to snatch a cracker. "It smells delicious."

"An old standby. Chicken cacciatore. Liz gave me the recipe years ago. I'm not the gourmet cook she is, nor Maggie, but I know my way around a kitchen."

"I never have time to cook, or I'm so beat by the end of the day, I can't be bothered."

"So, what do you eat?"

"I throw together a salad…add some oil and vinegar, sometimes a hard-boiled egg or cheese. I throw in some tuna or pick up a rotisserie chicken for more protein."

"No wonder you keep your lovely figure," said Erika, spreading cheese on a cracker and offering it to Lucy. "I must say that, despite your perky outfit, you look exhausted. Therefore, I insist that you allow me to wait on you hand and foot. I've been relaxing on the beach while you've been working your pretty little tail off."

Lucy mocked surprise. "You've been looking at my rear?"

"It was hard not to, especially with you in that sexy, red dress. What did you expect? I'd look the other way?"

"No, I wore it to get a rise out of you."

"I provided a satisfactory response, I hope."

Lucy laughed. "Yes, very satisfactory."

Erika settled back in her seat and gave her a long, measuring look. "What's your story, Lucy Bartlett? Are you a lesbian?"

Lucy took a moment to get over the shock, then laughed. "That's certainly a direct question. Yes, I love women, if that's what you're asking, but I don't really like labels."

"Fine. Let's dispense with the labels." Erika let out an exaggerated sigh. "I'm so glad that's settled. I was concerned."

"Not really. Not after I kissed you last night."

"That was just a friendly kiss, but what if I made a pass at the local rector, and it was poorly received? They might drive me out of town."

"Oh, I doubt that. Hobbs is a very friendly place. Besides, Liz and Maggie would stick up for you." Lucy mocked a frown of alarm. "Do you intend to make a pass at me?"

"Perhaps later. At the moment, I have a million questions for you."

"Please don't interview me tonight." Lucy sighed. "I'm too tired."

"I can see that. All right. I'll reserve the interview for another time."

"Thank you. That's very generous."

They clicked glasses in agreement.

5

Erika listened to Lucy's bright chatter as she watched her gobble down her food. It pleased her to see that Lucy enjoyed her cooking. Making a favorite meal had been one of the ways Erika had taken care of Jeannine when she was overworked or discouraged about a painting. It was how Erika's mother had shown love. Her daughter had unintentionally absorbed the lesson.

"Oh, shit," exclaimed Lucy when a drop of tomato sauce landed on her shirt, right over the left breast. Her hand flew to her mouth. "Sorry for the profanity."

"No need to apologize. I've been known to say that word myself. However, it does shock me a bit, hearing it come out of your mouth."

"Why? Because I'm a priest?"

"Well, yes."

"You'll find I'm the least holy person you'll meet. Although, I try. Excuse me while I do this." She dipped her napkin in her water glass and attempted to sponge out the tomato sauce on her shirt. That only succeeded in spreading the orange stain.

"I don't think that's going to work," said Erika, watching. She got up. "Liz gave me a little pen to take out stains because I'm forever dropping food on my clothes. Let me get it." Erika went into her little laundry room and found the detergent pen. She gave it to Lucy, whose attempts to remove the spot were hampered by the awkward position. "Here, allow me," offered Erika, reaching for the pen.

Lucy looked up at her with a wicked grin. "You just want to touch my boob."

"Yes, of course, I want to touch your boob, but that can wait for later. If you prefer, you can remove your shirt, and I can put it in a tub to soak while we finish eating."

"Now you want to take off my shirt," said Lucy, obviously trying to stifle laughter.

Erika hurried to explain, "I can give you one of my shirts to wear."

"Sit down and finish your meal. Now, that the damage is done, it can wait. Who knows? I may drop more sauce on my boobs, and you'll have even more reason to touch them."

"You are quite the sassy lady, Lucille Bartlett."

"No more than you. Am I a lesbian?" Lucy said in a mocking voice. "What did you think?"

"I had no idea what to think. You are a woman of the cloth. You have the most feminine appearance…"

"Stereotypes."

"And you're tight with Maggie and Liz," Erika added.

"Birds of a feather?"

"Precisely."

"In fact, I haven't come out to Maggie and Liz, and they never asked. We're just comfortable together. I'm sure they've assumed by now."

"Maybe not. Liz reserves judgment and takes things at face value. One of the things I like most about her." Erika frowned in the direction of Lucy's plate. "You'd best finish your meal, or it will get cold."

"Good idea. It's delicious, and I don't want to waste it," said Lucy with a radiant smile.

The rest of the meal proceeded without further mishap. When they finished eating, Erika got up to clear the table.

"Why don't you sit in the living room and listen to the music while I tidy a bit before dessert. Would you like me to give you a shirt, so I can put yours in to soak?"

"That's so kind," said Lucy.

"Come with me." Erika gestured with a beckoning finger. She led Lucy to her bedroom, pleased that she had made the bed and the room was tidy. She opened a drawer in the high chest and took out a neatly folded T-shirt. She closed the door behind her.

While she was putting the cacciatore in a storage dish, Lucy returned. "Thank you for taking care of this. I love this shirt, and I don't want the stain to set," she said hanging it over the back of a chair. Erika turned around and saw that Lucy was swimming in the T-shirt she had given her. It was a size too big for Erika, but it looked comical on tiny Lucy.

"I see that's rather large. Shall I find you another?"

"No, it's fine. It feels cozy." Lucy hugged herself to demonstrate.

"Let me put this in to soak. I've prepared a care package for you to take home. I don't want you starving yourself in that rectory of yours."

"Thank you," said Lucy, "I'll certainly enjoy it the second time around."

Erika ran some water into a laundry tub in the kitchen sink, rubbed a little detergent into the stain, and put the shirt into the tub to soak. "Do you mind if I finish tidying?"

"No, no. Do what you have to do. I'll help you."

"I won't hear of it! Go into the living room and enjoy the music. I won't be but a few minutes."

"Take your time," Lucy said, "There's no rush. I'm not going anywhere."

"I hope not."

Erika resumed loading the dishwasher. She put the rustic tart she'd baked earlier on a plate. Ordinarily, she wouldn't make such an effort at presentation, but this was Lucy's first time as a dinner guest, and Erika wanted to make a good impression.

Erika came into the living room to find Lucy sound asleep on the sofa. Her fists were balled under her chin. She looked like a large, beautiful child. She'd taken off her espadrilles. Her toenails were painted dark red, which made Erika shiver a little.

Although Erika's first instinct was to wake the sleeping woman, she took a moment to admire her. Lucy was heartbreakingly beautiful. Her pale skin was like porcelain. The faint freckles on her nose were visible now that her foundation had worn through after a long day. Her ear was small and delicate, like a pretty shell that had washed up on the beach. The tiny veins showed through the pink skin. Erika gently tucked a stray lock of red hair that had escaped from Lucy's French braid behind her ear, which caused her to stir. She stretched and opened her eyes, taking a moment to focus. She turned up her face and smiled. “Hello,” she said. “I’m sorry to have passed out on your sofa.”

“You’re tired. I understand.”

Lucy patted a place next to her. “Sit down.”

Erika sat where Lucy had indicated. “You’re welcome to spend the night. I assure you that means nothing except the offer of a comfortable bed in the guest room.”

Lucy yawned and turned on her back. “You’re very kind.”

“You say that as if you’re surprised.”

“When I first met you, I was a little afraid of your sharp tongue, but now I know it protects a kind heart.”

“I’ll thank you not to let everyone know my secret.”

“I won’t tell. Promise.” Lucy hooked her pinky around Erika’s. “Pinky swear.”

The little gesture was charming and girlish. Erika gazed into Lucy’s green eyes and saw them soften with affection and then desire.

“I want to kiss you,” said Erika.

“Is someone stopping you?” Lucy’s voice was almost a purr.

Erika leaned down and gently touched her lips to Lucy’s. She felt a hand come behind her neck to draw her closer. She gasped a little when the soft lips parted, welcoming her inside. She moved closer and explored Lucy’s warm mouth with her tongue. It tasted tangy from wine and tomato sauce. Her warm breath tickled her nostrils. Erika withdrew a little and soon found Lucy’s gently probing tongue in her mouth. The hand behind her neck was firmer, indicating it wasn’t about to let go. Lucy’s breathing changed. She let out a little moan as she continued to probe Erika’s mouth. She released her for a moment to say, “I love the way you kiss!”

“You’re kissing me,” said Erika.

Lucy laughed softly. “Yes, I am.” When the kiss resumed, it became more assertive and there were more moans. Tentatively, Erika reached up to weigh the soft breast just inches away, but a hand came up and gently pulled hers away.

"Not yet. Just kiss me," said Lucy, opening her eyes.

They went back to kissing. Now, Lucy relaxed and allowed Erika to take the lead. If this was all Lucy would allow her to do tonight, Erika wanted to make it count. She liked the way Lucy kissed too, and the way her breathing changed when she was excited. By now, it was obvious that she was very excited. Lucy had finally let go of her hand, but something about this woman made Erika want to honor her wishes to the letter.

When Erika ended the kiss, Lucy's breaths were still shallow and fast.

"Oh, I wish I could stay tonight."

"You can," said Erika. "I did invite you."

Lucy reached for Erika's hand and squeezed it. "I'm sorry. I can't make love tonight."

Erika sat up and frowned. "You're not celibate, are you?"

Lucy laughed softly. "No. But I don't believe in casual sex."

"I assure you there's nothing casual about my interest in you."

Lucy sat up and looked earnestly into her eyes. "I never thought so. But I also don't want us to get ahead of ourselves. I believe that making love is a sacred act."

Erika couldn't stop herself from rolling her eyes.

Lucy looked hurt. "I'm sorry, but that's what I believe," she said in a slightly defensive tone.

Erika glanced down. "No, I'm sorry. I shouldn't be mocking your beliefs. In some ways, they are very romantic and touching."

Lucy sighed. "You're still trivializing them."

"Not intentionally."

Lucy took Erika's hand. "If I give you my body, it will be because I love you. I know I want you. I really, really want you, but that's not enough. Please try to understand."

"I do, I suppose," said Erika, taking her hand back. She brushed off her pants as if the conversation had somehow sullied them. "Now, I've prepared some dessert. Please come to the table." She got to her feet.

Lucy remained where she sat. "I feel I've disappointed you."

Erika turned at the dining room door. "You haven't. Not at all. Now, please come to the table. I don't often bake, but when I do, I expect it to be eaten." Erika gestured toward the dining room table. Retreating into practicality felt satisfying. She went into the kitchen to bring out the rustic berry tart. When she returned, she was relieved to see that Lucy had taken a seat at the table.

"I'm going to have to up my game after this wonderful meal and return the favor."

"That sounds lovely," replied Erika. "I look forward to it." She cut the tart into quarters and put two portions on plates. She handed one to Lucy. "Are you certain you wouldn't like some coffee? Or tea, perhaps?"

Lucy shook her head. "Thank you, but the caffeine will keep me awake, and I definitely need some sleep. I'm so embarrassed I nodded off on you like that."

"I forgive you," said Erika. She realized her voice had become a little frosty and she regretted it. After that, there was silence as they ate. When it extended beyond a few minutes, Erika cleared her throat pointedly.

"When will I be able to hear you sing again?"

"Haven't you heard about the concert Maggie and I are singing?"

"I know nothing of this concert. Tell me more."

"At the Webhanet Playhouse on Labor Day Weekend. It's a fundraiser for the Playhouse and the Hobb's Women's Shelter. We're singing favorites from Broadway musicals and operettas."

"That sounds splendid. You can be sure I'll be there."

"There are three performances."

"Then I shall be there for all three. I am very much looking forward to hearing you sing again. Maggie too. You have very different styles, both equally valid, however. Will you sing any duets?"

"As a matter of fact, we will. We're singing some songs from *Chicago* and *Wicked* and *West Side Story*. I tried to convince Maggie to sing something from operetta, but she's shy about singing anything classical with me."

"I understand. In her shoes, I would be equally shy. I can't wait to hear you both."

Erika finished what was on her plate. When she looked up, she saw that Lucy was staring at her.

"What's the matter? Has my skin turned green?"

Lucy laughed. "No. I just want you to understand I'm not brushing you off. I really value our friendship. I don't want to ruin it by getting off on the wrong foot."

"I am an abysmal dancer, I should warn you, and I have no wish to tread on your toes."

Lucy's smile faded. "I'm serious."

"So am I. Very." Knife poised over the tart, Erika asked, "More of this berry thing?"

"No, thanks. I'm still full from dinner."

"I'll give you a portion to take with you."

"Thank you. I'll enjoy it." Lucy glanced toward the door. "I should be getting home."

Erika nodded. She got up and brought the dishes to the kitchen. She packed the tart and the dinner leftovers in a reusable shopping bag. "I'll thank you to bring back the bag," she said, handing it to Lucy.

"I will. I promise."

They walked to the door, but Lucy made no move to open it.

"When may I see you again?" Erika asked.

Lucy searched her face. "You can come to church on Sunday and see what I do in my day job."

This time, Erika managed to curb her disapproval. She became stony-faced instead.

Lucy nodded. "I know. That may be a bridge too far." She reached up and touched Erika's cheek. "It's okay."

"Perhaps someday, I'll wander in," said Erika vaguely. She bent to offer Lucy a kiss, which rapidly went from friendly to passionate. Erika didn't mind taking advantage of the opportunity. Lucy clung to her. Finally, she let go and stepped back.

"Now, I really don't want to go," Lucy said with a sigh. "But I have to. Thank you for dinner."

Erika nodded and handed her the shopping bag. She opened her mouth to speak, but Lucy jumped in. “I know. Bring it back.”

Erika stood on the porch until Lucy drove off. She went inside and closed the door. Leaning against it, she put her fingers to her lips and tried to remember the feel of Lucy’s lips on hers.

6

Lucy opened the window. It had been warm all morning, but now, it was stifling. She had already taken off her collar, then her stock. Now, she unbuttoned another button of her blouse. Any more and it would be obscene. She wished she had worn a skirt instead of pants. The rayon of the black dress pants didn't breathe and clung to her skin, but at least, she could get away without wearing panty hose.

She sat down and read what she'd written so far, which wasn't much. Her conversation with Erika had inspired her to write a homily about the material nature of Christianity. The ancient Greeks thought the material world was base and less holy than the world of ideas, but Christ had been embodied. He had been incarnated as a human being, in a human body. That was significant. Lucy remembered one of her professors at Union Theological lecturing on this subject, and she wondered if she had the notes handy, or if she'd have to dig through the boxes she'd put in storage in the basement.

Writing sermons was her least favorite clerical task. She knew she had a tendency to procrastinate, so she always tried to have a draft of her Sunday sermon done by Wednesday.

When the final text flowed well, she enjoyed delivering her homilies. They allowed her to connect with her audience not unlike when she sang. She tried not to make it a performance, although there was an element of theater in every religious service, despite the glare her liturgy professor had given her when she'd made that point.

Maggie understood. As a girl and a young woman, she had been an enthusiastic singer at what the Catholics then called "folk masses." It was only later that Maggie had turned away from the Church because of the pedophilia, but that early engagement had allowed Lucy to woo her back. Now, she never thought of her as a convert, only as her best friend.

There was a knock at the door. "Come in," said Lucy absently, still trying to remember where she'd hidden Professor Spangler's notes.

"Mother Lucy, Dr. Stolz is here to see you."

Lucy remembered that Liz had said she would stop by to work on the hookup for the washer and dryer. Lucy went to the outer office, where she found Liz, perusing the parish bulletin. She was wearing worn jeans, a T-shirt from some long defunct brewery and her beloved Keen sandals.

"Making house calls today?" Lucy asked, hugging her.

"Yes, but as you see I'm carrying a tool bag, not a medical bag. You don't mind PEX, do you?"

"PEX?" Lucy repeated, looking puzzled.

"Yes, you know, cross-linked polyethylene. PEX for short."

"I have no idea what you're talking about."

"It's okay. I do."

"Liz Stolz, don't give me that 'don't worry your pretty little head' brush off. I want to learn. I'm in charge of this place now."

"Okay," said Liz, obviously making an effort to be patient. "It's a kind of plastic pipe that comes in blue for cold and red for hot and white for general use. It's quick to install, and I only need to sweat a couple of connections to tap in. It lasts longer than copper pipe because…"

"That's fine. I get it. Do other people know their doctor doubles as a plumber?"

"You do, and the people at the fish and game. Don't spread it around," said Liz with a wink. "Remember what I told you about the code inspector. Tell him you did the work yourself."

"Like anyone would believe that."

"He might. You do wear a collar. You're supposed to be truthful." Liz grinned, then she was all business. "I need to turn off the water for about twenty minutes."

"Apart from the john, I can't imagine that Samantha or I will need the water. And I'm not going to complain after you've been so generous, and now you're doing all the work. I think we can live without water for a few minutes. Right, Samantha?"

The admin nodded in agreement.

"I might need you at the main supply valve to turn the water on and off when I say."

"You bet. Anything to get away from the sermon I'm working on," said Lucy heading for the basement door.

Liz put up her hand. "Not yet. I'll let you know when I need you." Liz turned to leave, nearly bumping into Erika, who was on her way in.

"Liz! What are you doing here?" Erika exclaimed, taking a step back.

"Plumbing. What are you doing here?"

"I am delivering a care package to Mother Bartlett. She's been looking a bit pale and thin."

"And you're trying to fatten her up? She looks just fine to me. In fact, more than fine." Liz gave Lucy a rakish smile.

Lucy shook her head at their banter. They were so ridiculous together, like a dysfunctional, stand-up comedy team. Lucy had finally figured out why they entertained one another but no one else. Each of them tried to be the "straight man," and their humor was so dry, few people understood it.

"Erika, if you have nothing better to do than delivering food, you could help me, and we can let Lucy get back to work."

"Please put this in the refrigerator." She handed Lucy the reusable bag. "Nothing fancy. A pasta primavera. It should heat up well."

Lucy caught Erika's hand as she reached out the bag. "Thank you. That's very sweet of you to think of me."

Erika opened her mouth to speak, then seemed to think better of it, but Lucy had sensed what Erika had wanted to say because she couldn't stop thinking about her either. It was even keeping her up at night.

Erika turned to follow Liz. "Let me help my friend stay out of mischief. If that's possible."

After they'd left, Lucy leaned on the admin's desk. "Please hold my calls, Sam. I need to finish this sermon this afternoon. I'm too busy tomorrow."

"Yes, Mother."

Despite the sounds of hammering and drilling coming from the basement and the room next door, Lucy worked steadily, finishing at least ninety percent of the draft. She had some open questions. Later, she'd find her notes from Spangler's class and fill in the blanks. She glanced at the clock on her desk and realized that Liz and Erika had been downstairs for over two hours.

"I'm going to see what the dynamic duo are up to," she told Samantha and headed to the communal kitchen to get two bottles of iced tea.

As she came down the stairs, she found Liz standing on a ladder, hammering in clamps to support the new pipes. Erica was lounging in a beach chair that she'd evidently found in the junk piled in the basement.

"I thought you might like a cold drink," said Lucy, offering a bottle to Liz.

"Thank you." Liz came down from the ladder. There was a dark Vee of sweat in the front of her T-shirt. At least, one of them had been working hard. Liz took off the bottle cap and gulped down some tea. "Thanks, Lucy, that hit the spot." She gestured to the rafter overhead. "I have the supply pipes run. I decided to tap into the main, so you don't lose water pressure in the kitchen. Now I'll just bore through the floor in the spare room where we're going to run the lines. I also have to make a hole for the waste pipe. Then I'll connect everything and clamp it to a stud."

Lucy nodded as if she knew what Liz was talking about because she didn't want to reveal her ignorance in front of Erika, who looked casually relaxed in the beach chair. "And what are you doing?" Lucy asked, handing Erika a bottle of iced tea.

"Liz was teaching me to sweat pipe. I've been holding the pipe while she hammers the clamps. It's not steady work, as you can see."

"Yes, you look very busy."

"I am. We've been discussing the state of the world. And Liz has been giving me valuable insights into how to deal with women."

"Is that so?" said Lucy, putting her hands on her hips. "Why? What have you been telling her?"

"Absolutely nothing. But now it seems you have revealed the facts."

Lucy turned to Liz, who raised her brows and lowered the bottle from her mouth. "I know nothing," she said. She replaced her dead-blow hammer in her tool belt and repositioned the ladder under the location of the next clamp. "I'll need to turn off the electricity to install the breakers, but the water is on now, in case you need it."

"Do you still need Erika?" Lucy asked, engaging Erika's gaze.

Liz snickered. "No, you can have her."

"Come with me," said Lucy, beckoning with her finger. She headed up the stairs. A moment later, she heard Erika following her.

"Come into my office," said Lucy when Erika came through the basement door. Erika's expression was a very good imitation of a guilty child caught at mischief by the teacher. Looking grave, she accompanied Lucy to her office.

Lucy shut the door and stood with her arms crossed. "Have you been telling Liz what's going on between us?"

"No, she guessed. She's pretty astute, you know. But I didn't give her any grist for the mill. And what, by the way, *is* going on between us? Nothing yet."

"But there's intention," said Lucy.

"There is?" asked Erika, obviously playing dumb.

"Erika!" Lucy put her hands on her hips.

"Lucy!" countered Erika, mirroring her pose.

They both smiled, then began to chuckle until they finally dissolved into laughter. Lucy fell into Erika's open arms. "You are wicked."

"I beg your pardon! And why don't you want Liz to know? She's our friend."

"I don't want anyone to know until we know. Otherwise, it sets up too many expectations, and it puts our friends in a difficult position if things don't work out."

"Oh, my dear," said Erika, pulling her close. "You worry so much about appearances."

"I have to," replied Lucy, enjoying the press of Erika's breasts against her. "I lead a very public life."

There was a knock on the door, and they sprang apart. Liz poked her head into the room. "Don't worry. It's just me. The power is back on in this section."

"Come in, Liz," said Lucy, reaching for Erika's hand. "Erika's right. We should be open with you and Maggie."

Liz waved dismissively. "It's no one's business, but I figured it out." Liz began to sing, "The look of love is in your eyes..."

"Never mind that. Sit down and tell me what you've done." Lucy gestured to the visitors' chairs opposite her desk.

Liz sat down and slouched. Erika took the other chair. As Lucy sat down behind her desk, she noted how interesting it was to see them side by side—Liz, iron-gray, with a bit of a tummy from the beer she liked so much, her grin slightly lopsided, tan, almost leathery from the outdoors; Erika, a bit prim, hair so blond it was nearly white, those enormous, pale-blue eyes, one blond brow permanently higher from being raised in skepticism.

"I ran all the wiring and pipes," Liz said. "Sorry about the smell from the PVC cement. I opened the window. It will be gone soon. Using the spare room next to your office isn't ideal, but at least you'll hear the signal when your laundry is done. You're all set for the delivery on Wednesday. I'll leave all the final hookups—the pigtail for the dryer and the supply and drain hoses for the washing machine. If they have any trouble with the installation, just call me."

Lucy nodded. She had understood most of what Liz had said. Although Lucy had never owned or managed any real estate before, she was pleased to realize she wasn't as incompetent as she'd thought.

"Liz, how did you learn so much about fixing things?"

"When I was a girl, I used to follow my father around like a puppy. I was probably more interested in fixing things than my brothers were." Liz frowned thoughtfully. "In another era, I might have become an engineer, like my father, instead of a surgeon." Liz slapped her thighs. "I'm done here, so I'm heading home. I promised Maggie I'd take her to the beach this afternoon."

"Maybe I'll see you there," said Erika.

"That would be nice. I'll tell Maggie to pack more food for our picnic. She's making her famous chicken wings. I made the salads. You're welcome too, Lucy, if you'd like to join us."

"I don't know…" Lucy began to say. She still had work to do on her sermon.

"Oh, say yes, Lucy," Erika said. "We all want to see you in your bathing suit."

"Do you?" Lucy raised an auburn brow. "Now that the townspeople won't be looking at my bras and panties anymore, I suppose my bathing suit is the next big reveal."

Liz and Erika, each wearing a leering grin, leaned forward at the same time.

Laughing, Lucy shook her head. "Get out here, both of you, so I can finish my sermon!"

***

"Lucy, I never thought I'd find someone paler than I am," said Maggie, slathering super-blocking sunscreen on her friend's back. "You really need to be careful." It felt good to have someone rub her back, even with sticky sunscreen. *Am I that desperate for human contact?* Lucy wondered. Maggie stopped rubbing and touched a specific spot. "Lucy, you should have Liz look at this." Before Lucy could protest, Maggie was calling to Liz.

"What's the matter?" asked Liz, running back from the ocean's edge where she'd been looking for rocks with Erika. Liz wasn't the kind who sat still very well, nor was Erika.

"Liz, take a look at this," said Maggie.

Lucy squirmed at being the object of so much attention. She felt Liz's gentle fingers on her back. "That's nothing. Just the biopsy scar from the last time I sampled it. Sometimes the scars discolor." Liz's hands patted her shoulders. "You're fine, Lucy. Don't let my wife drive you crazy. Since she found out about her BRCA2, she's become an eagle eye where sunspots are concerned."

"Thanks, Liz," said Lucy. She looked up and saw Erika watching the exchange with a little frown.

Erika dropped her gaze. When Lucy followed her line of sight, she realized those pale eyes were admiring her breasts. In an effort be modest, Lucy had chosen her least revealing swimsuit, a navy one-piece that looked like it could be a school swim team uniform. She had more enticing suits, including a bikini, but she would never dare wear them on the town beach where her parishioners might see her. Lucy tried to send Erika a friendly warning to avoid lustful inspections in front of their friends.

"Erika, would you like to walk down to the estuarine preserve?" asked Liz, antsy again. Erika nodded, and the two of them headed down to the water's edge to walk in the packed sand.

"Sometimes, I'm jealous of their friendship," Maggie said, following them with her eyes.

Lucy turned to her with surprise. "Really? Why? They've been friends for decades."

"I know, but they share something I can't. Liz is scary smart. So is Erika. Sometimes, I feel left out. But I know Liz needs the stimulation of brainy people around her."

"I don't think you're being fair to yourself, Maggie. You're a very bright woman. You even have a doctorate from Yale to prove it. Look at all you've accomplished. You were a full professor at NYU before they made you one at UNE. And you've had a stage career too."

"Yes, but they can talk about Hegel and Kant and *The Structure of Scientific Revolutions*."

"Sounds like you know something about those things too, if you can tell me about them."

Maggie adjusted the awning of her beach chair to block the sun better. "Liz talks at me about them from time to time. I try to listen carefully, and I do pick up things. I know enough not to sound stupid, but honestly, it bores me to death."

Lucy laughed. "Yes, I'd be bored too. Theology wasn't my favorite subject in divinity school. Abstractions aren't my thing." Lucy looked in the direction of the two figures growing smaller in the distance and frowned. "Sometimes, I worry I won't be able to hold my own in conversation with Erika."

"Then I'll say the same thing you said to me. You're a very bright woman, Lucy. You're a licensed counselor. You have a divinity degree, and you're an ordained priest. For heaven's sake, you sang on the stage of the Metropolitan Opera!"

"Yes, but I worry what we'll talk about after the sexual attraction wears off."

"I'm sure you'll find lots to talk about. Liz and I certainly do. There's the business of daily life. You know, the info exchange. But we also talk about politics and music, the kids, our jobs. Erika loves music and she's very literate. She can tell you the key of every Wagnerian Leitmotiv."

"Does she sing or play an instrument?"

"Piano, I think." Maggie turned to look Lucy in the eye. "Lucy, why didn't you tell me you're gay?"

"When you're a priest, you don't spread it around. Many people are still so conservative. They think if you're gay, you should be celibate. Same-sex marriage horrifies them."

"But I'm your friend."

Lucy gazed into Maggie's hazel eyes and saw that withholding the information had really hurt her. Lucy reached over and took her hand. "I'm sorry, Maggie, I should have told you. Please, forgive me."

Maggie nodded. "I do forgive you, Lucy, and you don't have to tell me everything. You have a right to your privacy. Liz picked you up on her gaydar, and you know Liz can be a little dense sometimes, but I kept saying no, I thought you were straight."

"The truth is, I'm probably bi. I've had male and female partners, but I prefer women."

"Are you interested in Erika?"

Lucy felt herself blush. She was so fair everyone could see when she was embarrassed.

"Never mind," said Maggie, "I can see you are." She patted Lucy's knee. "Just be careful, Lucy. Erika is a complicated person. You'll have a lot to handle there."

Lucy nodded. "Oh, I figured that out already."

"There's a lot you don't know."

"Well then, I suppose I'm about to find out."

7

The flag irises in Erika's cottage garden were blooming when she finally decided to see what Lucy did in her "day job." Their beach walks had been more sporadic since Lucy had opened the summer chapel, St. Mary's by the Sea. Minding two churches was more than a full-time job. Regular services at St. Margaret's were moved to an earlier time, so Lucy could dash to the other chapel five miles away to conduct services there.

When Erika had last seen Lucy, she'd looked harried and pale. Erika had stepped up her efforts to share her cooking, dropping off care packages when she went into town. In return, Lucy left little notes, sometimes hastily dashed off, other times full blown, handwritten letters that became warmer as time went by. For the first time, she had signed one, "Love." Erika didn't want to get too cocky, but she took this as a positive sign.

Purely out of curiosity, Erika decided to attend the Eucharist service at the summer chapel. Maggie had said it was a beautiful setting on a cliff overlooking the ocean. The gorgeous view made it a popular spot for summer weddings. If the couple hadn't chosen their own celebrant, that was added to Lucy's other duties. Erika had always thought Liz was the busiest friend she had, especially when she was chief of surgery at Yale. Now, she saw Lucy was a close second. She wondered how that boded for a future relationship. If they became a couple, would she ever see Lucy?

The Eucharist service at St. Mary's by the Sea was at 11:45. That suited Erika, who was a late riser in the summer when she had no classes to teach. To keep the brilliant sun from streaming in her window at five thirty, she'd installed light-blocking shades. When she awoke around 8:30, her room was as black as night. Meanwhile, outside, the summer sun shone brilliantly.

Erika lay in bed for a few minutes to accustom herself to being awake. Liz had said it was better for her blood pressure to avoid jumping right out of bed, and she always followed her advice. At least, that's what she told Liz.

Erika wondered what to wear to church. Did people dress up nowadays?

Except for formal occasions like weddings and funerals, it had been decades since Erika had been inside a church. If this was a summer chapel open only when the tourists came to Hobbs, it was likely to be a casual venue. Nonetheless, Erika decided that she should dress up a little to show respect for Lucy and to make a good impression. It was also vanity. Erika cared about her looks, which was why she made sure to keep her figure trim and resisted Liz's persistent attempts to ply her with beer and lobster rolls.

While she drank her coffee, Erika turned finding out more about St. Mary's by the Sea into a research project. The website showed that the setting was, indeed, beautiful: a rustic stone church and an outdoor chapel overlooking the waves. There was a portrait of the presiding priest, the Reverend Lucille Bartlett. Looking away from the camera, Lucy had smiled fully for the camera. Her perfect features and striking red hair made her look like a model standing in for the real priest. She wore a deep-red lipstick that made Erika want to pucker up for a kiss.

"Well, Mother Lucy," she said aloud to the photo, "I hope you won't be too shocked to see me today." She blew a kiss to Lucy's smiling face.

As Erika took a shower, she realized that it had been a long time since she had courted a woman, not since Jeannine. The others had found her. There probably would never have been others, except Jeannine, with her insatiable artist's appetite, had a roving eye. Erika was only trying to keep up with her. She never minded having the permission to stray but exercised it less frequently than her partner.

Erika carefully styled her blond hair, put on a full complement of makeup, including the pink lipstick she preferred for the summer. She looked through her closet for something to wear. Her first impulse was to choose white pants and a multicolored camp blouse. Then she saw one of her few summer dresses, a fitted sleeveless number with a muted floral pattern. Perfect. She finished dressing and gave herself another quick look in the full-length mirror on the back of her bedroom door.

As Erika drove to the church, she wondered if she should sit in the front where Lucy would be sure to see her or in the back to be less of a distraction. She chastised herself for being so self-centered as to think Lucy would even pay attention to where she sat, or if she did, have a reaction. Lucy had once been an international opera star. Surely, she would be just as professional in the pulpit as she had been on the stage of the Met. The thought made Erika think of the recordings she'd downloaded of Lucy singing, and she asked Siri to play one while she drove.

Lucy had only recorded two solo albums. Erika had downloaded them both but had also purchased the CDs on eBay. Lucy had appeared as a principal singer in numerous opera recordings. Erika had purchased every one. She'd added every YouTube video of Lucy to her favorites list.

Erika turned on to the road that led to the ocean. The chapel was at the very end. When she arrived, she was surprised to see the parking lot was nearly full, but the picturesque church was small and its parking area, small as well. A strong wind was blowing when Erika got out of her car. Her hair would be a mess by the time she got inside. Fortunately, it was completely straight and easily smoothed into some semblance of order.

Erika still hadn't decided on the most advantageous position as she surveyed the rows of pews. There were some spaces left on the outside aisle. Erika chose a pew halfway to the front and moved as far to the center as she could. She realized that would put her directly in Lucy's line of vision when she ascended the pulpit, but by then, it was too late to change her mind. People had moved into the pew, hemming her in on both sides.

An organ began to play, signaling the start of the service. Two acolytes in cinched, white robes approached the altar. One carried a cross mounted on a staff. The other carried a tall, white candle.

The congregations's singing was thin and reedy, but Erika recognized the hymn from her childhood. It was an old Lutheran anthem, "Holy God, We Praise Thy Name." Not wanting to seem belligerent, Erika joined her strong alto to the other voices, timidly at first, but then more strongly. The words meant nothing to her, but she knew every one of them. To her surprise, she enjoyed singing with the others. It felt like a friendly thing to do.

Then the words stuck in her throat. Lucy came down the aisle in full vestments, a beautiful green chasuble with a gold brocade cross. Her red hair was pinned up. Her eyes were fixed straight ahead. Erika's lips parted for a moment as she took it all in. This Lucy belonged not only to her. She belonged to everyone in that church.

The procession ended when Lucy bowed to the altar and turned around. Erika's eyes instantly went to the red toenails peeking out from high-heeled sandals below Lucy's cassock. Erika felt an immediate and distinctive nudge in her genitals.

To distract herself, Erika fished in the rack on the back of the pew ahead and found the bulletin with the order of the service. Lucy intoned the salutation in a clear voice that reached the back of the church. There was no microphone in the tiny chapel. "Blessed be God: Father, Son and Holy Spirit!"

The congregation replied: "And blessed be his kingdom, now and for ever, Amen." Lucy's eyes scanned the congregation. "Thank you for joining us this morning at St. Mary's by the Sea. All are welcome at God's table, and that means everyone, no exceptions. If you have been baptized, you are welcome to take communion with us no matter what Christian path you follow."

Lucy finally noticed Erika. Her green eyes grew wide for a moment. Then she smiled one of her solar-flare smiles. Erika wagged her hand at waist-height in a subtle wave. Lucy pursed her lips and gave her a sweetly indulgent look. Then she faced forward and was all business.

Erika recognized most of the rite from the Lutheran liturgy of her childhood. Her grandmother had taken her to church because her heathen father wouldn't. Erika took her cues for standing, sitting and kneeling from the others, although the impulse to do one or the other was mostly instinctual. She was pleased that Lucy's homily on the Sermon on the Mount was well-reasoned and thoughtful. Had Lucy been one of her undergraduates, Erika would have given her an A.

The ritual and the hymns, despite being from a different sect, felt as familiar as an old friend. Finally, the service proceeded to its high point. Lucy took the unleavened bread and held it up. "For in the night in which he was betrayed, he took bread, and when he had given thanks, he broke it, and gave it to his disciples, saying, 'Take, eat, this is my Body, which is given for you. Do this in remembrance of me.'" Lucy genuflected in front of the altar.

Erika felt deeply touched as she watched this sacred affirmation of Lucy's priesthood. The awe and tenderness she felt for Lucy at that moment went far beyond the titillation she'd experienced when she'd glimpsed the painted toenails. It was desire on a completely different level. This was a new experience for Erika, and she had no idea what to do with it.

The prayers continued. The people stood and kneeled. Erika followed their example. The time for communion came. Should she, an unbeliever, approach the altar? Lucy had said that all were welcome at God's table.

Erika decided to take a scientific approach. She wanted the whole experience, didn't she? When the people in her row rose and moved in an orderly line to the center aisle, Erika followed. She noticed that the man in front of her had dandruff on his collar. She lowered her eyes to avoid fixating on it. Fortunately, the line moved quickly.

Finally, she stood before Lucy. Subconsciously, Erika remembered from childhood how to hold her hands for communion, cupped open, one hand folded under the other. There was surprise in the green eyes that briefly searched her face before Lucy offered the bread. "The body of Christ, the bread of heaven." Erika gazed directly into Lucy eyes, where she saw a profound look of love. She felt the bread in her hand and had to remind herself to put it into her mouth. She moved away to drink the wine, but she felt Lucy's eyes following her.

The rest of the service was something of a blur. All Erika could think about was the look Lucy had given her when she had offered her communion. It wasn't sexual. Erika could recognize desire because she'd seen it in Lucy's eyes. This was an expression Erika couldn't find words to describe, and that frustrated her. Erika could always find the right words.

At the conclusion of the service, the procession filed out, and the congregation straggled out behind them. Erika considered slipping away, but then decided that, after coming this far with her experiment, she would see it to the end. She was one of the last to leave the chapel. Lucy was waiting outside to shake the hands of all those who had attended the service. When Erika approached, Lucy offered her hand, but instead of shaking it, she used it to draw her close. She placed a soft kiss on Erika's cheek and whispered into her ear, "Thank you so much for coming. Stay a moment." She released her hand so that she could greet the next congregant.

Erika lingered on the sidelines until everyone had moved away from Lucy, who was beaming when she approached. "Let me hang up my vestments, then please join us in the lower church for fellowship."

"What's that?" asked Erika.

"Coffee, donuts, and gossip," said Lucy with a mischievous grin. "You can come with me to the robing room, if you'd like."

Erika followed her back into the church. She watched with fascination as Lucy removed each of the ceremonial garments and carefully hung them in the closet among the other colorful vestments. She felt a bit like a voyeur watching Lucy change into her black clericals. She glanced at the red toenails and the stylish sandals for distraction.

"I like your shoes," said Erika idly.

"I would never wear these for a service, but I was rushing and broke the heel off my pumps on the stone walk in front of the rectory. These were the only dressy shoes I could find in that mess of a closet of mine."

Lucy had never struck Erika as a messy person. She was extremely tidy and fastidious about her personal appearance, but such people could be secret slobs. She hoped the disorder in Lucy's closet wasn't a bad sign. Erika couldn't stand disorder.

"Do you think people thought my shoes were too risqué?"

"Risqué isn't quite the word I would have chosen. Racy, perhaps."

"Oh, no!" Lucy blushed to the roots of her red hair.

Erika laughed. "It's not every day you see a priest wearing red nail polish, but I, for one, liked it very much. In fact, I found it rather stimulating." She leaned forward and kissed Lucy on the lips.

"Stop that, or I won't want to get back to my congregation."

"All right. Let's have coffee and a ration of gossip, and then I'll take you to the diner for brunch. All right?"

"Deal," said Lucy.

"You're spending too much time with Liz. You're picking up her expressions."

Lucy looked thoughtful for a moment. "Yes, I guess I am."

***

St. Mary's churchgoers were mostly "from away," as Mainers would say—summer visitors from the other New England states. Some were Canadians because the coast of Maine was closer to them than their own maritime provinces. Some were Hobb's residents who liked the picturesque setting.

During the fellowship, Erika hung back to observe Lucy in her element. The rector was charming and gracious and laughed easily as she greeted the people who had gathered in the basement for donuts from the world-famous donut restaurant on Route 1. The delicious donuts were accompanied by weak coffee dispensed from an industrial-sized urn.

Erika wasn't sure how she felt sharing Lucy with so many people. From Jeannine's exhibitions, she was accustomed to playing the role of significant other to a celebrity. Jeannine's stridently feminist paintings, an oeuvre that went back to the 1970s, went in and out of fashion. With the sudden resurgence of misogyny in the political environment, her artwork had suddenly become popular again. Erika had been the executor and heir to Jeannine's estate. Although the proceeds could have helped Erika with her early retirement scheme, she had used the money to create a foundation for women artists. She'd kept a few paintings for sentimental reasons, but they'd been consigned to storage.

Finally, the last stragglers in the lower church left, and Lucy breathed an audible sigh of relief. "Usually, I go home and crash after this," she confessed to Erika. "Three services in one day is a lot."

Erika was instantly sympathetic. "You do look exhausted. Would you rather go home and rest? I'll understand."

"No," said Lucy, taking Erika's arm, "It's been so long since I've seen you. I want to spend some time with you." Her smile was as radiant as always, but her eyes looked tired and bleary.

"Maybe you'll perk up after a bit of sustenance."

"Let's drive to the rectory, so I can drop off my car. Then you can drive us to the diner."

The lunch crowd jammed the small diner, but Lucy's collar earned her special treatment and a booth in the corner. After they put in their order, Lucy asked, "What made you come to church this morning?

"Candidly? Nothing but curiosity."

Lucy gave her an I-don't-believe-you look.

"All right, I'll be truthful. I'm a bit of a voyeur. I just wanted to look at you."

"You're still not being completely honest."

"Yes, fine! As I told you, religious people fascinate me. I am still trying to work out who you are. I look for clues wherever they can be found. Your Sunday service seemed like a good place to start."

Lucy sighed, making her fatigue evident. She managed a smile, somewhat less sunny than usual, but very warm. "I really don't care why you came. I'm just glad you did." She reached across the table and took Erika's hand. "Thank you."

"I found it very interesting. I may attend a future service. I found your homily well-constructed and quite elegantly presented. Well done, Mother Bartlett."

Lucy nodded slightly to acknowledge the compliment, but her eyes gazed deeply into Erika's. "Do you have any idea how much I've missed you?"

Erika blinked. "No, but from the look you just gave me, I assume you did…a bit."

"How have you been?"

Lucy's open interest touched Erika and momentarily lessened her defenses.

"Unfortunately, some bad news from my father. My mother has taken a fall and is in the hospital again."

"Oh, Erika, I'm so sorry. It's difficult to deal with aging parents."

"Are your parents still living?"

Lucy shook her head. "My father died quite young. My mother passed away a few years ago. Fortunately, she was relatively healthy until a few weeks before she died. Ovarian cancer."

"Ugh," exclaimed Erika.

"Yes," Lucy agreed, "but she went quickly and that was a blessing."

"My mother has been declining for years."

"I'm sorry to hear that. What's her situation?"

"She has severe arthritis, so her mobility is limited. She's also losing her hearing. The brilliant conversation between my parents was the glue that held them together. I also think her mind is beginning to go."

"That's sad. I'm sorry."

Erika sighed. "So am I."

A little, dark-haired girl appeared at Erika's elbow. "Hi, Aunt Erika."

"My goodness, hello, Katrina. Is your mommy here?"

Katrina nodded. "We're sitting back there, against the wall." She thumbed over her shoulder toward the other side of the tiny diner.

Alina hurried to retrieve her daughter. "Come back here, Miss," she said, taking Katrina's hand. She smiled at Lucy and gave Erika a half hug. "So sorry she's bothering you."

"She's no bother. Are you, love?" said Erika, returning the girl's warm smile. "Are your grandmothers here too?"

Katrina pointed in their direction.

"Tell them we say hello, will you?"

"Enjoy your meal," said Alina as she led her daughter away.

"I'm surprised Liz and Maggie are here," Erika said. "The locals almost never come to this place during the season."

A sturdy woman with a thick French braid stopped on her way to the counter. "Well, hello there, Reverend," said Brenda Harrison, the Hobbs police chief. She glanced at the open-toed sandals. Her eyes widened momentarily, but she quickly glanced away.

She tapped Erika on the shoulder. "Hey, Professor, I hear you're staying a while."

"Yes, I'm here for at least a year, maybe two. I'm on sabbatical."

"Lucky you."

"Yes, I am."

"Have a good day, ladies," said Brenda, moving to her place at the counter.

Once Brenda was occupied with giving the waitress her order, Erika said, "I'd forgotten we can't have any privacy here."

Lucy smiled. "It doesn't matter. I just want to look at you."

"That's my line."

"I know. I'm borrowing it."

8

Lucy bit into the peanut and jelly sandwich that Renee Langdon had brought. Lucy had been trying to discourage her from bringing more sandwiches—after all the woman, like most of her clients, had limited means. So far, Lucy's protests had fallen on deaf ears.

"You don't need to bring me a sandwich. I can certainly make my own."

"I make one for myself and my kids, so it's nothing to make one for you," Renee said with a smile.

"Do you have the same thing every day?" asked Lucy, worried. While the sugary grape jelly and peanut butter on white bread recalled childhood and the Monkees lunch box Lucy had carried in elementary school, she knew there were healthier choices.

"Depends," said Renee. "Sometimes it's leftovers, like chicken or meatloaf. Tuna fish some days. Kids love the peanut butter and jelly. Sometimes I make them a fluffernutter. Remember those? Peanut butter with marshmallow spread."

"I never had one," Lucy admitted. Her mother, despite her busy schedule as a voice teacher, had paid careful attention to what her daughter ate. She was ahead of her time in choosing "health food" for her family. "Sounds sweet enough to make your teeth hurt."

Renee laughed. "It does make your teeth hurt. You can be sure of that. I only make them for the kids once in a while. Pure sugar."

Lucy listened to Renee's gentle Maine accent with the long open A's, the swallowed R's. She loved the way people spoke in Maine, not unlike how they did in her home state of Massachusetts. As a city dweller in the western part of the state, Lucy's accent had always been faint. She'd lost it long before she headed to New York and Julliard.

They finished eating their sweet and sticky lunch. Lucy handed Renee a packaged wipe from the ample supply in her desk. Now that she knew to expect sandwiches from Renee, Lucy kept the stock replenished.

"We need to get started," Lucy said. "As much as I enjoy your sandwiches and chatting, I don't want to cheat you out of the time in your session."

"I don't mind. Sometimes, I feel better just sitting here with you and eating. You have the most beautiful smile. It warms me all up inside."

Of course, that made Lucy smile even more. "Thank you. I'm glad my presence is a comfort to you. But let's get started. How are things going at home? How's your son doing?"

Renee looked down into her lap and shook her head. "He got the flagman job, but he lost it already. He was late for work the second day. The fourth day, he didn't show up. With the unemployment so low, they can't find workers, so they kept giving him chances. Finally, they had to let him go."

"He told you this?"

"No, I have a friend in the department. He's the one who helped get Pete the job. Obviously, he's not only mad, he's embarrassed. So, no more DOT jobs for Pete."

"That's a shame."

"It is. It's steady work and it pays well."

"Do you still feel uneasy with him in the house?"

Renee glanced away, but she nodded. "It's a terrible thing for a mother to be scared of her own son."

"Is it only the guns that frighten you?"

"No, the guns are scary, but Pete's got some temper. Once, he ripped the door off the kitchen cabinet because it swung back and hit his knuckles. Then he smashed all the glasses inside."

Lucy felt dread at the thought of someone being so out of control he would rip a door off the hinges. "Maybe you can get him to come in and talk to me."

"Are you kidding?"

"No," said Lucy earnestly. "I'm serious."

"He would never talk to you. He's not much for religion, and I don't think he likes women very much."

Lucy tried to interpret this message. There were several possibilities. "Do you think he's gay?"

Renee laughed. "No. He likes women just fine, for sex."

"Then what do you mean, 'he doesn't like women'?"

"He thinks they're stupid and useless. He doesn't respect them.... Maybe that's my fault. I wasn't firm enough after his father left. Or maybe I was too firm. Who knows?"

"Stop blaming yourself. His friends probably have more to do with his views of women than you do. There have been studies..."

"So? Studies. Who cares what they say? I raised him. I made him who he is."

Lucy leveled her vision at Renee, hoping to emphasize the point she'd made. Why were the men she counseled always looking for excuses for their behavior, while the women couldn't wait to take all the blame?

"What about the guns? Have you asked him to get rid of them?"

"Yes, and he snapped at me, 'Mind your own business.'"

"Maybe you should go to the police. Chief Harrison is smart. I bet she deals with this kind of thing all the time. I'm sure she could find a way to talk to him without implicating you."

Renee shook her head emphatically. "He would kill me if I went to the police."

Startled, Lucy sat up straight. "You don't really mean that, I hope."

Renee made a face. "I don't really know what he would do. Sometimes, I don't recognize my own son."

"How can I help you, Renee? Please tell me how I can help." Lucy realized she was pleading, and her client was staring at her anxiously.

Finally, Renee said, "You're doing exactly the right thing, Mother Lucy. I need you to listen to me. You're the only one I can talk to. My mother thinks this is all my fault, that I drove my husband away because I kept leaning on him to get a decent job. Never mind a decent job, just one that he kept for more than a couple of months. I have no other family. I need you to listen to me."

"Is Dr. Stolz your doctor?"

Renee nodded. "Yes, she is."

"You could talk to her."

Renee looked down and shook her head. "Dr. Stolz has better things to do than talk to me about this."

"Is she Peter's doctor too?"

"She is, but I don't even know if he goes to the doctor anymore. He never tells me anything."

"Maybe she could talk to him. She knows about guns. She can talk his language."

"No. He can never know I even told you about them."

"Do you mind if I ask Dr. Stolz's advice about this situation?"

Renee thought for a long moment. "I trust Dr. Stolz. Sure. You can talk to her."

***

Renee remained on Lucy's mind during her usual Tuesday afternoon counseling sessions with the grieving widower and the woman who couldn't make up her mind about her pregnancy. By not making a decision, she was, of course, deciding. She was already into her second trimester. Time was running out to terminate the pregnancy. Lucy reminded her of this before she left. She gave her the number of the nearest Planned Parenthood. When the woman casually slipped the paper into her jeans pocket, Lucy knew she would never call the clinic.

After her pregnant client left, Lucy called Liz. Lucy hated to interrupt Liz during her office hours, but the urgency of the situation warranted it. She called her cell number instead of going through the office staff because of the sensitivity of the matter.

"And how's my favorite lady priest today?" Liz asked when she answered. Lucy could hear the smile in her voice.

"Great. How's my favorite lady doctor?"

"Eh, fair to middling. A busy day. Is this a social call or business?"

"Business…"

"What's the matter, Lucy?" Liz asked anxiously. "Are you sick?"

Lucy laughed softly. "Don't worry, Liz, it's not about me."

"That's good." Lucy imagined Liz's handsome face relaxing.

"I'm calling about Peter Langdon. Can we speak in confidence as one professional to another?"

"Absolutely."

"His mother is one of my counseling clients. She's a single mom, as you probably know, and has had some challenges with those kids."

"I do know. Peter had some issues with alcohol and pot in high school. A few times it landed him in trouble with the police, but I thought he'd gotten past that. Unfortunately, he's like so many boys up here. They just can't seem to find their way."

"Mrs. Langdon is worried about what she calls an arsenal in the basement. He got all of his father's hunting guns when Mr. Langdon left them, but he apparently also has pistols and some assault rifles."

"I wonder where he gets the money. Those aren't cheap. Maybe he's dealing or cooking meth."

"She doesn't suspect any drugs except marijuana, but maybe she wouldn't say anything if she did. Are you busy? I'd like to come over and talk to you."

There was a pause. Presumably, Liz was checking her schedule. "I'll be free in an hour. Is that good?

Lucy considered her own afternoon plans. She had invited Erika for dinner and needed to get to the supermarket. This was more important.

"Sure. I'll be there."

***

As Lucy sat in the waiting room of Hobbs Family Practice, she was glad she had changed into her civvies—today, cropped pants, a T-shirt and sandals. She remembered Erika's reaction to the nail polish on her toes and smiled. When Lucy had been an opera singer, it had been part of the glamor she'd needed to project. Now, it was one of the vanities she allowed herself. She never painted her fingernails, not because the Church prohibited it, but because she felt red fingernails would be a distraction during the Eucharist.

Unfortunately, she was used to being a distraction. As she sat in the waiting room of Hobbs Family Practice, she was aware of people staring at her. That was the price she paid for being an attractive woman. She knew it was nothing she did. Her perfect features were the result of good genes. Her beautiful mother had been a model while she was trying to break into singing.

Lucy had long ago given up thinking her pretty face was an asset, although it had certainly helped when she was coming up through the ranks in the opera world. Now, she mostly ignored the people who stared at her for her beauty, but it was especially annoying when she was giving a sermon, and the men in the congregation ogled her.

Lucy glanced at her phone. It was getting late and she needed to get to the supermarket. She got up and leaned over the check-in desk to speak discreetly. "Ginny, are these people all waiting for Liz?"

The practice manager looked up from her paperwork. "No, they're waiting for Dr. Pelletier. She has office hours this evening. Liz is almost done." As she said that, Liz came through the corridor with a patient. Lucy took a step back so that Liz could confer with Ginny about future appointments.

"Okay, Mother Lucy, you can come in now," said Liz with a wink, and Lucy followed her down the hall to her consulting room.

Liz closed the door after Lucy took a seat in one of the visitors' chairs. "May I kiss my favorite lady priest?" Lucy nodded and Liz gave her a quick kiss on the lips. "I never miss a chance to kiss a beautiful woman," she explained with a rakish grin.

"You're such a tease. Just like your friend, Erika."

"Erika isn't a tease. She's very literal. Very Teutonic. What you see is what you get."

Lucy frowned as she compared her impressions of Erika to Liz's. She wasn't sure they agreed.

Liz sat down in the other visitors' chair. "I don't have any lipstick on me?" she asked, frowning. "Maggie would kill me."

"No. You're fine. What do you think? I wear lipstick that smudges? I know better than that."

"Of course, you do." Liz assumed her doctor face, and she was instantly all business. The swiftness of the transition almost threw Lucy off balance. She guessed it was a holdover from when Liz was a surgeon and had no time to waste. "Okay, Lucy. What's going on with the Langdons?"

"As I started to tell you, I'm worried. Poor Mrs. Langdon is running in every direction trying to make a living and raise the younger children. She's been coming to me for counseling since February. She was depressed and couldn't shake it. I think she was suffering from seasonal affective disorder. She snapped out of it once spring came."

"Unfortunately, there's a lot of SAD here in Maine. Our winters are so long."

Lucy nodded in agreement. "Once Renee started feeling better, she began opening up to me about the situation at home."

"So, tell me your specific worry, Lucy," said Liz, cutting to the chase. "Is it domestic violence? A potential mass shooter?"

"I don't know exactly. All I know is that Renee is really frightened of her son, and he has a lot of guns."

Liz frowned. "Many people up here have a lot of guns. I have a lot of guns."

"I know. I just have a bad feeling about this."

"That worries me. After all, you have a direct line to the Almighty." Liz grinned and raised a brow.

"Be serious."

"Okay. What would you like me to do?"

"Give me advice. Should I go to the police?"

"You know you can't without breaking confidentiality. And even if you could, there's nothing they can do unless there's an immediate threat. Damn. I wish that red flag law passed last year."

"There's nothing we can do?"

Liz shook her head. "You can encourage Mrs. Langdon to go to the police. Then they'd know what's going on and can keep an eye on the situation."

"She won't go. She said he'd kill her if she went to the police."

That certainly got Liz's attention. "That's a pretty clear threat, Lucy."

"But you just said there's nothing we can do."

"There's not. She didn't say he'd threatened to kill her. It's speculation on her part." Liz gazed out the window with a frown. "We could hedge, I guess. I have my weekly breakfast at the diner with the chief tomorrow morning. I could drop a hint like, 'I hear there's quite a powerful collection in the basement at 127 Blueberry Road' or something vague like that. Brenda's sharp. She'll catch on."

"That's right on the edge, Liz."

"I know, but up here, we do things differently sometimes. It works for us." Liz winked. "Like dealing with the code inspector about your wiring and plumbing."

"I don't want to get you in trouble, Liz…or me."

"Don't worry. I'll handle it," said Liz in a confident voice.

"Okay. I trust you." That made Liz smile.

"I wonder if your parishioners appreciate having a licensed therapist as their counselor."

"Because I don't charge, there's no insurance involved. Hardly anyone knows I have the credentials."

"Maybe you should charge. Do you mind if I send you some of my patients who don't have insurance and could never pay for counseling?"

"If I have time, sure," said Lucy. "But now, I need some more advice."

"Lucy, I'm going to have to start charging you. Ginny will make me, you know."

"This is cooking advice. I don't think you can bill for that."

Liz laughed heartily. "No, I don't think so."

"I'm making dinner for Erika tonight. This is a big deal because she's always cooking for me, and I've never returned the favor."

"You can cook?" Liz asked, deadpanning.

"Oh, stop! Yes, I can cook, but it's not my favorite thing. And I've been so busy, I'm out of practice."

"What can I do to help an out-of-practice cook?"

"Do you know Erika's favorite dish?"

"She's an omnivore like me. But she likes fish and seafood. Especially, when she's here at the shore and can get it fresh."

"Salmon? I found a really good recipe with a soy sauce and honey glaze."

"Have you cooked it before? You have to time salmon just right, so it doesn't dry out. And it's tricky because it depends on the thickness, where it's from and—"

"But I want to prepare something she really likes."

"She really likes salmon," said Liz, nodding.

"Good."

"Just don't overcook it."

"I won't."

"Really, you have to be careful."

"I will be."

***

Lucy looked over the spread she had prepared for before-dinner snacking: tangy goat cheese from the farmer's market, local smoked cheddar, olives, multi-grain crackers, cut up vegetables and dip. It looked very tasty and appealing. She hoped her guest would be impressed.

She glanced at her phone and realized she had a few minutes before Erika arrived. She went into the bathroom and slicked on a fresh coat of lipstick. She released her hair from the ponytail and gave it a quick brush. She started to put it in a French braid, then changed her mind and decided to leave it loose. *I'm like a teenager getting ready for my first date. Can't make up my mind.* She had just finished brushing out her hair when the doorbell rang.

Erika stood at the door with a bouquet of flowers and a bottle of wine.

When she saw Lucy, her lips parted in surprise. "I've never seen you with your hair down."

"From the look on your face, I'm not sure if you like it or not."

"Oh, I do, indeed." She leaned forward to offer a kiss when Lucy yanked her inside.

"No kissing the rector on the door stoop," she said anxiously. She smiled to soften the warning.

"It's hard to resist. You look luscious as always." This time, Erika succeeded in landing the kiss. Lucy felt almost dizzy when they parted. "What's the matter?" asked Erika. "Do I have your lipstick on my face?"

Lucy chuckled. "No. Can't I look at you? You look pretty luscious yourself."

Erika blushed a little. "Thank you," she said modestly. She thrust forward a multicolored bouquet of flowers. "From my garden," Erika explained. "And this," she said, holding out the bottle of wine. "White. Liz says we're having fish for dinner."

"Liz told you that?"

"Yes, when I called to ask her to recommend a wine."

"Is she your wingman?"

"My wingman?" Erika repeated, looking puzzled.

Lucy laughed. "That's an expression for a buddy who looks out for you when you're picking up chicks in a bar."

"I'm not picking up any chicks." She frowned at Lucy. "You are quite up on the lingo, my dear. Do you frequent bars often?"

Lucy laughed aloud this time. "No, never. I'm a priest, remember?"

Erika gave her a cautious look. "Somehow, I don't think that would deter you."

Lucy glanced down at the bouquet, a lovely selection of June flowers: day lilies of every color, baby's breath, a few early roses, flag iris. "Let me put these in some water. Come in."

She could sense Erika inspecting the place as she followed her through the halls to the rector's quarters—an ample apartment with a full kitchen, living room, dining room, and a large bedroom.

"It's rather spacious," observed Erika, giving the artwork in the living room a brief, critical look. "One could be quite comfortable here."

"It was remodeled once the rector no longer had the means to employ a housekeeper and had to fend for himself. I'm the first female rector of the parish. Down the hall, there are two efficiency studios for curates, but now we only use them for visiting clergy. There's also a common room, downstairs and a communal kitchen."

"This is a big place. I never realized."

"But it's an old building and it's hard to heat in the winter." Lucy gestured to the sofa. "Have a seat. I've prepared some snacks. Dinner won't take long. Let me open the wine." Lucy returned in a few minutes with a glass for each of them.

Erika took a sip from her glass. "Very good. Liz never fails me." She inspected the snack tray and selected a cracker, which she spread with goat cheese.

"Do you ask her advice about women?" Lucy asked, sitting beside her.

"I need no advice about women," replied Erika in a cocky voice that surprised Lucy. "I am perfectly capable of figuring them out on my own."

"Is that so? And what have you figured out about me?"

Erika chuckled. "There's an interesting backstory to why you quit singing. Not exactly a Pauline conversion, but something dramatic, I'm quite sure of that. Perhaps you will tell me."

"It's a long story."

"I'm not going anywhere," said Erika, selecting another cracker and slicing off a piece of smoked cheddar.

Lucy knew Erika's casual attitude was almost a dare to get her to open up, but one that she wasn't about to take. "I'll tell you another time, when we know each other better."

Erika nodded sympathetically. "All right. But you will tell me?"

"Yes," Lucy agreed.

"Will you tell me after we make love?"

The question startled Lucy. "You're pretty confident that's where we're headed."

Erika gave her a sly look. "I have no doubt, do you?"

Lucy looked down and shook her head.

"So, then will you tell me?"

"If we become close enough to make love, yes, I will tell you."

"Have I told you I've been collecting your recordings? I find hearing you sing very erotic. I think I have every recording, every video. I listen to them over and over again. When I hear your voice, it's like a caress." Erika's pale eyes gave her a penetrating look, which Lucy found very stimulating, almost like being touched in an intimate place.

"There's the concert in September," said Lucy brightly, trying to divert her.

"I can't wait that long," Erika replied, her gaze unwavering.

"Then I'll tell you a secret. I sing every morning in church to keep my voice in shape. I always leave the side door open in case I forget the key."

"Ah, I could slip in and listen to a private performance. At what time does this recital occur?"

"Around seven o'clock."

Erika made a face. "A bit early for me but certainly worth it."

"Maybe not. I sing nothing but exercises for the first twenty minutes or so."

"Good to know. I shall delay my arrival. My body will thank me for a few extra minutes of sleep."

"I should get dinner started," said Lucy.

Erika caught her arm. "There's no rush. I just arrived. And you've set out all these lovely treats. Sit and talk to me a bit."

Lucy smiled. "You don't want to talk. We talk all the time. You have other things in mind."

"Perhaps, but I definitely do not want you to busy yourself with domestic activities when I have this rare opportunity to be alone with you." Erika looked at her through half-closed eyes.

"You are incorrigible," said Lucy leaning into her. She didn't resist when Erika took her in her arms and began to kiss her. She allowed her head to fall back on Erika's arm and her tongue to explore her mouth. Erika's hand tenderly caressed her breast, the fingertips drawing circles around the nipple. Lucy felt it hardening to the persistent touch. Then the hand found its way under her T-shirt. It pinched the nipple through the lace bra. Lucy's body was saying, *Yes! Pinch harder*! And Erika was kissing her exactly the way she liked.

Lucy broke the kiss to say, "Keep doing that, and we'll never eat dinner."

"I don't care," said Erika. "I'd much rather kiss you."

"But I care." Lucy slipped out of Erika's arms. "I'm going to make dinner now," she said and headed to the kitchen.

9

Erika munched on a cracker as she thought. She felt frustrated and, if she were willing to admit it, slightly angry. One moment she'd been holding Lucy in her arms, and then, she was gone. Lucy's reticence was confusing. She said she wasn't celibate, but sometimes she acted as if she were. What, after all, were they waiting for? All that nonsense about giving her body and sex being a sacred act. Absurd!

Suddenly, Erika heard a sharp cry of dismay, "Oh, no! NO!" Erika scrambled to her feet and went into the kitchen, where she found Lucy staring at the pan she'd just taken from the oven. "It's ruined. Ruined!"

Erika evaluated the situation in a glance. The salmon on the pan looked a bit toasty. She picked up a fork and flaked the fish. "We can eat it," she said, "but it will be dry."

"Liz told me over and over again not to overcook it!"

"Is the salmon wild caught?"

"Yes. I wanted the best for you," said Lucy, looking perfectly miserable. "I thought it must be good because it was the most expensive."

Erika nodded, understanding. "That's very generous, but wild-caught salmon requires a different approach. It's not as fatty as farm raised. It needs less time under the broiler."

Lucy began to cry. "I'm sorry. I only wanted to show you I could cook! That I'm not a complete zero in the kitchen." She began to sob outright. Erika realized that it had less to do with the ruined dinner than fatigue. Lucy was overextended. Her many duties had finally overwhelmed her.

Erika took her in her arms. "Don't cry, love. I can help you fix this, or we can go out to eat. Which do you prefer?"

"Can you really fix it?" Lucy asked in a small, hopeful voice.

"Yes, I think so," said Erika, rubbing her back soothingly. "Would you like me to show you how?" She drew back to look at Lucy's face.

Pouting, Lucy nodded solemnly. Erika was reminded of a small child after a crying jag.

"Do you have pasta?" Erika asked.

Lucy nodded.

"Butter?"

"Yes."

"Cream?"

"Half and half."

"That will do."

"Parmesan cheese?"

"Yes."

"Let's collect what we need. Then I'll show you how we can rescue your dish. No one will be the wiser." Erika tapped the side of her nose with her forefinger, then pushed up the three-quarter sleeves of her T-shirt even though they weren't really in the way. "I also need a stock pot and a large sauté pan."

Erika felt Lucy watching intently as she organized the ingredients. "An Alfredo sauce is ridiculously simple, but you need to pay attention to keep the sauce from breaking and turning into a nasty goo." Erika put up the water to boil. The pasta was multi-colored penne, but it was all Lucy had, and it would have to do. While the water heated, Erika flaked the edible parts of the salmon and cut up the asparagus that Lucy had roasted along with the fish.

"This will be tasty. Wait and see," said Erika.

"You make it look so easy," Lucy murmured.

"Like everything, it's easy when you know how."

The water began to boil, Erika added some salt and threw in the pasta. She melted the butter and warmed the cream. The Parmesan cheese had come already grated, which saved her a step.

"How did you learn to cook?" asked Lucy, watching carefully.

"My mother taught me," Erika explained. "She is quite good at it. When we first landed in London, and times were hard, she supported us as a cook in a small restaurant. Then Cambridge gave my father a job as lecturer, and she had to give it up. A shame, really. I'd never seen her happier than when she ruled that little restaurant kitchen." Erika looked at her watch to judge how long the pasta had been on to boil. "Another minute." While she waited, Erika incorporated the grated cheese into the warm butter and cream.

Lucy put her arm around Erika's waist and leaned against her. "You are amazing!"

Erika wasn't sure how she amazing was, but she liked the feel of Lucy's arm around her and her head on her shoulder. Her hair smelled of something smoky and sweet. After puzzling for a moment, Erika identified it as incense.

"Time to test the pasta, love," said Erika, gently untangling herself from Lucy's embrace. She removed a piece of pasta with a slotted spoon, allowed it to cool a moment, then popped it into her mouth. "Perfect," she pronounced. She drained the rest of the pasta and added it to the sauté pan. She tossed in the salmon and asparagus. "Do you have pasta bowls? Otherwise dinner plates will do."

"I do have pasta bowls," said Lucy proudly, taking them down from a cabinet.

Erika served two portions of her creation. "Unless we have enormous appetites, you will have leftovers for tomorrow. Heat it gently in the microwave, or the sauce will separate."

"I am so embarrassed. I finally invite you for dinner, and you have to cook for me."

"It's nothing, as you saw. Very simple. The sauce will make up for the dryness of the salmon. Let's sit down." Erika brought the bowls to the table, which had been carefully set for a romantic dinner. Lucy lit the candles. As always, she bowed her head in silent prayer before she ate. Erika appreciated that she never expected her to participate in this ritual, nor did it in restaurants.

Lucy tasted the pasta. "Oh, my word! This is so delicious!" The pure pleasure on her face was all the reward Erika needed for saving the meal.

"You saw how simple it is. Next time you can make it for me. You can put nearly anything in it. Cooked shrimp or chicken, herbs, peas, cooked broccoli...quite versatile."

Erika looked up and saw that Lucy was gazing at her with such admiration and love that she wanted to melt like the butter in the sauce. She returned the tender look, but said, "Eat your supper, Lucy, or it will get cold."

"You're amazing!"

"So you said. Your mother never taught you to cook?"

"She did. A little. My mother was also a singer. She made it to the Boston Lyric Opera as a principal before she married my dad. Afterwards, she taught music and gave private voice lessons. She never had much time for cooking."

"And your father?"

"Dad was a math teacher."

"So is mine."

"Your father is Clemson Professor of Mathematics at Yale. Not quite the same."

So, Lucy has looked him up. Interesting, thought Erika.

"He's still a maths teacher, or at least he was. He's emeritus now, of course." Erika took another taste of the pasta. It was good. "So, you came by being a singer honestly. Did your mother push you toward a career as a singer?"

"No, but she was my first voice teacher. When I got to Julliard, I discovered how common it is for singers to come from musical families. That, or church choirs."

"Ah, yes. Church choirs."

"I was raised Catholic," said Lucy. "We never had a real choir in my church, so that didn't apply to me. What about you?"

"My father is an atheist. My mother is nominally Lutheran but never went to church. As you know, I am an agnostic."

Lucy smiled one of her sunny smiles. "At least, you're not an atheist. There may still be hope for you."

"Don't get excited, dear. I am a hard sell."

"It always makes me smile to hear Americanisms come out of your mouth. You sound so British, except for that teeny-weeny German accent."

"I've tried, but I simply can't lose it, not even if I try to put on an American accent. After Father left Cambridge to come to teach at Yale, I wanted to sound American. My speech ended up sounding flat and toneless, so I stopped trying. By the time I got to Yale, I had completed my undergraduate education at Cambridge, so by then, I was already very, very English."

"So, you studied philosophy at Cambridge?"

"Maths, actually. It was at Yale that I discovered continental philosophy and fell in love." Erika crossed her hands on her heart and rolled her eyes toward the ceiling.

But Lucy didn't laugh. She gave Erika a long thoughtful look. "That's the most you've told me about your background since I've known you."

Erika chuckled. "I suppose we're at the point in our relationship for the background check. I could send you my CV. You can also download it from the Colby faculty page."

"Thanks, but I'd rather hear you tell me. I like listening to you." Lucy got up to toss the salad and brought it to the table.

"I see you've acquired the habit of eating your salad after the meal as we do in Europe."

"I lived in Stuttgart for three years while I was building my career. I was a principal soprano at the Stuttgart opera."

"*Sprichts du Deutsch*?"

"*Ja, ich kann Deutsch sprechen*."

"Then I'd best mind what I say to Liz in your presence!"

Lucy laughed. "Now, I'm sorry I told you. I've learned some interesting things from your German conversations."

Erika felt her face flame with embarrassment. "Such as?"

"I know you really like my butt and my boobs. And so does Liz."

Erika's fork stopped midway to her mouth. "Dear God! Why didn't you tell me?"

"Why? I enjoyed being a fly on the wall while you two crudely went on about me."

"Lucy! That's horrible! You should have said something!"

Lucy began to laugh. "Serves you both right for treating a woman like an object. You should be embarrassed. Shame on you! Both of you!"

"Oh, don't give me that feminist drivel," said Erika in a dismissive voice. "I had quite enough of it from Jeannine."

Across the table, Lucy gave her a sympathetic look. "You never talk about her."

"Why would I burden you with information about my dead partner?"

"Perhaps it would comfort you to talk about her."

"Thank you, Lucy," Erika said sharply, "but I don't need you to minister to me."

Lucy's expression instantly changed from sympathy to hurt. "I meant, I would listen as a friend, not as a counselor or priest."

Erika eyed her cautiously. Lucy's expression of sympathy touched her, but Erika wasn't ready to talk about Jeannine yet, and certainly not to the woman she was courting. "Thank you, but I'd rather not talk about it." She attempted a contrite look. "Forgive me for snapping at you."

"No need to apologize." Lucy got up to pick up her plate and Erika's. As she passed, she bent to kiss the top of Erika's head. "You're fine." She took the plates to the sink.

Erika rose. "I'll help you."

"No, you don't," said Lucy, nudging her aside. "Go out to the living room and put on some music. You cooked. I clean up. That's our deal, right?"

"We already have domestic rules? In fact, we both cooked."

"Never mind," said Lucy, bumping her lightly with her hip. "Go."

Erika surveyed the vast collection of CDs on the shelves in the living room. Being a singer, Lucy would prefer the superior sound quality of CDs. The collection was well organized, and Erika had no trouble finding her way around. There were boxed sets of complete operas, sometimes several recordings of the same opera. Erika guessed those were the operas in Lucy's repertoire. No doubt, she owned multiple recordings to study different interpretations.

Erika had already figured out from the music she'd acquired that Lucy was a spinto. Her voice was not big enough to sing the heavy, dramatic parts, but it had the heft to sing roles like Desdemona, Tosca, Cio-Cio San, or Aida.

While Erika was exploring the collection, she found a stack of noncommercial CDs in a box. Her heart skipped a beat when she realized these were demo disks and private recordings, some of which went back to Lucy's early career. Erika loaded one marked "MB 1995" into the disc player. Soon the sound of Cio-Cio San's famous aria from *Madame Butterfly* ,"Un Bel Di Vedremo," filled the air. The hair on Erika's arms stood up. This was Lucille Bartlett in her prime. Erika closed her eyes and allowed her imagination to transport her to Lucy singing this role on stage. When the aria hit its crescendo, Erika thought her heart might break.

She opened her eyes to see Lucy standing in front of her, frowning. "I didn't mean for you to play my personal recordings," she said with an edge in her voice.

"But Lucy, I can never get enough of hearing you sing. May I make duplicates of these discs?"

"I don't know," said Lucy, frowning more deeply. "Let me think about that."

"Don't tell me you're so self-critical, you don't want anyone else to hear."

"No, that's not it," said Lucy, ejecting the disc. She loaded a disc of Chris Botti playing jazz trumpet. Relaxing, but much farther from home. She gestured to the sofa. Erika reluctantly took a seat, and Lucy sat down beside her.

"Sometimes, it's difficult to hear myself sing. It reminds me of what I've given up. Can you understand?"

"Yes, but you are driving me insane by not telling me why you quit singing."

"Let's just say, I was going through a very hard time, and I needed to take a break. The break ended up being permanent."

"That's sufficiently vague."

Lucy turned to face her. "You know how you don't want to talk about Jeannine? Well, I'm not ready to talk about why I stopped singing. Okay?"

"Of course," said Erika. She touched her cheek. "Lucy, I need to kiss you."

Lucy turned up her face for kiss. As Erika explored Lucy's mouth, she eased her back on the cushion. She could feel Lucy's breathing change and allowed her hand to travel under Lucy's shirt, then under her bra. She pinched the nipple gently as she continued to kiss her. Lucy's soft moan reminded Erika of the aria she had heard a few minutes before. The sound of Lucy's pleasure was music of another kind. Encouraged, Erika slipped her hand into Lucy's pants.

She was startled when Lucy abruptly pulled away and got to her feet.

"I'm sorry, but I'm not ready to make love. I really want to, but I can't."

Erika nodded and got up too. "I should be going. After that kiss, I can't sit here with you innocently listening to music. What time did you say you practice singing?" asked Erika.

"Seven o'clock."

"No promises, but you may see me there," said Erika and kissed her lightly on the lips. She took her in her arms.

Lucy clung to her for a moment. "You need to go," she murmured, giving her a little nudge.

10

When Lucy awoke, she remembered she had been dreaming about Erika kissing her. Her genitals throbbed with excitement. She reached down to touch herself and found she was wet. Startled, she pulled her hand back. Since menopause, she'd found dryness to be the more usual state. Her doctor had suggested progesterone cream. Lucy was leery of the cancer risk from hormone replacement, although she trusted Liz, who knew more about breast cancer than almost anyone. She'd even written a book on it.

When Lucy had expressed her concerns, Liz had nodded, opened a drawer in her desk and produced a little jar. "All-natural ingredients, mostly thinned bee's wax, which also has mild antibiotic characteristics. Helps prevent the vaginitis that can accompany dryness. And it's rated food grade, so it's edible." Liz's face had been perfectly deadpan, her blue eyes completely serious, which Lucy had realized was her doctor look.

"And here's something that might help too." Lucy had been shocked to see a box containing a bullet-shaped vibrator. "You were really tight when I took your pap smear. Use it or lose it they say. Vaginal atrophy can be a real problem. You want to keep yourself open and prevent calcification."

"Do you give your other patients sex toys?"

The question had finally broken Liz's control, and she'd laughed aloud. "That's a pretty tame sex toy. No, I only give vibrators to my post-menopausal patients who complain about dryness. Stimulation increases blood flow to the vagina. If you're not having regular sex, masturbation is the best insurance for your sexual future."

At the time, Lucy wondered why she needed insurance. She hadn't had any sex partners since Susan, and that was five years ago. It wasn't that she lacked opportunity. She'd had plenty of suitors of both sexes. Up to now, she hadn't really been interested. That was another symptom of menopause, Liz had explained: diminished libido, but something about Erika had awakened Lucy's sleeping sex drive.

Officially, the Church recommended waiting until marriage for sex. Not long ago, the church insisted that gay clergy remain celibate. With her lack of interest in sex, Lucy had no trouble following that rule. But now everything had changed. She had opportunity in a beautiful, brilliant woman, and the Church had approved gay marriage. In fact, Lucy's own bishop, a wonderful man, who practically glowed with the love of God, was married to a man.

She recalled Erika gently pinching her nipple. Lucy felt a flush of arousal in the present. She reached down to touch herself and found herself hot and swollen. She could hear the sound of her wetness, which excited her even more. In her fantasy, she allowed Erika's fingers to reach their goal. Lucy came within seconds.

Pent up demand, thought Lucy, as she waited for her breathing to come back to normal. There was no doubt her sex drive had returned, or that she wanted Erika, but was it love?

Her alarm clock buzzed. Lucy reached over to shut it off. She wondered why she still set an alarm clock when she always slept with her cell phone next to her bed in case some parishioner needed her during the night. The rectory landline was set to forward to her mobile after business hours. She could be called at any hour to say prayers for the dying and sit at their bedside through their last hours.

Usually, Lucy took a quick shower, but this morning she felt languorous after making love to herself, so she ran a hot bath. As she sat in the hot water, she thought about Erika and wondered if she was awake yet. She'd said she wasn't an early riser during summer break. How could she resist the bright sun shining through the window? It rose earlier every day. Right now, it streamed through the bathroom window and bathed Lucy in golden light.

Lazy bones, get up! She told herself, but she really wanted to drowse in the hot water. She reached down to wash between her legs and found herself still stimulated. She undressed Erika in her mind. She imagined touching those soft breasts. Erika had such a lovely female figure, well-proportioned.

She was tall but wore it well. Her legs were shapely and toned. She was so obviously a natural blond. Was her pubic hair blond too?

After the orgasm, Lucy wondered what time it was. If she didn't get out of the hot water now, she wouldn't have any time to sing. She hauled herself out of the tub. Her hair had gotten slightly wet, so she gave it a quick blow dry and put it up, slightly damp, in a French braid. She put on her makeup, choosing a dark red lipstick. She had a funeral later that morning, so even though it was promising to be a warm day, she put on a skirted suit over a clerical blouse and collar.

She never ate before singing, but she filled a sports bottle with water and drank it on her way to the church because her throat needed moisture in order to sing.

Lucy unlocked the rectory-side door as she always did. She needed to throw her weight against the heavy, carved-panel door to open it. St. Margaret's By the Sea Church wasn't as old as some of the churches in the county, which went back to Revolutionary times, but it was an old-style church with a choir loft in the back and a magnificent full-throated pipe organ.

Lucy sometimes used the organ to find the key. The organ tuner had said the instrument needed to be played to keep it in tune, so she didn't feel guilty about turning on the power to run the bellows. Liz's off-handed comment, "use it, or lose it" suddenly came to mind, and Lucy smiled.

Since her earliest vocal training with her mother, Lucy followed a regular routine. She began scales and arpeggios to warm up, first, *sotto voce* and then, opening her voice gradually. Taking so much air into her lungs also served to wake her up. Singing always blew away the dusty feeling from sleep. She tried to give her voice at least an hour every day. If she were still singing professionally, that would hardly be adequate, but it was better than nothing.

Once the exercises were done, Lucy flipped through the playlists on her smartphone. Pre-recorded accompaniment was a Godsend to a singer. First, she'd practiced with a piano or special LPs, then cassettes, CDs, and now she had a whole collection of full accompaniment on her phone. Best of all she could hook into the church sound system with her Bluetooth. She wondered if younger singers appreciated how easy they had it now.

Lucy scrolled through her list. Sometimes, she decided on a program the night before or on her way to practice. This morning, she felt adventurous. She listened to the accompaniment to the "Ave Maria" from Verdi's *Otello*. That felt like something she'd like to sing. She followed the plaintive aria with Schubert's "Ave Maria." By then, she decided she'd had enough. She turned off the power to the pipe organ and the sound system. She carefully descended the spiral staircase to the first floor.

She nearly bumped into a tall woman standing at the bottom of the stairs. Erika gazed at Lucy with a look of pure adoration. "That was exquisite!" She snatched Lucy's hands and bent to kiss them.

"I didn't think you'd come," said Lucy. "It's so early for you."

"Now that I know you do this, I shall be here every day! You are magnificent! I adore you." Erika brought Lucy's hands to her lips and kissed them. "You are a diva! *Das Ewig-Weibliche!* A goddess! I would happily worship at your feet."

The effusive declaration made Lucy want to laugh, until she saw from the look in Erika's eyes that it wasn't sarcasm.

"Erika," said Lucy, squeezing her hands gently. "I don't want to be worshipped. I only want to be loved."

"And I do love you, but I also worship you. Your voice is such a gift. How could you ever give it up?"

"I haven't given it up. I still sing."

"But here, alone, where no one hears you."

"I still perform occasionally. But I've found another calling." She put her arms on Erika's shoulders to draw her closer. "Thank you for coming." She kissed her lightly on the lips. "Come back to the rectory. Have a cup of coffee and some toast with me."

"If I'm alone with you, I can't guarantee I won't try to seduce you."

Lucy laughed. "Not this morning. I have a funeral at nine, so I don't have much time. Let's not waste it standing here talking."

Lucy took her hand while they headed to the front of the church but released it once they reached the door. “We have to behave so we don’t give my congregation the wrong idea.”

“If they perceive that I’m madly in love with their rector, it wouldn’t be the wrong idea at all.”

Lucy gave her a tender look. “And here I thought all Germans were cold and unemotional.”

“That is a total misreading of us. Not only are we emotional, we are sentimental to excess and sometimes, grandiose. Think of Wagner!”

Lucy gazed at Erika in amazement. “Sometimes, I don’t know how to take you. You come out with the most unexpected things.”

“I find the element of surprise to be especially useful when courting women,” said Erika, falling into stride with Lucy as they headed across the quadrangle to the rectory.

“You’re so cute, Erika.”

“Cute? How can a five-foot-nine, sixty-year-old woman be cute!”

“Trust me. You are.” Lucy unlocked the rectory door. “Come in, and I’ll explain.”

Erika gazed around the kitchen as Lucy filled the coffee carafe with water from the sink. “It’s been ages since I’ve been here.”

“You were here last night.”

“Exactly!”

“Oh, sit down!” said Lucy. “It’s too early for your silly wit.”

Erika sat down at the little table and gazed out the window. Lucy took the opportunity to admire her. Erika looked particularly attractive this morning in a blue blouse and white Bermuda shorts that showed her nice legs. Lucy had never thought of herself as a “leg woman,” but she certainly liked Erika’s.

“Thank you for coming this morning.”

“I wasn’t joking when I said I shall come every day. I find your singing very erotic, an opportunity for me to sublimate, so I don’t jump you in public.”

"Now, that would really get the town talking." Lucy took a loaf of cinnamon raisin bread out of a drawer. "Would you like some toast?"

"That would be lovely. Thank you."

Lucy put four pieces of bread in the toaster. She leaned against the counter while she waited for them to brown. "We should probably have a talk about where this is going. Are we dating?"

"I should think that would be obvious."

"Erika, be serious."

"I am being serious." Erika deadpanned. "Let's talk."

"We don't have enough time this morning."

"This evening? Let me take you to dinner at Nathan's. The food is good, mostly local ingredients. It's a nice place. An opportunity to dress up a little. You can wear that sexy, red number and knock my eyes out again."

"I do have other dresses. Let me surprise you. I like the element of surprise too," said Lucy, taking out the toast. She buttered two pieces, cut them into triangles and put them on a plate for Erika. She poured coffee into two institutional white mugs. "It's nice to have company for breakfast."

"Have you ever lived with a partner?" Erika asked as Lucy buttered her toast.

"No. I traveled too much to have a live-in relationship. What about you?"

"Jeannine and I decided it was better to maintain separate households. She had her own space with all her artist's paraphernalia, all those smelly oils and mineral spirits, and I had mine. Besides she was untidy when it came to housekeeping. I like things neat. She'd spend the night. Then I'd send her back to her mess."

Lucy glanced around the kitchen and wondered what Erika thought of her housekeeping. She was very glad she had done all the dishes and cleaned up the kitchen the night before.

"Living with someone requires a lot of compromise and negotiation to be successful," said Lucy.

"And you know this without the benefit of having lived with a partner," said Erika and bit into her toast. Lucy watched her smile at the taste of the raisins in the bread. Cinnamon raisin toast was Lucy's favorite quick breakfast.

"I have training as a marriage counselor. As a priest, I have to counsel couples before I can marry them in the Church."

"And you advise them without the benefit of experience?" Erika clucked her tongue. "You know what Kant says, 'concepts without experience are empty.' Bad business to give advice without knowledge."

Lucy's body tensed at the criticism. "You don't have to experience everything to have a useful perspective. I don't have to be a man to counsel a man."

"True," said Erika, nodding. "Do you have many men as clients?"

"Some. Mostly women. Men don't really go in for counseling as much."

Again, Erika nodded. "Your toast is very good. I didn't realize how hungry I was. Thank you for breakfast."

That made Lucy glance at the clock. "Finish your coffee. I need to kick you out in a few minutes."

When the time came, Lucy didn't want to part from Erika, who held her in her arms in a long, close hug. "I'll pick you up at six." Erika bent to kiss her. "I can't wait to see you again."

***

Lucy tried to focus as she reviewed the homily for the funeral. The deceased was a ninety-year-old woman. Most of the information had come from her daughter and emphasized her mother's role as an active volunteer in the community. The fact that the woman had founded and run a thriving retail business for over forty years had been almost completely glossed over. Lucy was determined not to let her hard work and success go unacknowledged. She had discovered the archives of the local paper to be a rich source of information. In addition, Liz had given her access to the Hobbs Chamber of Commerce records.

Some celebrants never tried to get to know the people involved in their services and backfilled with scripture. Not Lucy. Liturgy was meant to speak directly to each person. If it was just a dry exegesis of a text, she was missing an opportunity to help someone connect with God.

Today, Lucy prayed she could keep her mind on what she was doing. Feeling so disoriented was strange to her. Usually, she was precisely focused on her performance and nothing could distract her. Before Erika, no one had ever affected her like this. It was very strange and uncomfortable feeling.

Lucy was relieved to get through the funeral without a hitch. After she made an appearance at the brunch the family had sponsored, she headed to the hospital to bring patients communion. Her next stop was the hospice facility to talk to the patients and facilitate the care-givers group. Those were her regular Tuesday activities and usually the day flew by, but today, it dragged.

As Lucy drove home, she thought about how to frame the conversation with Erika. They were at the point where they needed to talk about what should come next. Should they become sexually involved or remain friends and step back? Lucy was well aware of what her body had to say about that. The muscles below tightened at the mere thought. She had to will away the sensations to stay focused on the road.

Instead, she thought about what to wear to dinner with Erika. She had a beautiful green silk dress that was more elegant than revealing. That would be a good choice because she wanted Erika's mind on the content of the conversation and not looking down into her cleavage.

Lucy wanted to make sure they agreed on certain basics before they got in too deep. It was very important to Lucy that Erika take the act of love seriously. Lucy was absolutely not interested in recreational sex. For her, sex was the ultimate communication between two people, and, as a reflection of God's love, a sacred act. Yes, it should be fun, joyful and enjoyable, but it was not something to be taken lightly. She also wanted to know whether Erika was willing to be monogamous. Lucy was not willing to share her with anyone. Finally, she wanted to know if Erika saw a future for them, specifically a future that could ultimately lead to a commitment.

She was a little worried that Erika would see her concerns as too "religious." Maybe the agnostic philosopher in her would see them as "quaint" and look down on them, but Lucy really didn't care. They were important to her, and if Erika wanted a relationship, they'd need to agree on these points.

Lucy had just decided which shoes to wear with the green dress and was mentally choosing her jewelry when a call came in through the dashboard Bluetooth. Erika's number. Lucy pushed the button on the steering wheel to answer.

"Hello, Erika. I'm surprised to hear from you."

"Oh, my dear, I fear I must cancel our date for tonight."

Lucy felt a little stunned by the news. Now that she'd screwed up her courage to have this important talk, it wasn't going to happen.

"My mother is not doing well, and I'm on my way to New Haven."

Lucy's instantly dismissed her own feelings and worried about Erika's. "Oh, no! Is it serious?"

She heard a long sigh. "It's hard to say. This is how it is with elderly parents. We go through one emotional disaster drill after another. Then one day, it isn't a drill."

"Oh, Erika. I'm so sorry!"

"Thank you for your sympathy. I'm sorry to disappoint you. I was looking forward to our date."

Lucy wondered if Erika would be so enthusiastic if she knew what was on the agenda. "I guess we'll have to hold our talk for another time," said Lucy.

"Perhaps we can have our talk while I drive. I'm going to be on the road for hours."

"Not this talk. I need to see your face when we talk about this."

"Oh, dear. Sounds ominous."

"No, but we do need to talk."

Erika didn't respond immediately. Finally, she said, "Do you intend to explain to me that you are not interested in a sexual relationship?"

"No, I was going to explain that I *am* interested in a sexual relationship, but I want to know more about how you feel. I mean, besides the obvious."

"So, we could talk about it while I drive to New Haven?"

"I want to see your face, so, no."

"Well, then. Let's talk about something else. You can keep me company for a while."

"All right, I'll stay on until I get home. I can call you later, after I change and see what's for dinner, now that my date is unavailable. What would you like to talk about?"

"Do you think Callas was as good as everyone says?"

Lucy laughed. "Good question!"

11

"Erika, I have to eat something. I'm practically fainting with hunger!" said Lucy's voice through the dashboard speaker. "And I desperately need to pee."

Erika chuckled. "Yes, do that and then eat. I'm in the homestretch now, passing the Yale bowl as we speak. I'll be there in a few minutes."

"Text me when you get there."

"I promise. Thank you for staying with me through the drive."

"Well, most of it anyway." They'd been on the phone discussing opera stars, politics, and plans to visit Acadia National Park that fall with Maggie and Liz—anything to pass the time and keep the other talking. During the few pauses in the conversation, Erika had found herself thinking, that's what lovers do. But they weren't lovers yet. Perhaps if this important date hadn't been postponed, they would have moved on to the next step. Now, it was a lost opportunity.

"Go pee," ordered Erika.

"Erika..."

"Yes?"

"I love you."

A little surprised, Erika hesitated momentarily. "I love you too, Lucy."

"Good luck with your mother. I'll pray for the best possible outcome. Keep me posted."

"I shall."

Erika sighed as she took the turn near Yale-New Haven. She could get off here and visit her mother. No, she decided, let me go home first and see if Papi wants to come along.

She headed into downtown New Haven and Wooster Square. Her parents had purchased the co-op in the late 1980s after the real estate collapse. They had lived there since her father had taken the professorship at Yale in 1980. When the owners of the crumbling building offered the apartments to the tenants at bargain prices, Stefan Bultmann had made one of the best investments of his life. Now, the place was worth over a million dollars. The spacious apartment, which had been large enough for the three of them while Erika was still in graduate school, had an amazing view of Wooster Square and its famous cherry blossoms.

Erika drove into the below-ground parking garage. Her father had given up his car, a blessing because at the end, he was always smacking into other motorists. Fortunately, he could walk anywhere he needed to go or take a bus. Since her mother had started to fail and no longer cooked, he picked up prepared meals at Ferraro's Market, just a few blocks away.

Despite giving up the car, Erika's father continued to pay for the reserved parking spaces, one for himself, and one for Erika's use when she visited. When she looked over her parents' finances, she always recommended he give up the parking spaces to save money.

"Why? It's only thirty dollars a month. People who visit can use them."

"Who visits? All your friends are gone."

Her father would turn his eyes on her, as pale as hers and give her a hard look. "Not all of them!" he would protest in heavily accented English. "And there are your friends to think about."

"You should save your money. You might need it someday."

"Don't worry. You're getting it all anyway. You won't miss the thirty dollars a month."

Both parents were in their nineties now. They'd waited until they'd saved enough money for a Berlin apartment before having a child, and then they could afford only one. It was lonely to be an only child, but her parents had never given her a sibling, despite her pleas. Erika had always dreamed about having a big sister, which is probably why she and Liz had became so close. They shared so much besides philosophy and loving women. Liz's father had been an officer in the German army during the war, so she understood the odd guilt all Germans felt afterwards, and Erika found it comforting to have an American friend who could speak her language.

Erika parked in her reserved space. She took two black suits, one with a skirt and one with pants, and two dress blouses, off the hook behind the driver's seat. She wanted to be prepared in case her father had understated her mother's decline. For the same reason, her bag was heavier than it would usually be for a summer visit, when there was no need for multiple layers. She'd packed extra of everything because she had no idea how long she'd need to be away from Hobbs.

When her father opened the door of the apartment, she instantly saw the toll this latest stage of her mother's health crisis had taken. Stefan Bultmann was a very tall man, six-foot-three. Based on his height, Erika would have undoubtedly been taller, but her period came early, which abruptly cut off her growth. He stooped a little now, pressed down by the unspeakable burden of his wife's illness.

As a young man, he had been a white blond like Erika. Some of the blond could still be seen in his hair, which was now the palest yellow. Like Erika, he had a lanky figure and handsome planes in his face, a quintessentially professorial face with a lined forehead from many hours in thought, a permanently raised skeptical left brow, strong chin and thin lips. His daughter was a younger, feminine version of her father with her own distinctive professorial face.

Erika half hugged her father as she laid her suits over the back of the sofa. Then she held him close. "Papi, I'm so sorry."

Her father released a long sigh. "We all come to this eventually."

When they were alone, they always spoke German, cultured *Hoch Deutsch*. Occasionally, the hint of a guttural Berlin accent could be heard, but not often.

"Let me unpack a little, and we can go to the hospital together."

"I was hoping you would say that. I want to bring your mother some food. She won't eat the hospital food. She says it's tasteless, so I've been bringing her soup from Ferraro's."

"That's good," said Erika, nodding. "I need a few minutes."

"Take your time. There's no rush. Your mother isn't going anywhere, and neither am I."

Erika took her bags to her old bedroom to unpack. She hung the suits and some of the clothes from her bag in the closet. The rest could wait until later. She sat down on one of the beds. There was a full-size bed and a twin bed in her room for a guest. Her mother had gotten the idea from traveling in England where such arrangements were common in the bed and breakfasts.

In the corner of the decent-sized comfortable room was the writing desk on which Erika had written her doctoral dissertation on Habermas. Shelves of childhood books still lined the walls. Someday, she would take them back with her, but to where? The faculty residence at Colby wasn't really home. Maybe she should pack them up and take them to Hobbs, but if she went through with the renovation, she wouldn't want boxes cluttering the place.

Erika felt her phone buzzing in her pocket. She took it out and saw it was Lucy calling. Erika tapped the call open and put the phone to her ear.

"You said you'd text me when you got there," said Lucy in a slightly accusing voice, but Erika realized she was more anxious than angry. "Are you there?"

"Yes, sorry, dear. I was talking to my father."

"How is he?"

"Sad," said Erika, "Very sad."

"Poor man. I'll pray for him. This must be so hard."

"Yes, it was only ever me and Mom. We are his only family."

"Give him a hug from me."

"I will."

"I love you," said Lucy.

Erika was startled. This was the thing now, saying "I love you." She liked the sound of it. "I love you too. I'm going to the hospital with my father now. I'll call you tonight. How late is too late to call?"

"For you, it's never too late."

"Really? What time?"

"I sleep with my phone by the bed. Sometimes I'm called away in the middle of the night to comfort the dying. Call whenever you can."

"I promise," said Erika before she ended the call.

She returned to the living room and found her father sitting with his head in his hands on the sofa. His hearing was rapidly declining, and he hadn't heard her approach, so she touched his shoulder.

"Come, Papi. I'll drive us to the hospital."

"I'll get the soup."

They drove in silence to Yale-New Haven. When they pulled into the parking space, her father said, "I need to call Elizabeth and thank her for her help with the surgeon. I couldn't understand what the man was trying to do."

"I'm sure Liz would love to hear from you. What did she do?"

"When they discovered the fracture in your mother's leg, they weren't certain they could fix it or if she could survive the surgery. I called Elizabeth, and she found a young orthopedic surgeon, who specializes in unusual traumatic fractures. She called him and explained the situation. I didn't expect your mother to make it through the operation, but she did."

"Why didn't you call me? I would have sat with you during the surgery."

"There was nothing either of us could do."

Erika gave her father a hard look. "Papi, you know I am always here for you."

Her father nodded. "I know, but it wasn't necessary to disturb you. I could manage."

She took his arm as they walked to the elevator. The parking area smelled of stale gasoline, filth, and urine. There was debris in every corner. The hospital wasn't in the best part of the city. Homeless people slept in the parking garage in the winter. Usually, the police ignored them.

They took the elevator to the lobby so Erika could get an ID badge for the visit. Her wallet was new and stiff. The guard looked impatient as she struggled to remove her driver's license from the window compartment. Her driver's license was returned with a badge bearing a bad black-and-white transfer of the photo. *That could be anyone*, Erika thought as she inspected it. She wondered why they even bothered with the pretense.

They took the elevator to the surgery department on the fifth floor. Erika knew her way around. This had once been Liz Stolz's domain when she was an attending and later chief of surgery. After Erika had moved to Colby, she often met Liz there.

Erika swallowed hard and took a deep breath before entering her mother's room. She never knew what she'd find lying in that hospital bed. Over the last months of steady decline, her mother had become gray, shriveled and tiny, as if she were disappearing before their eyes. She was relieved to see her mother open her eyes, as pale blue as her own, and smile.

"Erika, you came," she murmured.

"Of course, I came Mutti. How are you?"

"Tired. Very tired."

"Are you in pain?"

"No, no pain."

"I'm going to heat up the soup," said her father.

"No, Papi, you stay here with Mutti. I'll do it." She took the brown bag from her father and headed to the solarium. She waited until the nurse, who was heating up her dinner, finished with the microwave.

Erika put in the paper container of soup. It smelled good as it heated. She guessed it was potato leek soup, her mother's favorite. While she was waiting, she found a plastic soup spoon in a drawer and some napkins.

Her father had raised the head of the bed while she was gone, and her mother looked much more alert. He reached out for the soup and took off the lid.

"It's too hot," he said, testing the temperature with his lips over the open container. "Let it cool a little."

Erika found a clean towel in the bathroom and put it under her mother's chin. Her father blew gently on the spoonful of soup before offering it to his wife. His hand was trembling.

"Papi, why don't you let me do that?" offered Erika.

For a moment, it seemed he would argue with her, but then he simply nodded and put the soup down on the rolling table. Erika changed places with him and spooned the soup into her mother's mouth. Helga Bultmann smiled at her daughter. "This is my favorite soup. My mother used to make it. We had no leeks. That was too fancy, so she would use onions." Erika thought of her grandmother. She never saw her again after they left the GDR. She remembered her as a tiny woman like her mother, who had the same light blue, gentle eyes. "I'm sorry you have to feed me, but my hand isn't much good since the stroke."

"It's all right, Mutti. I'm happy to help you. Enjoy your soup."

By the time Erika had gotten halfway to the bottom of the container, Helga had fallen asleep. Erika nudged her gently to encourage her to swallow the last mouthful.

Her father put the top on the container. "We'll put it in the refrigerator for tomorrow."

Erika wiped her mother's mouth with the towel.

"We should go now and not tire her more," said Stefan. "She'll sleep now."

"If you don't mind, Papi. I'd like to sit here a few minutes."

"Of course," he said, nodding. He sat down in the other chair.

Erika lowered the head of the bed a little. Her mother was obviously in a deep sleep. She sat down and took her mother's hand. When she glanced at her father, she saw he was nodding off too. She sat in the gathering twilight and watched her parents sleep.

Erika recalled the research about near-death experiences and the reports that the dying recall important events from the past, a more scientific assessment of the old phrase, "watching your life pass before your eyes."

She wondered what her parents would remember when their time came. Would they recall her father's daring escape during a mathematics conference in the West? He defected and applied for refugee status, knowing his wife and child could be in danger of imprisonment or worse. Before he left, he had arranged for some friends to help his family escape, but it was months before the plan could be implemented. It was too dangerous. They were watched all the time. Erika knew that a Stasi agent followed her to school. She saw him waiting for her every day when class was dismissed. He leaned against the building, smoking a cigarette, which he flung into the gutter when she headed for home.

Fortunately, the government never tried to use them as leverage against her father. They weren't important enough politically, and things were already unraveling in East Berlin. Everything was beginning to fall apart, especially the substandard buildings hastily thrown up after the war. When Erika and her mother were driven to the West, they left everything behind except the clothes on their backs. They hid in the trunk of an old car owned by a sympathetic East Berlin police officer. Erika still remembered the smell of camphor and old wool from the blanket that covered them as they passed through the gates. She could hear the guards talking outside, and her heart pounded until they opened the trunk in the West.

Erika glanced at her phone. More than an hour had passed. Both parents were still sound asleep. There was a text message from Lucy. *How are you doing?*

Erika texted back. *Okay. Visiting with my mother. She's sleeping.*

Call me later. Please.

I promise.

Red heart emoticon.

Erika smiled.

12

Lucy set her phone to remind her when to return to the rectory for her counseling appointment. Saturdays were always busy because so many people who came for counseling had full-time jobs. She found that she could squeeze in one or two after-work sessions, but it wasn't her preference. After a full day at work, people were often tired and wanted to go home and relax. The single women among her clients sometimes had to go to another job or rush home to prepare dinner for their children.

Saturday sessions put a special burden on Lucy because she could have used that time to put the finishing touches on her Sunday sermon. That's what most priests would do, but Lucy sympathized with the people who came to her. Hobbs might look like an affluent, happy town on the surface, but many were struggling. She had been called to serve the people of God. In her mind, that meant making the opportunity to receive God's comfort and healing love as convenient as possible.

Lucy found a place in the second pew and knelt down. Kneeling was hard on her back and her knees, but she'd always found it to be the best position for prayer. For the same reason, she clasped her hands under her chin and bowed her head. This posture signalled to her body as well as her mind that she was opening a channel of communication with God.

Today, it was particularly difficult to find the quiet space in her mind necessary for prayer. Worry about Erika and her mother had nagged her through the day as it had for the last week since Erika had left. Lucy wished she knew more about what was happening in New Haven, but she'd restrained the impulse to call. She remembered from dealing with her own mother's last illness that people's requests for updates could be overwhelming and infuriating. It was enough to deal with the patient's needs and communicating with the doctors and hospital staff without well-intentioned phone calls or annoying texts demanding to know: how is she? Instead, Lucy waited to hear from Erika, who sent text messages at all hours and wrote long emails ruminating on life and death. The conversations by phone were quick and sporadic.

Lucy savored those brief moments of hearing Erika's voice with its British accent and hint of German. She still found it unique and a bit exotic despite many hours of conversation while walking on the beach or at dinners in Erika's cottage.

She'd been so disappointed they'd had to cancel their date, but it certainly wasn't appropriate to complain or whine. Under the circumstances, her one and only goal was to support her friend. *Her friend*. Perhaps more, depending on how the serious talk about their future had played out. With Erika sitting by the bedside of her failing mother, that conversation would have to wait.

After prayer, Lucy had an appointment with a young couple preparing for marriage. This duty always gave her pleasure because nowadays, so few young people bothered with prenuptial counseling or church weddings. During prenuptial sessions, Lucy directed the couples to discuss the same questions she had hoped to ask Erika. Were they ready for a lifelong commitment? How did they manage conflict? Were they open in their communication? Did they genuinely enjoy spending time together? Were they sexually compatible?

This last question always made people uncomfortable because they assumed it meant she was pruriently interested in their sex life. Nothing could be farther from the truth. She really wanted them to talk to one another about the importance of physical intimacy in the marriage. How often did they expect sex and how much was enough to keep them close? Were they willing to be open with their partner about their sexual needs? Would they consider experimentation to keep their sex life fresh? Sometimes when Lucy asked the questions in a prenuptial session, she wondered what Erika's answers would be.

Lucy took out her phone and glanced at it. Half of her time had been taken up with these meandering thoughts. She ordered her mind to be still and open, borrowing a yoga breathing trick to encourage it. Finally, she heard a voice in her head that was different from the voice she heard when she thought or debated with herself. It was the same voice she'd heard when she realized she had been called to the priesthood. It was clear and very direct. She could speak to that voice and ask questions. Sometimes, she simply listened or saw things, little scenes and snippets she couldn't see with her eyes.

Today, she saw Erika sitting by her mother's bedside in the hospital. She imagined laying a comforting hand on her shoulder. "Yes," said the voice, "Human love can be divine. It is a mirror of my love. Nurture and love my people. Visit the sick. Comfort the grieving. Bury the dead."

Lucy remembered Erika recognizing the corporal acts of mercy in the conversation they'd had about Lucy's duties. Erika had more grounding in religion than she was willing to admit. She might not say so, but she could be open to God's healing love. Like every human being, she had the potential for redemption.

Lucy was deep into her meditation on human and divine love when she heard the sound of footsteps behind her. Whoever had come into the church had been extremely quiet about opening the squeaky door, so it was likely a member of the congregation. The efforts to preserve the quiet were thwarted by the creak of the pew as the person sat down behind her. Almost no one came into the church at that hour unless it was important. As much as Lucy didn't want to leave her meditation, she crossed herself and got up.

Maggie Fitzgerald was sitting three rows back. "I'm so sorry, Lucy. I didn't mean to interrupt your prayers," said Maggie getting up to greet her with a kiss on the cheek. "Your admin said I might find you here. She didn't tell me you were praying."

"She doesn't know. And I don't want her to turn away anyone who might need me."

"You're too good, Lucy. Set some boundaries. You need to take care of yourself too."

"I know, but there's so much need in this community. I want to be available."

Maggie shook her head. Her white hair was striking. She still wore it long even now that she had let it go natural. Always the actress, she was beautifully made up, so different from Liz, her wife, who needed to be prodded to dress up or put on makeup.

"I thought you might be missing Erika, so Liz and I decided to invite you to dinner," said Maggie. "My daughter, Alina is coming down with the kids, if you don't mind sharing a meal with them."

"No, I love Alina, and I'm so glad I could help her make progress in moving on from the domestic abuse. It will be nice to see her."

"Good. So, it's a plan. When can you get away from here?"

"Four-thirty."

"Perfect. Come right over." Maggie gave Lucy's arm a little squeeze. "See you later."

Lucy watched her friend walk out of the church. She recognized the perfect posture and carefully measured steps from her own stage training.

***

Lucy found she was looking forward to a social evening. Her life had been much too quiet while Erika had been gone. She wondered if that was a bad sign. Perhaps she was becoming too dependent on Erika's company. Parishioners often asked her to have a drink with them in the local pub or to join them for dinner in their homes. She more often than not declined because she didn't want to take advantage of the hospitality of people who had less than she had. Now, she saw that there was some selfishness involved. Her real reason was to leave her calendar open for walks and dinners with Erika. Maybe that was wrong. Her congregation should come first.

When she arrived, she saw Alina, standing on the side deck, where Liz had set up a kiddie pool for the children.

"Mother Lucy!" Alina called and waved to her. Lucy knew that she'd have to climb the stairs to the deck to greet her. Alina would never leave her children alone in the pool without supervision, not even for a second. Her early life in a Romanian orphanage had left her especially protective of her own children.

The dark-haired woman was shorter than Lucy, which made her feel tall. Really tall women like Erika and Liz made her feel like a midget. Alina gave her a tight, full-body hug. "I was so happy when Mom said you were coming. It seems like forever." Despite the broad smile, Alina looked tired. It wasn't easy trying to hold down an important job like regional news producer and raise two small daughters alone.

"Mother Lucy!" squealed Katrina, Alina's eldest daughter. She jumped out of the wading pool and hugged Lucy's legs with her wet body, leaving dark water marks on the black skirt.

Her mother pulled her back. "You're all wet. Go ask Grandma for another towel and dry yourself off." Katrina ran into the house. "I'm so sorry," Alina apologized.

"It doesn't matter. It's rayon and goes into the washing machine your stepmother was kind enough to install. I would have changed into my civvies before I came, but I was too lazy."

"I'm sure Mom can lend you a pair of shorts and a shirt if you want to change."

"I don't care. I'm just glad to be here. And I'm so glad to see you!"

"Me too," said Alina, putting her arm around Lucy. "Let me get Nicki out of the water and we can go inside." Alina hauled the protesting toddler out of the pool. "Come on, you. Let's get you dry and presentable."

Lucy had loved the relaxed atmosphere of the Stolz-Fitzgerald home from the moment she'd stepped into the house. A plaque proclaimed that it had been designated a "barefoot home," so she took off her black pumps and placed them on the rack inside the door. Besides maintaining a casual atmosphere, it also kept down the sand everyone in Hobbs dragged inside their living spaces, whether it came from the beach or sanding the roads in winter.

Maggie swooped in and caught Lucy in a hug. "Thank you for coming. We've missed you."

"Where's Liz?"

"In the kitchen skewering chicken curry kabobs."

Lucy followed Maggie into the kitchen. "Hello, my dear," said Liz, bending to kiss her. "Sorry I can't give you a hug. My hands are full of chicken goo."

"I can see." Lucy put her arm around Liz and gave her a half hug. "Looks good."

Liz finished the last kabob and carefully scrubbed her hands in the kitchen sink. She used a surgical brush on her fingernails, a habit, Lucy guessed, from the compulsive cleanliness her profession demanded.

After drying her hands, Liz scooped her up into a fierce hug, stopping just short of crushing her. "So good to see you, Lucy. How are you holding up?" Liz released her and gave her a doctor's quick once over. Her blue eyes against her tan were compelling, but not like Erika's.

"I'm worried about her, of course," said Lucy in a soft voice.

Liz nodded. "So am I. I've talked to her mother's surgeon a few times and the hospitalist. It's not looking good. Her mother stopped eating. Won't take any fluids by mouth. They're hydrating her by IV. They've started a palliative drip. If I know Erika, she's rolled up in a ball over this."

"Even if you think you're prepared, a parent's death hits you hard."

"She hasn't called you?" asked Liz, cocking an eyebrow.

"Yes, a few times, but she doesn't stay on the phone long. She texts and emails me more."

Liz nodded. "That sounds like her. Don't take it personally."

"I wish I could help her."

"You'll get your chance," said Liz and let out a big sigh.

Katrina had come into the kitchen and pulled on Lucy's hand. "Mother Lucy, come see the rocket I built with Grandma Liz."

"Excuse me, Liz. I'm being summoned," said Lucy, allowing herself to be dragged away by Katrina into the screen porch. Maggie was there, putting away the supplies and extra parts for the model rocket.

"She's great at doing these projects with the kids but she never cleans up afterward," grumbled Maggie. Lucy knew it was a lighthearted complaint.

Maggie adored Liz. Lucy wondered if one day, she'd be complaining about Erika that way.

Katrina showed Lucy her project, a sleek model rocket painted tractor green. The nose cone and fins were bright yellow. The paint had run down the body of the rocket, but it was an excellent effort for a seven-year-old. "We're going to put on our decals tomorrow," said Katrina, "after the paint dries completely. Otherwise, it peels, and that's not good." Lucy could hear adult advice behind Katrina's explanation. "Then we'll shoot it off."

"Where are you going to shoot it off?" asked Lucy, leaning on her knees so that her face was level with Katrina's.

"At the ball field behind the middle school," replied Katrina matter-of-factly. "You can come watch, if you want."

"Ask Grandma Liz to call me before you go. I'll come if I can."

"We're staying over tonight and tomorrow night because Mommy is going to New York for a big meeting."

"Lucky you. Do you like staying with your grandmas?"

"Yes. They let me do things Mommy doesn't let me do."

"Like what?"

"Like eat popcorn in my pajamas and stay up late and watch movies. I like movies about super heroes. So does Grandma Liz. Wonder Woman is my favorite."

Maggie finished putting away the remnants of the rocketry project. "What can I get you to drink, Lucy?"

"White wine would be wonderful, thank you."

Katrina left to watch cartoons in the media room, and Lucy was glad for the moment of quiet. Despite her pleasure in visiting this busy household, she had become used to solitary living. She needed to get out more.

Maggie returned with her wine. "You look beat," she observed, giving Lucy a critical look.

"Oh, I've been running myself ragged again."

"Better conserve your energy. Someone we know is going to need you soon."

"What are you trying to say, Maggie?"

Maggie glanced in the direction of the kitchen with a guilty look. "Liz wouldn't want me to share this, but she says it won't be long now."

"How can she be so sure? People do rally."

"It's past that now."

Lucy sighed. "Oh, dear."

"Yeah, not good."

Little Nicki came out on the porch, dragging a stuffed animal. She gave Lucy a beaming smile. "Mother Lucy, pick me up?"

"Sure, Nicki," said Lucy, hauling the dark-haired two-year old into her lap. The child had the most beautiful brown eyes.

"Bless, Stitch!" the girl demanded.

Lucy looked at the grinning blue monster with sharp teeth made of white felt, a classic Disney cartoon character. "But Stitch is just a toy, Nicki."

"You blessed Kitty," protested Nicki. Lucy realized she was referring to the annual ritual of Blessing of the Animals. Nicki had brought her cat.

"But Kitty is alive, and Stitch isn't."

"Bless Stitch!" Nicki insisted shrilly.

"All right," said Lucy, putting her hand on the stuffed toy. "God bless you, Stitch. Be a good and faithful companion to Nicki."

"Good," pronounced Nicki and put her thumb into her mouth. Maggie reached over and pulled it out.

"Big girls don't do that, Nicki," her grandmother scolded.

Nicki gave her grandmother a foul look and returned her thumb to her mouth. Lucy smiled and gave the girl a little squeeze.

"You're very good with children, Lucy. Do you ever regret not having your own?"

Lucy felt that cold dread inside whenever anyone asked her whether she had children, but she smiled at her friend and said, "Of course. But we can't have everything, can we?"

Maggie smiled indulgently. "I think you would have made a very good mother. I can't even imagine not being a mother. When I found out I couldn't have kids, I had to adopt. I'm so glad we were able to give the girls a good home. Those Romanian orphanages were a horror show."

Liz came out to the porch on her way to the deck. "Dinner will be ready shortly. Maggie, will you round up the troops?"

Maggie patted Lucy's knee. "We'll catch up after dinner."

13

Erika set the plate of food in front of her father. He sighed and shook his head. "I'm not hungry."

She was disappointed because she had taken the trouble to make her father's favorite meal—Schnitzel with capers accompanied by boiled potatoes and green sauce. It was a fussy dish that took time to prepare and left too many dirty dishes, but her father hadn't been eating much. He needed nourishment, so she'd made the extra effort, but now, annoyance competed with her concerns.

"Papi, please eat. It's enough to worry about Mutti without having to worry about you too." It was a blatant plea, but it came out gruffly and sounded like criticism.

Her father looked up and gazed at her with his pale eyes. "I know you're trying, but I don't know what I will do without her. I have been caring for her for sixty-two years."

"Start by taking care of yourself," Erika said bluntly, picking up her knife and fork. When she was at home or with other Europeans, she ate with both utensils. She'd only learned to eat American-style later, and it still felt odd to her, like trying to sound American instead of British. Being a refugee, she had once wanted so much wanted to fit in. Now, she really didn't care. "Mutti would want you to look after yourself," said Erika. "She took care of you too."

"I don't want you thinking you have to take care of me. I don't want to be a burden."

"Then eat, and I won't need to take care of you," she replied in a firm voice.

Stefan heaved out another great sigh and picked up his knife and fork. Erika was pleased to see him dig into the cutlet hungrily. He reached over to sample the cucumber salad she'd made. "It's good," he said. "Almost as good as your mother makes."

"I hope so. She taught me how to make it." For some reason, that made her eyes fill. She blinked back the tears so her father wouldn't see them. He was already sad enough. She sensed he was holding back too, being Teutonically stoic. What a ridiculous game they were playing, trying to fool one another.

"I think I shall be retiring after this double sabbatical," she said to change the topic.

Her father looked up from his plate with surprise. "Retire? You're only sixty."

"Yes, but by the time I finally retire, I'll be sixty-two, old enough for my pension and social security."

"I taught until I was seventy-five."

"I know. That's because you never saved any money."

"No, because I loved to teach."

"I hate it. I despise those bratty trust babies. They act like they know everything when in fact they know nothing. Idiots. They have no idea what it is to do philosophy."

"Philosophy is the mother of sciences, but she herself is sterile," her father quoted. "You should have been a mathematician like me. You would have found it more stimulating."

"You keep saying that, Papi. Mathematics is too abstract. It never compelled me."

"You threw away your talent. You're more brilliant than I ever was."

"Says the man who was short-listed for the Fields Medal." Erika put down her knife and fork. The conversation had stolen her appetite. "It's too late now. I'm done with academia. I'd rather do other things with my life." After she said that, she gave her meal another look and decided she was still hungry. When she glanced at her father's plate, she saw that, despite his protests, he had been hungry too.

"They say it's very important for the caretakers to take care of themselves," Erika said. "I'm glad you liked my Schnitzel."

"You beat it thin enough, like your mother. You can't find good food like this in any restaurant."

"There are very few German restaurants anymore. Our food is too plain for most people."

Stefan wiped his mouth and pushed his plate away. "Good food. Thank you."

Erika nodded.

"We should talk about the funeral," said Stefan.

"She's not dead yet, Papi."

"No, but she will be soon, and we should have a plan."

"Has she ever expressed thoughts about her funeral?" asked Erika.

Her father shook his head. "No, she never spoke about it. I think she was afraid it would upset me, and she was right."

"You could have asked her before she had the stroke and could barely speak."

"I know, I could have done a lot of things," he said, nodding, "but I didn't." He looked so sad and lost. Erika thought of getting up to hug him, but she was still a little angry with him from earlier and didn't want to be a hypocrite. "I couldn't talk about it because I never wanted to face the fact that one day, I might lose her. She trusted me to take care of everything. Even when I arranged to have you taken out of Berlin. It was so dangerous, but she was very brave."

"Yes, she was," Erika agreed.

"I never listened to her when she was alive. I was always the one speaking. I would talk and she would listen."

Erika remembered. As a younger man, her father had been so dominant in her mother's life and in hers. Everyone listened to Professor Bultmann because he was so brilliant.

"You've known her longer than anyone, Papi. What do you think she would like?"

Staring into a place over Erika's shoulder, Stefan thought for a long time. "We should have a wake so that our friends can pay their respects. Your mother was a kind woman. She made many friends. She volunteered at the parish thrift shop even though she never officially joined the church. My colleagues from the department will want to come as well."

"All right, but I think the casket should be closed. Since the coma, she has shrunken to nothing."

Her father nodded his agreement. "I think she would like someone to say some prayers." The statement took Erika by surprise. Her father was a devout atheist, and her mother never went to church.

"I never knew she was religious."

"She was. She thought no one knew, but she kept a Bible in her bed stand, and I caught her reading it a few times."

"I'm surprised. I would have thought you'd frightened the religion out of her. You were quite vocal on the subject."

He looked sheepish. "Yes, I once thought I knew everything. Just like you."

Erika laughed. "I know nothing. Nothing at all."

"Skepticism is an honorable philosophical position."

"It's not a position, Papi. It's an admission."

Her father looked her in the eye. He knew what she was trying to say and was about to elaborate. Then he evidently thought better of it.

"Is there someone who can say some prayers at Mutti's funeral?" Erika asked.

"I called the Lutheran pastor, but he said he wouldn't do it because she wasn't a member of his church."

"How Christian."

Stefan grunted. "Erika, you will find that those who wear the cloth are often the least Christian of all."

"Some are genuine. I have a friend, who is a priest."

Stefan's eyebrows rose. "That's not the company I would expect you to keep."

"Nor I, but Liz invited me to a Christmas service at her church."

"Her? A female priest?"

"She's an Episcopal priest. They ordain women now."

"So, they do," said Stefan frowning. "It's all nonsense. All those sects fighting with one another. The bitterest wars have been fought over the smallest differences in doctrine. They burned people at the stake for it. Tortured them horribly. You saw the torture museum in Augsberg." He shook his head. "And now there are women priests. Hopefully, that is the beginning of the end!"

Erika chuckled. Her father could never resist the opportunity for a tirade.

He narrowed his eyes. "Are you interested in this lady priest?"

"Maybe," replied Erika slyly.

Her father shook his finger at her. "Be careful, Erika. I don't like the sound of this."

Erika laughed out loud. "Why not?"

"A lady priest?" He screwed up his face and looked sour. "But I suppose it's no worse than that crazy Jeannine with her paintings of fat, naked women. Blue. Orange. Green. Giant hairy vaginas!" He waved his arms. "Like a bottomless pit or a tunnel through the Alps."

Erika laughed harder. "Papi, it's bad luck to speak ill of the dead. And vaginas are not hairy. Only the pudenda."

Stefan would never acknowledge being corrected. He scowled at his daughter. "That woman was crazy. I never knew what you saw in her."

"You didn't like her because she was as strident as you are. She wouldn't fall silent when you spoke. How could you ever stand having female students?"

"I never had many, thank God."

"Now, you invoke the deity."

"It is a figure of speech."

"That's part of the reason I dropped out of maths and went to the philosophy department. I would have had you as a professor, at least for upper level courses."

Stefan gave her a filthy look. "We could have made other arrangements. That was just an excuse."

"Maybe it was," replied Erika. She sighed. "Would you like me to ask Lucy to say prayers at Mutti's funeral? She was once an opera singer. I could to ask her to sing."

"A singing lady priest?" Stefan's eyebrows rose almost to the lank, blond hair overhanging his forehead. "An opera singer?"

"Yes, her name is Lucille Bartlett."

Stefan cocked his head and narrowed his eyes. "I think I have heard of her. Yes, I'm quite sure. I think I heard her sing in the 1990s." He frowned. "She sang Elsa in *Lohengrin* at the Met."

That was entirely possible. The role of Elsa was in Lucy's *Fach*. Erika was instantly angry at the injustice of it and insanely jealous. Her father had heard Lucy sing on the Met stage, yet she would never have the opportunity. Erika revealed nothing of her feelings. She maintained her composure as she'd been brought up to do.

"Shall I ask her to officiate at Mutti's funeral?"

"Let me think about it," said Stefan. "But you may ask her to sing. That would be a nice touch."

"Do you have any preference what she sings? Can it be religious?"

"You choose. You have good taste in music."

As Erika washed the dishes and cleaned up the kitchen, she realized Lucy deserved some warning that she would be asked to sing and possibly to pray at her mother's funeral.

Erika wrung out the dish cloth and hung it over the faucet. She heard her father coming into the kitchen. He set something down on the kitchen table. She recognized it as her mother's jewelry box. She remembered as a child inspecting the earrings, necklaces and bracelets in the tiny compartments, everything organized and pin-neat.

"Erika, your mother would want you to have her jewelry."

"Papi, she's not gone yet."

"No, but she will not be wearing these things again in this life."

He picked up a ring set with a deep blue sapphire. "I gave this to her when I asked her to marry me. It belonged to my mother. She said to give it to the woman, who would be my wife. I had no diamonds to give your mother. In Germany, after the war, who could get diamonds? When she put on her wedding ring, she never wore this ring again. You should wear it."

Erika tried it on her finger. It fit perfectly.

"Thank you, Papi."

He nodded. "Good night, my dear." He leaned down to give her a kiss on the forehead.

Erika waited until she was comfortable in her sleeping Tee and shorts before calling Lucy. She knew she would have privacy because her father was on the other side of the apartment, reading in the living room. It really didn't matter where he was. He turned down his hearing aids when he was alone or took them out. Without them, he was nearly deaf.

Her heart took a little leap of joy at the sound of Lucy's voice. "Erika! I'm so happy to hear from you. I've been thinking about you and your family all day."

"I miss you," was all Erika could say. "Oh, Lucy! I miss you so, so much!"

"I miss you too. I'm sending you a hug." The transmission went silent for a moment. "There. Could you feel it?"

"Yes, I think so." Erika wrapped her arms around herself and squeezed. "I'm sending you one too." On any other occasion, Erika would feel silly for playing this game, but with Lucy, it felt entirely natural.

"How is your mother?" Lucy asked gently.

"The same. She's comatose. Her kidneys are beginning to fail and her liver. Her urine is the color of coffee. One by one, her organs are shutting down. It's a horrible process."

"Death is never pretty."

"No. It's not."

"I'll pray that it goes quickly, and it's not painful."

"They're pumping her full of morphine."

"Even so."

There was a long silence. Lucy asked, "Do you really miss me?"

"I do. I miss you so much my heart aches when I hear your voice."

"Oh, no!" said Lucy. "I don't want to cause you pain."

"Never mind. It's a sweet ache." Erika imagined the tender look on Lucy's face. "I told my father about you today."

"Is that a good thing? What did he say?"

"He said he heard you sing Elsa at the Met in the early '90s."

There was another long moment of silence. "That's possible I did sing *Lohengrin* in 1993. It was my debut role at the Met."

"Really? I never fancied you a Wagnerian. You're so tiny and slight."

"Only the lighter roles—Elsa, Elisabeth in *Tannhäuser*."

"Damsels in distress awaiting their noble knight. Suits you perfectly."

"Watch your step, Erika. You're on thin ice."

"It's summer. There's no ice here. And I know you're in Maine, but there's no ice there either."

"You're so silly sometimes. I love it!"

"I volunteered you to sing at my mother's wake. I hope you don't mind."

Again, the long silence. "Erika, I don't mind, but you should have asked me first. What would you like me to sing?"

"Something religious, I imagine. My father finally admitted that he knew my mother was secretly religious. He was trying to arrange a church funeral, but the Lutheran pastor refused."

"Why?" asked Lucy in a slightly angry voice.

"My mother was not a member of his church."

"Bastard!" said Lucy.

"My sentiments exactly." Erika hesitated for moment. "I suggested you instead."

"What?"

"You can officiate at the funeral, can't you?"

"Well, yes, but I have to contact the local parish. Do you know the name of it?" Before Erika could answer, Lucy said, "Never mind. I can look it up. I'm just glad you gave me a heads up. I need to speak to the vicar there. Just so you know, I already arranged for the deacon at St. Anne's to cover for me while I'm in New Haven with you."

"But I never asked you to come," said Erika, surprised and touched.

"I know, but of course, I'd be there for you. I love you."

Again, the words. They brought tears to Erika's eyes. "Thank you."

"You don't need to thank me for loving you. I just do."

14

Lucy's hand searched on the bedside table for the blasted phone. She'd left it on vibrate during her counseling session, and now it was dancing all over. She finally sat up. According to the red numerals on her alarm clock, it was four-forty-five in the morning. She blinked to clear her vision so that she could focus on the screen. Liz Stolz was calling.

"Liz! Is everything all right?"

There was slight hesitation. "Yes and no. Erika's mother died during the night."

"Oh, no!"

"I think the hospice people showed them the trigger for sending a morphine bolus, but that's between us."

"Of course, it is. When did she pass?" As she asked, Lucy wondered why Liz was calling and not Erika herself.

"A little after one this morning. Erika called me around two. She asked me to wait until morning to call you, but I'm on my way to get coffee and then my walk."

"Do you mind if I come with you?"

"Sure," said Liz, but she didn't sound sure. "I'll bring you coffee. Cream, one sugar, right?"

"Yes. You have a good memory."

"Training. It's all in the training. I'll pick you up in ten minutes."

After she ended the call, Lucy checked her messages. There were two from Erika. The first was from 1:10: *My mother just passed*. The second one, a minute later: *I love you*.

Lucy texted back: *I love you too*, and filled the screen with red heart emoticons.

She jumped out of bed and pulled her nightgown over her head. She danced into a pair of panties and running shorts and wiggled into a sports bra. She had no more clean T-shirts, so she took the one from yesterday off the hook in the bathroom. She took her plastic hamper with her as she headed downstairs to the office area. She'd throw in her laundry before she left for her walk. By the time she got home, it would be done, and she'd throw it in the dryer. As she headed to the new laundry room, she sent Liz mental hugs to thank her for the convenience.

Once the wash was going, Lucy sat on the back stairs to lace up her running shoes. She mentally reviewed the day's schedule. She had no services and just one counseling session that evening. She'd ask Samantha to cancel it. She grabbed her phone armband and sweatshirt from the hook by the door.

Liz was just pulling into the parking lot in front of the rectory. She pulled up to the door and got out of the truck. When Lucy came down the stairs, Liz opened her arms. Lucy threw herself into them.

"I feel so bad for Erika," Lucy murmured, hugging Liz, who felt so sure and solid compared to willowy Erika.

"Get in," said Liz, releasing her. "I brought you coffee."

Lucy climbed into the cab. "Thanks for letting me come along."

Despite the remote camera on the dash, Liz looked over her shoulder to back up the truck. "You could come with me every day if you could get up on time. But I know you'd rather walk with that cute blonde." She turned around and grinned.

"You walk too fast."

"I have long legs. Comes with the territory. Why didn't you say something? I would have slowed down."

"I just did. I was afraid to tell you before."

"That's ridiculous," scoffed Liz. "Erika says I scare people. Do I scare you?"

"In the beginning, but now I know you're just a rough, tough cream puff."

Liz frowned. "Don't spread it around."

Liz took Lucy's coffee out of the cup holder and handed it to her. "Hope it's right. They have a new kid at Awakened Brews. Since the job market improved so much, they have trouble getting help."

Lucy tasted the coffee. "Perfect. Thank you for bringing me coffee."

"You're welcome." Liz turned on to Beach Road. Lucy's head automatically turned to look as they passed Liz's office. "Now, you'll have to go out of your way to bring me back."

"Doesn't matter to me," said Liz.

"You're such a good woman. I hope Maggie appreciates you."

"Oh, she does. She takes very good care of me. In every way," Liz turned and winked. "We're going down to New Haven this afternoon after my office hours. You're welcome to come with us. That is, if you plan to go."

"Of course, I'm going!" Lucy said more sharply than she'd intended.

"Well, I didn't want to assume. You're a busy woman. An important person in this town."

"So are you!"

"Yes, but I have backup. I guess we'll see if that new PA I hired is worth anything. She just finished that crash course in family practice I had to take. There's such a shortage of primary care providers the state is doing everything it can to attract them. But it's hard for a specialist to go back and relearn the basics, humiliating and humbling."

"She just started, and you're throwing her into the deep end of the pool?"

"Sink or swim, they say. She seems sharp, and she has background in mental health. She was a psychiatric social worker before she went to PA school. That could ease some of the burden on you and the mental health clinic."

The mention made Lucy wonder about Erika's mental state. "Did Erika say how she's doing?"

"You know Erika, closed-mouth German. Never talks much about her feelings. She gave me the facts. There's no need for an autopsy because the death was attended. They're holding off until tomorrow to make arrangements because her father is a wreck. He's always been in control, but you can't control death."

"I wish I were there already."

"Can you get down there today?"

"Yes, I'll cancel my counseling session. St. Anne's has two deacons. One can cover for me. I'll consecrate enough bread, so they'll have communion to distribute while I'm away." Liz turned and gave her a strange look. "I'm a priest, remember? That's part of my job."

Liz shrugged. She pulled her truck into a parking space by the chain-link fence overlooking the beach. "It's a little chilly this morning. We can sit here and watch the sun rise while we drink our coffee. Then we can go for our walk. The exercise should keep us warm."

Lucy was grateful for Liz's companionable silence while they sat watching the rising sun throw pink and orange ribbons across the sky. She loved sunrises because they symbolized another chance for everyone to make things right. Only two things diminished her happiness at witnessing the beautiful sunrise. Erika wasn't there with her, and Helga Bultmann would never see this sight again with her mortal eyes.

"We're staying with my ex, Jenny, while we're in New Haven," said Liz. "It's a big house. There's room for you too. I just need to tell her to expect you. Do you want to drive down with us?"

"Thanks, Liz. I think I'll drive myself and stay with Erika. That is, if her father doesn't mind. From what Erika says, I may be involved in the plans for the funeral."

"That's a surprise. Her father is a staunch atheist."

"Apparently, he's softened a little."

Liz raised her brows in surprise. "Don't expect much and you won't be disappointed."

"I don't expect anything. If I'm called upon, I'll be glad to help. It's the least I can do for Erika in her time of need."

Liz turned and gave her a penetrating look. "Are you...involved?"

To Lucy's surprise, her face warmed, but in the predawn light, Liz wouldn't be able to see her flushed cheeks. "Not yet," said Lucy. "But close."

Liz nodded. "Sorry. That was none of my business."

"Sure, it is. You're her wingman. You're just looking out for her."

"Yes, I am," said Liz with a little chuckle. "Just looking out for her, I mean."

***

Lucy's evening appointment was a woman in a domestic crisis, so she decided not to cancel. That meant she couldn't leave Hobbs until six o'clock. At least by then, rush-hour traffic would have abated.

She streamed the accompaniment for one of the possible selections to sing at the wake: "Schafe konnen sicher weiden" from Bach's *Cantata 208*—a beautiful mediation Lucy hoped would appeal to the Lutherans in the audience. She began to sing. The air filling her lungs woke her up, and the sound of her voice making music made her happy. How had she given this up? Lucy dismissed the thought and gave herself over to the music.

Next she sang. "Laudate Dominum" from Mozart's *Solemn Vespers.* Completely out of character from the rest of the selections, because it was so modern, she had added "Pie Jesus" from Faure's *Requiem.* If none of those selections suited the Bultmanns, Lucy had an entire repertoire of Bach and Handel arias to substitute. She sang a few a capella as she drove until a call interrupted.

"Are you on your way?" Erika's voice asked.

"Yes, I'm sorry to be so late. My counseling appointment was too important to cancel."

"Don't apologize. I'm glad you're coming down. I set aside dinner for you."

"It will be after ten by the time I get there."

"If you're hungry, you can eat it. Otherwise, I can give you something lighter to eat."

"You're always feeding me."

"It was my mother's way of taking care of people." Lucy heard Erika's voice break.

"Oh, sweetheart, I'll be there soon!"

Erika's voice instantly became businesslike. "Ring me when you're approaching the building. I'll meet you in the parking area and show you where to park."

"The GPS says I'll be there in a little over two hours. I can't wait to see you."

***

As she'd promised, Erika was standing at the entrance of the parking garage when Lucy pulled up. She got into the car to direct her to the reserved parking space.

"Wearing your collar, I see," she said casually.

"I didn't want to take the time to change. I wanted to get on the road and come down here to see you." Lucy turned off the engine. For a long moment, they simply looked at one another. Then Erika took Lucy's face in her hands and kissed her, sweetly at first, but then deeply. Lucy's head began to swim. Her eyes nearly crossed as she drew back. "Let me look at you for a minute. I missed you so much!" Lucy whispered.

Erika's dreamy expression faded, replaced by a practical look. "Come upstairs and let's get you settled. Then you can look at me all you wish." She helped Lucy with the clothes hanging on hooks behind the passenger seat. "What's all this?" she asked, frowning at the black garments on hangers.

"Suits. A cassock. If your father really wants me to officiate, I'll need one. I'm so short, it's unlikely they'll have one in my size."

"The traveling priest show. I get it." The cynical tone reassured Lucy that, despite the loss Erika had suffered, she was basically all right.

***

Lucy heard sniffling in the dark. It was indistinguishable from the sound of a summer cold or congestion. She leaned up on her elbow to listen more carefully and heard the sound again.

"Erika," she whispered into the dark. "Are you crying?"

"No," came the muddy protest from across the room.

"Yes, you are."

"All right. Yes, I am," replied Erika gruffly.

Lucy got out of bed and headed across the room. She pulled up the covers and slipped into the double bed.

Knees to her chest, facing the wall, Erika was lying in a fetal position. Lucy gently stroked her shoulder.

"It's all right to cry," she soothed. "Go on. Let it out."

When Erika began to sob, Lucy could practically feel her horrible anguish, made more acute by every painful heave of her chest. The transferable pain was the hardest thing about being empathetic. Fortunately, joy could also be communicated in this way. Lucy leaned her chin on Erika's shoulder.

"It's okay, sweetheart. It's okay to cry. Scream your lungs out if you have to."

"No, I don't think so," Erika managed to say between sobs. "Not my style."

Lucy gently thumped her hip with her open fist. "You really are a hard case!" She laid her cheek against Erika's back. "You loved your mother, and you'll miss her. I'm sure it's a horrible pain you're feeling." That brought on more sobs. Lucy held her tight until the sounds changed. The pitiful sobs gave way to sniffles again. Lucy pulled on Erika's shoulder. "Turn around. Let me see you."

"No," murmured Erika into the pillow.

"Please." Erika rolled over. Lucy wiped her tears with her hands and said, "You're a mess."

"Thank you. There are tissues on the bed stand, if you wouldn't mind..." Lucy sat up and yanked a few tissues out of the box. Erika impatiently took the tissues out of her hand when Lucy made an attempt to dry Erika's face. "I need to blow my nose," she explained, sitting up. She accurately pitched the balled tissues into the trash basket next to the desk. "You have no idea how much practice that took."

Lucy lay down and patted her shoulder. "Come here. I'll snuggle you. Maybe that will help a little." She could feel Erika eyeing her suspiciously. "Come on. I don't bite."

Erika settled against Lucy's shoulder. "You smell good," Erika said. "Chanel No. Five. Classy scent. You have good taste for a priest."

"You think so? I always put a dab between my breasts. Chanel said a woman should put perfume everywhere she wants to be kissed."

There was an extended silence. "And do want to be kissed between your breasts?"

Lucy debated this question for a long moment. Then she unbuttoned her nightgown from the collar to her waist. She encouraged Erika with a light touch behind her head.

Erika leaned over and kissed the space between her breasts. "Yes, there it is. Very clever." She caressed Lucy's breast. "Beautiful," she whispered, teasing the nipple, which puckered into a little knot. "More beautiful than I'd ever imagined." She took the nipple in her mouth and sucked gently. Lucy's hand came up behind her head to encourage her. The sucking became harder, almost painful, but it was very stimulating.

"Yes, please. Do it more," Lucy whispered.

Erika abruptly sat up. "You don't think it's odd that my mother just died, and I'm lusting for you like a beast?"

Lucy put her hands on Erika's cheeks. "Erika, get out of your head! No! In the face of death, wanting to make love is the most natural thing in the world. It's an affirmation of life!" She sat up and kissed Erika so deeply, her own head began to swim. That brought out a side of Erika she had never seen before, wild and uninhibited, kissing her aggressively, biting her shoulder. She would have a bruise tomorrow. Erika's hand slipped between her legs. "Poor girl," Erika whispered into her ear, "You're a bit dry, but I can solve that in a jiffy! Lie down, love."

After a flush of embarrassment, Lucy lay on her back. Erika gently opened her legs and lay between them. "I detect some Chanel here too," she said kissing the soft mound above her sex. "I see you planned well, my Lucy." Then she kissed her fully and deeply, insinuating her tongue inside, withdrawing, then teasing her on the outside. After that, Lucy gave herself over to the sensations and stopped thinking. She was on the very edge of a climax, when the delicious kissing stopped. "No, you don't," whispered Erika moving up to lie beside her. "I'm not ready for you to come yet, but now, you are wet enough for this." Two fingers came inside her, then three. "There."

"Yes, please. I've wanted you inside me," Lucy said, as the fingers went deeper with every stroke. She put her arms around Erika's neck to draw her closer. Erika kissed her and filled her until Lucy just wanted to squeeze those fingers tight. A moment later, a powerful orgasm gripped her. Erika kissed her harder to stifle her cry.

When she settled down, Erika said, "My father is mostly deaf, but just in case, let's pretend he can hear."

She pulled up the covers and held Lucy tightly until her breath returned to normal. She raised Lucy's hand to her lips and kissed it. "Now that I have you in my thrall, I shall continue the bit below that I interrupted. If I may..." Erika slipped out of her arms and moved between her legs. Lucy wanted to jump out her skin when she felt a tongue delicately caressing her. "Oh, but you are luscious, Mother Lucy," Erika murmured. "I want to eat you alive!" She took her into her mouth and sucked gently.

Lucy's second orgasm was more powerful than the first. Her field of vision went white and she thought her head might implode.

"There now," said Erika, she sat up and yanked off her shorts. Climbing up Lucy's body, she lay between her legs and pressed her pubic bone against her sex. "To remind you that I'm still here."

"Oh, my gosh! Believe me, I know it!"

Erika pressed closer, rubbing gently. "Too much after you've come?"

"No," Lucy managed to say. "It feels good."

She rested her weight on Lucy's body. "I'm not too heavy, am I?"

"No, absolutely not." Lucy wrapped her legs around Erika's thighs as she pressed her pubic bone against her and undulated gently.

"Can you come this way?" Erika whispered in her ear.

"Maybe. Don't stop." The sweet pressure continued, until Lucy shuddered and came again. Erika let down her weight gently. "I love the feel of you," said Lucy, squeezing her one last time with her legs, before letting them down. "Don't ever move."

"I'm afraid that's not possible," said Erika, "but I wish I could lie between your legs forever."

Lucy slipped her leg between Erika's and deftly flipped her over, enjoying Erika's look of shock as she sat down on her hips.

"Dear God!" exclaimed Erika. "Where did you learn that trick?"

"Don't take the Lord's name in vain, Erika."

"My apologies, but where did you learn it?"

"Self-defense classes. I have a brown belt."

"I bet you do."

"You are my captive. I want you naked." Lucy peeled her nightgown over her head.

"May I sit up to disrobe?" Erika asked in a surprisingly formal voice.

"Yes, but then you're mine."

Erika sat up and took off her shirt. She looked shy while Lucy gazed at her body, touching and caressing as she explored it. She wasn't surprised that Erika was beautiful. Her breasts were perfect. "You are so beautiful," said Lucy, cupping her breast. "So womanly."

"Womanly," Erika repeated with disdain. "Fat and soft."

"No," said Lucy. "Feminine. Wonderful!" She stretched out on Erika's body and nudged her legs apart with her knee. "Can you come with my rubbing against you?"

"I don't know," Erika admitted anxiously. "I have to tell you it takes me time to adjust to a new partner."

"Don't you trust me?" Lucy asked on a warm breath of air into her ear. She rubbed her hip against Erika's sex. Feeling how wet she was excited her.

"Yes, I trust you," said Erika in a breathless voice.

"I may not be as skilled as you are, but I will make up for it with one important thing. Do you know what it is?"

"No, but you want me to ask." Erika's eyes closed. Obviously, Lucy's movements were giving her pleasure.

"I love you. Love is the ultimate aphrodisiac. When you love someone and give her your body, and she gives you hers..."

Erika moaned. "Please touch me."

Lucy reached down and began to stroke her.

"Do you want me inside you?"

"Yes, please."

It took only a few careful strokes and Erika came, arching her back. By then, they were both exhausted. Naked, wrapped in each other's arms, and sticky with the fluids of their lovemaking, they fell asleep.

***

Lucy opened her eyes to the sight of Erika wrapped in a bath towel. She was standing in front of a mirror to brush out her hair. She allowed the towel to drop and bent to dry her feet. Lucy was reminded of the French impressionist paintings entitled *Woman after Bathing*. When Erika stood again, Lucy admired her figure. Her buttocks were as perfect as was the way her shapely, long legs met them. Her shoulders and back were gently muscled. In all, it was a feminine and beautiful body.

"I can feel you staring at me," said Erika, looking over her shoulder.

"I'm not staring. I'm admiring you. It's the first time I've seen you naked."

Erika turned around and stood casually as if she were an athlete ready for a physical. Lucy's eyes caressed her breasts, devoured the curve of her waist and hips, and then dropped to the little thatch of pubic hair as blond as the hair on her head.

"And do I please you?" asked Erika in a surprisingly shy voice.

"Very much so."

Erika smiled and approached the bed. "Then let me see you, my luscious woman." She pulled down the sheets and bent to kiss her.

"Not fair. You're all clean and showered. You've brushed your teeth."

"I don't care. Kiss me."

Erika gave her a long soulful kiss. Then her lips traveled down her chin, to her neck and finally her breast. She took the nipple in her mouth and sucked it gently.

"Keep doing that and I'll drag you back into bed."

"I would like nothing better, but I must accompany my father to the funeral home this morning."

"Now?"

"Shortly," said Erika.

"Give me a few minutes, and I'll shower and go with you."

"I can handle it."

"I know you can, and I don't want to intrude, but if you'd like me there, I'll go with you."

Erika frowned slightly as she thought about it. "Yes, please. You know more about this funeral business than I do. But you must be quick. My father is ready to walk out the door."

Lucy decided to wash her hair later and kept it out of the shower spray as best she could. While she washed, she thought about what to wear. She hated to put on her clericals when not on duty, but being an attractive woman of small physical stature, she'd learned that her collar gave her more authority during important negotiations. She brushed her hair, tied it back, and dressed quickly.

15

"My father has decided that it's cruel to deprive you of a cup of coffee and some breakfast," said Erika. She could see that it had taken Lucy a moment to realize that she'd been addressed in German.

"How kind of him," replied Lucy in perfect German.

When Lucy had entered the kitchen, Erika's father stood at once, dropping his napkin on the floor. Lucy stooped to pick it up and smiled as she returned it. Stefan stared, as all men did at the first sight of Lucy.

Stefan dropped his chin in a little courtly bow. "You are welcome in my home, Miss."

"Father, may I present the Reverend Lucille Bartlett. We call her Lucy."

"It's is an honor to meet you, Professor Bultmann," Lucy said in correct *Hoch Deutsch*. Her accent was amazingly good, barely a hint of American intonations. Erika guessed they had been removed by the diction training given to every opera singer.

"Please sit, Lucy, while I get you some coffee. Help yourself to whatever you see on the table. If you need something else, I shall get it for you," Erika said, watching Lucy survey the platter of cold meats and cheese. There was also a basket of rolls. "Would you like a three-quarters soft-boiled egg? I made one for you too. Otherwise, Father will be happy to devour it."

"I don't want to take food out of your father's mouth, but I would love an egg. I haven't had such a wonderful German-style breakfast since the last time I sang there. And that's some time ago."

Stefan eyes had never left Lucy's face. As always when turned out in her clericals, Lucy wore subtle makeup, but her natural beauty simply shone through, no matter what she wore. Erika felt a little thrill of pride that this beautiful woman had finally given herself to her. As she poured Lucy a cup of coffee, she stole glances at her.

Lucy reached over and put her hand over Stefan's. "Professor Bultmann, you have my deepest sympathies over the loss of your wife."

The brilliant admiration in Stefan's eyes dimmed. He looked down at his plate and nodded sadly. "Thank you. She suffered greatly in these last years. I am grateful she is no longer in pain. But I will certainly miss her." He looked up at Lucy. "We all have our time."

"My father has become a philosopher in his old age," said Erika and smacked open her egg with her butter knife. "Not a very good one, I'm afraid."

Her father frowned in her direction. "I am as good a philosopher as you are a mathematician. Not a very good one, I'm afraid."

Lucy glanced at Erika for an explanation. "We are still arguing over the fact that I chose philosophy over maths," Erika explained in English. "It's an argument that has been going on for more than forty years. We will never agree on this subject."

Stefan had been looking over Lucy's outfit while this sidebar had been going on. "I have never met a lady minister before," he said, speaking in English, evidently sensing that Lucy was more comfortable speaking her own tongue. Erika knew he was also signaling that English would now be used for the conversation.

"If you went to church more often, you would see more of them," said Erika between spoonsful of egg. "There are many women of the cloth these days."

"I will go into a church this one time for your mother's sake. Otherwise, I have no use for God, and He, if he exists, has no use for me," said Stefan scowling. This sentiment had a visible effect on Lucy. Her eyebrows rose, and she gave him a sad look of sympathy. To her credit, she did not attempt an argument. Not that she could ever win a debate with Stefan Bultmann. He was a master, who could argue Erika to a draw, if not defeat.

"I see you are dressed in your uniform. Do you plan a battle?" quipped Stefan with a little chuckle at his own joke.

Lucy smiled. "Not exactly, but I find that the collar gives me some authority. Otherwise, some people don't take me seriously."

"Some people will never take a female priest seriously," Erika said before she could stop herself. Lucy gave her a pleading look. "I meant, there is still prejudice against women in the clergy."

"Unfortunately, there is," Lucy agreed. "I try to deal with it by being the best priest I possibly can be…to set an example as a good priest, who happens to be a woman."

"As we all do in every profession. A woman has to be ten times whatever a man is to be just as good. And my dear, you are an excellent priest. Don't ever doubt it."

"Which brings me to a request," Stefan said. He allowed a long pause to develop as he focused intently on Lucy's eyes. "My daughter tells me you could officiate at my wife's funeral."

Lucy glanced at Erika before she spoke, "That's true. Just in case, I've taken the liberty of contacting the local rector. He's in agreement, so it is only a matter of finding a good day and time for you and Holy Trinity Church, which is your local parish. It's nearby."

"That's good," replied Stefan. "Yes, I wish you to perform the service." He turned to Erika "What do I call this woman priest?" he asked, frowning. Stefan never did well with social uncertainty.

Erika gestured toward Lucy. "Ask her yourself, but she goes by Mother Bartlett or Mother Lucy with her flock."

Lucy took Stefan's hand and looked into his eyes. "Please, call me Lucy. Just Lucy."

Erika's heart swelled at the gentleness and compassion Lucy was showing her father, and as always, it was completely genuine.

"Now, we just need to decide whether the funeral should it be High Church or Low Church."

"What's the difference?" asked Erika, very curious.

"High Church is very much like a Catholic service. It is often a High Mass with a choir and singing. I would wear full vestments including a white chasuble to signify the resurrection. If it is Low Church, it is more protestant in tone. I would wear only a priest's choir robe, a cassock and surplice and a white stole. There can be some singing, readings from scripture and a homily. Holy communion can be distributed if the family wishes."

Erika realized she had been frowning during this explanation. So had her father. In fact, he'd looked perfectly aghast while Lucy was describing the High Church service. "I don't want to speak for my father, but I think our Lutheran friends would be horrified by something like a Catholic Mass. Most of our friends are unbelievers, so the less flashy the service the better."

"Whatever you decide is fine with me."

"I would like you to sing," said Erika.

Lucy looked pained. "I can sing at the wake. I've picked out some pieces for you to approve, but I can't officiate and sing at a funeral. It's too much."

"It would be nice to have some singing," said Stefan, glancing at Erika to support the request. "Most of all, I would like singing. My wife loved music. She would listen on the stereo whenever she could."

"Ask Maggie Fitzgerald," said Lucy quickly. "She sings at funerals at St. Margaret's when the family asks for a cantor."

"But she's not you," Erika said, surprised to find herself pouting.

"No, but she has a very fine, well-trained voice. Just don't ask her to sing coloratura. Stick to Bach or hymns, and Maggie will do an excellent job."

Erika still looked skeptical.

Lucy took her phone out of her pocket. "Here, I'll call her right now and you can ask her. I'll bet money she'll be happy to do it." Before Erika could reply, Lucy called Maggie's number, and she was on the phone. Lucy explained briefly what they'd been discussing and held out the phone to Erika.

"Erika, I am honored that you'd want me to sing at your mother's funeral," said Maggie. "Truly honored."

With that said, Erika knew she couldn't refuse. "Let's get together this afternoon and plan what we're doing."

"Hold on. Liz wants to talk to you."

"Jenny and Laura would like you and your father and Lucy, of course, to come for dinner tonight. Don't worry. I'm cooking so it will be edible. Ouch! Don't!" said Liz in warning voice, obviously to someone on the other end of the call. "Jenny just pinched my arm," Liz explained. "Hard."

"Maybe we shouldn't come tonight," said Erika. "It sounds dangerous there."

"Don't worry. I'll get her under control by the time you get here. Are you going to make the arrangements this morning?"

"Yes. Lucy is coming along to help."

"Good. Glad she got there in one piece." Liz lowered her voice. "Thanks for asking Maggie to sing. She's very flattered, especially with Lucy there."

"Lucy says she can't do both, and I have to take her at her word, but I am very grateful to have Maggie sing."

"You know her. Any opportunity to perform."

While the conversation had been going on, Lucy had cleared up the breakfast dishes and put away the perishable food. Stefan had slipped away to finish dressing. He returned wearing a tweed sports coat over a dress shirt and a tie. He looked every bit a professor from an earlier era.

***

The funeral director was as unctuous as Erika would have expected, a small, white-haired man who spoke too quickly. He showed them caskets because Stefan was terrified of fire since his Berlin apartment building burned down during the war, and insisted his wife be buried instead of cremated. He'd purchased a burial plot years before, so that part was all arranged.

Erika was startled when Lucy stepped forward and firmly managed the man after he suggested that a high-end metal casket would be a greater honor to the deceased.

"This is a simple family with simple tastes," Lucy said sharply. "A reasonably priced casket honors the deceased just as well as a fancy, high-priced one."

The man's eyes widened as he realized he'd been challenged by a diminutive, female priest. His other suggestions were more economical. He was equally deferential when he and Lucy made the arrangements for the service during the wake. Erika perceived that they'd all been deftly managed by the formidable Reverend Bartlett.

"I'll need a way to stream the accompaniment through Bluetooth," Lucy explained to the man.

"No problem," he said, showing her the way to link into the sound system through the WiFi connection.

"Now, I just need the family to choose a selection from the pieces I proposed."

"You sing for wakes?" the funeral director asked. "That's rather unusual, isn't it?"

"Mother Bartlett was once a principle singer at the Metropolitan Opera," Erika proudly explained.

"You were?" asked the funeral director, looking very impressed.

Lucy blushed a little. "Yes. But I've retired from the stage."

Erika looked up from the paper Lucy had handed her. "Sing them all. Each is beautiful and together, they will make a wonderful tribute to my mother."

Lucy stared at her with surprise. "Are you sure? They're such different styles. They don't really go together."

"Erika is right," Stefan agreed. "The people coming to the wake are mostly our friends from Yale. They are cultured people. They would rather hear you sing than give a speech."

The remark appeared to hurt Lucy, but after a moment, she said, "I never intended to give a speech…or a concert. I was only going to lead the group in the Lord's prayer and offer a blessing. I agreed to sing one piece and only because Erika had asked."

Erika noticed that, despite Lucy's mask of professionalism, the conversation had confused and disturbed her. She put her arm around her shoulders. "Please, Lucy. Please do it for me."

"You're the only one I would do it for," said Lucy. "The *only one*."

"Thank you. I am enormously grateful," said Erika. "I shall never forget this."

***

"Your father seems fine with being the only man…and the only straight person in the room," said Lucy as she dried the last pan.

"He's quite the lady's man, in case you hadn't noticed." Erika let the dishwater out of the sink. "And women love his debonair ways. We used to spend a great deal of time here when Jenny and Liz were together. Liz loved to throw lavish dinner parties for her friends and colleagues. My parents were always invited because Liz adores my father. My mother and Liz would cook up a storm. Things have come down a bit since she moved to Maine. I shouldn't say that. Let's say, they've become much more casual."

At the sound of female laughter from the living room, Lucy glanced in that direction. "I find it hard to picture Liz with Jenny. Liz is so down to earth. Jenny is, well, not."

"It was always an odd relationship, but they were *the* lesbian power couple in this town."

"Ritzy place."

"Guilford? Oh, God yes! Especially, here on the shoreline. But there are many artist types as well."

"This house is amazing, and the view of the sound…wow!"

Erika lowered her voice to speak confidentially. "Liz promised Jenny she would never force her to sell it. It was quite the bone of contention between Maggie and Liz, but Liz stood her ground. She's very loyal."

"I can see that." Lucy affectionately rubbed the small of Erika's back, then moved down to rub her behind.

Erika turned and took her into her arms. "I can hardly wait to get you home," she said and kissed her. Soon, they were lost in one another's mouth.

"Whoops!" Erika heard as Jenny came into the kitchen. "Sorry. Just looking for ice."

Erika reluctantly released Lucy. "Nonsense. It's your house. You see, we're new at this. We're in the I-can't-keep-my-hands-off-you stage."

"I think it's sweet," said Jenny, putting her arms around both of them. "Let me get my ice and I'll leave you to it." She squatted as she exited the room as if she could make herself small.

"We'd best join the party and not be unsociable," Erika suggested. "Later, I shall have my wicked way with you."

Lucy rubbed Erika's crotch gently. "I'm looking forward to it."

"Stop that. Someone else will come in and find us."

"You don't really want me to stop, do you?"

"No, but we should. We can continue this later," said Erika, kissing her lightly on the lips.

Lucy pulled her down into a hug. "I love you," she said, and Erika melted into her.

***

"Thank you for staying up and listening to my father reminisce," said Erika as they undressed for bed. "He likes to hear himself talk. I apologize that he kept you up so late."

"I love your father. He's adorable and so smart. Just like his daughter."

"His eyes are on springs when you're in the room," said Erika about to step into her sleeping shorts.

Lucy put a hand on her arm. "Forget those. You won't need them tonight. Get into bed."

Erika raised a brow. She wasn't used to being ordered around by a woman, but she slipped, naked, into bed. Lucy pulled off the white T-shirt she wore under her clerical stock in the summer. Underneath, she wore the sexiest lace bra Erika had ever seen. Lucy reached down to unfasten the front hooks. Erika couldn't take her eyes away as Lucy slowly opened the bra, and her breasts sprang free. She tossed the bra aside and pulled down her slip and lace panties.

"You have very nice underwear for a priest," said Erika as Lucy climbed into bed beside her.

"Every woman needs a few feminine things, even if they're hidden. Women are full of secrets." Lucy blew into her ear and gently probed it with her tongue until Erika was nearly writhing. Erika wanted to flip her over on her back, but Lucy held her down firmly. "Just relax," whispered Lucy. "Relax and let me take care of you." She caressed each of Erika's breasts, kneading them gently. "You are so beautiful."

"You are driving me mad, you know."

"That's the idea," Lucy breathed into her ear. She sat up and straddled Erika's hips.

"Am I allowed to touch you?" asked Erika.

"I hope you will." Lucy took Erika's hand and placed it on her breast. "You like my breasts. You look at them a lot."

"I adore your breasts," said Erika, attempting to sit up so she could kiss them.

Lucy put a firm hand on her shoulder. "No, no. Just relax. I'm making love to you now."

Lucy began to kiss her aggressively. She trailed hot kisses down Erika's neck, nipped her shoulder with her teeth. She kissed Erika's breasts, sucked one hard while she pinched the other. This Lucy was a stranger Erika had never seen before nor imagined. She fought the impulse to get up and take control. Lucy had her hips pinned, but she was slight, and Erika could have easily rolled her off, yet she let her take the lead. Lucy continued her tour down Erika's body, bathing her with her tongue. She released her hips and insinuated one knee between her legs, then the other. She nudged her leg. "Open up," she urged. "I want to taste you."

After that, Erika stopped thinking and focused on what Lucy was doing with her enthusiastic tongue.

16

"Erika! Stop looking at me like that!"

"How am I looking at you?"

"Like you're going to eat me alive."

"I want to eat you alive. Certainly, not dead. I'm not that kind." Erika batted her eyelashes, but they were so blond that it undercut the effect.

Lucy had paused her singing because Erika's smoldering look was so distracting. "If you don't behave, I'm going to banish you from the room."

"Stop arguing, or you'll wake my father."

"If my singing hasn't awakened him, why would an argument?" Lucy had been singing sotto voce to avoid disturbing Stefan's neighbors. Fortunately, the apartment was in an old building with very thick walls. And it was a weekday, so most of the residents were at work.

"When he takes out his hearing aids, he hears next to nothing. Fortunate, as you're not the quietest woman when you come."

Lucy's face warmed, but she enjoyed the flashback to their night together.

Unfortunately, their lovemaking had been punctuated by bouts of sobbing when Lucy held Erika against her breasts and stroked her hair. What a horrible, yet strangely beautiful combination—passionately wild lovemaking alternating with pitiful grief. Lucy wanted to open herself completely to Erika so that she would feel enveloped by her love. When Lucy kissed her, she willed that her kisses would heal the awful grief. Lucy could remember her own pain when her mother died. The death was expected after all the poor woman had suffered, but when it came, it had hit Lucy like a blow to the chest.

Lucy sat down beside Erika on the sofa and pulled her close. She only wanted to touch lips to reassure her that the little tiff had past, so she stopped the kiss from becoming too involved. They still had so much work to do before the wake. Erika had ordered a catered luncheon after the funeral, and the apartment still needed tidying.

"Promise me you'll behave when I sing at the wake tonight," Lucy said to Erika when the kiss ended. "Try to get a grip for your mother's sake. No, staring at my crotch or my boobs."

Erika chuckled. "I promise. I shall look adoring, not lustful, but it's extremely difficult to keep my eyes off your breasts. They rise and fall so beautifully with each breath you take."

"Try!" Lucy ordered. "I don't need you distracting me. I don't want to screw up, especially not on an occasion like this!"

Erika snapped herself into a more controlled persona. "Mother Bartlett, I assure you that I shall observe proper decorum in every possible way." She gave Lucy a quick kiss. "Meanwhile, there's something I want to discuss with you while my father is asleep."

Lucy settled back on the sofa to show that she was ready to listen.

"I think I should encourage my father to move to Maine where I can keep an eye on him." Lucy opened her mouth to speak, but Erika raised her hand to silence her. "I know what you're going to say. Elderly people find leaving their homes and familiar environment stressful. That's true, and I know of the risks in that regard. However, my father is still very sharp and socially aware. He makes friends easily. I think he has the potential to adapt. Yes, he will leave behind his beloved Yale and his old friends, but quite honestly, those people are dying out. He is ninety-one, after all."

Lucy had waited patiently with her hands folded in her lap until this pause. "May I speak now?"

"Of course, you may speak. As if I, or anyone, could prevent you!" Erika rolled her eyes.

"If you move your father to Maine, it will be a big responsibility. You'll need to help him build a new social network."

Erika looked pensive for moment. "He'll have me and you. He'll also have Liz, whom he considers another daughter. He'll love walking on the beach. Although there may be a waiting list, there are senior apartments near the beach and in walking distance to a convenience store. It won't be his beloved Ferraro's, but I'm sure it will be fine."

Lucy gave her a hard look. "I think you need to discuss this with him before you make all these plans."

"But the point is, I do need a plan."

"Yes, you do. And I'm happy to help in any way I can. I love your father. He's such a character!"

"Perhaps you can even convert him," said Erika raising a brow.

"I have to convert you first."

"Impossible," said Erika, folding her arms on her chest.

Lucy gave her a suggestive look. "We'll see. God's love comes in many forms. So does her grace."

"You persist in this idea that God is female."

"God is male and female. Scripture says we are made in her image. Of course, God has no gender, but all genders. In my mind, She is female."

"Nonsense, as is all theology."

Lucy screwed up her face in disapproval. "That's really harsh, Erika. Theologians can be very good philosophers. Take Augustine, for example, and Anselm. Duns Scotus. Ockham and his famous razor. Thomas Aquinas…"

Erika's frown deepened. "You're worrying me. You're quite well versed on this subject."

"We had to read their works when I studied theology." Lucy cocked a shoulder. "What did you think? I'm just a pretty face?"

"No, I knew you were more. Nor are you just a pretty voice. You are quite something, but I haven't figured out what yet."

Lucy laughed. "For that, you get a quick round in bed before your father wakes up."

Although their lovemaking was intended to be quick, they didn't rush. Lucy loved the discovery of so many ways to make love. Susan had been a generous lover but limited in her experience, and Erika had confidence on her side. She took what she wanted. Lucy liked both her aggression and her tenderness.

It was so different with women, like an endless dance with new moves and rhythms at every turn. She especially liked it when Erika lay back and let her make love to her in any way she chose. Lucy had intuited how much Erika liked to be in control, so she considered those moments a special gift.

When they got up, Erika went to take a shower while Lucy finished cleaning up the kitchen. While Lucy showered, Erika tidied the living areas. By the time Stefan awoke from his nap, the apartment looked presentable.

"Let's try to keep it tidy, shall we?" said Erika with a stern look to her father.

"You'll have no argument from me." Stefan yawned and made his way to the bathroom.

***

Lucy found her way to Trinity Church on the Green with little trouble, although New Haven wasn't the easiest city to navigate. Compared to Boston, where she'd been posted as a curate, it was a cinch. Once she got to the church, she realized how close it was. She could have walked.

Trinity was enormous compared to St. Margaret's. The old stone building looked like a minor cathedral. The history of the church on the website had proudly proclaimed that it was the first Gothic-style church in North America, over 300 years old. The stained-glass windows were vibrantly colored. The scenes they depicted from the life of Christ were inspiring.

Lucy felt a sense of awe in the vast and beautiful interior of the church. She genuflected in front of the altar and wondered if this setting was too Anglo-Catholic for her ex-Lutheran friends back on Wooster Square. Too late now. They were committed to this venue. The location of the service had already been announced on the funeral home website.

She'd called ahead, and the rector, Father Simmons was in the church to meet her. He was a friendly, gray-haired man with a ruggedly handsome face and a carefully trimmed beard. He approached with his hand extended.

"Hello, I'm Tom Simmons," he said warmly as he shook Lucy's hand. "Call me, Tom."

"Call me, Lucy," she said, her smile mirroring his.

"Forgive me for asking, but are you by any chance related to Lucille Bartlett, the opera singer? When you called, your name sounded so familiar."

Lucy's smile faded, and her heart sank because now she needed to engage on this subject. Very few people recognized her any more, but this man was about her age or perhaps a little older. "I'm afraid I am more than related. I am she."

Tom clapped his hands together. "Oh, that's wonderful! I am so honored to meet you. I was a great fan of yours. I was so disappointed when you retired."

"As you can see, I found a higher calling."

"Some time, you must share your vocation story," he said to Lucy's discomfort. "I love hearing people's stories. Every one is so unique!" His exaggerated gestures, the tone of his voice and his careful grooming led Lucy to suspect that Tom could be gay. "Let me show you around," he said, opening the gate in the altar rail. "I found that I'm free tomorrow during your funeral. I would be happy to concelebrate with you."

Although Lucy found Tom's friendliness a little overbearing, she said, "That's very generous, Tom. Thank you."

"It avoids awkwardness in case you're looking for something during the service and can't find it."

"Thank you, Tom, I've been a visiting officiant in other churches and somehow, I always manage to find my way around."

"I'm sure you do," said Tom, eyeing her cautiously. Maybe he'd perceived that he'd been put in his place.

"But you are welcome to concelebrate," said Lucy, feeling a little guilty about jumping down the man's throat. It was instinctual after being marginalized and mansplained to by male clergy, which happened to her regularly as a female priest. This man, however, seemed genuinely kind.

"Professor Bultmann was a professor of mine when I was at Yale," Tom said. "It would be an honor to co-officiate at his wife's funeral."

"Small world," remarked Lucy casually, unwilling to encourage too much conversation about her friends.

"Are you close to the family?"

"Yes."

"So, you know Erika," he said, fishing for more. He looked at her expectantly.

"We're friends," said Lucy vaguely.

Tom nodded. "We were graduate students together. Bultmann was my mentor in the math department. You can be sure he was none too pleased when Erika switched to philosophy."

Lucy stared at Tom, frowning a little at his over-sharing. "Can you show me where the robing room is? I brought my own cassock and surplice. Few churches have vestments my size."

"Oh, you'll find we're very well stocked here. Trinity has a lot of visiting clergy. We even have shorter chasubles in a variety of colors."

"The family has made it clear they prefer Low Church."

Tom nodded and his expression suggested he had expected such. "Not surprised," he said, confirming Lucy's impressions. "The old man's an atheist. Although, I must say, he's very broad minded."

"Sounds like you've spent time talking to him about this subject."

"Yes, while I was his student. He has very interesting ideas, and I think he liked to talk to me because, as a would-be mathematician, I understand some of what he was talking about. Most of what he said is just beyond me." Tom passed his hand over his head.

"Yet you never succeeded in converting him."

Tom laughed heartily. "No. And I wouldn't even try. That man has a deeper understanding and respect for the Almighty than most people will ever have, including me."

"Interesting," Lucy said, nodding. She regretted not taking the rector's warmth at face value. "Please show me what I need to know here. I don't want to take up your time."

"It's no bother," said Tom as he led her to the robing room. When he showed her around the sacristy, he explained that they used commercial hosts rather than real bread because there was usually such a crowd.

"Will you sing during the funeral?" he asked casually.

"No, it's too difficult for me to do both. Maggie Fitzgerald, a friend and parishioner of mine will sing during the funeral."

Tom stroked his beard pensively. "Maggie Fitzgerald. That name is familiar too." Lucy could actually see the moment when recognition dawned. "Ah! She was on Broadway."

"Long ago. You can tell we're all of a certain age," said Lucy. "I wish we had more time to plan this funeral. I would love to do something choral. Selections from Rutter's *Requiem* perhaps."

Tom sighed. "Rutter is so comforting and restful," he said, nodding. "We have a famous choir here at Trinity. I can ask around to see who is available tomorrow, and, of course, we can provide an organist. There is even a chamber ensemble. Many of our members are retired and available on short notice. I'll see what I can put together."

"That would be wonderful. Thank you so much."

"How can you resist joining in?"

"I may sing. I always sing with the choir. That is, if I'm not occupied with some part of the liturgy."

Tom sighed. "I am so disappointed I won't hear you sing."

Lucy hesitated for some reason she couldn't put her finger on, but then she said, "The family has asked me to sing at the wake tonight."

"Really? Now, that's unusual. What are you singing?"

"Mozart's "Laudate Dominum," "Schafe können sicher weiden" from *Bach's Cantata 208*, and Faure's "Pie Jesu." An eclectic mix, but the family insisted I sing them all."

"Tell me where, and when, and I'll be there," said Tom in an excited voice. His face was bright with anticipation.

Lucy gave him the address of the funeral home. "If you come tonight, you'll meet Maggie Fitzgerald too. Seven o'clock."

"I can hardly wait!" Tom rubbed his hands together to demonstrate his enthusiasm.

***

When Lucy returned to the Wooster Square apartment, she found Liz and Maggie there. Everyone was standing around the dining room table, which was covered with open pizza boxes.

"Lucy, you're just in time," said Maggie, pulling her into the room. "Liz brought in pizza from Pepe's. She says it's the best pizza in the world!"

"Here you have to try this one," said Erika, putting a slice on a plate for Lucy. "Papi loves it. White pizza with fennel, pancetta and black olives." Lucy saw that Stefan, seated at the head of the table, was happily slicing up a piece of pizza with a knife and fork. Lucy sat down next to him. Stefan put a piece of pizza in his mouth and smiled with pleasure. "My favorite," he explained after he'd finished chewing.

"Professor Bultmann, I met one of your former students today."

"And who is that?"

"Tom Simmons. He's now the rector of Trinity Church on the Green."

"Ah, yes, Tom. I remember him. Not a very original thinker, but talented. I'm sure he makes a better priest than a mathematician."

"Not everyone can ascend to the upper rings of paradise with you, Papi." Erika patted her father's shoulder. "Tom. My God, I haven't seen him in ages."

"He remembered you Erika," Lucy said. "He asked me to say hello."

"I would hope so. We dated for a time."

"Really?" said Liz, her brows shooting up. "You never told me that."

"I don't have to tell you everything! Besides, you were having your own dalliances with men at the time."

"Not my greatest hour," said Liz and took a large bite out of a piece of pepperoni and onion pizza. "I needed to prove to myself empirically that I wasn't interested in them. Clumsy oafs. All of them."

"Be careful, Elizabeth," said Stefan, tapping his cheek near his ear. "My new hearing aids work very well. I can hear you."

"Present company excepted, Stefan. I'm sure you were never clumsy in the sack."

"My wife never complained," replied Stefan dryly.

"Papi, I don't think I want to hear this."

"Where do you think you came from?" Stefan challenged. "A Quadratic equation?"

"Nothing so banal," quipped Erika in reply.

Stefan reached out and patted Lucy's hand. "Ignore them, Lucy. They are all lunatics. We are the only sane ones here."

"Thank you, Professor. I see I am in good company."

"Stop with the professor. Call me Stefan." The old man gave her a positively seductive look, and Lucy saw she had made another conquest.

***

Lucy left early for the funeral home to make sure her Bluetooth hooked up smoothly to the sound system. Alone in the room where Erika's mother lay in a simple oak coffin, Lucy felt a strange sense of peace.

For so many, death was a horror, but to Lucy, it was another passage in life like all the others. She had no illusions that the afterlife looked anything like the way it was depicted in religious art. She was certain there was no father God with a big white beard like Santa Claus. Since she had read Bishop Spong's book on the afterlife, her vision of it had changed completely.

At first, she was devastated at having her childhood images shattered, but now she had reformed her ideas around a less mythological view. The resurrection of Christ and the resurrection of the body was a core belief of Christianity, but she had begun to see it more metaphorically. Officially, she preached the words of the Bible as the living word of God, but privately, she held other beliefs. She knew she was not alone. Many clergy held beliefs that differed from the doctrines of their faith.

Lucy laid her hands on the casket and said a silent prayer. She blessed the casket and the mortal remains of the mother of the woman she loved. Tomorrow, she would do it more formally, but it comforted her to have this private moment with Helga Bultmann. Her only regret was not having met Erika's mother while she was alive.

Lucy heard the funeral director come into the room behind her. "Did you find everything you need, Mother Bartlett?"

"Yes, everything's working fine," Lucy replied.

"Were you really an opera singer?"

"Yes, I was." Lucy sighed. "In another life."

"Quite a change."

Lucy didn't want to engage on this subject, so she shrugged.

"The family will be here soon," he said. "We always let them in a little early to make sure everything's right before the public arrives. Plus, it's a time for a last, private goodbye. Do you know the family well?"

"I'm a friend of the daughter."

"I'm sorry if I seemed too pushy with the caskets. It's my job."

Lucy frowned. "I know, but adding guilt to grief isn't very kind."

"Unfortunately, it works and it's very effective." He extended his hand. "I'm Jim, by the way."

Lucy took his hand. "Lucy."

They both gazed at the casket. "The funeral business is dying out," said Jim. "Many people just want a quick cremation and a memorial service afterward. They don't really need us for that."

"The church business is dying out too," said Lucy, sympathizing. "It's not what it once was." She was sorry now that she had jumped down the man's throat, but not sorry she had defended Erika and Stefan from his predatory business practices.

The sound of the main door scraping open made them both turn around at once.

"That will be the family," said Jim. "Excuse me, please."

Lucy took a seat in one of the chairs along the wall to be out of the way while the family viewed the casket. She was surprised to see Liz and Maggie with them. Maggie looked wonderfully turned out as always, but Lucy stared at Liz. She was used to seeing her in shorts and a polo shirt, not fully made up and dressed to the nines in a designer suit.

Liz and Maggie stood a respectful distance away while Erika and her father approached the casket. As he drew near, Stefan visibly crumpled. Erika reached for his arm to hold him up and Liz was instantly at his side. The two of them helped him to a seat in the front row. Lucy could see Liz's hand reaching for his wrist to take a pulse. Erika was rubbing his back.

Maggie sat down beside Lucy. "It's been quite a day, hasn't it?" she said. "I feel so bad for Stefan. He adored her. They were married for sixty-two years."

"Did you know her well?"

"Not really. She was very quiet. A typical woman of her generation. She always allowed her husband to take center stage. Liz knew her better. They used to cook together. Liz extracted all of her best recipes. She still cooks them."

"Then something of her will live on."

"There's also her daughter."

Lucy gazed fondly at Erika, sitting with her father, gently stroking his back. "Yes," said Lucy with a sigh.

Maggie smiled slyly. "You're involved now, aren't you?"

Lucy nodded. "Since I came down."

Maggie gave Lucy's hand a little squeeze. "A shame to have this sorrow hanging over you right in the beginning."

"You and Liz did too...with your cancer."

"Yes, we did. It creates a deep bond when you have to face adversity right out of the gate."

Lucy nodded in agreement. "I'm sure it won't be our last challenge."

"No," agreed Maggie.

Tom Simmons appeared, wearing an ordinary dress shirt under a sports coat instead of his collar. Lucy guessed he was trying to avoid stealing her thunder. She appreciated his tact.

Lucy watched as he curiously glanced in Erika's direction while appearing to be in conversation with another mourner. Finally, he approached her. Their reunion seemed warm, but it was very strange to see Erika standing with the man who had once been her lover.

Lucy was thinking about her own spotty past with men when Maggie suggested they step outside. "I always hate these things," Maggie confessed.

"They're never pleasant. But it's an opportunity for people who haven't seen one another for years to meet and catch up. Like Tom and Erika."

"Weddings and funerals." Maggie sighed. "Thank you for agreeing to come out. I really needed some air. Are you anxious about tonight?"

"No, but it's an odd venue for what has turned into a concert."

***

Lucy and Erika had agreed that they should wait until eight o'clock for the prayer service. Meanwhile, Erika insisted that Lucy stand beside her, although she wasn't a member of the family. But when Liz asked Erika outside for few minutes, Lucy didn't follow, knowing that three would be a crowd.

When the two of them returned, she smelled smoke on Erika's clothes, and realized that Liz had asked her out to share a forbidden cigarette. She was sure the single malt scotch would come out later. Maybe if Lucy offered an alternative, the scotch might remain corked.

"I think it's time," Erika whispered in Lucy's ear. Lucy found her bag and took out Susan's white stole. As always, before putting it on, she kissed the embroidered cross.

Lucy used her stage voice to get people's attention over the murmur of conversation. "Good evening, everyone! The Bultmann family has asked me to thank you for coming tonight. My name is Lucille Bartlett. I'm a priest at St. Margaret by the Sea Church in Hobbs, Maine, where Erika has a summer house. The family has asked me to lead you in prayer and to sing some music they thought you might find comforting. First, let us pray the Lord's prayer."

Lucy bowed her head and began the prayer. Out of the corner of her eye, she saw Erika's lips moving. She was praying along, as was her father.

Lucy felt the "Laudate Dominum" could have been better. The tempo of the accompaniment was slower than she preferred. With a live orchestra, she could push the conductor, but not with canned music. After singing, she invited people to share their memories of Helga Bultmann.

The Bach went better. Her voice had warmed up. She asked for more reminiscences after that. Liz praised Helga as a cook and told funny stories of some kitchen disasters they'd shared. Liz was a natural storyteller with good comedic timing. She soon had the mourners laughing. Lucy always considered laughter at a wake a positive sign.

Finally, Erika got up to speak. "My mother was the bravest woman I knew." Erika's voice was a little shaky, but it grew stronger as she went on. "She encouraged my father to leave the GDR so that we could all be free. She knew how dangerous it was to trust his friends to get us out, but she went ahead with the plan. We were terrified, hiding in the trunk of a policeman's car so we could escape to the West. Hardly anyone remembers the Cold War nowadays. It's part of a history we all want to forget. But my mother so wanted to be with my father, she risked everything, even her life…and mine…to be with him. She was small but tall. She was quiet but loud in her courage. I shall always miss her." Erika had kept her emotions in check to make that little speech, but during the last few lines, tears had begun streaming down her face.

Lucy felt her eyes sting. Every funeral brought back memories of her own losses, other deaths—her parents, dear friends gone before their time. She'd learned to control her feelings when she was officiating, but Erika's grief was personal. Lucy felt it as if it were her own. She swallowed the lump that rose in her throat and was about to go to Erika, but then Liz got up, put her arm around her friend, and led her back to her seat.

Lucy returned to the front and stood in front of the casket. "I will now sing the 'Pie Jesu' from Faure's *Requiem.* Let us all ask for the peace of Christ in this moment of sorrow."

Lucy heard Erika sob, and it took all she had to maintain her composure. She streamed the accompaniment and began to sing. "*Pie Jesu, dona eis pacem…*"

As usual when Lucy sang, she took in the crowd as a whole. Then Erika's face came into focus. She was gazing at her with such a look of tenderness that Lucy thought her heart would break.

17

Lucy wrapped her legs around Erika's hips. Her breath caught for a moment. "Yes, deeper. Like that!" Erika had never had a more passionate, sensual woman in her bed, although she'd had artists, writers, dancers, once even a prostitute, but that was long ago when she was young. Lucy opened her green eyes, which were misty with need. "I want to come with you," she said breathlessly.

Erika was reluctant. Being touched now would be too distracting, and she wouldn't be able to focus. "No, let me make you come first."

"I want to come with you. At the same time," Lucy insisted. Her legs tightened their grip and suddenly Erika was on her side and Lucy's fingers slipped inside her. They withdrew and stroked her in the most delicious way. Erika was so excited it took barely a touch, and she felt herself coming at the same moment Lucy had a tumultuous climax.

"How do you do that?" Erika whispered into her ear.

"Do what?"

"Drive me mad with excitement."

Lucy laughed softly. "I told you. Love is the greatest aphrodisiac of all." She pulled Erika to her breasts and purred as she stroked her hair. "I love you with all my heart." She reached between Erika's legs and gave her a friendly caress. "Do you need more?"

"Any more of that and I won't be able to walk today. And I must walk because I need to hear you preach."

"I don't preach," protested Lucy.

"So you said."

"But I will say nice things about your mother. Now, that I know you better, I know much more about her." Lucy sat up. "We should shower and dress. Your father will be awake soon and be looking for his breakfast. I need to go over my sermon and get to the church for a brief rehearsal. Thank heavens the service isn't until eleven. It gives us some time to pull everything together."

"Have you worked out all the details with Tom and the rest?"

"Yes, the choir will sing selections from Rutter's *Requiem*. Liz will do one of the readings. Tom will read the Gospel. Maggie will sing "Amazing Grace" as the communion meditation."

"You are like a general, Mother Bartlett, marshalling your troops with aplomb."

Lucy stroked Erika's arm. "That's what I love about you. You use words no one ever uses in day-to-day conversation anymore."

"That's what happens when you learn a language through books rather than speaking it."

"Do you think in German?" asked Lucy.

Erika thought for a moment. "Sometimes. When I'm with my father, or I've been speaking German with Liz. Other times, no. It's too much trouble to translate in my head."

"I still translate in my head. But I learned German as an adult."

"What other languages do you speak?"

"I studied French in school. I can speak enough Italian to get by."

Lucy started to get up, but Erika pulled her back and kissed her. "I shall miss you so much when you leave this afternoon." She kissed Lucy's breast and gave the nipple a little squeeze.

"I know. But I need to get back to my flock."

This time, when Lucy got up to leave, Erika let her go.

***

Liz ascended the pulpit to read. Erika always marveled how her friend could transform herself from her casual drinking companion to a powerhouse who could command a room with a mere glance. Erika was glad that as a professor her transitions between the professional and the personal had been less dramatic. Liz nodded toward Lucy and Tom to acknowledge them. She paused for a moment to get the attention of the congregation. *She's good at this*, Erika thought.

"A reading from the prophet Isaiah…." After a few moments, Erika realized that Liz was reciting from memory. "…On this mountain, the Lord of hosts will make for all peoples a feast of rich food, a feast of well-aged wines, of rich food filled with marrow, of well-aged wines strained clear…" Erika smiled. Of course, given options for the readings, Liz would choose one about food.

Maggie sang the Goodall arrangement of Psalm 23 with the choir. After Tom read the Gospel, Lucy went up to the pulpit. Her sermon was on quiet heroes. It hit exactly the right notes. Erika's heart swelled at watching her friends work together to create this beautiful send-off for her mother. The choir sang selections from the Rutter *Requiem* during communion.

Erika felt her father's eyes following her as she approached the altar rail. She remembered the ineffable look in Lucy's eyes from the first time she had given her communion. Seeing that look again was worth drawing Stefan's disapproval. The person ahead of her moved away, and Erika stepped up to take his place. Lucy's calm eyes were so full of love that Erika shivered.

"The body of Christ, The bread of heaven." Erika felt the host touch her palm, but she couldn't release Lucy's gentle gaze. Finally, Lucy nodded to encourage her to move on.

As Erika sat down beside her father, she tried to sort out the confusion she felt. How could those same eyes invite her to penetrate her body at one moment, then look at her with such otherworldly love? Was Lucy, the woman, separate from Lucy, the priest? Erika tried to parse this distinction. It was completely different from how Liz stepped into the role of Dr. Stolz, the surgeon. Despite the white coat, she was still Liz Stolz, her friend. When Lucy donned the vestments of a priest, she was transformed. Erika had no idea how to manage this conundrum. It was a puzzle that stubbornly resisted her usually incisive analytic approach. It was simply baffling.

Maggie stepped up to sing "Amazing Grace" as a post-communion meditation. She sang it better than anyone Erika had ever heard. Her voice lacked the purity of Lucy's but made up for it with character. It was so plaintive that Erika was moved to tears. Beside her, Liz cut a tear from her cheek.

As Erika walked behind the casket with her father, she finally realized this was goodbye. They had declined the undertaker's invitation to take a last look at the body. Now, Erika wished she had asked him to open the casket. Her mother's body had not been made pretty for public viewing, but Erika ached to see her one last time. Too late now.

Erika felt a hand on her shoulder. She turned around and saw it was Liz, who was taking her arm. Liz always had good instincts in difficult situations. Lucy, in her ceremonial role, was far away, but Liz was near, shoring her up when she needed it most.

The casket was loaded into the hearse. A small group would head to the cemetery for the grave-side ceremony. Erika and her father rode in the limousine with Lucy, still wearing her ceremonial robes.

As they gathered around the wound in the earth where her mother would lay, Erika was numb. Lucy read Psalm 121, "I lift up my eyes to the hills whence comes my help." The words were familiar and comforting.

Finally, Lucy said the last benediction. The funeral director distributed red roses. One by one, the mourners laid roses on the casket. Maggie helped Stefan navigate the uneven grass as they walked down from the knoll. Liz's arm, hooked in Erika's, was sturdy and sure. She clung to it. Erika looked over her shoulder to see Lucy walking behind them. Her eyes were clouded with sorrow. For the first time, Erika realized that Lucy was grieving too.

***

The caterers were very efficient and laid out a nice spread for the guests invited back to Wooster Square. Erika was relieved that part had gone well. This awful day was nearly over. They would eat and drink, and then the people would leave. As much as that thought was welcome, it also meant that Lucy would be leaving too.

Erika looked down and saw a glass of whiskey at her wrist. "Go on. Take it," said Liz.

"I shouldn't. There are all these people here."

"Take it. Doctor's orders. Maggie and I will manage your guests."

"You've already done so much."

"That's what friends are for." Liz offered one of those off-centered grins that were so endearing.

Erika gratefully took the glass and took a deep swallow. It would be so easy to lose herself in the smooth liquid, but the relief would only be temporary.

She saw a flash of red hair behind the people standing nearby. Lucy had been quietly packing her car while everyone was eating. Now, she was carrying her cassock double hung on two hangers to avoid dragging it on the floor. She slipped out the door. Erika momentarily panicked that she might leave without saying goodbye, but the red hair passed behind the guests again. Then Lucy was at her side.

"I need to leave soon. Can we speak alone?"

"Meet me in my room."

Lucy nodded. Erika strained the rest of her scotch through her teeth. What a waste to bolt down such wonderful liquor, but she needed to talk to Lucy before she left.

She found Lucy pacing behind the closed door. She could almost feel the jittery energy emanating from her body. It was clear she was anxious to leave.

Erika kissed her. "I don't want you to go."

"I know, and I don't want to go, but I have to get back. Bring your father to Maine soon. Don't let him get too settled. Get him out of here. The sooner the better. Do you understand?"

"There are things I need to do…oversee disposing of my mother's clothes, arranging for the sale of the apartment…"

"Don't make it into a project. Just do it and come home." Lucy's look was firm. "I love you."

"I love you too."

"When you come home, we'll have our talk."

Erika frowned. Lucy reached up and touched the pucker between her brows with her fingertips. "Don't frown. It's nothing bad." She allowed her fingertips to trail down Erika's cheek. "Kiss me goodbye."

Erika grew weak as Lucy's tongue explored her mouth. When they parted, she was dizzy. Was it the kiss or the scotch?

"Take care of yourself, my love. Come home to me. Soon!"

After Lucy left the room, Erika realized she'd been given an order.

***

The caterers finished taking away the tableware and dishes on little wheeled carts. Liz and Maggie were walking around in stocking feet as they helped put things back in order. Soon they would be gone too, and Erika and her father would be alone. Stefan was exhausted and had gone to his room to lay down. Liz insisted on giving him a quick examination to make sure it was only fatigue and not something more serious.

"He'll be all right," she pronounced, stuffing her stethoscope into her pocket. "Let him rest. No more stimulation tonight." Liz patted Erika's arm. "Are you sure you don't want us to stay? We can."

Erika shook her head. "We'll be fine."

"You don't sound very convincing."

Erika rubbed her forehead. A fierce headache was coming on. *Damn scotch.* "Really. We'll be fine. I'm actually looking forward to some time alone."

"Enough said." Liz gave her a quick hug. "Maggie, we're out of here!"

Maggie looked up. She came over and hugged Erika. "Remember we're here if you need us. Just say the word. I'm off for the summer, so if you need help with your mother's things or anything at all, just call me."

"I promise," Erika assured her.

Maggie kissed her cheek. "Be well. Call me tomorrow to let me know how things are going. Okay?"

Erika nodded.

Maggie and Liz stepped into their shoes, and then they were gone. Finally, Erika was alone. There had been so much noise an hour ago, but now it was stunningly quiet. The silence was wonderful and terrifying. She sank down in a chair at the kitchen table in gratitude. That was the strangest thing about funerals. For days, people were everywhere, trying to show their respect. And then, they vanished.

Her phone flashed. Lucy was calling. Erika wondered why it hadn't rung. Then she remembered she had put it into silent mode for the service.

"Are you almost home?" asked Erika.

"I'm seeing signs for Portsmouth, so I'm close."

"You must be exhausted. That was quite a performance."

"Nothing compared to singing Wagner, but I'm pretty tired."

"I bet you are. It was a beautiful funeral. Simply magnificent. How can I ever thank you?"

"Take care of yourself until I see you again. By the way, if you're looking for that bottle of scotch Liz gave you, I have it."

"What?" asked Erika with surprise.

Lucy chuckled. "Lead us not into temptation. I'm bringing it home with me. Something to look forward to when you get back."

"You are wicked."

"Sometimes, it's for a good cause."

"I won't miss the scotch, but it will be very difficult to sleep without you tonight."

"For me too. But you can dream of me making love to you."

"Then I'll have to make love to myself."

"What do you think I'll be doing?"

"Oh, Lucy. I miss you already. I can't stand to be away from you."

"Then finish up there and come home!"

They talked about nothing for the next five minutes. By then, Erika heard her father beginning to stir. When he came into the kitchen, Erika wound down the conversation and reluctantly ended the call.

"Hello, Papi. Did you have a good nap?"

"Yes, it felt good to sleep." He ran his fingers through his yellow hair. "Sometimes, sleep is the only respite. You can dream of something nice and forget for a while."

That morning, Erika had experienced something similar. She'd awakened in Lucy's arms and felt safe and wonderful until she recalled that her mother was dead. So many things in life could be changed, fixed, amended, but death was final.

"Would you like me to make something for you to eat?" Erika asked her father.

"Eat? I am still stuffed like a pig from that party. The food was good."

"The refrigerator is full of leftovers. We won't have to cook for a few days."

Stefan sat down at the table opposite his daughter. Erika could see how the last few days had aged him. Like many blonds, he had a slightly golden tone to his skin, but tonight, he was ashen. His pale eyes looked faded. As she looked at him, she wondered if she looked equally bad. She was afraid to look in a mirror.

"Was that your lady friend on the phone?" Stefan asked.

"Yes," Erika admitted. "She's almost home."

"She's very pretty. No, more than pretty. She is beautiful."

"Yes, I saw your eyes follow her."

Stefan grunted. "Too young for me, but just right for you."

"You think so?"

"You should ask her to marry you."

"What?" exclaimed Erika, stunned.

"You heard me. Lucy is a good woman. Kind. It's obvious that she loves you. She would be good for you."

Erika waved dismissively. "I don't believe in marriage."

Stefan gave her a hard look. "And why not? Marriage is a good thing. It provides stability."

"Marriage is an instrument of the patriarchy. It's how a man demonstrates his ownership over a woman. It ensures that she will be his possession, and that he alone will have access to her sexually."

Stefan made a sour face. "That's feminist drivel. Something your friend who painted hairy vaginas would say. Fat women with hairy vaginas."

For some reason, that made Erika laugh until she was giddy. "Those hairy vaginas made a big impression on you, Papi."

He wrinkled up his nose. "That woman painted ugly women. Women are beautiful. Like your mother and you. Like Lucy." He wagged his finger at her. "Listen to your father for a change. Ask Lucy to marry you."

"I'll think about it, Papi."

"Not that you ever listen to me." He grunted as he got up. "I think I'll make some tea."

18

Lucy was afraid to blink because she might miss something. She pressed pause and glanced at the desk clock to see how much time she had left. In about five minutes, Samantha would be knocking on the door to announce her next appointment.

Lucy pressed play and her eyes widened. *There are strapless dildos? Who knew? How do they work?* She strained to see the details. All the while, her conscience nagged her, reminding her that many porn actors were often sex trafficked and exploited.

It's education, she told herself, but she could tell from the sensations below that it was something else. Education wouldn't make her want to touch herself. But she was so ignorant about lovemaking with women, and she didn't want Erika to know she'd been learning on the job. Lucy grinned. *Bad pun. Here I am watching lesbian porn videos in my office.*

Susan had known less than Lucy. She'd been in the convent for twenty years before she'd felt called to the priesthood. They had fumbled together and learned everything they knew about love between women, led mostly by Lucy, who had been with men sporadically during her busy career. Unfortunately, none of Lucy's male lovers had been sexual geniuses, so they'd only gotten so far.

If Susan hadn't decided she must be celibate to be an Anglican Catholic priest, would they still be together? No amount of pleading could change her mind. When she left for the Midwest, she'd asked Lucy not to contact her. It was too painful, she said. "Not even a letter?" Lucy had asked. "An email?" No. Nothing. Silence.

Lucy didn't want to stop the video before the end, but she realized she must. She needed enough time to unlink her personal laptop from her phone hotspot and wipe the history before someone came in. She'd finally figured out how to do that without deleting all her passwords. She stowed her laptop in its padded sleeve and put it in the bottom drawer of her desk. As she raised the lid on her office laptop to open the schedule, she noticed a banner announcing a call flashing across her phone. The ringer was turned off, of course, because her first client would be arriving soon. She had just a few minutes, but she so wanted to hear Erika's voice.

"How are you?" Lucy asked.

"Eh, it's coming along. Father finally agreed to come to Maine. Thanks for talking to him last night. I really think he's agreed to move so he can see you."

"How's the packing going?"

"The men came to pick up the storage cube and move it to Hobbs. We can't completely clean out the place until it's been sold, of course. It will show better with some furniture. I never thought anyone could have more books than I do, but Papi has proven me wrong."

"When are you coming home?" asked Lucy. "I miss you so much!"

"Tomorrow afternoon, if all goes well."

"I can't wait. Come to the rectory. I'll make dinner for you and your father."

"Are you sure that's wise? I might not have the energy to rescue you this time." Lucy felt a little hurt by Erika's reminder of her cooking disaster. She brushed it off because she knew Erika was grieving and under tremendous stress.

"This time, I'll make something I've cooked before. I promise it will be good."

"I'm sorry, Lucy. I never meant to be unkind. I'm so absolutely tired."

"I know. You're forgiven."

"God! I miss you so much."

There was a knock on the door. "Mother Lucy, your one o'clock is here."

"Have to go. I'll call you tonight. Around seven. Okay?"

"Perfect."

***

Lucy had decided to stop protesting the peanut butter and jelly sandwiches. She'd finally figured out it was Renee's way of thanking her for the counseling sessions. Instead, Lucy brought fruit to add to the meal. Today, it was local strawberries. They were deep red and richly flavored, not like the strawberries in the supermarket. She offered Renee iced tea.

"I have good news for a change," Renee said when they'd settled down to their meal.

"Oh, yes? What's that?"

"Peter signed up for Dr. Stolz's gun safety class."

Lucy opened her mouth in surprise. "How did that happen?"

"He had a lump down there." Renee pointed to her crotch.

"A lump? What kind of lump?"

"On his testicle. Fortunately, it was only a cyst, but he was scared enough to tell his mother about it. That's the first time he's told me anything about his health since he was in high school. He was practically in tears. He let me make an appointment with Dr. Stolz for him."

"That's good. I'm glad he's okay. But how did he get into Liz's…Dr. Stolz's gun class?"

"You know how she is. How she chats with you while she's examining you, to make you relaxed and comfortable. I guess she started talking about her class."

Lucy knew that family doctors were encouraged to talk about firearms in the home to assess the risk for domestic violence and gun accidents. Liz had probably figured out how to work it into her routine.

She also convinced him to lock up his assault rifles in the safe at the gun club. She gave him trigger locks for his pistols, and I watched him put them on."

"Wow. That's a big step. Does it make you feel better?"

"Of course. But now all he talks about is Dr. Stolz. It's Dr. Stolz this, and Dr. Stolz that. Supposedly, she's trying to get him a job with one of the tile contractors in town. I hope she knows what she's getting into. Peter isn't the most reliable person."

"Dr. Stolz is pretty astute. I'm sure she made the offer with her eyes wide open. But how about you, Renee? How are you?"

"I'm feeling pretty good. I'm even feeling good enough to stop taking up your time. I think I can stop our sessions."

Lucy smiled. "That *is* good news. But I will miss the peanut butter and jelly sandwiches." *It's only a white lie*, thought Lucy.

Renee looked concerned. "I can still bring them for you. I drive by here on my way to the bank."

"No, that's all right. I can make them for myself." In fact, Lucy had had enough peanut butter and jelly sandwiches to last a lifetime. One was a treat. Once a week was deadly.

After Renee left, Lucy congratulated herself on a successful conclusion. She had no illusion that Peter was reformed and wouldn't continue to be a problem, but having Liz involved as an ally was a positive step. Liz's solution was unconventional, but that's how things seemed to be done in Maine. Trained to pay attention to regulations and carefully document everything, Lucy wasn't sure what to think about that.

Lucy finished her afternoon appointments and couldn't wait to go home and change into shorts and a T-shirt. She'd been wearing her hair up because the heat for the last few days had been unbearable. The humidity made her feel so uncomfortable, and the temperature was only eighty-five degrees. The rayon of her clericals clung to her. She could never live in the South and was so glad when St. Margaret's had hired her. The alternative had been a church in Virginia. Fortunately, God had listened to her prayers and had sent her to Maine instead.

She wondered what to make when Erika and Stefan came for dinner. She decided to head to the supermarket for inspiration. Fortunately, it was mid-week, and although the town was full of tourists, the supermarket wasn't unusually busy.

Lucy surveyed the meat counter. She rarely ate red meat nowadays, not only for health reasons, but because it had become so expensive. When the summer visitors were in town, the store upped its prices.

She could make barbecued chicken. That was pretty basic. Yes, chicken, her mother's homemade potato salad recipe, and a green salad. As she passed the seafood counter, she saw Liz and waved to her. Liz waved back and beckoned to her.

"What are you doing here?" asked Lucy.

"Well, my wife is in Connecticut helping our friend, so I am buying myself a treat."

The fishmonger called to her. "That's half a pound, Doc. Is that good?" Liz looked over the counter at the scale. "Just a minute." She turned to Lucy. "Do you like sea scallops? Maggie hates them, so I only make them for myself when she's not home."

"I love scallops."

"Good. Come for dinner."

Lucy had no opportunity to protest before Liz asked the man behind the counter to double the order.

When the scale registered the price, Lucy protested, "Liz that's too generous."

Liz shrugged. "I decide when it's too generous. Okay? Come over after you unpack your groceries."

"What can I bring?"

"You. See you later." Liz took her package and headed toward the produce aisle.

Lucy shook her head and checked her shopping list. She wanted to stock up on things she knew Erika liked—Cinnamon bread with raisins, Greek yogurt, goat cheese, rice crackers, fruit. Hopefully, she'd be seeing much more of her once she got back.

***

When Lucy arrived, Liz was on the phone. She opened the door and gestured to the screen porch, where Lucy found olives, cheese, and crackers set out on the coffee table. Still on the phone, Liz brought her a glass of white wine. Lucy tasted it and found it delicious—light and moderately dry. Perfect for a warm night.

"Sorry about that," said Liz, coming out to the porch with a glass of wine for herself. "I think I found Stefan an apartment in the senior housing on Ocean Road. That will be close to Erika, but far enough away for privacy." She raised her hand with her finger crossed.

"How did you manage that? There's a waiting list a mile long."

"I have friends in high places."

"You're dangerous since you became president of the chamber of commerce. What about some poor, old lady who's been waiting for a place for months?"

Liz frowned. "You're not serious."

"I am. Some of my parishioners have been trying to get in there for a long time."

"There's another senior complex across Route 1, and it's cheaper. There's even a special trolly that can take them to the beach." Liz sat back and crossed her arms on her chest. "I have no sympathy."

"Liz..." Lucy reached over and put her hand on her arm. "I'm sorry. I know you're trying to do a good deed and help Stefan. I don't want to quarrel."

"Who will rid me of this troublesome priest?" Liz quoted with a scowl.

Lucy laughed. "You invited me. Remember?"

"So I did." Liz helped herself to cheese and crackers. "I don't know why. I love my bachelor nights. I can stay up all night watching superhero movies, drinking beer, and farting to my heart's content."

"You're drinking wine," Lucy reminded her.

"I'm trying to be on good behavior because you're here."

"That's nice of you," said Lucy with a chuckle. "Do you miss Maggie?"

"Of course, I miss Maggie. I can never get enough of Maggie."

"That's very sweet and romantic."

"Romantic? No. I'm not the romantic type."

"But you gave her that big diamond ring."

"Maggie is a romantic. It's important to read your audience." Liz winked. "Don't get any ideas. Erika is not into diamonds. And you should probably let her propose to you, not the other way around." Liz nodded as if affirming the wisdom of her own statement.

"I'm not into roles," said Lucy. "Just because I look feminine doesn't mean I'm the femme."

Liz gave her a long, measuring look. "Erika's not exactly butch either. But you'd scare her away if you proposed to her. She's not a big fan of marriage. She tried to talk me out of marrying Maggie. When I explained I was trying to reassure Maggie that I'd stand by her through the cancer, she backed off. Erika knows how to read her audience."

"I never knew that about you and Maggie. Is that the real reason you married her?"

Liz shook her head. "No, and don't ever tell her I told you. I married Maggie because I love her, but there were plenty of good reasons to marry her, practical reasons. It made our life simpler, especially when she was being treated for cancer. Her daughter, the oncologist, was always fighting me. After we married, I could say, 'Buzz off. She's my wife.'"

"You never said that."

"Of course, not. I'm a doctor. I would never say such a thing."

"Liz, I never know what you'll say."

Liz laughed. "Neither do I." She took a long swallow of wine. "Marriage also ended the arguments about who would pay for expenses. After we married, it was our money."

"All very practical reasons."

"Marriage is practical. It's a social and economic contract."

"Marriage is sacred."

"Definitely don't tell Erika that."

"I don't know. I think she's weakening."

Liz spread some cheese on a cracker and offered it to Lucy. "Believe me. After decades as an agnostic, she is not weakening. Don't get your hopes up."

"Liz, do you mind if I ask your professional advice about something?" Lucy wondered how to frame her question without making Liz uncomfortable, but, after all, she was the one who had given Lucy the vibrator.

Liz glanced at her watch. "Meter's running. Anything beyond fifteen minutes, and I'll bill your insurance."

"You will not," scoffed Lucy. She looked Liz directly in the eye. "What do you think about dildos?"

Liz's face was a completely impassive mask. She had assumed her doctor face. She shrugged. "They're perfectly fine as long both parties agree, they're correctly sized to the partners' anatomy, and people maintain proper hygiene."

"Correctly sized?"

"Yes, you know. The average erect penis is a little over six inches and a little under five inches in circumference. Anything bigger could be painful." Liz frowned. "And you were tight, so you need to be careful."

"Not anymore. I've been following my doctor's recommendations."

Liz raised an eyebrow. "Good. I like patients who follow my advice."

"And the hygiene part?"

"Certain materials are porous and absorb bacteria, but made of the right stuff, dildos are not hard to keep clean. Some people put them in the dishwasher."

"Really?" That was something Lucy hadn't thought of. "And what do *you* think about dildos?"

Liz glanced her watch. "I turned off the meter. Sounds like you're asking me a personal question."

"I am."

"You are the damn strangest priest I ever met."

"I'm trying to learn. I'm new to all this. Besides, one of my clients might ask about sex toys. I have no idea what to say."

Liz let out a long sigh. "I enjoyed sex toys with other partners. Maggie is strictly a natural woman and doesn't care for them. They're not for everyone. Does that answer your question?"

"Yes, thank you."

"If you're really interested in this subject, you should call my ex, Jenny. She's a gynecologist and knows a lot about sex toys. She taught me everything I know."

Lucy recalled Liz's sharp-tongued ex. "Thanks. I'll consider it," Lucy said, but she had no intention of calling Jenny.

"Now, are we finished with the dildo discussion?"

"Yes, I think so."

"Good. Now, would you like me to show you how to make pan-seared scallops with wilted spinach? Erika really likes them too."

The idea of learning how to cook another of Erika's favorite dishes was incentive enough. Lucy followed Liz into the kitchen.

The scallops were succulent. Everything else was just right.

"Maggie says she married you for your cooking," said Lucy. "This is soooo delicious."

"She's wrong. I married Maggie for *her* cooking."

After dinner, they sat on the screen porch, eating pieces of cantaloupe right out of the common bowl. Lucy remembered she had a wedding in the morning and needed to put the final touches on her sermon, but she felt comfortable and relaxed. She didn't want to leave.

"I should go," she said, but she made no move to get up.

"It must be lonely in that rectory of yours at night. I wouldn't want to go home either."

"I keep myself busy. I read. I watch old movies, thrillers from the 1950s."

"Sounds so exciting I could go right to sleep, but Erika will be home tomorrow."

"I can't wait."

"The apartment in the senior residence won't be available until the first of the month. That's only a week and a half away. Stefan could stay with us until then…to give you ladies some privacy."

"I think Erika and her father need one another right now. But thank you." Lucy finally got up. "I really should go."

Liz walked her to the door. When Lucy hugged her, Liz's strength felt comforting.

"It's a good thing I'm married," said Liz, seemingly unwilling to let her go, "or Erika might have something to worry about."

"You're such a flirt, Liz." Lucy gave her a light punch on the shoulder. "Thank you for dinner. It was wonderful."

19

"Hold on, dear. Let me go where I can talk." Erika patted Maggie's hand to apologize in advance for any unintended offense and headed into the bedroom. She closed the door and sat down on the bed. "I thought you'd forgotten me."

Erika could hear the fatigue in Lucy's sigh. "I'm sorry. I should have texted you that Liz invited me for dinner. We bumped into one another in the supermarket. She showed me how to make pan-seared scallops."

"I'm jealous," said Erika.

"No, please don't be. She was just being Liz…taking in a stray."

"Don't be silly, Lucy. I'm jealous she made you scallops. I adore them."

"Well, now I know how to make them too."

"Good. You can make them for me when I get home."

"When you get home, first things first. You know what I mean."

Erika's sex tingled at the thought of Lucy's legs wrapped around her thighs. She resorted to humor to help her stay focused. "We've been apart so long I've nearly forgotten what you look like."

The phone rang in Erika's hand, indicating that Lucy was trying to open a video chat. Erika tapped the button and Lucy's face came into focus. Erika was so happy to see her, a lump formed in her throat.

"Is that better?" Lucy asked. Her lips parted a little and Erika wanted to kiss the screen.

"Woman, you are a temptress!"

"Really? Tell me how," said Lucy in her sexiest voice.

"Phone sex? Oh, I wish, but I need to maintain some composure. After all, I have my father just outside, and I have a roommate tonight."

"Now, I'm jealous."

"Don't be. Maggie's beautiful and wonderful company, but she's not you."

"Maggie is good company, a real chatterbox. And so funny. Her wit is different from yours…or Liz's. Half the time I don't get your jokes."

"I admit that German humor is…odd. Philosopher humor is not funny in the least."

"But you and Liz do a very good job of amusing one another. That's enough." Lucy suddenly looked serious and very tired. "How are things going down there?"

"Pretty well. My father signed the contract with the real estate agent and received the sign off from the coop board, so that's done. All the odd bits bound for Maine are on their way to storage until we find a place."

"Oh! I forgot to tell you. Liz thinks she found an opening at Beach Terrace for your father."

"Yes, she called. That Liz. She has the most extraordinary knack for getting her way."

"Must be that philosophy training."

"Oh, I doubt that. I can't convince anyone to do anything."

"You talked your father into moving to Maine." On the screen, Lucy raised her auburn brows.

"He only agreed because you're there."

Lucy laughed. "I'm a little young for him."

"Doesn't matter when you're a lady's man."

"Sorry to disappoint him, but it's his daughter I love." She sighed. "I miss you soooo much!"

"Patience, love. I'll be home tomorrow. What time is dinner?"

"Any time after five. I can't wait to see you!" Lucy kissed the air. "Sleep well, my dearest Erika."

When Lucy's image vanished from the screen, Erika felt a hollow ache. She almost called her back to blow her another kiss. But Lucy looked so tired. Instead, Erika texted a string of heart emoticons.

Erika returned to the living room where Maggie was talking to Stefan. It was obvious that he was trying to charm Maggie, but it was she who had him wrapped around her finger.

"Lucy good?" Maggie asked.

"Tired, but well," Erika said. "Your wife invited her for dinner and made sea scallops."

Maggie made a little face. "I hate them. I'll eat the little bay scallops, but the big ones, no. I can't stand them."

"I'll eat your portion. I love them." Erika turned to her father. "We're going to Lucy's tomorrow for supper, Papi. All right?"

A twinkle formed in Stefan's eyes, and he smiled broadly. "Oh, yes," he agreed enthusiastically. "That would be very nice."

Erika could feel Maggie's eyes studying her.

"Stefan, we have no one visiting us at the moment," said Maggie. "Wouldn't you be more comfortable staying with me and Liz instead of in Erika's little cottage?"

Erika looked up and saw Maggie nodding. She understood that her friend was encouraging her to endorse the idea, but after her father had suffered such a loss, sending him to stay anywhere but her cottage felt like a betrayal. She stared at her wine glass and remained silent while she waited for her father's response.

"It's an idea," her father said slowly. "I'm sure my daughter is sick of me by now. I've seen more of her in the last three weeks than in thirty years!"

"Maybe you're sick of me, Papi," said Erika.

He reached over and patted her hand. "I would never get tired of being with you. But I understand you like your privacy too. Here, we have been cheek to jowl."

"I'm sure Liz will take you out in her new boat," Maggie said enthusiastically. "Maybe you can do a little fishing."

Stefan sat back and smiled. "Fishing. What a pleasure. Something I haven't done in years."

"You can walk with me on the beach…" Maggie said.

"Enough," said Stefan, raising his hand. "You have convinced me." He glanced slyly at his daughter. "As long as Erika is in agreement."

"You can do whatever you want, Papi. If you want to stay with Maggie and Liz, my feelings won't be hurt."

"They do have more room," her father said, smoothing the legs of his trousers. "Your little cottage is small for two people."

"It will only be for a short time until you move into your new place," said Erika. "Liz has found you a nice studio right on the beach."

"Beach Terrace?" asked Maggie. "That's a great place! I hear the food is very good. You can walk to Erika's cottage. There's a little café, and they don't care if you sit for hours. There's a little convenience grocery with a very good deli. It's not Ferraro's, but not bad. And of course, the seafood restaurant is open all summer...."

Stefan turned to Maggie and smiled knowingly. "There's no need to sell me on the place. I know it's time to move on. I've lived in this flat with my wife for over forty years, but now it's time to go elsewhere and begin again."

Erika took his hand and squeezed it. "You're very brave, Papi. Not everyone would welcome a new adventure with such optimism."

"Optimism is the only thing that kept me going when we were stuck in the GDR. Optimism and the fervent hope that one day, we would be free. And now the wall is down, and people come and go as they please. Things change. The delta is the only constant."

"Do you mean mathematically, Papi, or are you being philosophical?"

"In the broadest sense only. Don't be fresh, Erika." He grinned. "Don't tread on my toes and I won't tread on yours." He raised a blond brow.

He got up to use the bathroom. As soon as he was out of earshot, Erika asked, "Are you sure Liz will be all right with this arrangement?"

Maggie waved her hand in a dismissive gesture. "Of course. She suggested it. You know how Liz is. She loves company...unless the kids are crawling into bed when we have other things in mind."

"Yes, that could be disconcerting."

"Liz will love having someone to take out on the boat. I always get seasick."

"You hate scallops, and you get seasick on her boat. This doesn't sound like a match made in heaven."

"Don't worry," said Maggie with a sly look. "We are compatible in all the important ways." She finished her wine and got up. "I'm going to bed. I have a long drive tomorrow. Hopefully, my better half will be available to help me unpack on the other end."

"It's kind of you and Liz to store my father's things."

Maggie shrugged. "It's summer. We don't need to park in the garage." She headed to the sink to rinse out her wine glass. "I'll see you later."

Maggie was in bed with a book when Erika came in to undress for bed.

"Do you want me to turn off the light," Maggie asked.

"I'm so exhausted, I think I could fall asleep with the light on."

"No, I'm tired too. I'll turn it off, so you can sleep."

The light went off. Erika was grateful for the dark and the quiet. She undressed and got into bed. "It's very generous of you and Liz to take in my father. He's been getting on my nerves."

"It must be hard returning to the parental home after being gone for all these years. But I'm sure you have many happy memories of this place."

"In fact, I was never that fond of New Haven. That's why when Colby offered me a tenure track position, I jumped at it. My father and his pals had a hand in it. He knew I'd be waiting for years for tenure track at Yale."

"Sounds like he's always had your best interests at heart," said Maggie. "I'm sure he'd rather stay with you, but he knows you want to get back to your sweetie."

"You think so?"

"Of course, he does."

"He told me I should marry her."

"You should."

"I don't know…"

Evidently, sensing Erika's reluctance, Maggie quickly said, "It's still early. You have time to figure it out."

"You and Liz didn't wait long."

"We waited for forty years."

Erika rearranged her pillow. For some reason, it was annoying her tonight. "Are you glad you got married?"

"Absolutely! The smartest thing I ever did."

Erika made a face in the dark even though no one could see her.

"This is fun…sharing secrets in the dark like teenagers," said Maggie.

"It is fun. I never had a sister. Liz is the closest thing to a sister I ever had…and now you too. Thank you for being here to help with my father and packing."

"You're welcome," said Maggie. "I'm sorry to poop out on you, but my eyes are rolling in my head. I need to sleep."

Erika could sense when Maggie nodded off, but Erika's mind was working overtime and she couldn't settle down. She lay with her hands behind her head staring up at the ceiling. Her phone, sitting on the bedside table, suddenly lit up. She realized it was a text message coming in. *I'm going to bed now. Sleep well, sweetheart. I love you.*

I love you too, Erika texted back. She added a red heart.

She imagined Lucy curled on her side like a child, her red hair in a thick braid on her pale, slender neck. Now that she'd seen Lucy asleep, it was easier to imagine the scene.

Erika took the extra pillow from under her head and hugged it. She felt a bit silly doing it, but for once, she didn't care.

***

After Maggie left with her SUV packed solid, Stefan sat in the living room and stared at the nearly bare bookcases. Only a few volumes with attractive spines remained to make the apartment more attractive to prospective buyers. All of the valuable books had already been packed. Erika brought the last box down to her car and locked it carefully. Wooster square was one of the more affluent, safer neighborhoods, but one couldn't be too cautious.

"Ready to leave?" asked a familiar voice. Erika turned around and saw Tom Simmons standing behind her. He was wearing jogging pants, a baggy Yale T-shirt and running shoes.

"Tom. Off for a run?"

"I don't run anymore. My knees can't take it. I thought I'd walk over to say goodbye."

"Well, come in, then. Father will be glad to see you."

They took the elevator to the third floor because Erika was exhausted from going up and down all morning with boxes. She unlocked the door and Tom followed her in.

"Hello, Professor Bultmann," said Tom offering his hand. Stefan tried to get up, but he was having a little trouble today. It seemed he had aged in only a few days' time. "Don't get up, sir," Tom urged and sat down beside him. "I heard you're leaving today."

"Yes, my daughter is driving us to Maine. I will be staying with her friend Elizabeth until my apartment is ready."

"That should be fun. Liz is good company."

"Yes. She is going to take me fishing." His response was noticeably less enthusiastic than when Maggie had first suggested the idea. Erika wondered if she should decline their invitation and take her father to her cottage. "But I am very much looking forward to walks by the ocean," her father continued. "There was no ocean nearby when I was growing up. The closest thing to a beach was at Wannsee."

"I remember your telling me," said Tom.

"Tom, would you like some tea?" asked Erika, belatedly remembering her mother's lessons in how to be a gracious hostess.

"Sure, that sounds great," said Tom.

"Papi, tea?"

Stefan shook his head. "No, I just want to sit here and look around. Who knows if I'll ever see it again? I want to remember it."

Tom frowned sympathetically. "I'm sure you'll be back for the closing."

"I doubt it. Erika says it can all be done through an attorney," replied Stefan in a matter-of-fact voice.

"I'll just be a minute with the tea," said Erika. When she turned around, she saw that Tom had followed her into the kitchen.

"Can he hear us in here?" Tom asked.

"No, not unless he turns up his hearing aids to full volume. He never does that."

Tom glanced in the direction of the living room. "He seems very despondent today."

Erika shrugged. "He misses her. Of course, he does." She finished filling the kettle and turned on the gas. "So do I."

Tom laid a comforting hand on her shoulder. "It will take time."

"Yes, it will."

Erika turned around. "I haven't yet had the chance to thank you for helping Lucy with the funeral."

Tom smiled and his gray mustache twitched up. "She didn't need any help. She's quite a firecracker, that one."

"Yes, she is. It wears me out trying to keep up with her sometimes."

"Are you a couple?" asked Tom, taking a seat on a counter stool. Of course, he knew they were a couple. By now, anyone who knew them could see that.

"How did you guess?" asked Erika with more sarcasm than she'd intended. Then she was sorry. Tom had been nothing but kind.

"You lucky dog, partnered with the great soprano, Lucille Bartlett."

Erika sighed. "The great soprano Lucille Bartlett is no more. She's been replaced by Mother Lucy."

"Kind of like me. Changed my mind later in life."

"About women too?"

"Yes."

"Ironic that we pretended to want one another when it was our own sex we really wanted. Do you have a partner?"

"Not at the moment."

"You'll find someone," said Erika without conviction.

"It's not easy for older men. Worse for us, I think, than for women."

"Have you ever been a woman, Tom?" asked Erika, looking over her shoulder as she opened a tin of shortbread.

"No, of course not," he said, frowning.

"Then you know nothing about it, so your opinions are meaningless."

Tom laughed aloud. "You haven't changed a bit, Erika."

"Oh, I've changed all right, but not in the essential ways."

"I envy you living in Maine. What a beautiful place. Will you stay there?"

"Yes, now that my Father is moving there, I think I must. I have a double sabbatical, and then, I think I shall retire."

"I'm sure you'll inherit some money from the old man."

"He's not dead yet," said Erika, frowning in his direction.

"I didn't mean anything by that."

"I know."

"Maybe Lucy needs a curate, and I could come to Maine."

"Why? You're the rector of one of the most important churches in the state."

Tom sighed. "I know, but once you've accomplished all you can in your career, what else is there? I've had enough."

"I know what you mean. That's why I'm retiring."

"Do you think she could use a curate?"

"You're not serious."

"I am."

"I have no idea. You'll have to ask her. I know she's ridiculously busy, especially in the summer." She gave Tom a long, inspecting look. "Why Maine?"

"I hear there are a lot of gay men in Webhanet."

"There are, as a matter of fact." Erika arranged the shortbread on a plate. "You'd really work for Lucy?" she asked, peering at him.

Tom nodded dramatically. "I would. I've changed, Erika. Really."

"I don't believe it. You were so competitive you stole my notes!"

"That was a long time ago!"

Stefan came into the room. "I hear raised voices in here, children."

"I'm sorry, Professor," said Tom, looking contrite.

"You missed your opportunity, Mr. Simmons," said Stefan with a scowl. He turned to Erika and wagged his finger at her. "And you too!"

Baffled, Erika and Tom exchanged a look. When Stefan snatched a shortbread from the plate and went into the other room, they smiled at one another.

***

Erika finally trudged over the rectory threshold after a six-hour drive. They'd hit stop-and-go traffic on I84 and I495. Stefan grumbled about being hungry, but Erika knew that if they got off to eat, the traffic would be worse when they returned to the road. She offered him a granola bar and a nectarine, which temporarily seemed to satisfy him. Most of all, she didn't want to disappoint Lucy, who was undoubtedly laboring over this special welcome-home meal.

Stefan got an enthusiastic hug from their hostess; Erika, a quick peck on the cheek, but Lucy whispered in her ear. "I'll get you later."

Lucy anxiously served her meal and watched to see whether her guests were enjoying the food. Erika found it easy to praise the potato salad. She tactfully overlooked the fact that the chicken was a bit dry, although tasty. Stefan ate happily and smiled at Lucy, who was carefully watching for any indication that her meal wasn't being well received.

Erika dreaded unloading the contents of the car, but when she arrived at Liz's house, Maggie led Stefan off to entertain him. "Don't' worry," said Liz as Erika's eyes followed him. "We'll take good care of him." She squeezed Erika's shoulder.

"Thank heavens, we're this far," said Erika with a sigh.

"Come on. Let's get his done, so you can go back to your hot girlfriend."

"I hope I can stay awake when I get there."

"Oh, I'm sure you will."

Liz and Erika formed a fire brigade and soon all the cartons were neatly stacked. Liz draped some plastic sheeting over the boxes and household items.

"The contract should be ready for your father to sign tomorrow," Liz said. "We'll all feel better when he's settled in his own place."

"Yes," Erika agreed. "It's been a long, hard slog."

Liz made a shooing motion. "Well, go on. Get out of here. Go bed your girlfriend."

Erika texted Lucy before leaving Liz's: *On my way.* With the load removed from the back of her car, Erika herself felt lighter. She knew it was an illusion. They hadn't been carrying that much weight. Although she couldn't wait to see Lucy, she tried not to speed as she headed down Route 1. With the summer visitors in town, the Hobbs police were everywhere.

When Erika arrived at the rectory, she was rushing so much, she tangled herself in her seat belt and practically tripped getting out of the car. *Relax*, she told herself. She'll wait for you. She got to the door and found a yellow sticky note that read: "Come upstairs. I'll be waiting for you."

She smiled as she turned the knob and found the door unlocked. She came in and locked the door behind her. As she went up the stairs, she willed herself to slow her step. She wanted to savor every moment of her reunion with Lucy. She wanted it to be perfect.

When Erika arrived at the door to Lucy's personal quarters, she found it slightly ajar. A candle glowed on the table in the dining room; an oil lamp burned in the kitchen. She took these as trail markers and, smiling, followed them to Lucy's bedroom. She had never seen it. The door had always been closed when she'd visited before. Now, it was slightly open, and she could see candlelight glowing from within. There was also a wonderful spicy scent. Incense, Erika realized. She slowly opened the door and stepped inside.

Lucy, in a beautiful white negligee, lay on the bed. Her red hair was unbound. She smiled fully, one of those radiant Lucy smiles.

Erika realized she'd seen something very similar before. Her brain kicked up the source from long ago: *Otello* at the Metropolitan Opera, March, 1995. Erika had been going through a difficult time, and Liz thought a night at the opera would distract her. She'd taken her to dinner at O'Neal's Balloon across the street. Afterwards, they'd dodged traffic as they jaywalked across Columbus Avenue to the Met.

Until this moment Erika had almost forgotten the scene of the beautiful woman lying in wait for her jealous husband. The Desdemona that night had been Lucille Bartlett.

"What's the matter?" asked Lucy. "You look like you've seen a ghost."

"I have," Erika admitted.

"Please," begged Lucy. "I've waited for you. I wanted it all to be perfect."

"It is...perfect."

Lucy reached out her arms. "Come to me. Please, come to me."

Erika took off her sandals and approached the bed.

"I want to feel your skin against me. Take off your clothes."

Erika peeled her T-shirt over her head and unhooked her bra. She stepped out of her shorts and panties. Finally, she was in Lucy's arms. Her green eyes were misty with desire. "I've missed you so much," Lucy said, stroking Erika's cheek. "I've wanted you so much." Her voice was slightly husky. She raised the beautiful nightgown and her thighs parted. "I want to feel you between my legs."

As Erika lowered her body onto Lucy's, she thought her heart would explode.

20

"Wake up, sweetie. You have to go home." Lucy stroked Erika's blond hair and kissed her temple. Her eyelids fluttered before they opened.

"What time is it?" she asked in a scratchy voice.

"A little after two."

"I don't want to go home." Erika pulled Lucy closer. She sucked her breast until she began to moan. She released the nipple and kissed it. "Don't send me home. Please. I want to stay with you forever!"

"I know you do."

Lucy felt gentle fingers slipping inside her, opening her again. There had been so many openings and climaxes. Her insides were so swollen and sensitive it was easy to arouse her again. Erika made her come with her tongue. When she climbed up her body and let her weight down on her, Lucy wanted to enfold her and hold her in her arms forever.

"I love you, Erika, but you have to go."

"You're serious." Erika rolled off and sat up.

"Please understand."

"No, I don't understand."

"Your car can't be parked here all night."

"What?"

"People can't know we're together."

"You're not joking."

"No."

"This is absurd!" Erika jumped out of bed and began to dress. She thrust her legs into her shorts and pulled her shirt over her head. She stuffed her bra into her pocket as she headed out the door.

Lucy grabbed her robe and wrapped it around her. "Wait. Erika, wait!" she called down the stairs.

"We'll talk in the morning," snarled Erika. She slammed the outer door as she went out.

Lucy went downstairs to lock the door behind her. She watched as Erika backed up too quickly and roared out of the parking lot. Lucy hoped she was awake enough to make it home in one piece.

Yes, it was absurd, an old-fashioned norm that almost no one followed anymore, but she was a female priest. She would be held to a higher standard. There were whole websites devoted to advice on dating for gay clergy. All of them advised one thing: discretion. If this relationship had a chance, they must keep up appearances. If and when, they married it would be different, but for now, no one must know they were a couple.

Lucy looked at the relics of her carefully set reunion scene. The incense had long since smoldered into ash. The candle had melted, and fingers of wax had run on to the table. Fortunately, the top was formica and it could be scraped with an old credit card. She'd learned that trick from Liz. Afterwards, no one would be the wiser. She wished Erika's disappointment could be so easily remedied.

When Lucy awoke to the sound of her phone, she hoped it was Erika calling but knew it wasn't. Lucy had finally changed the ring tone for her alarm. Time to get up and practice singing.

Lucy took a very brief shower to rinse away the fluids of their love-making. As she washed between her legs, she felt how swollen she was. She thought of Erika as she touched herself, but she got right back to washing. Finally, she turned off the water. The last bill had been high enough. Later, after her walk, she would take a more cleansing shower and wash her hair.

Lucy sang her scales as usual. Every morning, she sang one operatic piece. This morning, she chose "Elsa's Dream" from *Lohengrin.* Although she hoped Erika might come to hear her sing, her sixth sense told her that she was alone in the church. When she finished the aria, she went down the winding staircase. As she'd feared, the church was empty. She genuflected as she passed the altar. For the first time since she had been ordained, her priesthood felt like a heavy burden.

She dressed quickly and tied up her hair in a loose ponytail. She set her power-walk pace along Route 1. She kept her arms pumping to keep her momentum as she waited for the light on Beach Road. She passed Hobbs Family Practice and saw Liz heading to the back door from the parking lot. "Liz!" Lucy called, waving.

"Good morning!" Liz called back and waved.

Lucy passed the café door and saw some of the early risers sitting on the porch, nursing a coffee or nibbling one of the pastries while reading the morning news on their phones. Some of the old timers read print newspapers from the convenience store next door.

Ten steps beyond the café door, Lucy turned around and went back. She waited on the line, which fortunately, was moving quickly. She always kept a twenty-dollar bill in her phone holder for emergencies. She bought two croissants to bring to Erika as a peace offering. She turned on Ocean Road, heading in the direction of Erika's cottage.

When she stepped on to the little porch, she saw that all the blinds were still drawn. That didn't surprise her. After all, it had been late when she'd sent Erika home, and the poor woman had driven in summer traffic for hours.

Lucy knocked cautiously on the door. No answer. She took a deep breath and rang the bell. She put her ear to the door and listened but heard nothing from inside. *Be bold*, she told herself. *You need to talk to her.* She leaned on the button to ring the bell again. Now, she heard stirring within. The door opened. Standing in the brilliant morning light, Lucy was momentarily blind looking into the completely darkened space.

"Well?" asked a cold voice. "Are you coming in?"

Lucy stepped inside, and an unseen hand closed the door behind her. After a moment, her eyes began to adjust to the light. Erika was standing there rubbing her eyes. Her hair was a mess. She was wearing a sleeveless T-shirt and cotton shorts. Her feet were bare.

"What do you want?" she asked irritably.

"I brought us breakfast," said Lucy in a hopeful voice as she proffered the brown bag of croissants.

"I'm not hungry at the moment," Erika growled.

Lucy took a step back, then two steps forward. She would not be dismissed so easily. "At least, have a cup of coffee with me."

"Well, all right. Come into the kitchen." Erika switched on a lamp so they could navigate.

Erika filled the coffee maker with water from a glass milk bottle. "Go on. Sit down." Lucy sighed as she took a seat. She set the paper bag containing the croissants on the table. As Erika prepared the coffee pods, Lucy admired her legs and imagined her shapely buttocks inside the baggy sleeping shorts. The sight of her made her want to jump out of the chair and put her arms around her. She wanted to hug her so hard that she would know how much she was loved.

But Lucy remained in her seat. This was a moment for negotiation, not passion.

"I'm sorry I had to throw you out this morning," she said cautiously to Erika's back.

"So am I."

"I need you to understand."

Erika turned around and leaned against the counter while the coffee maker spit dark liquid into the cup.

"I don't understand. In fact, I find it ridiculous. Do you think the people of Hobbs really care that you're sleeping with me?"

"I'm a priest and the rector of a parish. That makes me a public figure, so yes, my reputation is important."

"Yes, Mother Lucy, whatever you say." Erika handed her the coffee cup and started her own coffee brewing. She opened the refrigerator and took out a container of milk. "Here. Don't wait for me."

But Lucy did wait until Erika sat down with her coffee to prepare her own. "We need to talk," said Lucy.

Erika winkled up her face and looked stricken. "For fuck's sake woman! I am not awake, and you want to talk!"

"Not now. I want to make a date to have that talk we were supposed to have before you left for New Haven."

"Oh, that," said Erika in a disparaging voice. "Yes, I suppose that bit was run over by my mother's death. Perhaps you shouldn't have seduced me that night."

"It wasn't my plan, but I would do it again. You desperately needed comfort, so I gave you my body."

"And I gratefully accepted it." Erika stirred her coffee. She gestured toward the brown bag. "What have you brought for breakfast?"

"Croissants."

"My favorite."

"I know."

Erika sighed. "Oh, Lucy, I love you with all my heart, but I have no idea what to do with this priest thing. It is totally alien to me. And I will not be hidden away like the idiot in the attic!"

"I know. That's why we need to talk."

Erika beckoned, rolling her fingers toward herself. "Give me a croissant, please, and thank you."

Lucy opened the bag and handed her a croissant. She took two napkins out of the holder on the table and handed one to Erika, who bit into the croissant and chewed with a thoughtful look on her face. "There's butter. Would you like butter?"

"No, this is perfect the way it is."

"When would you like to have this talk?"

"The sooner, the better," said Lucy. "Tonight?"

"Very well. I'll take you to dinner."

"Not in town. I don't want anyone to hear our conversation."

"No, that would not be good. I know a restaurant in Scarborough that's the perfect setting for an intimate conversation. It's a nice place. You can dress up, if you like."

"You like it when I dress up."

"I do. I prefer to see you as a woman and not a priest with that fucking collar!"

The piece of croissant in Lucy's mouth went down hard. She watched

Erika happily bite into hers and realized she had no idea how much pain she was causing.

"I am both, Erika, and if you want me, you have to take them both."

Erika let out a long, frustrated sigh. "Then let's talk later and see how it goes. At the moment, I am not optimistic."

Lucy's heart fell, but she took a deep breath and tried to be optimistic for both of them.

At the door, Erika pulled Lucy into a hug. Lucy could feel the softness of her breasts against her, and her sex instantly responded. In another world, she would drag Erika back to bed and make love to her, but Lucy couldn't stay. She needed to get back soon to meet with the vestry. As it was, she'd have to cut her walk short.

***

Lucy searched through her closet looking for something to reflect the serious purpose of the evening. She rejected anything remotely provocative. Instead, she chose a simple navy dress that flattered her figure without being too revealing. The neckline was modest, not even a hint of cleavage would show. Lucy knew how much Erika appreciated her breasts, and she wanted no distractions tonight.

For the same reason, Lucy put on conservative makeup and put up her hair. As she inspected herself in the mirror, she thought of the dinner meetings she used to have with producers and opera directors to negotiate fees and schedules. She looked all business.

She opened the door for Erika and saw that she'd had similar ideas while dressing. Erika looked somber in a black pants suit, but her floral print blouse was soft and feminine. The color made her eyes even bluer. Erika kissed her chastely on the cheek.

"You look lovely as always," Erika said, giving her a long, appreciative look. She nodded as if she understood the intention behind the conservative outfit. "We must go. The reservation is for seven. It's high summer. Who knows what the traffic will be like?"

As they drove north on I95, Erika played light classics. The sound system in the Audi had amazing acoustics. Liz was an audiophile, so she had chosen the best when she'd purchased the car. Now, Erika and Lucy were the beneficiaries. Erika asked Siri to play a recording of Lucy singing "Ave Maria" from *Otello*.

"I remembered last night that I had seen you live on the stage of the Met," said Erika.

"Really? When?"

"In the fall of 1995. Liz and Jenny had a subscription to the Met, and I often went with them, but Liz specially bought these tickets to cheer me up. Perhaps it was a bad choice. *Otello* is so grim. The good news is I finally remembered and realized how much I liked your voice."

"But the performance didn't stick in your mind."

"I blocked it because of the occasion."

"What occasion?"

"I'd just found out my first partner had committed suicide. Understand that we weren't together at the time. Our affair was long over, but we'd stayed in touch and were on friendly terms. I'd been growing increasingly impatient with her because she had panic attacks and would call me in the middle of the night. I think she'd worn out her welcome with most of her other friends, so I was the remedy of last resort. She was quite dramatic. It seems I have a weakness for dramatic women. A few nights before she killed herself, she called me. I was working devilishly hard on a paper, and I fear I was rather curt with her. The next I heard, she had opened her wrists in the bath."

Erika's voice had remained matter of fact through the entire tale, but Lucy had been holding her breath. Now, she finally took a big gulp of air. "Oh, Erika. I'm so sorry. What guilt you must have felt."

"Yes, for some time, I felt quite guilty. Liz finally talked me out of it. There is some value in having philosophers as friends. They are so reasonable." Erika glanced at Lucy and smiled. "Maybe there is also some value in having priests as friends, but I have to think about that." She turned her eyes back on the road. "My chief regret now is that my brain had blocked the memory of your lovely performance. You were exquisite. Your voice was a marvel and your acting superb. I wept when Desdemona met her end."

"I'm glad you finally remembered. It's not uncommon to block memories associated with something traumatic. What made you remember?"

"The scene you set last night. It was quite inventive. It made me very excited."

"I could tell." Lucy smiled at the acknowledgement of her plan.

"At least, now I can get over my insane jealousy of others who have heard you sing at the Met. I've heard you too."

They arrived at their destination and Erika searched in the parking lot for a space. She rejected an obvious spot. "Liz will kill me if she sees a scratch on her bloody car."

"It's your car now."

"Let's just say it's on permanent loan. Liz is very possessive when it comes to her vehicles. About nothing else, mind you, just her cars."

Erika placed a gallant hand at Lucy's back as they walked up the stairs into the restaurant. "I reserved a table in an alcove so we can speak privately. It has a nice view of the salt marsh."

After they were seated, Lucy admired the vast expanse of multicolored grasses. The tide was in and the tidal rivers and lakes reflected the brilliantly blue sky. "I always enjoy our dates," Lucy said. "You pick the best places."

"We haven't had enough dates," said Erika. "Yet here we are lovers, and in quite deep."

"That's why I wanted to talk before you left for New Haven."

"I know. Life interrupted. It's hard to make plans sometimes, especially when dealing with elderly parents." Erika opened the menu. "I recommend the seafood pasta. As you're wearing navy, you won't have to worry about tomato stains tonight." She smiled ironically.

The waiter came and Erika ordered a bottle of wine. Lucy admired how well Erika played the wine ritual, inspecting the label, aerating the wine with a quick swirl, then swishing a mouthful before she swallowed it. Lucy had learned these little customs when she'd traveled in opera circles. Everyone was so sophisticated, especially in Europe. Erika came from an educated, cultured European family, so it came more naturally to her. After the waiter had poured the wine, Erika raised her glass to Lucy, and she did the same. "To a productive talk," said Erika.

As Lucy gazed into Erika's pale eyes, she knew she could lose herself in them, so she snapped herself back into business mode. "I thought we could share thoughts about where we are as a couple."

Erika wagged her finger in disapproval. "Don't you dare use your marriage counseling techniques on me, Lucy Bartlett! I have the first word tonight."

Lucy was surprised at the adamance of the warning, but she sat back and clasped her hands on the table. "Go ahead."

"I am pretty much an open book," Erika said. "You've met my family and friends. You can read about my career online. You've even met one of my male lovers in Tom Simmons. You know much more about me than I know about you."

"That's true." Lucy sat back. "What would you like to know?"

"You know what I want to know, and don't deflect. You promised you would tell me after we made love."

Lucy felt her shoulders tense. "You want to know why I quit my singing career."

"Exactly."

Lucy nodded and took a deep breath before she began. "As I told you, it wasn't one thing. It was a series of events. Unfortunately, they all came together at the same time." She hesitated, trying to figure out how to begin.

"Go on. I'm listening."

"I found my overnight success overwhelming. It's not unusual for singers to have a crisis once they finally make it to the big leagues. All those years of competitions and sacrifice, being marooned in small European cities while you struggle to build your credentials. Then suddenly, you're in a major role on the stage of the Metropolitan Opera. It's the dream of every American kid, who ever sang in church or glee club and dreamed of being an opera star. I can't even describe how that feels when you first stand on the stage of the Met. In the beginning, you feel like a fraud, even though everything you've done for years was meant to prepare for that day."

"But you were brilliant. I've read the reviews of your debut. Elsa in *Lohengrin*."

"I was the understudy. You hear about those lucky breaks in opera mythology, but there I was, actually living it."

"A superbly clear, stunning voice," Erika quoted from her memory of the review. "Lucille Bartlett is our greatest young Wagnerian soprano."

"Yes, they were talking about grooming me for Wagner because there was a dearth of up and coming dramatic sopranos, but I'm petite, and I didn't have strength in my core, despite exercising to support the column of sound those roles demand. After I read how Berit Lindholm destroyed her voice singing Brünhilde at the Met in 1975, I swore I would never push my voice beyond its capacity. I'm a spinto, and I know my limits. I stopped singing Wagner but continued to sing the other roles in my *Fach*—Desdemona, Butterfly, Tosca..."

"That sounds wise, but how did it go wrong?"

"It wasn't my voice that went wrong. It was everything else. I found out my agent was embezzling from my accounts. I had to fire him. That was a mess because he'd been managing me since I went professional. I had to sue him to get back my money. The lawsuit dragged on and forced me to remain in New York, so I had to turn down some very important engagements."

"I'm sure that didn't help your career."

"No, it didn't. He also wasn't paying my taxes as he was supposed to, so I owed a lot of money. Birgit Nilsson wouldn't perform here for years because of back taxes."

"I remember that."

"As a U.S. citizen, I didn't have the luxury of running away to Europe. They would have put a lien on my bank accounts."

"Of course, they would."

"I was at a low point and very vulnerable. A big producer at the Met had been hitting on me. Mostly, I ignored him. I tried to avoid any sexual relationships with people in the opera world. It can mean trouble, and I'd seen too many female singers hurt their careers by screwing around. But this man was sympathetic to the mess with my agent and the taxes. I needed to talk to someone on the inside, someone who understood the intricacies of my problems. He took me out to nice restaurants. He listened to my tale of woe. He had a magnetic personality, and I found him attractive. He was very handsome, crazy smart, and enormously talented."

Lucy had been watching Erika's face carefully while she told this part of the story. She looked sincerely interested, but there was no judgment in her eyes. She was listening intently.

"One night, he invited me back to his apartment for a drink. Of course, he tried to seduce me. Men were always trying to seduce me in those days. That's the curse of a pretty face and big boobs. That's all they see. It must trigger some primal need of theirs."

"Did you give in to this man?" asked Erika, obviously focused on the narrative.

"I was interested at first, but then I remembered who he was, which was a very big deal. He oversaw some of the most important casting decisions at the Metropolitan. When he came on to me, I asked him to stop. He didn't."

"What do you mean?"

"He forced himself on me."

"What!"

"He raped me."

Erika's mouth gaped open.

"And he was pretty brutal. I had a bruise on my cheek for a week. But I was proud of myself. I gave him a black eye."

"Good for you. Go, Lucy! But how horrible! Is that why you learned martial arts?"

"Yes, long afterwards. Taking self-defense classes was part of my recovery. Susan suggested it."

"And who is Susan?"

"She was the one who helped me heal after the rape and brought me back to God."

Lucy saw Erika make a profound effort to maintain a neutral expression, but she could see the distaste in her eyes.

"That's another story. Let's stick with this one for now."

"All right," Erika agreed.

"I went straight to the general manager and told him. He said if I wanted to have a career at the Met, I'd better forget the whole thing ever happened. He said I wasn't the first singer to complain about this producer, and I wouldn't be the last. I was stunned."

"Unfortunately, that was the way things were done in those days. Did you go to the police?"

"I did go to the police. They took a rape kit, but the assistant district attorney said it was very difficult to prove date rape. She asked if the bad publicity was worth it, considering my career. Meanwhile, the producer found out I'd gone to the general manager and threatened to sue me."

"So, you were fighting lawsuits on every front and trying to recover from rape?"

"Fortunately, he never actually sued me. Instead, he offered me money to drop out of sight for a while. He encouraged me to go to Europe until everything died down."

"Did you go?"

"No, I took the money, I'm ashamed to admit. I needed the cash for the lawsuits against the agent. It was a big enough sum to live on for a couple of years, even after I paid my legal bills. I kept a low profile for more than a year. I bought a little house in the Catskills and came down to New York only for depositions and hearings. Then a friend asked me to sing a solo for an ordination at Union Theological. I thought, 'well, none of my opera friends will ever notice if I do this, so why not?' At the reception afterwards,

I met Susan. She was enrolled in the divinity school and studying to be a deacon."

"Ah, the intersection point. Had you ever been with a woman before this Susan?"

"No, she was the first, and the only one before you."

"Oh, my dear, you're practically a virgin!" declared Erika, grinning.

"Erika, that's not funny."

Erika instantly assumed a straight face. "In the context, no. Forgive me. But after the hullabaloo blew over, why didn't you resume your career?"

"It's not that easy once you lose momentum. The mess with my agent made it hard to find another one. They all embezzle to a greater or lesser degree. Most of it is pretty harmless, like booking expensive travel and dinners, renting fancy cars, but some of them are outright thieves. I tried to make a comeback. I went to Europe. I sang a few roles at the City Opera. I'd been pretty much banned from the Met."

Erika gazed at her with a frown for a long time before speaking. "You have quite a storied past. Who else knows about this?"

"You. Susan. The man who raped me, but he's pretty much disappeared. His career went downhill soon after this happened. Karma, I guess. Other people know bits and pieces. I told Maggie and Liz about the mess with the agent. Maggie knows about the rape."

Erika studied her face carefully. "Thank you for your honesty. It all makes much more sense now. I could see how difficult it was for you to tell me, but I assure you it was worth it."

"I hope so," said Lucy with a sigh.

21

They agreed to observe a break in the conversation while they ate. Erika was glad for the hiatus. She needed some time to absorb Lucy's revelations.

After the waiter cleared the table, Lucy studied Erika's face. "What are you thinking about? You've gone away."

Erika gave Lucy a quick smile to reassure her. "I was thinking how things have improved marginally since that fool, Volpe, blew you off. At least now, women are speaking out. And men, for that matter. There's the case of James Levine. What an idiot! That was on Volpe's watch too. And Placido Domingo. He was venerated in those circles."

"It's been going on in music, movies, and the theater since forever."

"And universities, board rooms, the Supreme Court…everywhere…" Erika sighed. "My poor, dear Lucy. If I could get my hands on the man who raped you, I would wring his bloody neck!"

"I wouldn't bother. I hear he's dying from prostate cancer. Besides… 'thou shalt not kill.' Part of my healing was learning to forgive him."

Erika divided the remaining wine in the bottle into their glasses. "You are a better woman than I. I would have killed the bastard."

"And what would that have gotten me? It's in the past. I've long since put it behind me. I want to talk about the present." Lucy reached across the table and took Erika's hand.

Erika took a deep breath. "The relationship…"

"Yes, that. We need to talk about it."

"Why? Can't we simply enjoy it? We like being in one another's company. The sex is phenomenal…"

"I told you. I don't believe in casual sex."

"My dear, our sex is anything but casual."

"Don't be a smartass. You know what I mean." Lucy released her hand. "We got ahead of ourselves by having sex before we talked about our relationship. Many couples do. If they don't catch up, the relationship is over before it even gets started."

"You mean, when the desire ends, the relationship ends? At the moment, I don't see that happening."

"No one does when they're having hot, satisfying sex."

The idea that Lucy saw their love life as "hot and satisfying" pleased Erika. "We have more than sex," she said. "We were friends first. I love being with you. In fact, I can't spend enough time with you."

"And that's a good start. But there are some things we should agree on before we get in too deep."

"Aren't we already in too deep?"

"Possibly. If I said after this conversation, let's end it here, how would you feel?"

"Devastated."

"Me too. So, let's back up a little and figure out what we want together."

Erika gave Lucy a fish-eyed stare. "Why do I have the feeling you're doing prenuptial counseling with me?"

"Because I am, but I'm part of it too. We're in it together. And don't worry. We're just talking." Lucy gave her one of those warm smiles that could melt Erika into a puddle of agreement.

Erika sighed. Lucy was going to have this talk no matter what she said, so she might as well be cooperative. "All right, carry on."

"Let's start with the basics," said Lucy brightly. "Can you see yourself being faithful to one person?"

Erika allowed herself a long moment of thought before responding. "That's a good question. I have, in fact, been monogamous for long periods. Those relationships eventually died from natural causes, but I was faithful. Jeannine and I had an open relationship, which was one reason why we never lived together. She was the kind of woman who could never be satisfied with one partner. As for myself, I had other partners because she did. She encouraged me, perhaps out of guilt, but she did encourage me, and I went along."

"It sounds like your heart wasn't in it."

"It wasn't."

"Were you jealous when Jeannine had other partners?"

Erika scanned her feelings to come up with an honest answer. "Sometimes. Mostly, I tried not to think about it, especially when I knew she planned to spend the night with someone else. My mind would imagine the scene in her bed, and that was uncomfortable. That's one of the reasons why I insisted we have sex in my bed."

"Did you love Jeannine?"

"Yes. On some level. In the beginning, I found her very sexy and exciting."

"What did you find so exciting about her?"

"She was an artist, very creative, and she had a brilliant mind. She was unfettered by ordinary norms and openly disparaged them. Being German, I am naturally drawn to rules. Jeannine hated rules and thought they only existed to be broken."

"So, she was your opposite?"

"Not in everything. For a relationship to survive, there must be areas of compatibility. But I admit I was drawn to her differences. It's true that opposites attract. Look at how different we are from one another."

Lucy, nodded. "Back to monogamy. You're not against it?"

"No, not in principle. However, I am opposed to the institution of marriage."

"Why?"

"It was designed to benefit men, to ensure their ownership of and sexual access to a female. I know you're a bit younger, but there was a time when heterosexual marriage was looked upon as a great evil by lesbians. It's no coincidence that the so-called 'conservative argument for same-sex marriage' won the day at the Supreme Court."

"But marriage also benefits women by protecting them physically and economically. It ensures a supportive environment for children."

"I'm pleased that you are using sociological rather than religious arguments."

"Oh, I'm not finished making my case. I started with the practical arguments because Liz said they would appeal to you."

"You discussed marriage with Liz? Before talking to me?"

"Oh, don't get yourself into such a lather. It was a theoretical conversation. And she explained how reluctant she was to marry."

"Liz was reluctant to marry anyone other than Maggie because she was still in love with her. I know it sounds sentimental, and very romantic, but it's true. But before they reconnected, Liz had gotten into the habit of seducing women because she could. It was the thrill of the conquest. In her day, Liz was quite the hot number. She had the added appeal of being a surgeon. For some reason, women still fall for that. Watch out for her. She's quite the flirt."

Lucy laughed. "I've figured her out. And I'm used to dealing with flirts. Don't worry. I find her attraction to me entertaining, but I'm not interested."

"That's good," said Erika, wiping imaginary sweat from her brow.

"Besides, Maggie is my best friend. I could never hurt her."

Erika pouted. "I thought I was your best friend."

"It's different," said Lucy with a little smile.

"Returning to the subject of marriage…Apart from the argument on principle, I'll allow that legally and economically, it has practical benefits such as protecting joint property, ensuring the orderly transmission of wealth. It automatically creates a health proxy in the case of illness or death."

Lucy grinned. "I love it when you make my case for me."

"You've been leading the witness."

"You're not that difficult to lead," said Lucy, raising her chin. Erika eyed her and realized that she might have underestimated Lucy. Not only was she intelligent, she was also incredibly shrewd. "So, you could be monogamous," Lucy continued, "and you might consider marriage, despite your objections in theory."

Erika nodded. "I think that's fair to say. What about you?"

"You have to ask?"

"No, I guess not. I can assume you're interested in a monogamous relationship and eventually, marriage. Is that correct?"

Lucy nodded.

"And beyond that, what do you want from this relationship?"

Lucy's green eyes searched her face for a long moment before she said, "I want to get to know you more and more each day until our intimacy is as perfect as two human beings can have in this life. I want to love you as you've never been loved before. I want to give you pleasure and comfort with my body. I want to stand beside you every day for the rest of my life."

Erika sat up straight as if knocked back by Lucy's words. "You don't want much do you?"

"If you listened carefully, you would have heard, not what I want, but what I'm willing to give."

Erika allowed the words to sink into her mind. She swallowed hard. "You know that already?"

"Yes, once I realized I love you, there was no question. That's why I gave you my body."

Erika's attempt to smile was disabled by her anxiety. The best she could do was twitch her mouth up for moment. "Oh, dear, I feel a religious argument coming on."

"In my world, marriage is sacred."

"So, you've said."

"I wish you could see how your face changes when I talk about my faith," said Lucy with a sigh.

"I suppose I look very disapproving."

"No, you look frightened as if I'm trying to force something on you that you might really like."

Erika grinned. "Like a dildo?"

Lucy's face flamed crimson.

"Ah, hah! So you know about dildos and have thought about them regarding me. Interesting, but you have many interesting facets, Mother Lucy."

Lucy looked moderately flattered.

"I'm sorry if I've given you the wrong impression," said Erika. "I may be an unbeliever, but I don't begrudge you your faith. If I am honest with myself, I am moved by it. I don't understand it, and yes, sometimes, it makes me feel uncomfortable, but not in a bad way. No, that's not completely true. Sometimes in a bad way. I want to make faces, roll my eyes, and sigh. Sometimes, it makes my skin crawl."

"That's because there may be something there for you."

"Lucy, don't push me!"

"I try never to push people. I try to be the best person I can be, so that people can see Christ in me and be attracted to Him."

"Lucy, one would have to be a stone not to be attracted to you!"

"As a priest and a Christian, I want people to see the God Light in me. That's what I want to shine, not my personal beauty."

"But you are beautiful. That certainly helps."

"Not always."

"Well, it works with me. I am particularly moved when you offer me communion. I get a very strange feeling. I can't explain it. It's not sexual, but I am sexually attracted to you, so I can't completely separate the two. And I am human and so are you, so I can't cleave off your humanity from the spiritual side of you."

"That's why Christ was embodied. Why Christianity has a material component, and why marriage is sacred. It's why in the most sacred ritual of the Church, a priest says, 'This is my body.' And we believe that the bread transforms into the body of Christ."

"Forgive me, Lucy, but as a philosopher, I find that doctrine absurd."

"Yes, it's scientifically impossible. I understand that. So, don't think about it that way. Think of it as a metaphor, as poetry. 'This is my body which is given for you.' Imagine it. Let it roll off your tongue, hear it in your mind."

Erika tried to force down her skeptical left brow. "Why is this important?"

"Because when I make love to you, I give you my body. It's the greatest act of love one person can offer another. It's sacred."

"I hope your bishop hasn't planted listening devices under the table. I think you may be skirting heresy, if not blasphemy."

To Erika's surprise, Lucy laughed merrily. "I don't think so. There are many metaphors of mystical marriage in Christianity. Christ's relationship to the Church is a marriage. Nuns are said to be brides of Christ. Sex and religion are often interwoven."

"What does this have to do with us?"

"If you want me, you must accept the whole package, not just lusty Lucy in your bed, not just Lucille Bartlett, faded opera star, not just your walking buddy. You must also love Mother Lucy, the priest, and accept that she's coming along for the ride."

Erika shook her head. "I would make a terrible parson's wife. As much as your faith fascinates me, I'm not a believer, and don't expect to convert me."

"I don't. I'm asking you to accept me as a whole, just as I accept the skeptical philosopher in you."

"I think I can manage that."

Lucy gave her a cautious, sidelong look. "That was too easy."

"You will find that I am extremely reasonable. Make a compelling argument, and I will fall for it every time." Erika reached over and patted Lucy's hand. "In fact, it's often easier to agree on the big picture because it's, well...big. Hegel says, when things don't fit neatly into categories, make a bigger category."

"I don't know anything about Hegel."

"Perhaps not, but I do, and it goes both ways. I accept you as a priest, you tolerate Hegel. He's not my favorite, but he's part of the pantheon. So, we love Hegel, right?"

Lucy looked doubtful, but she said, "I guess so."

"Now, to conclude, we've agreed to consider monogamy and marriage. I shall accept you as a priest, and you..." Erika nodded in Lucy's direction. "...will tolerate Hegel. Agreed?"

Lucy nodded.

"But the ordinary bits are harder to negotiate. Like your throwing me out of bed this morning. I hated that. And I have no intention of being with a woman who feels she needs to hide me. I came out a long time ago."

"I'm sorry, but I have to hide you for now. I'm a priest. People expect me to behave a certain way."

"Well, isn't that nice of them? And what do they expect? You to be celibate while we figure out what our relationship will be?"

"Yes, as a matter of fact. That's exactly what the Church says. No sex until marriage."

"And yet you counsel couples who would marry on sexual compatibility. How are they to find out if they are compatible?"

"That's a good question, and one we wrestle with regularly."

"Lucy, I want to sleep with you after we make love. Is that too much to ask? Can't you sleep with me at the cottage?"

"Yes, I suppose so, as long as we're discreet."

"Which means?"

"Your car isn't always parked behind the rectory. And mine isn't gone from the rectory parking lot every night."

"Then walk, you lazy thing, or I'll pick you up and drop you off. Just bring your walking clothes and all will be well. When I bring you home tonight, you can pick them up."

Unconsciously, Erika had been spinning her mother's ring around her finger while they'd been talking. Now, she became aware of it and realized the action was not as completely unconscious as she'd thought.

"Look, Lucy. I want to give you something. My father gave it to me." Erika wiggled the ring off her finger, struggling a little over the place where arthritis was beginning to thicken the knuckle. "It was my mother's engagement ring. This is not a proposal, but a sign of my intentions. Will you wear it?"

Lucy looked at the ring. "It's beautiful, and it's wonderful that it belonged to your mother. I will be honored to wear it, when it is a proposal. Meanwhile, you keep it safe for me. Put it back on."

Erika nodded and returned the ring to her finger.

***

They decided to pass on dessert. Instead, they headed back to Hobbs for ice cream from the local stand. On the way, they picked up Lucy's walking clothes, a change of underwear and her toiletry bag.

After they ordered their double-scoop cones, chocolate truffle and cookie dough fudge for Erika, wild blueberry and strawberry for Lucy, they sat in the car in their dress clothes to eat them. They held their cones for one another so they could get a taste of each flavor.

"We're like two children," said Erika wiping some blue ice cream from Lucy's cone off her chin.

"There's nothing wrong with that," said Lucy, rescuing her fingers from ice cream melt with her tongue. Erika found it very erotic and stared.

"Don't look at me like that in public," said Lucy.

Erika glanced around to see if anyone had been watching. "Doesn't it bother you that everyone recognizes you? That girl who said, 'hello, Mother Lucy.'"

Lucy shrugged. "I'm used to people recognizing me. With the red hair, I always stood out in a crowd."

"It's hard being in love with someone who belongs to everyone."

"Instead of seeing it as a problem, try being proud," said Lucy, licking the strawberry ice cream more aggressively because it was melting faster. "It will make it easier."

"I thought pride was a sin."

"Don't be difficult." She looked at Erika's cone. By then, most of the ice cream had been consumed. "I can't eat that fast. I get brain freeze."

Erika bit off the bottom of the cone and sucked out the remaining ice cream.

"That looks oddly sexual," Lucy observed.

"You have sex on the brain."

"I do," Lucy agreed.

Erika drove back to the cottage while Lucy continued to work on her cone. She timed it perfectly because she finished as they were pulling into the parking space.

On the porch, Erika stepped out of her heels and carried them in. "Thank heavens," she said with a sigh. "It's fun to dress up, but even more to dress down." In the bedroom, she slipped out of her suit jacket.

"Stop there," ordered Lucy. "I want to undress you."

"Then let's draw the blinds and not entertain the neighbors." Erika engaged the pull and dropped the blinds.

"Will you help me with the zipper?" asked Lucy, turning her back to her.

"With great pleasure. There's something so erotic about freeing a woman from a beautiful dress." Erika kissed the nape of Lucy's neck before opening the zipper. Beneath, Lucy was wearing a black lace bra and matching panties. "Oh, woman, you are the sexiest thing I have ever laid eyes on. I adore you."

After they made love, Erika leaned up on her elbow and studied Lucy's face. "Are you satisfied with the results of tonight's conversation?"

"Yes," said Lucy, "…for now."

22

Perched on a ladder, Lucy placed Stefan's books on the shelves, while Erika, sitting below, opened the boxes of books and directed their placement. Liz was unpacking the truck with the help of one of the boys from Awakened Brews. The place was coming together faster than anyone expected.

"Erika! Are you looking up Lucy's skirt?" asked Liz with exaggerated shock as she came into the room.

Lucy looked down and saw Erika blushing.

"Serves her right for wearing a skirt for a task like this," said Erika defensively.

"I didn't have time to change. You shouldn't be looking!"

Liz put the box down next to Erika. "Get a room!"

After Liz left to bring in more boxes, Erika laughed.

Lucy climbed down from the ladder. "Erika, that's not funny. Don't I give you enough sex?"

"Yes, but I can't resist you. Isn't that how it's supposed to be at this stage in a relationship?"

"Don't ask me. You're the one who has all the experience with women."

Liz returned with more boxes and a new helper carrying a box. "I found this guy wandering around downstairs. He says he knows you."

Erika got up, looking a little stiff from sitting cross-legged. "Tom! What are you doing here?" After Tom Simmons put down his box, Erika hugged and kissed him.

Lucy noticed something different about him. He was wearing a gold stud in his ear. "Thanks for coming to help," she said, shaking his hand. She turned to Erika, "Didn't I tell you Tom asked to spend his vacation up here to see if he'd like being a curate at St. Margaret's?"

"No," said Erika, regarding Tom with a frown.

"It was a last-minute decision, but I was so happy when Lucy said, yes."

"You weren't kidding about that," Erika said, raising a brow.

He shook his head. "I have to get out from under being rector. It's overwhelming between all the choirs, the maintenance on an old historic building, civic demands. I'm just done!"

"So, now you plan to horn in on Lucy's gig?"

"No!" protested Tom. "That's the whole point. I just want to be a curate, live my life, and mind my own business."

"Lucy, can St. Margaret's really afford a curate?" asked Erika.

"We can, but the decision isn't mine alone. If Tom's really interested, I'd have to put it to the vestry. Tom has a meeting with them on Wednesday evening."

"God knows, you could use the help," said Erika, but she regarded Tom suspiciously. Lucy realized their shared history could be a problem. She hadn't thought of that.

Stefan came into the room. "I heard a new voice and I wondered who is here." He saw Tom. "Mr. Simmons!" he said, reaching out his hands. "How nice to see you again!"

"Papi, Tom has a doctorate in theology. He should be addressed as Dr. Simmons."

Stefan made a face. "A doctorate in theology? Hah! What's that? He'll always be Mr. Simmons to me."

Tom laughed. "You can call me anything you like, Professor, but I wish you'd call me, Tom."

Liz came in carrying another box of books. "Why are you all standing around? Get to work!"

Tom groaned. "She's tough, isn't she?" he said, but he followed Liz to bring up more boxes.

Stefan sat down and surveyed the work on the bookshelf. "It's beginning to feel like home now that my books are here. And the old neighborhood is coming to visit."

"So, you like it here, Papi?" asked Erika.

"My books, my daughter, and a beautiful view of the ocean…what more could I need?"

Lucy thought, but didn't say, *your wife*, but Stefan was surrounded by people who cared about him. Things could be much worse for a man of his age.

Lucy and Erika resumed their positions to sort and place the books, while Liz and Tom brought in the remaining boxes.

Finally, Liz stretched backwards, and rubbed the small of her back. "That's all of them. Looks like we're almost done here. How about I take you all out to dinner at Dockside?"

"Oh, Liz, that's far too generous," protested Erika.

"I feel like having a lobster dinner by the harbor with my friends. I'll go home and pick up Maggie. I'll make the reservation on the way. Six for six. It will be fun."

Lucy climbed down from the ladder. "If that's the case, I'd like to change. I'll take Tom back with me so he can settle in."

"Very well," Erika agreed, "I'll finish putting away the books. We'll meet you there."

"If you get there before us," said Liz, "open a bar tab in my name. They know."

Lucy watched in her rear-view mirror as Tom followed her back to St. Margaret's. With all the summer traffic and people changing lanes on Route 1, she wanted to make sure he stayed behind her. Finally, he pulled into the rectory parking lot beside her.

"This place is nuts in the summer," he said, getting out of the car.

"Yes, but you should see it in January. Those streets we just drove are deserted. The restaurants close on a rolling basis for two weeks at time. At least, some of them stay open in Hobbs. There are places up north where everything closes down."

"I see," said Tom, looking over the rectory building.

"Tom, I'll be honest with you. Living up here is not all walks on the beach. Winters are hard. It's wicked cold, as they say. Sometimes, we have a hundred inches of snow." Lucy gave him a hard look to make sure he was paying attention. "I just want you to understand what you're getting into."

"I appreciate the preview."

"Come on. I'll show you where you'll be staying."

Tom pulled his duffle bag out of the back of his SUV and followed Lucy into the rectory. They went up the stairs to the clergy quarters, and Lucy led him down to the end of the hall. She opened the door with the key in the lock. "This will be your place while you're here."

Tom stepped into the pleasantly furnished room with a daybed, a desk, and a small table in the efficiency kitchen. It was a large space with good light. "I could be happy here," he said, smiling.

"I'm sure it's nothing compared to your old rectory in New Haven. This is pretty humble."

Tom sighed. "It is, but it's just what I need."

Lucy glanced at her phone. "We have an hour before we have to meet them. I'll meet you downstairs in forty-five minutes. We can drive together. This time of year, parking will be a problem. The fewer cars, the better."

"Okay," he said. "That will give me time to get cleaned up. That was quite a drive."

"It's better off season."

He smiled pleasantly. "Something to look forward to."

Before she closed the door, she pulled the key out of the lock and gave it to him. "We lock our doors here only because there are a lot of people through the rectory during the day. You never know. The other key opens the back door."

He nodded and thanked her for the keys.

While Lucy changed her clothes, she thought about Tom. She wondered if he was really sincere about downsizing his career because she had no intention of moving over to make room for him.

She couldn't deny that she needed the help. The bishop, when she'd asked him about taking on a curate, was in full agreement, especially when she'd told him of her plans to expand her counseling role. They had agreed the time had come for Lucy to start taking insurance for her work, but charge on a sliding scale, depending on the client's ability to pay. The income would be split between Lucy and the parish, which would partially offset the cost of taking on a curate.

Lucy put on capris and a boat neck shirt. She'd learned from experience to avoid low-cut shirts around Erika, especially in public. She smiled as she slipped on open-toed sandals. She knew that Erika found her red toenails exciting. Erika had made her promise that, when and if they ever got away on vacation, she'd paint her fingernails to match.

The numerals on the bedside clock indicated there was still plenty of time before meeting Tom. Lucy opened her laptop to check her email. She almost deleted a suspicious message that looked like it was from a lawyer, but her spam filter usually blocked anything dangerous. Lucy knew it could still be risky, but curiosity compelled her to open it.

Dear Ms. Bartlett,

I work for an agency dedicated to helping adopted children locate their birth parents. A girl has contacted us, and we think she may be your daughter. She is sixteen years old and has recently become an emancipated minor in New York State.

Of course, there is no obligation for you to meet with her. We will not reveal your name or location unless you give us permission. If you wish to know more, please call me at 914-628-3500.

Sincerely,
Melanie Peters
Lost Child Network

Lucy's heart was pounding as she re-read the email. *How did they find her?* she wondered. *Hadn't the adoption been sealed?* Her lawyer had assured her it was final, and she could never see the baby again. Never.

When she'd handed over the beautiful girl with her soft pate of red hair, Lucy's arms had ached. She knew it was for the best, but it had hurt so much. She'd cried herself to sleep for months. It still hurt. Despite all the pain, she was sure that giving up the baby for adoption was much better than an abortion. After she'd held the baby in her arms, she knew she had made the right decision. Although she firmly and completely believed in a woman's right to choose, when it came to her own child, she just couldn't deprive it of an opportunity for life.

Lucy had thought about the baby over the years, especially at her birthday. She'd wondered what she looked like. Did she resemble her or Alex? The fine, red hair at her birth gave her some clues, but who could tell what form that innocent face would take?

Lucy glanced at the clock. Ten to five. If she called right away, she might get Melanie Peters in the office. "No obligation," the email had said. Did she really want to see this child she'd thought was lost forever?

The red numerals on the clock flipped to the next minute. Time was running out. Lucy tapped out the number on her phone and listened to it ring on the other side. Part of her hoped it wouldn't pick up. But it did.

"Lost Child Network, Melanie Peters speaking," the friendly voice announced.

Lucy had been holding her breath. Now she took a huge gulp of air. "Hello, this is Lucille Bartlett. I received an email from you today."

"Oh, Ms. Bartlett, thank you so much for getting back to me so quickly. You understand that you are under no obligation to reply to this girl's request."

"Yes, I understand, but I'm curious."

"Of course, you are. First, let me get a little information from you. The girl in question was born in Kingston, New York on May twenty-third. Does that seem right?"

"Yes," said Lucy, "but how did you find me? The adoption was supposed be sealed."

"We found you through a routine background check. The Kingston address for that period came up. New York maintains an adoption information registry for adopted children seeking their birth parents. The girl we think is your daughter had already petitioned the court for her original birth certificate before getting us involved in her case. She's a pretty smart girl. In fact, there's something you should know before we go further."

"What's that?"

"She's slightly handicapped. She's on the spectrum, a very well-adapted and extremely high functioning case of ASD. You wouldn't notice it except she won't give you eye contact when she's stressed, and she becomes socially awkward. But only when she's really stressed."

"So, you've met her?"

"Yes, I'm her caseworker. And I want to remind you that there is no charge to you or to the child. Our organization is completely funded by donations."

"Yes, fine," said Lucy impatiently. "Tell me more about her, please."

"As I wrote in my email, she's recently become an emancipated minor."

"Why isn't she with her adoptive parents?"

"I'm sorry. I can't tell you that. She can tell you if you decide to meet her."

"Where is she living now?"

"She's in a women's shelter."

Lucy audibly gasped. Evidently, the woman on the other end heard it.

"Don't worry," she assured her. "It's a very nice, safe shelter, not like you read about. We place a lot of clients there."

"What else can you tell me?"

"That's it. If you decide you would like to speak to the girl, I can arrange a telephone call, and we can go from there."

"Yes, please," said Lucy quickly without thinking. "I want to speak to her." *What am I doing?* she wondered. She'd thought she'd left that part of her life behind her completely, but the fact that her baby was in a shelter horrified her. "The sooner, the better."

"Is tomorrow too soon? Do you want to think it over first?"

"No, tomorrow is fine. You can call me at this number." Lucy gave the woman her cell phone number.

"Any particular time better?"

"Please call after five thirty." By then, Lucy's office hours would be over, and she could wrap up anything outstanding.

"All right, then, Ms. Bartlett. I'll get in contact with my client to see if that works for her. If there's any problem, I'll be in touch by email. In the meanwhile, you might think about what to say when she calls. These calls can be really awkward, and you want to be prepared."

"I understand," said Lucy. "Thank you." She said goodbye and ended the call. Shaking, she closed her eyes and prayed that she had made the right decision.

❊❊❊

Tom was waiting in the foyer when she came downstairs. "I can drive," he offered, "if you tell me where to go."

"Thank you, I appreciate it," Lucy said curtly.

Tom gave her a curious look. "Are you all right? You look upset."

It annoyed Lucy to be reminded that she wasn't always good at hiding her emotions, but she made a special effort to be cordial. "I'm fine, Tom. Thank you for driving."

Lucy's mind was on her conversation with Melanie Peters. Except for giving Tom directions, she was silent as he drove to the restaurant.

"What kind of restaurant is this place?" Tom asked.

"Seafood mostly. Wonderful views of the harbor and the salt marsh. Great food. Expensive, but Liz is paying, so we don't have to worry."

"That's nice of her."

"She's very generous."

"Always has been," said Tom affably. "I remember when Liz was just a resident in surgery. She had huge student loans to pay off, but she was generous back then too."

"You go that far back?" asked Lucy.

"Yes, hard to believe. Over forty years."

"It's nice to have old friends."

He shrugged. "It's a mixed blessing. They remember things about you you'd wish everyone would forget."

"Oh, really," said Lucy, finally drawn in by Tom's warmth. His easy manner made it easy to talk to him. "You'll have to tell me sometime."

Tom chuckled. "Maybe."

Lucy felt more relaxed after the conversation with Tom, but as soon as she saw Erika, she instantly tensed. Obviously, Lucy needed to tell her the news as soon as possible, but she wanted to wait until they were alone.

The others were making toasts to Stefan's new apartment when Lucy and Tom joined them on the deck.

As soon as Liz noticed them approaching, she got up to get drinks for them. "What do you drink, Tom?"

"What's the local beer?"

"What's the local beer?" Liz repeated, almost hooting. "There are dozens of them! What's your poison? IPA? Stout? Lager? Porter?"

"Pick for me, please."

"I will. And white wine for the lovely Lucy?"

Lucy nodded. "Thanks, Liz."

"Sit by me, lovely Lucy," said Stefan, raising his hand in her direction. "Lovely Lucy. I like that. I think it should become your new name." He put his arm around her. "This beautiful woman will soon be my daughter in law.

The conversation at the table instantly stilled. Finally, Erika said, "I think my father just proposed for me."

Everyone laughed. Lucy wanted to sink in her chair and disappear.

"So?" asked Maggie. "Is it true?"

"That we're getting married?" Erika's smile looked forced. "Yes, someday, I would like that."

"Let me get the drinks," said Liz. "Poor Lucy looks like she needs one."

23

When their table was called, Erika held Lucy back from following the others by catching her arm. "I want to apologize for my father. He had no business saying such a thing."

Lucy turned around and stared at her. "We need to talk later."

"You're not angry I didn't confirm his statement?"

"No! Why would I be? It's not true."

"Good thing our friends just laughed it off. It was so embarrassing!"

Erika noticed that Lucy was very pale and her face looked pinched.

"Lucy, you don't look well. Are you sure you're all right?"

Lucy nodded. "We should catch up with the others. They're watching us. They probably think we're having a fight."

Liz was ordering wine for the table when they sat down. "I ordered a single malt for each of us, Erika. We deserve it after all we accomplished today."

"Thank you, Liz," said Erika, but she noticed Lucy giving her a strange look.

Everyone settled down to study the menu. Erika stole glances at Lucy. Her usual rosy complexion was pale, almost gray. Was she angered by Stefan's remark? No, that made no sense. Lucy was not one to hold grudges. She forgave as easily as the sun shone on a beautiful day. Just to make sure, Erika whispered in Lucy's ear, "I love you."

Lucy turned and gave her a little, muted smile, but her eyes were full of worry.

"Are you sure you're all right?" Erika asked in a soft voice.

"We'll talk about it after dinner."

Liz ordered the double lobster special. When she cracked into a claw, the cooking water burst out and sprayed all over Tom's face. "Oh, my God! I'm so sorry!" said Liz, getting up to offer him her extra napkins.

It took a moment for everyone to process what had happened. Then they were all laughing as Tom tried to wipe the lobster juice off his glasses.

The only one not laughing was Lucy. Her mouth was turned up in a smile, but her eyes remained serious.

Erika leaned over to say, "Finish your supper and we're leaving."

"Okay," said Lucy.

Erika noticed that Liz also looked concerned. She was studying Lucy carefully. She could imagine her physician's eyes assessing the situation and forming a differential diagnosis. Liz never missed a thing. "Lucy, are you feeling okay?" asked Liz in a confidential tone.

"Yes, I'm fine," Lucy answered instantly. "Just tired. Long day, and my friend here was working me to death while she sat there looking beautiful." She managed a defective smile.

Liz nodded, but Erika could see she wasn't satisfied with that explanation.

The delicious stuffed haddock stuck in Erika's throat as she watched Lucy pick at her food. Erika caught Liz's eye. "I think I'm going to take Lucy home and give her some tea."

"I think that's a good idea," said Liz. "Excuse us," she announced, getting up. She ripped off the plastic lobster bib and tossed it on the table. "Lucy's not feeling well. I'm just going to walk them out to the parking lot. Don't worry. I'm not running off. I'll be back in time to pay."

It was meant to be funny, but no one laughed. Everyone's eyes were fixed on Lucy.

Once they were on the deck overlooking the parking lot, Liz felt Lucy's forehead with the back of her hand. The other hand reached for her wrist to take a pulse. Lucy shook it off. "It's not physical, Liz. Don't worry. Go back to your guests."

Now, Liz looked even more worried. "Okay. I'm glad you're not sick…I guess." She looked over Lucy's head to Erika. "Good idea to take her home. Call me if you need me, and I'll be right over."

Erika nodded, and Liz went back into the restaurant.

"Liz is so kind," Lucy murmured.

"Yes, she is, but I'm really worried about you."

"Take me home, and I'll explain."

"Home to the cottage?"

Lucy nodded, and Erika led her to her car. Despite the sweltering temperature, Lucy was hugging herself as they drove to Ocean Road. Erika fumbled with the key because she was hanging on to Lucy's arm and not paying attention. Once inside the cottage, Lucy flung her arms around Erika.

"Please hold me. Hold me really tight."

Erika pulled her close. "Oh, Lucy. Whatever is the matter?"

Lucy began to sob. "She wants to see me."

"Who? Who wants to see you? Your ex who never wanted to speak to you again?"

"No. Not Susan."

"Who, Lucy?"

"My daughter."

Erika was so startled she sucked in air quickly, but then forgot to let it go. She finally allowed herself to breathe. "What?" It came out sounding as if someone had just turned on the light in a dark room. It was a small, curious question.

"We should sit down," Erika said, slipping out of Lucy's embrace. She took her hand and led her to the sofa. Uncertain, Lucy allowed herself to be led. She dropped onto the sofa cushion. Erika sat beside her and took her hand. "What daughter?"

Lucy's eyes were filled with anxiety. "There was something I left out when I told you why I quit singing."

"The rape left you pregnant," Erika guessed.

Lucy nodded.

"Good God!" Erika exclaimed softly.

"Having a child would have meant the end of my career. I thought about having an abortion, but when I got to the clinic, I couldn't go through with it."

Erika tightened her grip on Lucy's hand. "I understand."

"I looked in the *New York Times* real estate ads. They always had bargain houses in remote areas far north of the city. I found a place, and I went up there to wait out my pregnancy. When the baby was born, I arranged for an adoption through my lawyer. Then, I came back to New York to try to restart my career. You know how the story goes from there."

"Who else knows about this?"

"Besides the medical personnel who assisted at the birth and the lawyer? No one. Well, now my child knows, the judge in New York who unsealed her birth certificate, and the agency she signed up to find me."

"Not even the father?"

"No, I never wanted him to know. That's why I left the city. No one knew me up in Kingston. I said my husband had been killed in a car accident. It was a small town, and the people were sympathetic, but I kept to myself. After the delivery, I listed the house. It was an impulsive purchase, not a good investment. It took almost a year to sell it."

"Did you tell Susan?"

"No, I wanted to tell her. All those months, while she was bringing me back from the dead, I wanted to tell her. She was so kind and loving and deserved to know, but I found it too hard to admit I gave away my child for my career."

Erika sighed. "You did what you had to do."

"But it was pointless, because my career never came back. I gave away my baby for nothing."

"Look at it this way, you could have aborted her and then she wouldn't even have life." Erika laid a gentle hand on Lucy's cheek. "My poor, dear Lucy, you look so miserable."

"Oh, Erika. I'm sorry I didn't tell you."

"I'm sorry too. I wish you had trusted me enough to confide in me, but I understand why. You thought it was all behind you."

"I did. The adoption was supposed to be sealed. That idiot lawyer screwed up everything else, why not that too?"

Erika took Lucy's hand. "What are going to do?"

"She wants to see me."

"Will you?"

Lucy nodded like a forlorn child. "I have to. She's living in a women's shelter. She's declared herself independent of her adoptive parents. Oh, my God, I hope they weren't abusive! I would never forgive myself." Lucy began to sob.

Erika took her in her arms. She held her tight and rocked her gently. "It's all right, Lucy," she soothed. "It will be all right."

When the sobs stopped, Lucy sat up and wiped her face with her fingers. Erika got some tissues from the bathroom.

"Thank you," murmured Lucy. "Thank you for being kind."

"Oh, my God! How could I not be kind? I'm sure this is so painful for you."

"You don't hate me for not telling you right away?"

"No, we all have secrets. There are many things you don't know about me."

"Such as?"

Erika took a deep breath. Whatever she shared now must be of equal magnitude, or it would be of no comfort to Lucy. "I once slept with a woman and a man at the same time. She got pregnant. She was my partner at the time. Unlike you, she chose to have an abortion. I was quite broken up about it. I'd nearly forgotten until now."

Lucy sat up to look at her. "So, you know how hard it is."

"If I'd been the one who became pregnant and not she, I don't know what I would have decided. I know it's not politically correct to admit it, but deciding to abort your child is very difficult."

"It is. That's why I will fight for free access to birth control for every woman."

Erika chuckled. "Here we are, two post-menopausal lesbians. It's certainly not our problem, and yet, we make it our fight."

"All women must be free to choose, or none of us are."

Erika nodded. "So right you are." She took Lucy's hand. "You said this child is emancipated from her parents and living in a shelter. How old is she?"

"Sixteen."

"That's young to be on her own. What can be done for her?"

"I don't know. I need to find out more. We're talking by phone tomorrow."

Erika took a deep breath. This was not the time to ask too many questions or offer advice. This was the time to listen. "Lucy, let me call Liz to give you something to calm your nerves. I've never seen you so upset."

"I'm fine, Erika. Just let me catch my breath."

"Would you like something to drink? I have some scotch."

Lucy made a face. "Please, not that. I'll be sick for sure."

Erika laughed. "Then something else? A glass of wine?"

Lucy nodded. Erika got up to pour her a glass of wine.

"Sip it," Erika advised. "You're jangled now. It will go right to your head."

"Thank you for being kind to me. Now, I feel so guilty about not telling you."

"Please stop," said Erika. "It's in the past. All of it. Now, we need to figure out what to do in the future." She got up to pour herself a glass of scotch. "You don't mind if I have one, do you?"

Lucy chuckled weakly. "Of course not."

"Well, I can't send you home to Tom in this condition. You'll just have to spend the night."

"Thank you, but I don't think I'll be good for much. I don't feel very sexy at the moment."

"Oh, my dear, you are sexy taking a breath, but I understand. I don't feel very sexy myself. I'm stunned."

"Take me to bed and just hold me. Please?"

Erika nodded and put aside her glass of scotch. She took Lucy by the hand and led her into the bedroom. Lucy lay in the crook of Erika's arm and snuggled against her breast. From time to time she sniffled a little, but there was no more sobbing.

"I can't believe this is happening," she murmured.

"I know, love. Relax. You're safe. I'm here with you." Erika stroked her hair. After a while, she realized that Lucy had fallen asleep. Erika watched the gentle rise and fall of her chest. When her arm became numb, Erika decided to wake her. "Lucy, darling, would you like to sleep or get up? It's only eight thirty."

"I'm so tired," Lucy murmured.

Erika brought some makeup wipes from the bathroom and took an oversize T-shirt out of the drawer of her bureau. "Sit up, love. I'm going to help you take off your makeup."

"I can do it," said Lucy, sitting up. She wiped off the eyeliner and mascara but ended up looking like a raccoon.

Here. Let me help," said Erika, taking the wipe out of her hand. Lucy held up her face like a sleepy child. Erika took a fresh wipe and tidied the mess. She took another wipe and removed the foundation and finally the lipstick. Erika pulled the shirt over Lucy's head and unhooked her bra. She pulled Lucy's arms through the T-shirt she'd brought for her to sleep in.

"Lie down, love." She pulled off Lucy's capris and panties because she knew she didn't like to sleep wearing anything below. Then she pulled back the covers, and Lucy got under them.

"I love you, Erika," murmured Lucy.

Erika smoothed back her hair and kissed her temple. "I love you too, lovely Lucy."

24

Lucy awoke to a wonderful smell and realized it was fresh coffee. She opened her eyes and saw the coffee cup being offered to her. She looked around to get her bearings. She was in Erika's cottage, in her bed, and it was morning.

"Good morning, love. If you sit up for me, I'll give you your coffee."

Like an obedient child, Lucy sat up. Erika put the coffee in her hand and watched her take a few tentative sips. It was nice and hot but not scalding.

"Thank you," said Lucy.

Her eyes roamed the room, taking in the details. Usually, she was in such a state of sexual excitement when she arrived here, she missed everything. Now, she decided the white-painted, tongue-and-groove paneling was appropriately nautical as well as the framed watercolor paintings. The light blocking cellular shades had been raised, which was why she could see. Her clerical blouse and a black skirt were hanging on the door.

"Where did those come from?" Lucy asked between sips of coffee.

"I drove over to your rectory last night after you fell asleep and fetched your clothes and those black flats," she said, waving a finger at something in the corner. "I hope I brought the right things. Your makeup kit is in the bathroom." Erika's pale eyes smiled. Then her mouth curved up slightly. Erika's smiles were subtle like her wit. "You look better this morning," she said.

Lucy nodded and took a deep breath. "I feel a lot better."

"There's no need to rush about. Tom and I hacked into your schedule last night. Tom's taking your hospice and hospital visits this morning."

"That's so nice of him."

"He said he would leave the afternoon home visits to you because the elderly can be so finicky, and they don't know him."

"He's right about that. Maybe he'll make a good curate after all."

"Would you mind if I make myself a cup of coffee and join you? Or would you rather be alone?"

"No, get some coffee and come back."

Erika got up. She was wearing short shorts this morning. Lucy admired her long legs as she walked away.

After a few more swallows of coffee, Lucy remembered the events of the previous night—her embarrassment at Stefan's announcement blurted out to their friends, Liz taking her pulse, Erika wiping away her makeup. After those scenes replayed in her mind, she remembered the conversation with the caseworker at Lost Children Network. Today was the day her daughter would call.

Erika returned and sat down on the bed with one ankle on the opposite knee. Although there were faint broken veins in her ankles, she had the legs of a woman much younger.

"You have nice legs," said Lucy.

"Now, I know you're feeling better," said Erika, brushing the hair away from Lucy's face. "If you're looking at my legs, your sex drive has returned."

Lucy laughed softly. "Yes, I suppose that's a good sign."

Erika gave her a critical inspection. "You look adorable in my T-shirt, but it doesn't really suit you. For one thing, it's much too big." Erika's T-shirt was almost long enough to be a nightgown on Lucy, or at least, a nightshirt.

"May I keep this shirt? I like wearing it. It's like having your arms around me. You were so kind last night…especially after I'd thrown a bomb in your path."

"More like a land mine discovered years after the war is over. And like a mine, we must treat it with respect and walk around it *very* carefully." Erika patted Lucy's thigh. "When I saw Tom last night, I explained that you were ill, and I was keeping you for the night. He's just arrived. There's no need for him to know everything."

"You didn't let on that I wasn't physically ill?" Lucy asked anxiously.

"No, not a word. He accepted my explanation. It was harder to keep Liz away. She threatened to stop by, but I fended her off by saying you were still asleep. It wasn't a lie. You were."

Lucy's eyes began to sting. Then a few tears rolled down her cheeks.

"What's the matter?" asked Erika, "Have I said something wrong?"

"No, I'm just moved by all the kindness. Everyone here is so kind."

"We love you, Lucy. You are a beautiful, brilliant, loving woman who gives so much. It's not hard to be kind to you. It's an honor that you would accept it."

Lucy's hand crept across the blanket and found Erika's. She gave it a little squeeze. "Wait til they find out what I did."

"What you did," Erika repeated in a disparaging voice. "You made a difficult choice when your world was falling apart. You are not the first woman to make such a choice, and certainly not the last." Erika reached under the covers and ran her hand along the inside of Lucy's thigh. Lucy made a little cooing sound as the gentle fingers approached her crotch.

"Hah! You are fully recovered," Erika declared. "Why don't you get up, and I shall make you a nice cooked breakfast?"

"Let me take a shower first."

"Go on, then. You know where everything is."

Lucy took a leisurely shower. It was such a luxury to have so much time in the morning. She could get used to having a curate to shoulder some of the burden. If the vestry approved Tom, they would still need to get permission from the bishop to hire him, but that was a formality. Lucy mentally crossed her fingers.

She still didn't completely understand Tom's motives, although after hearing Liz complain about her life as chief of surgery at Yale and why she needed to retire, she understood a little better. Burnout was a real thing for ambitious professionals. In Lucy's time on the stage, she'd seen many opera singers burn out, some in their forties, comparatively young for a classical singer. The whirlwind international travel took its toll, never mind the stress of singing for hours and hours, sometimes on little sleep. Family life was non-existent.

It was now obvious to Lucy that Tom was gay. She liked the addition of the stud earring. Perhaps in deciding to leave his important post in New Haven, he was finally willing to make a bold statement about his sexuality.

He'd certainly come to the right place. In the summertime, Webhanet was a mecca for gay men and lesbians. The bar in the center of town and the rainbow flags everywhere proclaimed how gay-friendly it was.

Lucy said a quick prayer that Tom would find someone. He seemed so hearty at times, but as a savvy counselor, she could sense how lonely he was.

Knowing him now, it was amazing to think that he and Erika had once been together, but weren't they all so unsettled back then? Nowadays, young people took their gender choices and sexual preferences for granted. They had no idea that gender roles were once so rigid.

"Should I worry about you drowning in there?" asked Erika, opening the bathroom door a crack.

"Maybe you should come in and see."

"Now, now, Mother Lucy. Don't tempt me. It was difficult enough to resist you last night. A sexy woman in my bed, and all I could do was look at her! Come out of there and get your breakfast. Sausage or bacon?"

"Both."

"Greedy, little thing."

"I'm hungry," Lucy protested.

"No surprise. You ate almost nothing last night. Now, come out of there before you drown."

Lucy dried her hair with Erika's hair dryer and tied it into a ponytail. She'd wait until the steam cleared from the bathroom before putting on her makeup. She dressed in the outfit Erika had selected, pleased that it had been freshly laundered and all fit together perfectly. She wasn't surprised. Erika knew how to put herself together and always looked sharp.

Lucy sat down to a breakfast of fried eggs, bacon and link sausage. There was a pile of buttered toast, cut into triangles, and even a grilled tomato and a small dish of baked beans. "Full English this morning," Lucy observed. "Everything looks delicious."

"Unfortunately, the best meal in England is breakfast…except for Sunday roasts, perhaps."

"Fish and chips."

"Yes, and fish and chips. And curries." Erika dipped the corner of her toast into an egg yolk. "Did you perform much in England?"

"I sang at Covent Garden. A few times at Saddler Wells. I like England."

"So do I. We should go there sometime…to the lake country, perhaps. And I'll show you around Cambridge." Erika picked up her knife and fork and dug into her breakfast with gusto. She always enjoyed food, which was probably why she was such a good cook.

Lucy gazed across the table at Erika. The emotions she felt were overwhelming. Desire, yes, but so far beyond that. She felt an ache in her heart that only Erika could soothe. As the morning sun shone through the window, Erika's blond hair was brilliant. When she looked up, her pale eyes were languid and cool.

"Why are you looking at me like that?"

"You were so tender with me last night, washing my face, undressing me, holding me against your breasts." Tears came to Lucy's eyes.

"I love you," said Erika. When Lucy continued to gaze at her, Erika made a little face of discomfort. "Eat your breakfast, Lucy, or it will get cold."

***

Lucy decided to update her files while she waited in her office for the call. She knew there was a distinct possibility the call would never happen. All of this was so tenuous and fluid. The girl might change her mind now that she was faced with the concrete reality of speaking to her birth mother. Lucy herself had second thoughts. Deciding to speak to this child had been made in the emotion of the moment, completely without consideration.

There were so many questions. How would this new person fit into her life? Would it be a remote relationship where the support was merely financial? Lucy had saved a considerable sum for her retirement from her opera days. It was invested with a big brokerage house that actively managed it. As a priest, she needed little money and certainly had enough.

Perhaps she could help the child access social services, set her up in a place of her own with some supervision from local organizations.

Secretly, Lucy hoped that the girl would see her as the mother she had always dreamed of and want to be a family, but she knew that was pure fantasy. She couldn't just waltz into her daughter's life after sixteen years and announce, "Here I am!"

While she waited for the call, Lucy lost herself in the details of the counseling case she was annotating. The cases had become both more interesting and challenging since she had decided to expand her practice. Some of them were clearly psychiatric cases, and she'd referred them to the hospital clinic. Many involved substance abuse. She'd been developing more relationships with rehab organizations to cope. Liz had a backlog of mental health referrals, although her new PA had a mental health background and had taken on a few. Now that Lucy was faced with her own challenges, she wondered if she'd have the time and energy to keep up the momentum.

She glanced at the time. Five-thirty-five. The ring of her phone made her jump. She answered with her usual greeting. "St. Margaret's by the Sea, Lucille Bartlett speaking."

"Thank you for being available today, Ms. Bartlett. This is Melanie Peters at the Lost Children Network. I'm here with a young woman who's very anxious to speak to you. Her name is Emily."

Her name is Emily. Lucy hadn't been allowed to give the baby a name when she'd given her away. She was so glad the adoptive parents had given her a good name.

"Hello, Emily," said Lucy warmly. "How are you today?"

There was a long, tense pause. "Good," said a young voice.

"That's great," said Lucy, taking the initiative as she would with a new counseling client. "Can you tell me something about yourself? How old are you?"

"Sixteen."

"That's a great age. I had so much fun when I was sixteen." *Stop patronizing her*, Lucy ordered herself. *Have a substantive conversation. Ask open-ended questions.* "Ms. Peters says you've left your adoptive family. Why?"

"My parents are Witnesses of Jehovah. They don't believe people should go to college. I want to go to college."

Lucy was impressed that the girl could summarize her reasons so concisely. "That's an admirable goal, Emily. Education is important."

"What do you look like?" Emily asked.

"Oh, what do I look like? I'm petite. I have red hair and green eyes. I have very pale skin. I have to avoid the sun."

"Are you pretty?"

"Some people think so," said Lucy. "What do you look like?"

"I'm tall. I have red hair and blue eyes."

"Lucille?" Melanie Peters interrupted. "Do you want to open a video chat? That is, if you and Emily agree. Then you can see one another."

"Is that allowed?" asked Lucy.

"If you agree…"

"All right," said Lucy cautiously. A moment later, her phone rang. She tapped the screen to open the video chat. Suddenly, she found herself looking at a girl, who was clearly a blend of both birth parents. She had Lucy's delicate features but Alex's square chin. She also had her mother's red hair, but Emily's hair was still coppery and bright, whereas Lucy's had mellowed to auburn. The girl's eyes were a luminous blue. She got that from Alex too. "Hello, Emily," said Lucy, after nearly being overcome by the sight of her child.

"You're very pretty," said the girl, her eyes wide.

"So are you, Emily."

"I can tell you're my mother. You look like me." She frowned. "Why are you wearing that collar? It's a minister's collar, isn't it?"

Lucy's hand flew to her throat to cover it. She hadn't thought to take it off because she never expected to be seen. "Yes, it's an Anglican collar. I wear it because I'm a priest. I am the rector of an Episcopal church in Maine."

Lucy watched the girl's face darken as she digested this news. She tried to imagine the girl's thoughts. Here she'd abandoned one set of parents over religion only to find her mother was a priest.

"Do you think girls should go to college?" asked Emily, leaning her head to one side, her eyes fixed on the collar.

"I absolutely believe girls should go to college. I did."

"You did. Where?"

"I went to Julliard to study voice. Then I went to Union Theological Seminary to become a priest and Columbia University to become a psychiatric social worker."

"I want to be a mathematician," the girl said proudly.

"You do? Then I know someone you'd very much enjoy meeting."

"Who?"

"Stefan Bultmann."

"He wrote the Orion theorem," said Emily matter-of-factly. "It's very controversial."

"I'm afraid I don't know very much about it."

"I can explain it to you when I see you."

That seemed hopeful. "Would you like me to visit you?" asked Lucy. She had no idea whether that was a proper request during the first conversation. Maybe there were rules about when and how there could be further contact.

The girl's face lit up. "Yes, please!"

"Ms. Peters, is that all right?" Lucy asked. Emily glanced away, evidently looking for confirmation too. Lucy heard a voice in the background but couldn't hear what was said.

"She said yes, you can come." Emily was beaming. "You would like me. I'm very smart. I play the piano very well, and I compose music," said Emily, listing the reasons Lucy would like her. It hurt Lucy to think the girl felt the need to sell herself to her.

"That sounds wonderful. I'm looking forward to hearing all about it." Lucy flipped through the calendar on her computer screen. "I could come on Friday. Would that work for you?"

Again, Emily glanced away, looking for direction. "Yes, I can meet you on Friday, here at Melanie's office," said Emily. "She says she'll send you the time and address."

"All right."

"Thank you, Lucille," said Melanie, coming on the screen. "I'll send you the location and time, as well as directions. Is afternoon all right?"

"Yes, that would be best. I'll be driving down from Maine. It's at least five hours."

"I'll take that into account when I set up the time. Also, I'll suggest a time when we can speak more about Emily's background and your options for further contact. All right?"

"Yes, thank you," said Lucille. The view changed back to Emily. "Would you like to say goodbye to Lucille, Emily?" said Ms. Peters' voice.

"Goodbye, Lucille," Emily said.

"Goodbye, Emily. I'll see you on Friday."

"I can't wait to see you." The girl's smile was naturally enthusiastic. Lucy realized she was seeing her own smile reflected in her face.

Once Lucy was sure the call had ended, she began to cry.

***

Lucy ran into Tom as she came out of her office. "Lucy! I thought we could have dinner together tonight."

"I'm sorry, Tom, but I can't tonight. I have to talk to Erika about something very important. I was just going to change and walk down there."

He nodded. "The old man was just joking, wasn't he?"

Lucy felt her face warm. She really didn't want to talk about this now, but she said, "No, he unwittingly blurted out the truth. I think we will get married…eventually." She said it confidently, and on most days, she was confident.

"I'm so jealous."

"No, Tom, you can't have her. She belongs to me now."

"That's not what I meant. I'm jealous you've found someone. It's so hard at our age."

With all the anxiety and excitement, Lucy had overlooked the fact that she needed someone to fill in for her while she was in New York. "Tom, I have an important appointment in New York on Friday, and because of the distance, I'll likely stay over until Saturday. There are the usual hospice and hospital visits. Nothing major. But if something comes up, could you handle it?"

"No problem," he said. "Happy to do it. That's what curates are for. If you'd like me to take the Sunday services, I could do that too."

"But you're on vacation."

"I'm sure you'll return the favor and give me a few days off so I can sit on the beach. And maybe you can tear yourself away from your lady love long enough for us to have dinner. I'd like to share my thoughts on my role here if all goes well."

"And I would like to hear them, but unfortunately, I can't tonight."

"In that case, maybe I'll go down to Webhanet and prowl around. That bar on the main drag looks very interesting, although I haven't been in a bar in decades."

"It's a nice place, mostly men. Not dingy like most bars. I should put you in touch with Tony Roselli, the director of the Playhouse. He knows a lot of people. You don't want to waste your time with the summer people. Tony and his husband live here year-round. Maybe we could invite them to dinner while you're here."

"You'd do that? That's so kind!"

Lucy smiled. "It's no trouble. I'll ask them to scare up a friend to bring along." Lucy wiggled her eyebrows suggestively.

Tom reached out and touched her hand. "Thank you!"

Lucy hurried upstairs to change into her civvies. She packed a soft bag with a fresh stock, carefully folded a black skirt and suit jacket and added a pair of black ballerina flats. Her makeup kit was still at Erika's. Now that this routine was becoming established, she'd be wise to leave extra clothes and makeup there. Then she wouldn't have to go through packing every time.

Walking at a brisk pace, Lucy headed to Ocean Road. As she passed the café, she saw Stefan Bultmann engaged in animated conversation with two older men. She waved, but he was so engrossed, he didn't notice.

She found Erika sitting on her front porch with her laptop on her knees. She didn't look up until Lucy opened the porch door.

"Well, well, well. Look what the wind blew in." She glanced at Lucy's bag. "And from the looks of things, it seems she intends to spend the night." Erika closed her laptop and set it on the table beside her.

"I'm sorry. I should have called first. I just wanted to get down here and tell you what's going on. Did I interrupt you?"

"Yes, but I've had enough for today. I mean to finish this damn book this summer. My partner wants all of my time, so I must fit my work in between her demands."

Lucy affected a pout.

"You look adorable when you pout. Sit down, and I'll get you a glass of wine." Erika took her laptop and Lucy's bag inside. She returned with two glasses of white wine and sat down beside Lucy. "Fortunately, the piece of salmon I purchased is enough for two. I always like to make myself a salmon salad the next day for lunch, but I'll share with you this time. Hopefully, I can teach you how to cook a piece of fish properly."

"You'll never let me forget that disaster, will you?"

"Oh, maybe someday." Erika smiled a little ironic smile.

"I don't always know when you're kidding."

"That's the point, isn't it?" Erika reached out her hand and took Lucy's. "I'm so glad you came. You look much better. I assume the telephone call went well?"

"Yes, it was great. We did a video call so I could see her. It was scary and exciting."

"And…?"

"She looks like me."

"Oh, what a pleasure. A little Lucy."

"She also looks like her father."

"Of course, she would. A bit. So, what's the plan?"

"I'm going to New York to see her."

"When?"

"On Friday."

Erika's head snapped around to face Lucy. "So soon? Do you think that's wise?"

Lucy felt a little hurt that Erika was putting a damper on her enthusiasm, but she understood. Besides, it wasn't personal. It was Erika's nature to be reasonable and cautious.

"If I'm going to meet her, why not right away? It's been sixteen years."

"Are you driving to New York?"

"Yes. Flying into Albany would be the only option, but I'd have to change planes in Philadelphia, if that makes any sense."

"Unfortunately, it does. When I traveled to conferences, which were almost always in strange places, the connections were awful. Between that and being practically cavity searched in every airport, travel has become a nightmare." Erika took a sip of wine. "I shall go with you to New York."

Lucy looked at her with surprise. "That's so nice of you, but you don't have to."

"I know, but now that I am your partner, I must make these little investments in our future."

"You think of me as your partner?" asked Lucy, studying Erika's face. As always, it was calm and inscrutable.

"Yes, certainly your bed partner, but more as well. We make a good team." Erika nodded as if to confirm the thought conclusively. "Now, drink up, dear, and then your cookery lesson! You will learn to cook edible salmon yet!"

25

Erika couldn't take her eyes off Lucy's hands on the steering wheel. As she'd promised, Lucy had painted her fingernails dark red to match her toenails. They would be gone from Hobbs for a few days, and Tom was filling in for Lucy at worship services. Lucy's nails wouldn't be a distraction to anyone but Erika, who found them incredibly erotic. She could hardly wait to see them touching her body.

She hoped the motel room she'd reserved was clean and decent, not a dump smelling of stale cigarettes, darkened with heavy insulated curtains so no one could see the dirt. There were no chain motels near the Lost Children Network office and few options.

"Do you mind if I sing while we drive?" Lucy asked. "We left so early I didn't have time. Actually, I didn't want to get up an hour earlier to sing."

"Do I mind if you sing?" Erika repeated in a mocking voice. "You know how I love to hear you sing."

Lucy glanced in Erika's direction and smiled. "I won't inflict my exercises on you. That's asking too much."

"I don't mind, dear. Do what you need to do. If it gets unbearable, I always carry ear plugs when I travel."

Lucy laughed. "That's my Erika, always prepared. Like a girl scout."

"I believe that's the boy scout motto."

"And she knows everything," said Lucy, sounding a bit peeved, but when she turned, her smile was as brilliant as ever. "All right, just enough scales and arpeggios to warm up. Then I'll take requests."

Erika endured the exercises because she knew it was the price of living with a gifted singer. If she was patient with the monotony of the scales, she would be rewarded with something wonderful.

"All right, my dear. What's your pleasure?" asked Lucy, reaching for her water bottle in the console.

"You choose. Something operatic."

"Aida? That will wake us up. Here. Find "Qui Radames" on my phone, please."

Erika located the track. Hearing Lucy sing the aria was thrilling. As she listened, Erika couldn't decide what excited her more, hearing Lucy sing or making love with her. Lucy was a generous lover, and when she gave herself, it was absolute. She knew exactly what she wanted in bed and was completely uninhibited in saying so. And there were all the other levers of erotic stimulation, Lucy's exquisite beauty, her lacy undergarments, her dabs of cologne, and now her red fingernails. Sexually, Lucy could not be more perfect.

"Well? Did you like it?"

Erika realized Lucy had stopped singing. "Did I like it? You ask such silly questions."

"You didn't say anything. I thought you had gone into a coma." Lucy laughed at her own joke.

"I was thinking how perfect you are for me."

Lucy took her eyes away from the road long enough to give her a penetrating look.

"You're in love with me. It colors your perceptions."

"I know. I'm completely besotted with you, but I continue to find new depths of love for you. It's been a very exciting journey. Now, I'm about to discover who you are as a mother. I admit I find that a bit unnerving."

Lucy was silent for a long time. "We never talked about children."

"Why would we? Menopause has made that subject moot."

"Not always. Look at your friend, Liz. She became the stepmother of two in her fifties."

"That's quite different from dealing with a teenaged girl. God, sixteen is such a terrible age for female children. I remember my own adolescence with great shame."

"I bet you were adorable. Too tall, too gangly, much too smart for everyone. I bet you had a quick tongue and gave everyone a run for their money."

Erika turned to Lucy, who was smiling a little as she innocently kept her eyes on the road. "You have me pegged perfectly. How did you know?"

"I know grown-up Erika. She probably hasn't changed that much. Perhaps you've developed a few grooves on your tongue and don't say everything you think. Maturity will do that to a person."

"Maturity," scoffed Erika. "So overrated."

Lucy's smile faded. "I have no idea what I'm going to find when I get there. According to Melanie Peters, the rift with Emily's parents is permanent. They are more religious than most other Witnesses of Jehovah. They wouldn't let Emily have a cell phone or a computer. There was no internet access in the house. She had to go to the library to use it. Not only didn't they want her to go to college, they wanted her to drop out of school to help the mother with her cleaning business."

"That's tantamount to child abuse. Sounds like the Taliban."

"I agree. I can see now why she had to get away from them. She is a smart girl. Her IQ tests in the high 160s. She is in AP and honors classes in her high school and was taking some advanced math classes at the local college. Her autism is apparently very mild, or she is extremely well adapted."

"Good God, depriving a child like that of an education is simply cruel."

"Don't take the Lord's name, Erika. You know I don't like it."

"Oh, don't be so bloody pious." Erika frowned and stared out the window while she got over her annoyance.

"I know it's not easy being with a priest."

"Especially not one who's a hypocrite and has been known to use vulgarities herself."

Lucy sighed. "You're right. Guilty as charged."

"I'm sorry. I shouldn't push you today. I don't envy you this situation. What are your options?"

"Emily can go into the foster care system until she's eighteen. She could be an emancipated minor under the supervision of child protective services. According to Melanie, she's very mature and independent, so she probably could manage. One thing I mean to see to before we leave is making sure she's out of that shelter."

"How will you accomplish that?"

"I haven't figured it out yet."

"Is there a possibility you will take her back to Hobbs?"

Erika could see Lucy was struggling to answer this question. Finally, she said. "Yes."

Erika took a deep breath. "I'm sure you realize that is an act with many implications. You'll have to wear your scarlet letter in front of your congregation."

"What scarlet letter? I was raped."

"That fact might garner more sympathy, but I doubt you want to make a public announcement about that."

"No, definitely not. But a pregnancy out of wedlock is so commonplace nowadays. And we are all sinners. The Church teaches that God forgives the penitent."

"That's not what you say when you have to sneak around for our assignations."

Lucy turned and smiled. "I'm not repentant about being your lover."

"That's good to know." Erika took a deep breath. "But where will you put the girl? You have only one bedroom in your cozy lair."

"There's the other curate's studio."

"So, you have been giving this some thought."

"Of course, I want to be prepared. A German friend of mine admires that trait." Lucy turned and winked. "Let's see what happens today."

***

Erika looked up at the clock. It was an antique wall clock that belonged perfectly in the old-fashioned chrome diner shaped like a railroad car. The floor was linoleum and looked like it went back to the fifties. Despite the ancient look of the place, the diner had broadband WiFi.

No one seemed to mind that Erika had remained in the booth after she'd paid the lunch tab. She could have gone to their motel, but the light from outside was pleasant, as was the view of pine trees overlooking a brook, so she'd agreed to wait for Lucy there.

While she'd been waiting, Erika had made some progress on the next-to-the-last chapter in her Habermas book. She wondered what she would do after it was done. Maybe something on Hegel. Her conversation with Lucy had brought him to mind again. She'd always wanted to tackle something on the *Phenomenology of Spirit*, especially since it was out of her core area of expertise. Such a project would demand that she look at it with fresh eyes and do some research. Now that she was about to retire, who cared what she wrote?

She drained the last swallow from her coffee cup. Despite everyone's lack of interest in her squatting at the booth, she felt guilty about sitting there without paying for something. She glanced at the menu on the white tile board. It had slots and removable red letters that could be rearranged for specials. Today's feature was a chocolate malted. Erika hadn't had one since she had first come to the U.S. in the late seventies. Only a forgotten place like this would have such a thing on the menu.

When the waitress at the counter looked up from her newspaper, Erika signaled to her. She approached with her pad.

"Yes, Miss?"

Erika smiled. No one called her "Miss" anymore.

"How is the chocolate malted? Is it good?"

"To die for," said the woman.

"I'll have one, thank you."

"Should I keep a tab open for you? Will you be a while?"

Erika glanced at the clock. "Yes, I think so. I'm waiting for my friend to return."

The chocolate malted turned out to be very good. Erika allowed her straw to gurgle as she sucked out the very last sweet bit. When she gazed out the window, she saw Lucy's car pulling into the parking lot. A glance at the clock told her that she was back early. The meeting was to last until four. Perhaps something had gone wrong, and they'd ended it early. The driver's door opened, and Lucy got out. She looked in Erika's direction. She was smiling. That was good sign. Then the passenger door opened.

The girl was tall, not unusually so, but much taller than Lucy and as slender as a twig. She had the beginnings of a nice figure and long red hair. She resembled Lucy so completely that Erika gasped.

Mother and daughter climbed the steps into the diner and approached the booth. "Here's someone I want you to meet," Erika heard Lucy say. That was Erika's cue to get up. She closed her laptop and got to her feet. "This is my dear friend, Professor Erika Bultmann," Lucy said.

The girl shyly extended her hand. "Lucy says Stefan Bultmann is your father."

"That is correct."

"And you teach philosophy at Colby College."

"That is also correct, although I happen to be on sabbatical at the moment." She gestured toward her laptop. "I'm finishing a book."

"Do you mind if we sit with you?" asked Lucy.

"It's a bit snug in this little booth, but I think we'll manage." Erika put her laptop into its sleeve and stowed it in her bag. She gestured with her hand. "Sit down."

There was a long awkward silence. Even Lucy, whose counseling skills enabled her to navigate almost any social situation, seemed at a loss for words.

Finally, Erika opened the conversation. "I've just had the most amazing chocolate malted. Would either of you like to try one?"

Emily grinned. "I've never had one before. Are they good?" Her voice was musical like her mother's.

"They are an experience not to be missed!" said Erika. "When I first came to this country, I couldn't get enough of them."

"Okay. I'll try one," said Emily eagerly.

"Me too," said Lucy.

Erika signaled to the waitress and called, "Two malted for my friends, please."

Emily gave Erika a long, measuring look. "You sound English."

"I'm not. I'm actually German. Well, now, I'm a naturalized American citizen."

"Your father is from Berlin."

"Yes, that's where we lived, before we escaped to the West."

"Wow," exclaimed Emily. "That's pretty cool."

There was something old-fashioned about this girl, including her expressions. Erika guessed that she'd been isolated from the mainstream living with her religious parents.

"Your mother tells me you're interested in maths. I studied them before I changed my concentration to philosophy."

"Really?" Emily leaned forward. She was definitely interested. Erika had taught enough lower-level courses to know when she'd hooked a young mind.

"And I hear that you're quite the musician. You even compose. What style? Twelve tone? Minimalist?"

"I prefer more traditional, melodic music. You could say it's pretty derivative, I suppose."

Erika glanced at Lucy and saw that she was beaming over how well the exchange was going.

The conversation about Emily's composing went on while the two drank their malted milk. Emily made noises at the bottom with her straw when she'd finished. She looked around as if she wanted more.

"Would you like something to eat?" Erika asked.

"I don't want to be any trouble," said the girl, lowering her eyes.

"It's no trouble if you'd like something." Erika pulled the plastic menu out of its holder. "Here. Take a look."

Lucy looked at Erika with such a tender look that it was disconcerting, especially in that context. But it wasn't the sort of tender look she gave her during lovemaking, more like the look when she offered communion.

"Do you think we can reserve another room at the motel?" Lucy asked.

That burst the bubble of tenderness. Erika had made the reservations, so Lucy was asking her to call about another room.

"Of course," Erika said, trying to keep her brow from puckering into a frown. "Does this mean…?"

"Yes, Emily's coming home with us."

26

Lucy watched Erika talking on her phone in the parking lot. She'd gone outside to arrange for another room at the motel. She seemed relaxed and casual, but by now, Lucy knew her too well not to recognize it was an act.

She didn't know how to read Erika's reaction to Emily coming back with her, but after seeing the shelter where her daughter had been living, Lucy knew she had no choice. The place was full of homeless women, some of them intellectually disabled, others obviously psychotic. There were recovering drug addicts and beaten wives. Melanie had told her most of the residents had fled domestic abuse.

The organization that ran the shelter made an effort to keep the place clean and safe, and compared to other places Lucy had seen, it wasn't that bad, but it was no place for a sixteen-year-old. Lucy couldn't leave a child there, any child.

Erika leaned against the fender of the SUV after she ended the call. She looked deep in thought, which made Lucy anxious. The conversation before Erika knew Emily was coming home with them had been going so well. Erika had been wearing her professor's hat. She'd easily slipped into entertaining a young mind with her cleverness. Afterwards, she'd regarded Emily with a slight frown. Her efforts to make conversation stopped. She wasn't surly or rude, just quiet.

On her way into the diner, Erika ran her fingers through her hair and smoothed down her shirt, no doubt, putting her thoughts as well as her appearance in order.

"We're set," she said, standing over the table. "I was able to get a room right next to ours. The rooms are ready if we want to drive over there."

Lucy went out to the car with Emily while Erika settled the bill. She clicked open the doors. Emily climbed into the backseat, but Lucy waited outside for Erika so that she could ambush her on the way to the car.

"I'm sorry I didn't have time to explain. There was no privacy to talk."

"I'm sure you did what you had to do," Erika said in a cool voice.

Lucy caught her arm. "Please, tell me you understand."

"I do understand." Erika glanced at the hand on her arm, so Lucy released it.

They rode to the motel in silence. Erika checked in and came out with the keys. The old-fashioned place still used real keys instead of electric locks. "This town is like the land that time forgot." She handed a key over her head to Emily. "Sorry, but you get the smaller room."

"I don't mind. I'm used to a small room, but it will be nice to sleep in a real bed tonight instead of a cot. It was really hard and narrow."

Lucy could feel Erika's eyes on the side of her face. Maybe now she'd begin to understand why she had to bring Emily back with her.

She saw to settling Emily before joining Erika in the other room, where she found her stretched out on the bed with a book.

"I assume you explained the nature of our relationship to our young friend," said Erika, without looking up. "In case she wonders why you are sleeping with me tonight."

"Yes. I felt it was important to be honest right out of the gate. I'm not sure she completely understands. She's led a very sheltered life."

"That's all right, I didn't completely understand when I was sixteen either."

"It didn't seem to faze her at all, so I suppose it's all right for now."

"I have to give the girl credit. She seems pretty even keeled, considering what she's been through. Then she discovers her long-lost mother is not only a priest, but a lesbian. That's a lot to swallow." Erika spoke in her usual dry tone, but Lucy still couldn't read her feelings. She sat down on the bed beside her.

"Are you angry with me?"

"Not exactly. I don't know how I feel about this. When I sort it out, I'll let you know."

"At least, that's an honest answer."

"It's the best answer I can give at the moment."

"You think I should have done something different."

"I wasn't there. I don't know what the circumstances were. However, I think your decision was rather impulsive. But it's too late now. It's done, and you'll have to live with it."

Erika went back to her book. Lucy remained on the bed for moment to study her. She knew it was too much to ask that Erika enthusiastically endorse her actions. Lucy, herself, wasn't sure she had made the right decision. Now, that she had, she would have to live with it, just as Erika had said. But why couldn't Erika at least pretend to be more supportive? Why couldn't she say, "I don't agree with you, but I love you"?

Instead, Erika was acting like the reasonable philosopher. She probably saw this as some kind of decision tree exercise or an ethical dilemma instead of the messy human problem it was. She loved Erika's calm personality, yet at moments like this, she almost wished Erika would yell and call her names, so they could have a big, loud fight and then kiss and make up. That wasn't Erika's style, so it would never happen.

Lucy let Erika choose the restaurant for dinner. There were few choices, so it wasn't difficult. The local steak house was the best they could do. During dinner, Lucy felt she was doing all the work to keep the conversation going. She experimented with stepping back, but that resulted in deadly silence until Erika began talking about opera. She described the night she'd heard Lucy sing Desdemona in *Otello*.

"Your mother was truly phenomenal that night," Erika said, gazing at Lucy proudly. "Tomorrow, when we're driving home, you must ask her to sing for you."

Lucy breathed a sigh of relief when they began to discuss twelve-tone music. Erika thought it was ridiculous, but Emily went on about the mathematics behind it. After a while, they were so deeply into the discussion, they didn't seem to notice they were completely leaving Lucy out.

She knew that Erika's and Emily's brains operated on a different level, but now, the conversation was completely over her head and that frightened Lucy. This was a bond she could never have with her daughter, no matter how she tried. And this was a place she could never go with Erika either.

After dinner, Erika took a shower and got into bed with her book. Lucy showered and put on the new nightgown she had bought solely with Erika in mind. She was disappointed when she came out of the bathroom, and Erika didn't even look up. She gently raked her red fingernails down Erika's bare thigh, which finally got her attention. Lucy could hear her breath catch.

"New nightgown?" asked Erika, closing her book. "Very pretty."

"You finally noticed. I was about to take your pulse."

"My heart is working fine, but I'm reading at the moment."

Lucy ran her hand into the leg of Erika's shorts. "Are you sure you can't take a little break?"

Erika stopped the movement of Lucy's hand by gently pressing it against her leg. "Lucy, you are beautiful and very luscious, but I'm not really in the mood for sex."

The rejection stung more than Lucy would have expected. Up to now, Erika had never refused her sexual advances. Lucy might not be able to speak the heady language of philosophy and mathematics, but she could always communicate with Erika through a loving touch.

"If you don't want to make love tonight, that's fine," Lucy said. "But bringing Emily back to Hobbs doesn't change anything between us."

Erika carefully put her book aside. "I can't believe I am hearing you say such a thing. Of course, it does."

"Withholding sex is a cheap way to show disapproval," said Lucy. "If you have something to say, say it, but don't use sex as a weapon."

She could see from the persistent motion in Erika's temples that she was gritting her teeth to stop herself from speaking. When she finally spoke, her words were deliberate and measured. "Emily coming to Hobbs changes everything. I wasn't prepared for an instant family."

"Neither was I, but it's what we have."

"It's what *you* have."

"I thought I could count on you!" Lucy was shaking. She fought to control her tongue from saying more. As hurt as she was, she didn't want to lash out at Erika. Instead, she got into the other bed and turned her face to the wall. She wept silently because she didn't want Erika to know how deeply she'd been wounded.

Erika finally turned off the light. Lucy could feel her lifting the blanket and crawling into bed beside her. A gentle hand moved aside Lucy's braid. Soft lips kissed the nape of her neck.

"I'm sorry if I upset you. I'm having great difficulty with this. Everything's happened so suddenly."

"Can you imagine I might be having a hard time too?"

"Of course, you are. It must be an enormous shock." Erika kissed her neck again and allowed her lips to linger. "Go to sleep. We'll talk tomorrow."

"I love you," said Lucy.

Erika didn't instantly respond. When she did, it was to say, "I know you do."

For a few minutes, it seemed that Erika intended to sleep beside her, but then she got up and went to the other bed. Lucy tried to fight back the tears, but they came hot and silent. They rolled down her cheek into her pillow. She dared not even sniffle for fear Erika would know she was crying.

***

Erika was nearly silent on the way home, driving as Lucy and Emily got to know one another in the back seat. From time to time, Lucy noticed Erika's pale eyes studying her in the rear-view mirror. While Lucy drove, Emily dozed in the back seat. Erika was focused on her book.

"Is your book *that* interesting?" Lucy asked.

"Yes, actually, it is."

"More interesting than me?"

"Do you want my attention, Lucy?" asked Erika impatiently. She closed her book and put it into her bag. "I am happy to talk to you, but now our conversation must be more circumspect."

Lucy glanced in the rear-view mirror and smiled at the sleeping face of her daughter, the daughter she never imagined she would see.

"She's sound asleep."

"You don't know much about adolescents, do you?"

"And you're an authority?"

"I taught college students for thirty-five years. A few years older than our young friend, but not much." Erika leaned forward and looked at Lucy's hands on the steering wheel. "You took off your nail polish."

"You finally noticed? I figured I might as well. You didn't seem very interested."

"That's not true. I liked it very much." Erika sighed. "This arrangement will make it more difficult for us to be together."

"What do you mean?"

"You're responsible for a minor. You can't just waltz down to my cottage to spend the night."

"You can come to the rectory."

"Back to what your congregation will think." Erika gazed out the window. "I don't think you've thought this through very well."

"Well, what do you expect?" Lucy snapped. "It all happened so fast. We'll just have to make it up as we go along."

Erika nodded. "Good plan," she said in a very sarcastic tone.

"I wish you weren't sitting there in judgment. I'm going to get plenty of judgment as it is. I'd feel a lot better if I knew you were on my side."

"I am on your side, but I think you don't appreciate the magnitude of your decision."

"Oh, I appreciate it just fine. I think you don't appreciate how much your disapproval hurts me."

"I don't intend to hurt you."

"I'm sure you don't."

After a long, brittle pause, Erika dug into her bag and took out her book.

The silence was disheartening. Lucy was glad when they finally crossed the Piscataqua Bridge into Maine. In twenty minutes, they'd be home. Once they were there, all the changes the last few days had brought would become real.

27

Erika went over the bibliography one last time. Critics might disagree with her arguments, but they always praised her research. Her notes and documentation were meticulous.

This could be her last book, and if it was, it was an appropriate bookend to her career. It mirrored her dissertation on Habermas. Now, if the old man would only have the courtesy to die, it would be the definitive work, but like Stefan Bultmann, Jürgen Habermas seemed to go on forever.

Erika closed her laptop and gazed at the tidal marsh, lush now that it was August. A white crane alighted and walked delicately across the tall grass. Intrigued, Erika watched, reminded of a ballet dancer doing a pas de Basque.

The back deck was the place she came to commune with nature. The architect's plan called for it to be expanded and a screen enclosure added. The renovation would also add two large bedrooms on the second floor and another full bath, including a tub. Erika liked a soak once in a while, so that was essential. The kitchen would be renovated to be more modern. Minimally, it needed to be rewired, so the toaster didn't throw the breaker when the coffee pot was on.

The cost of the improvement was within her budget. The only reason she hadn't already gone forward was her indecision about where to retire. Living in Berlin was pure fantasy. Now that Stefan was in Hobbs, Erika wasn't going anywhere. She'd call the builder in the morning to make arrangements to start the work.

The only wrinkle in the plan was the request from the academic dean at Colby to suspend her sabbatical. With the book done, Erika had no excuse not to end it, although she was entitled to the time by contract.

Their arguments for returning to teaching were compelling. The country was more polarized than ever. As a disciple of Habermas, Erika was the leading expert on political discourse. The college also wanted to add one of her courses to Coursera and do a tie in with PBS. Obviously, they'd been busy planning their proposal. They knew their offer must be well thought out, or she wouldn't even talk to them.

The preliminary conversations with Morgan Collins, the new head of the department, had been productive. Perhaps they could do something with the schedule. It was less than a two-hour drive to Waterville, doable but not desirable. Morgan had put out the idea of holding all of Erika's classes on one day, but that was draining. Erika had always taken a dim view of online teaching, insisting that philosophy required face-to-face dialogue, but Morgan was dangling the possibly of interactive video classes. "We can do amazing things with technology now," she'd said.

With those thoughts racing through her mind, Erika opened her laptop and transmitted the final file of her book to her editor at Oxford University Press. She was pleased they'd held the contract open for all that time. When she'd mentioned it, her editor had laughed and said they'd once had an open contract for almost seventy years. The book was finally published, completed by the man's students.

Now that the file was on its way, Erika suddenly felt a void. She knew that she'd been using the book to block the anxiety of being separated from Lucy. Erika had worked not only steadily, but compulsively. She'd spent three days finishing the penultimate chapter. Then, despite years of procrastination, she'd barreled through the final chapter. It was the summation of her life's work and hard to lay out in a dozen pages. The day she'd finally written it, she'd awakened inspired. She'd eaten nothing all day, never showered, or brushed her teeth, but she'd finished the book.

Today, she'd showered when she got up because she couldn't stand her own filth. Plus, it had refreshed her enough to face the tedious task of checking the footnotes and bibliography.

With a sigh, Erika finally got up and made herself another cup of coffee. She checked her phone, which had been banished so that she could concentrate on her work. There was no email or message from Lucy. Erika hadn't expected one. Lucy had communicated only once since their trip to New York. She'd sent a text message: *No matter what happens, remember that I'll always love you.*

I know, Erika had replied. *I love you too.* After that, she hadn't known what to say. She'd let her silence do the heavy lifting, but now, she felt like a coward.

As the coffee ran through the machine into her cup, Erika heard her phone ping. When she saw it was from Lucy, she wondered if her thoughts had drawn her notice. *No, that's superstitious nonsense. Nothing happens for a reason beyond the obvious causal net.*

Erika poured cream into her coffee and sat down to read the message.

Maggie and Liz are throwing a party tomorrow night to welcome Emily. I already invited your father. He said he would come. I would REALLY like you to be there. The message was followed by five red heart emoticons.

Erika texted back: *Thank you for the invitation.* That sounded sufficiently vague. She could always decline at the last moment. Erika felt instantly regretful. She knew if she didn't appear, it would embarrass Lucy and make a big statement to their friends. *What time?* Erika texted.

Five o'clock.

Good. Thanks.

Lucy replied with another five heart emoticons.

Erika spent the next hour tidying the kitchen and the living room. She made the bed. Then she was at a loss for something to do. It was a splendid day with bright sunshine streaming down, but not too hot—perfect for a long walk on the beach.

As she passed the senior residence where Stefan lived, she thought about asking her father to join her. Then she decided she didn't really want company. Her father's conversations were always so engaging, and she needed to give her mind a rest after finishing her book.

While she walked to the estuarine preserve and back again, enjoying the bright sun overhead, she thought of Lucy's smile. It was completely appropriate that her name meant light. Erika's mind could be a dark place at times, but with Lucy in her life, there had always been illumination.

***

Erika awoke to some idiot pounding on her door. She turned over to grab her phone to see the time. It was dark in the room. The blinds were drawn, but she couldn't even see even a sliver of light at the bottom, which meant it was still dark outside. Her phone said it was only 5:15.

Erika threw off the covers, ran to the door, and flung it open. "Oh, for fuck's sake, what do you want!"

Grinning, Liz stood on the porch outside the door. "Well, good morning to you too. Get up. We're going for a walk."

"Like hell we are! I need coffee first."

Liz stretched out her hand to offer a large container of coffee from Awakened Brews.

"You are a beast!" said Erika, taking the coffee from her.

"Ayuh, I am."

"Liz, you're beginning to sound like a Mainer."

"That's good. About time."

Liz took a seat in one of the porch chairs and Erika sat down beside her. For a few minutes, they drank their coffee in silence.

"Doesn't your bell work anymore?" Liz asked.

"It works fine, but I don't always hear it in the bedroom, especially when I'm sound asleep. What are you doing here so early? You know I like to sleep in during the summer."

"It's an intervention. Hurry up and drink your coffee. I want to go down to the beach to watch the sun rise."

"Hold my coffee while I go in to throw on some clothes…and a bra, particularly a bra. I hate my boobs bouncing when I walk. I never had that problem when I was younger."

"Neither did I." Liz took Erika's coffee and rested it on her knee. The porch table was still full of the stuff Erika hadn't gotten around to clearing away since her book marathon.

Erika pulled on some clothes. The T-shirt and shorts didn't match, neither did the socks, but she reasoned that no one would be looking at a sixty-year-old woman at that hour. Besides, it was still half dark. She laced up her shoes on the porch. "All right. Let's go."

They walked through the access path to the beach. "Sunrises always make me happy," Liz said. "Each one is a new start."

"Liz, you are so simple sometimes."

"Sometimes, it's good to be simple. Occam's razor."

"Oh God! It's too early for philosophy."

"I heard from your father that you finished your book and sent it to your publisher."

"Big mouth! He can't resist crowing over my achievements. I suppose I should be grateful. At least, he praises me to someone. He never tells me he's proud."

"That old Prussian thing. Spare the rod…"

"Fortunately, he was never into corporal punishment. My mother, on the other hand, was quick to give me a whack with her cooking spoon."

"Builds character, they say."

Erika chuckled. "Right."

They didn't speak while the sun rose in the sky. It was a moody sunrise with dark clouds over the horizon. Finally, the sun flashed orange above the dark band, and their faces were bathed in golden light. They pitched their empty coffee cups into the rusted oil drum that served as a trash container and headed to the packed sand at the water's edge.

"You're not walking at your usual rapid pace," Erika observed.

"That's because I'm saving my breath to talk to you."

"Maybe you should just save your breath."

Liz barked a laugh. "You know when I have something to say, no one can shut me up."

"I know, and I even know what you mean to discuss."

"Good, then I won't need any throat clearing to introduce the topic." Liz stopped walking to look at her. "Erika, you're being an asshole."

Erika laughed. "That's what I love about you, Liz. You never mince words."

"You have to come to Emily's party. First of all, it will be an enormous embarrassment to Lucy if you don't show up. Second, we all need to support

Lucy in this new venture. It won't be easy to step in as a parent after sixteen years of absence. They have no history, no deep bond. There could be rocky times ahead, and we all need to be there for her. Third, if you don't come, it will break Lucy's heart, and I won't allow that."

"Whew! How can I refute those arguments? Compelling. All of them. Your professors at that Catholic college did well with you."

"I don't give a shit about the quality of my arguments. I just want you to come to the party."

Erika stopped in her tracks, forcing Liz to stop too. They eyed one another as if sizing up for a fight.

"Liz, think about it from my side. When I met Lucy, I wasn't looking for a relationship. I was still grieving Jeannine's death. Then my mother died—"

"When your mother died, Lucy came right away. She came without question. She even sang at the wake against her own better judgment. She did everything you asked. She was there for you when you needed her most."

"Yes, she was," said Erika, staring at her feet. "And she came without my needing to ask."

"That's because Lucy is full of love, and her love spills into everything she does, her singing, her preaching, her counseling. I've never met anyone so full of love as Lucy." Liz yanked Erika by the arm. "Come on. We're supposed to be walking." She headed off at a good pace, and Erika followed her. When Erika caught up, Liz said, "Do what you want, Erika. I'm your friend, and I'll always be your friend. But don't hurt Lucy. She doesn't deserve it."

"I know," Erika agreed. "She deserves much better than I've given her."

"Then you'll come to the party tonight?"

"I suppose I must, or I may find you outside my door with your gun!"

"That's not funny. Not even remotely."

Erika gave her a sheepish smile. "Sorry. I tried."

28

The party to welcome Emily had been Maggie's idea. After Lucy returned from New York, she realized she should tell her friends the whole story. They had adopted her like a member of the family. She knew they'd be there for her no matter what. That's why she wanted to tell them about Emily before they heard it from other sources.

Not long after Lucy first came to Hobbs, Maggie had shared that she'd been the victim of marital rape. She confessed it one night in whispered tones, while Liz cleaned up after dinner. "Please never tell Liz," Maggie pleaded. "She hates my ex-husband as it is." Of course, Lucy assured her that she would never tell, and being mellow after a few glasses of wine, she felt comfortable enough to tell her new friend the story of her own rape. She left out the part about the pregnancy.

When Lucy called on her return from New York and said she needed to talk, Maggie instantly invited her to come over for wine and hugs. Because Maggie already knew about the rape, Lucy could tell her the short version. When Liz arrived home and heard the longer version, she insisted on driving Lucy home to pick up Emily. Meanwhile, Maggie made a dinner of comfort food: her famous chicken wings, egg potato salad, and coleslaw.

Her friends' spontaneous generosity was not unexpected, but still touching. After dinner, Lucy helped Maggie with the dishes, while Liz and Emily talked on the screen porch.

"The big brains always find one another," Maggie said, watching them through the kitchen window, which allowed a view of the porch. "I have no idea what they're talking about half the time. I'm just glad they have each other for company."

"Yes," Lucy agreed with a sigh, reminded of the conversation in the restaurant in Kingston. She was not surprised that Emily had formed an instant bond with Liz, just as she had with Erika.

"We should have a party to introduce Emily to the family," Maggie suggested. "What do you think? We have lots of room for a party. We can have it here."

"That's so generous of you."

"Lucy, you give so much to everyone. Time for you to receive for a change."

The memory of those kind words made Lucy smile as she leaned toward the mirror to put on her makeup.

At least, she'd see Erika at the party. Lucy's heart had skipped a beat when Erika's text came in saying she would be there. In the time since they'd been apart, it had been so difficult to resist trying to "make it all better." There was nothing to say. If Erika was going to accept this, she would have to talk herself into it, not Lucy.

Lucy put the finishing touches on her makeup. She gave her hair a last brush and put it up. She headed to Emily's room to see if she was ready to go.

Emily was wearing a brand new outfit. After looking through the bag her daughter had brought from New York, Lucy realized the girl needed an entire wardrobe down to the underwear. First, they'd shopped at Reny's and Marshalls, so they wouldn't break the bank. Then, Lucy had taken her to the outlets in Kittery to find a few special things. Emily was shocked by the prices and had refused at first to try on the pretty clothes her mother had picked out for her, but Lucy had insisted. She'd given her daughter nothing in sixteen years. Now, she wanted to shower her with gifts.

Emily was pitifully grateful when Lucy had reactivated her old smartphone and added Emily to her plan. She'd installed her television in Emily's room. Lucy never watched it, so she'd never miss it. When she was alone, Emily was glued to the screen as if she'd never seen such a thing. There had been no TV in her adoptive parents' house. The only phone was a landline.

It was as if the girl had been dropped in from another time and place. Emily had learned most of what she knew from library books and surfing the internet on public computers. She'd taught herself to play the piano on the old upright in the back of the high school auditorium. She'd even learned to tune it herself. Lucy had tested the girl and found she had perfect pitch.

Emily's compositions were amazing, but she had so much to learn about the basics of music. At least, that was one thing Lucy could teach her brilliant daughter; that, and the feminine arts. The makeup lessons had been so much fun, recalling Lucy's own mother, the one-time model, showing Lucy how to apply mascara and lipstick.

Emily modeled her new outfit for her mother by twirling around like a dancer.

"You look beautiful, darling," said Lucy, holding her at arm's length to scrutinize her eye makeup. "You did a great job. You're a real natural."

"Thanks, Mom," said Emily. Her hand flew to her mouth. "I mean, Lucy."

Lucy studied the girl's face. "Do you want to call me Mom?" she asked gently. "You can, you know. I didn't want to say anything. I don't want to force you."

"You're not forcing me. I *want* to call you Mom. You don't know how I dreamed of meeting you, my real mother. I wondered how you looked…"

Lucy touched Emily's cheek with her fingertips. "Well, now you know. I look like you." Emily took Lucy's hand and kissed it.

"I'm so glad. I was afraid I would look like my father."

This was the first time Emily had mentioned her father. Lucy waited to hear what might come next. Would Emily want to know about him? Would she want to meet him too? Lucy knew that Alex was dying. Should she allow Emily the chance to meet him before he left this world? He had no idea she even existed. One thing Lucy was absolutely sure about: she would never tell Emily that she was the product of a rape.

"What's the matter, Mom? You look sad."

"Nothing," said Lucy, shaking off the thoughts. "Let's go. I know you're anxious to meet Stefan Bultmann. I think you'll enjoy talking to him. He's quite a character."

***

Lucy hadn't intended to make an entrance, but the party was well underway when they arrived. Tom was in animated conversation with Tony and Fred. She was glad they'd been getting on well since the little dinner party she'd hosted at the rectory. Tony had already introduced Tom to some of their friends in the community. It was a promising start.

Liz was handing out martinis. Maggie set down the tray of canapés she'd been passing around and announced in her actress voice: "The guest of honor has arrived!" She began to clap.

Everyone began to applaud. Emily looked to her mother for direction. Lucy whispered, "Look gracious, dear. They're clapping for you."

Lucy's eyes scanned the group for Erika while the other guests gathered to greet Emily. The girl shrank back, and Liz stepped in to block them from crowding her. "Emily's shy. One at a time, please, and just a handshake." The guests formed a line to shake Emily's hand and introduce themselves.

Liz bent to whisper in Lucy's ear. "Erika will be here soon. She knows she'll have to answer to me if she doesn't show up."

A moment later, Erika and Stefan came through the door. Erika handed off her father to Liz, who led him to a seat. Out of the corner of her eye, Lucy noticed Emily regarding the old man with pure awe.

"Is that Stefan Bultmann?" she asked.

"Yes, I'll introduce you in a minute. Okay?"

Lucy turned around and saw Erika standing behind her. "Hello, Lucy. How are you?"

"Wonderful now that you're here." She beamed a smile and in a moment, saw it reflected in Erika's face.

"May I have a kiss?" asked Erika.

"Oh, please!" Lucy felt Erika's lips on hers, a soft, sweet kiss that lingered a moment too long.

"Get a room," said Liz over Erika's shoulder.

"Later," Erika said and gave Lucy a little squeeze.

"I hope so." She caught Erika's hand before she could get away. "Please sit with me after you've said hello to everyone."

Lucy was moved by the warm welcome her friends gave her daughter. They included her in their conversations as if she were another adult. At the dinner table, she was proud to listen to Emily hold her own in the political discussion. She could talk about movies she had never seen from reading reviews online. Despite her sheltered upbringing, Emily had filled in the gaps in her education by educating herself.

After dinner, the group naturally split into two. Liz held court on the deck with Erika, Tom, Emily and Stefan. The singers and actors stuck to the screen porch to avoid the bugs.

When Liz brought out some cigars, Lucy was glad she had chosen her position. She drew the line when Liz offered a cigar to Emily.

"Oh, don't be a spoil sport," Liz complained.

"Yes," agreed Erika. "Leave the girl alone."

Even Stefan gave her a disapproving look. Realizing she was outnumbered, Lucy retreated. She was relieved when Emily declined without her prompting.

"Let the nerds have their fun," said Tony. "All the best people are in here."

"Agreed," said Maggie, saluting him with her wine glass.

"The ticket sales for your concert are through the roof," said Fred. "We've always have a good crowd for the Labor Day Gala, but I've never seen anything like this. Even the standing room tickets are gone for all three performances."

"Who says two, old has-beens can't draw a crowd?" said Maggie, laughing.

"You're not old has-beens." Tony gave her a stern look. "If you were, people wouldn't be ticket gouging. Maybe we should have planned another show for Sunday afternoon."

"No, three's enough." Fred nodded decisively. "Leave them wanting, and they'll come back for more next year."

Lucy craned her neck to look over Fred's shoulder to see how Emily was faring with the adults on the deck. "They all look very grim now."

"Oh, that's how big brains look when they're having fun," said Maggie, which caused Tony to laugh so hard he was slapping his knees.

When dusk came, the crowd on the deck wandered back inside. Despite the mosquito traps, the bugs were out for blood. Plus, it was getting nippy. When Liz came in, she closed the porch windows and turned on the propane stove. "You can tell summer's almost gone. Nights are getting cool."

Erika, who was sitting beside Lucy on the wicker settee, put her arm around her protectively. "Are you cold? I have a jacket in the car."

"No," said Lucy, loving the feel of Erika so near. "But your arm feels good. Don't move it."

Lucy noticed Emily giving her a look between envy and approval. Then the chatter in the room receded, and Lucy was only aware of Erika's warm body next to hers and breathing in the same rhythm. She sat up so she could speak into Erika's ear. "Come to me tonight," she whispered.

"After I drop off my father," Erika whispered back. "May I bring the car?"

Lucy nodded.

"Really?"

Again, Lucy nodded. "Tomorrow, you'll see why."

"Tomorrow? What's tomorrow?"

"Sunday." Lucy squeezed Erika's thigh. She moved a little closer so their hips touched. She allowed her hand to remain on Erika's thigh to stake her claim.

Suddenly, Tony jumped up. "Why are we all sitting around mumbling when we can make our own entertainment?"

"Absolutely!" Maggie agreed. "She reached out her hand to Lucy. Come on, girl! Let's show them what we're getting ready for the concert."

Lucy was reluctant to leave the warmth of Erika's body, but she allowed Maggie to lead her to the media room. Liz had designed the space for perfect acoustics, and there was an expensive, high end sound system. There was plenty of space for everyone in the rows of home theater seats.

After a few minutes of milling around, everyone found a seat. In the front was a raised platform below an enormous TV, that could be raised into the ceiling. The platform was two steps up, high enough and deep enough to serve as a small stage. Maggie and Lucy often practiced there, especially when the rehearsal rooms at the Playhouse were occupied.

Liz adjusted the lighting so that only the lights over the platform were lit. Tony took a seat at the grand piano and played a run of scales. "God, I love this Steinway! I wish we had one at the Playhouse."

"Put it on the wish list, and the board will consider it," said Maggie. Being secretary, she had a lot of say about what the board considered. She reached out her hand and led Lucy to the stage.

"What will it be, ladies?" Tony asked, but he'd already begun to play "Ohio" from *Wonderful Town*. Lucy always enjoyed Maggie's wonderful gift for comedy. The difference in range made the song a wonderful venue for their voices. They sang "For Good" from *Wicked* and then "A Boy Like That" from *West Side Story*.

"Wow!" said Liz, jumping up, clapping enthusiastically. "That was fantastic! Lucy, sing something classical."

"Let's stick with the concert," said Lucy. "This is the first time we've sung these numbers in front of an audience, and we can use the practice. I'll sing "*Nun lasst uns aber wie daheim*" from the *Merry Widow*."

Lucy sang over the audience as she always did, but when she caught sight of Emily, she nearly stopped singing. Her daughter had the same look of abject adoration on her face as Erika, sitting beside her. Lucy forgot the stage gestures for the number, crossed her hands over her heart and nodded to them.

When Lucy finished the aria, there were whistles and wild shouts of appreciation from the tiny audience. What it lacked in size, it made up for in enthusiasm.

"Well, Lucy, I think we can safely say you brought down the house," said Tony, his big baritone filling the room. "Your voice is exquisite. Why on earth did you ever stop singing?"

"That's a long story. Someday, I'll tell you, but tonight's for fun! Let's have some volunteers up here!"

Maggie picked up her guitar and sang some Judy Collins songs with Liz. Tony belted out some numbers from the piano, followed by duets with Fred.

"Erika?" Liz reached out her hand to her. "Sing something with me."

"Oh, we all know I can't sing," Erika protested, "but I understand Emily plays the piano very well."

Everyone turned to Emily, who instantly averted her eyes. Lucy was anxious for a moment. Tony got up and gestured toward the piano bench. "I'm sure musical talent runs in the family. Come on, Emily. Give us a song!"

Emily gazed uncertainly at her mother. "It's all right, dear, if you don't want to play. We understand." Then, to Lucy's surprise, Emily got up and sat down at the piano.

"I only know classical things," she said in an apologetic voice.

"That's all right," said Erika. "We love classical things. Don't we?" she asked, looking around for votes of approval.

"Yes, we do!" said Maggie enthusiastically. Then everyone was saying, "Yes!" and clapping.

Emily launched into the "Second Hungarian Rhapsody" and played it so professionally Lucy's mouth gaped a little. She'd heard Emily play on the upright in the Parish rec hall, but this performance was nothing short of phenomenal.

For a moment, everyone sat there stunned. Then there was enthusiastic applause.

"Play something else," Erika encouraged.

Emily nodded demurely and launched into a Beethoven sonata, which she performed equally well.

"Holy shit!" Liz exclaimed. Maggie elbowed her. "I mean, that was amazing, Emily. You could go professional."

"And she's never had any instruction?" Tony asked, looking at Lucy.

"The music teacher at my high school taught me how to use the pedals," said Emily.

"Lucy, you need to get this girl a teacher *now*," said Tony. "And I mean, a *really* good one!"

"Definitely," Lucy agreed.

After the impromptu concert, they returned to the porch. When Liz brought out the single-malt scotch, Lucy was afraid Erika might be tempted to stay for hours, but she used her father as an excuse to leave early.

Stefan gave Lucy an especially tight squeeze. "You look beautiful as always," he whispered into her ear. "Don't worry. I'll have a little talk with her." When he let her go, there was conspiratorial glint in his eyes.

On the way home, Emily said, "I was proud of you tonight, Mom. Were you proud of me?"

"Oh, Emily, I was *so* proud of you, and we will find you a piano teacher. A very good teacher."

After settling Emily for the night, she left a note for Tom to lock up when he came in, confident that Erika would arrive before him.

Lucy went to the rector's quarters to get herself ready for bed. She debated as she put on the new nightgown whether it had too many bad associations. She decided if she was ever going to be able to wear it again, they would have to make new memories.

She set the scene, lighting candles and incense as she had when Erika had returned from New Haven. She had just gotten into bed when she heard the outer door to the rector's apartment open, followed by the sound of Erika's sandals dropping outside the bedroom door.

"Beautiful," Erika breathed. "Simply and perfectly beautiful." Erika peeled off her T-shirt and bra. The shorts and panties came off together. Lucy pulled up her nightgown and parted her legs so that Erika could lie between them.

After being deprived for so long, Erika got too far ahead of Lucy too quickly. Lucy reasoned that if she made her come first, the tension would be relieved, and they could make love more leisurely. She flipped Erika over with one of her martial arts moves.

"You could warn me before you do that!"

"Why? You like it when I surprise you, don't you?"

"I actually loathe surprises, and I would never allow any other woman to do that."

"I'm not any other woman," Lucy said as she caressed her. She could tell from Erika's breathing that she was close now. She slipped her fingers inside her to slow her down. Erika groaned in protest, so she came back out again and let her come.

As Erika recovered, Lucy lay on her, snuggling the soft skin of her neck, breathing with her in the same rhythm.

"I've missed you so much," said Erika, squeezing her.

"Then don't hide from me again, and you won't have to miss me."

Despite Lucy's wish for slow, sensual lovemaking, her orgasm came so quickly it took her breath away. After she came, she was sensitive. Her grip on Erika's fingers was so tight she asked her to withdraw them slowly.

Erika pulled up the sheet to cover them and stroked Lucy's hair. "Sometimes, I wish my fingers were longer. When you're excited you become so big inside, I keep reaching, but I can't plumb your depth."

"Maybe we should get dildo," said Lucy.

"What!" Erika sat up. "A dildo? Are you saying I don't satisfy you?"

"Oh, no. Never think that!" said Lucy, enfolding her in her arms and pulling her close. "You satisfy me completely and absolutely."

"Then why are you suggesting toys?"

"I saw them in a video. It looked like fun."

"Lucy, for the first time you are really shocking me. What kind of video?"

"You know, those, little free videos."

"You watched porn?" asked Erika in an incredulous voice.

"Yes, I did. I'm trying to learn. I don't really know much about sex between women. You're only my second partner. Susan knew next to nothing. I taught her pretty much everything she knew."

Lucy could sense that Erika was beginning to relax with this topic.

The tension was perceptibly leaving her body. "Well, it's a bit early to need enhancements. Can't our digits and mouths do for now?"

"Of course, they can. I just want you to know I'm willing to try things to please you."

Erika began kissing her face, her forehead, her cheeks, her eyelids, and finally her lips. "Oh, lovely Lucy, I adore you."

"Don't adore me. Just love me."

"I adore you all the same."

"I need you to do something for me," said Lucy. "It's a very special favor, and you can't say, no."

"Ask. I'll do anything for you."

"I want you to come to my 10:30 Eucharist tomorrow morning and bring your father."

"No, not that."

Lucy grasped her wrist. "Erika, you said, anything!"

"But church? Really, Lucy!"

"You said, anything. Right?"

Erika let out a long sigh of exasperation. "Very well. I'll come…and bring my father."

"And spiff up a little. I want you to look sharp. Now, we should get some sleep. I have a big sermon to give tomorrow. It's very important!"

29

Erika straightened her father's tie. She held his blazer while he put his arms into it. She was surprised he was making such a fuss, especially to go to church. The one and only time she had seen him in a house of God was at her mother's funeral.

"You look quite smart, Papi."

He nodded. "I want to look especially good today," he said, which, of course, made Erika wonder why. He looked her up and down. "And you don't look so bad yourself."

She had worn one of her best suits, one with a skirt. She was wearing a gold necklace and earrings. It was the sort of outfit she would wear to the dean's reception or some other semi-formal event at the college. She hoped Lucy would find her appearance sufficiently "spiffy."

Erika led her father out to the car. The church was just a little too far for him to walk.

"Elizabeth is taking us to brunch at The Cliff Manor afterwards," said Stefan as he clipped in his seat belt.

"You seem to know a lot about this, Papi. Is there a secret plan?"

Stefan faced forward with a determined look. "You'll see. Let's go."

Erika shook her head. Obviously, Lucy was up to some special Lucy mischief, and her father was more loyal to her than to his own daughter.

Stefan held Erika's arm as they walked into the church. They found Maggie and Liz sitting near the front. Maggie was beautiful in a subtly flattering summer dress. Liz was wearing one of her designer suits. Next to them was Emily in a lovely floral dress. She was all made up and looking nearly as gorgeous as her mother.

"Why is everyone so dressed up?" Erika muttered as she slid into the pew.

"Lucy says it's a big day and we need to support her," Liz replied. "Otherwise, why would I be here? You know I don't believe in their iron-age fairy tales any more than you do."

"Now, now, Liz, that doesn't sound very supportive," said Erika with a chuckle.

"Maggie dragged me here," Liz admitted with a sigh.

Maggie leaned over and kissed Erika on the cheek. "I'll see you later. I'm the cantor today." She headed to the choir loft at the back of the church.

The enormous pipe organ began to sound, and everyone stood. Erika searched in the pocket attached to the pew in front of them to find the bulletins with the order of the service. She handed one to Liz, who scowled, and one to her father, who opened it curiously.

The processional hymn was "A Mighty Fortress is Our God," a sturdy and familiar Lutheran hymn. Beside her, Liz sang in a ringing contralto. To Erika's surprise, Stefan joined in too. Had they abandoned her to be the last agnostic?

The procession moved toward the altar. The acolytes, one leading with a cross, followed by one with a lighted candle, walked ahead of Lucy, dressed in magnificent gold vestments, obviously from another era. St. Margaret's had once been the recipient of enormous amounts of money from wealthy donors—old-money, summer people who'd owned the beach houses on the ocean. Tom followed, wearing an alb and a priest's stole. Erika watched him walk humbly behind Lucy. Perhaps he was sincere in wanting to downsize his career.

The procession ended, and Lucy took the celebrant's chair. Erika tried to catch her eye, but they were trained forward. Then she saw a twinkle in the green eyes, followed by the barest smile and the slightest arch of an auburn brow.

Lucy rose and crossed herself, saying, "Blessed be God: Father, Son and Holy Spirit!"

By now, the Common Prayer rite was becoming familiar to Erika. The service proceeded as usual. Erika was lulled into thinking it was another Sunday, and Lucy was just playing some new trick to get her into a pew.

Maggie sang the antiphons and the Psalm. Then Emily ascended the pulpit to read from the Acts of the Apostles. Erika was amazed at the poise the girl had in front of audience. Her religious parents had, at least, gotten that part right. Tom rose to read the Gospel.

Finally, Lucy climbed the stairs to the pulpit. She looked radiant as always, smiling her solar flare smile at the gathered parishioners. "Good morning!" she said.

"Good morning!" responded the congregation.

"I have several important announcements to make today." Lucy paused to make sure she had everyone's attention. "I hope you've all had a chance to meet our visiting priest, Father Tom Simmons. He's been the rector of Trinity Church on the Green in New Haven, Connecticut. But now he's going to join us here in Hobbs. The vestry and the bishop have approved Father Simmons to be associate rector of St. Margaret's. He'll be joining us in a couple of weeks once the search committee in his home parish is formed. Father Tom, please stand up and let everyone see you." Someone started clapping, and soon there was enthusiastic applause. Tom nodded to acknowledge it.

Well done, Tom, Erika thought. *Maybe this is the first time you're not a fraud.*

"Now, I'd like you to meet someone else who's new to St. Margaret's. As someone very dear to me said, this will be my scarlet letter moment. I intend to preach today on God's forgiveness, which is there for all of us at any moment as long as we sincerely repent in our hearts. Today, I ask for your forgiveness and understanding.

"Some of you know I used to be an opera singer. I loved it, and I was very good at it. It's really hard work to get to the stage of the Metropolitan Opera, but I did it. I'm only telling you this because I want you to understand the circumstances behind my actions. As my career began to take off, I became pregnant. I knew I couldn't be a single mother and successful as an opera singer. Having both was impossible, so I had to choose." There was a low murmur in the congregation. "I chose to give up my child for adoption. It was the hardest decision I have ever made. Now, I realize how selfish it was, but then, it was the only thing I could do. The alternative was not something I personally could ever do, and now I'm glad. Dear Friends, I would like you to meet my daughter, Emily Cunningham, soon to be Bartlett, once her adoption is revoked. Emily, would you please stand so the people of St. Margaret's can meet you?"

Shyly, Emily rose. The applause was more thunderous than when Tom had been introduced. Emily instantly sat down. Liz took her arm and encouraged her to stand again. Then she stood beside her with her arm around her. Erika was never so proud of her friend, not even when she was appointed chief of surgery at Yale. The applause went on for some time. Finally, it sputtered out.

"There's one last person I want you all to meet. I'm hoping she will someday be part of our community, but I think I'll need all of your help in achieving that goal. Most of you know that I'm a lesbian. Some of you don't approve. I understand that many of you were raised in a different time with different ideas, and things have changed very quickly in this country and in our church. All, I ask is that you keep an open mind and accept me as Lucy Bartlett and not think of me as just a label. As you know, our church ordains gay men and women. We bless same-sex marriages." There was some tentative applause. Lucy held up her hand to quiet it. "No, I'm not getting married yet. But I would like you all to meet the woman I'm dating. She's very dear to me. She's a professor of philosophy at Colby College and a very special person, whom I hope you'll all get to know. Please meet Dr. Erika Bultmann. And that's her father sitting beside her, the famous mathematician, Stefan Bultmann. Professor Bultmann, senior, just moved to Hobbs, so let's welcome him too."

Liz pulled Erika to her feet. Again, the applause was thunderous. Despite the spontaneous demonstration of approval, Erika noticed a few people leaving through the back door.

"Thank you," said Lucy as the applause faded. "And now, I hope you'll be as attentive to my sermon. Please hold the applause until the end."

There was a burst of laughter from the pews.

Erika tried to listen to Lucy's homily, but after that stunning introduction to the congregation, she was distracted. Meanwhile, she felt Stefan giving her sidelong looks. He'd known all about this, she realized.

She stood, knelt, and sat along with the congregation. She even sang along mindlessly, but she remained dazed.

The last of the communicants were heading back to their seats, when Erika noticed Lucy staring at her from the communion rail. Tom stood beside Lucy, waiting. *They're waiting for me*, Erika finally realized. She climbed over her father's legs and headed to the front.

"The body of Christ, the bread of heaven," said Lucy putting the bread in her hands. Erika looked up and saw that look of ineffable love in Lucy's eyes. She almost forgot to move in Tom's direction to drink from the cup. Lucy nodded to encourage her.

The rest of the service was a complete blur. Erika heard Liz whisper, "Are you all right?"

"Yes, I think so," Erika replied.

Maggie led them all to the lower church for fellowship. This morning, there were breakfast pizzas, courtesy of Hobbs Family Practice. Erika had never had them before she'd come to Hobbs. She knew they were tasty, but she wasn't hungry. She accepted the cup of coffee Liz placed in her hand and watched as parishioners came up to Tom and Lucy and hugged them.

Lucy beckoned to her with a little wave. When Erika came to her side, Lucy linked her arm in hers. The parishioners began hugging her too. Erika was moved but felt awkward. She saw Liz wink and nod and finally realized she should hug the well-wishers back.

Lucy reached out her hand to Emily, but Maggie shook her head and protectively put her arm around the girl. It was too much to ask someone with Asperger's to hug all those strange people. Lucy waved insistently, so Maggie led Emily to Lucy's side. "Offer your hand instead," she suggested gently. "That's all right too. Can you do that?"

Emily nodded. Erika and Lucy stood close to her to block people trying to hug her.

"You're doing very well," Erika said. "I'm very proud of you."

Emily nodded. "Thanks."

***

"Liz, why must you always pay?" asked Erika. The brunch had been superb, and the view of the cliffs of Webhanet, even more so.

"Because I can," said Liz. "Just say, thank you."

"Thank you, Liz," said Lucy, insinuating herself into the conversation.

Liz raised a mimosa in her direction. "Congratulations on a truly brave sermon, Mother Lucy."

Erika raised her glass as well. "Yes, Mother Lucy, well done." She noticed that Stefan was watching them carefully. "I suppose I should get my father home eventually. He was up at the crack of dawn this morning. He looks like he could use a nap."

"Will you come over later?" asked Lucy. "I could use a nap too."

Erika raised a brow in her direction. Lucy gave her one of those canny Lucy smiles, which were much more frightening than the solar flare variety.

"We'll see," said Erika, rising. "Come on, Papi. The party's over."

"You want to stay? I can bring your father home," Tom offered, getting up.

"Thank you, Tom, but I think my father expects me to be the dutiful daughter. Perhaps I shall see you later. Lucy is threatening to cook for us tonight." She gazed at Tom fondly. "You'll be leaving for a while."

"Yes, I'll be gone for a few weeks until my bishop approves my resignation."

"Then let's have a hug in case I don't see you later."

Erika embraced Tom. His male scent prickling her nostrils seemed so alien, but his hug was reassuring. "Thank you for everything," she said.

"Now that I've signed up to live in this crazy place, you'll see a lot more of me, I think."

"I suppose that's not a bad thing. You're not the worst."

"How many double negatives can dance on the head of a pin?"

"Many more than you think," said Erika, patting his shoulder.

She drove Stefan to the senior residence and rode up with him in the elevator. She waited while he opened the door with his key, then leaned over to embrace him. He held on to her.

"Come in for a moment, Erika. I have something to discuss with you."

"Oh, dear," said Erika. "Should I be worried?"

"No, but come in and sit down. I'll make a pot of tea."

Erika was tempted to take over in the tiny kitchen, but she respected her father's wish to prepare the tea on his own. He carefully brewed it in a tiny floral tea pot, that had belonged to her mother, and arranged it on a silver tray along with a cup of sugar cubes and a pitcher of cream. Because of the tremor that had developed since his wife had died, Stefan allowed his daughter to bring the tray into the sitting room. He was silent while he added sugar and a little cream to his cup. Erika sensed he was struggling to find the right words to open the conversation. He glanced at her over his teacup.

"I'm listening, Papi."

He put down the teacup and nodded. "Your mother didn't want to marry me at first. She thought I was too serious. And she was right. It took me a long time to learn how to laugh."

"But now, you're very funny, Papi. You make everyone laugh."

"Making people laugh is a good thing. Don't be too serious."

"Good advice," she agreed with a nod.

"Yes, it is."

"But that isn't what you wanted to talk about."

"How did you know?"

"I've known you for sixty years."

"A long time," he agreed. "I was very lucky to have all those years with your mother. Sixty-two years. But no matter how long you live, Erika, you can never be together with anyone that long. Pay attention. Time runs out faster than you think."

"Papi, what are you trying to say?"

"That woman was very brave today. She stood up in front of all those people in that church. She told them she loves you. She risked her job for you. What do you risk for her? Nothing. You can walk away, and it would make no difference to you."

"That's pretty harsh, Papi. What have I done to deserve this?"

"I thought you were brave. Your mother risked her life for me. She would rather have died than live apart from me. She stood up for me, for us. Like your Lucy did today. Would you do that for her?"

"It's a complicated situation," said Erika, staring at her feet. "I had no idea she had a child. Lucy wasn't honest with me."

"You're not being fair. She gave up the child. She thought she was gone forever. It's a miracle she returned."

"You don't believe in miracles, Papi. You're an atheist."

"I do believe in one miracle. Love. When you find it, don't refuse it. That woman loves you."

"And I love her too."

"Then prove it. Stand up for her the way she stood up for you."

"Thank you for your advice, Papi. I shall consider it."

"Good."

***

In a grumpy mood, Erika took off her dress clothes and put on shorts and a T-shirt. She decided to take a nap. She'd gone to sleep too late and had been awakened by Lucy's alarm too early. She went out cold.

When she opened her eyes, she saw Lucy sitting in the chair beside the bed.

"What are you doing here?" Erika asked.

"Your door was open, so I came in. You were sleeping so peacefully I didn't want to wake you."

Erika stretched like a cat and yawned. "I suppose I should lock the door with all the tourists in town.

"I left Emily on the beach and walked up to ask if you're coming to dinner," explained Lucy.

"Haven't you seen enough of me today?"

Lucy's smiling eyes were patient. "I can never see enough of you."

"That was quite a speech you gave this morning. Aren't you worried you'll lose parishioners? I saw some people trying to escape while you spoke about being a lesbian."

Lucy shrugged. "I expected that."

"Was it wise?"

"I don't really care. I can't hide Emily, and I'm tired of hiding you. There will always be haters. I need to live my life in the open. I'm not ashamed of you. In fact, I'm very proud to have you as my partner."

"I wasn't expecting to be thrown out of the closet so publicly."

"Are you angry?"

"No, because now I can come and go from your place without worry. However, I'm not sure I would have been as bold as you were today."

"I'm sorry. Maybe I should have warned you."

Erika reached out her arms. "Come here, lovely Lucy and make amends."

Lucy climbed on the bed. "I have sand on my feet."

"It doesn't matter. I live at the beach. There's always sand in the bed."

After they made love, Erika brought Lucy up to date on what had transpired in the time they'd been apart. She told Lucy about the request to suspend her sabbatical and her decision to go forward with the addition.

"Afterwards, there will be enough room for all of us here. Emily would have a lovely bedroom on the second floor overlooking the salt marsh. But we'll have to live somewhere else while the construction is going on. Could I stay at the rectory?"

Lucy's languid, green eyes gazed into hers. "Yes, but we'd have to be married."

Erika sat up. "I thought that now, everyone understood."

"They understand that we're seeing one another, but if you want to live in the rectory, we should be married. There are some boundaries we can't cross."

"Then maybe we should continue to live apart. If I teach those classes at Colby, I should probably move back into the faculty residence."

Lucy sat up. "If that's what you want, Erika." She slipped on her sandals. "I need to get Emily. She's waiting. Are you coming for dinner?"

"Yes, I'll be there in a bit. Let me get myself together."

Lucy nodded and headed to the front door. After she was gone, Erika realized she had missed an important opportunity.

What a stupid question—can I stay at the rectory? Erika had known the answer before she'd asked, and it wasn't a matter of practicality. She could always stay with Maggie and Liz during the construction. They never turned away a guest, even if the hapless visitor had to sleep on the pullout in Liz's office.

Now, Erika had introduced new doubt into the conversation. Of course, she didn't want to move back to Colby. It had never really been home. More importantly, Erika wanted to spend every moment she could with Lucy. On the rare nights when they were apart, her longing for her bordered on pain.

Erika might have complained about an instant family, but she found Emily's young mind very stimulating. It touched her that the girl looked up to her with a kind of hero worship. In the short time she'd known the girl, she'd become very fond of her.

How could so much have changed so quickly? It was all extremely confusing. Erika needed to think.

She also needed to get up and dress or she'd be late for dinner.

***

Lucy made a very nice meal of broiled haddock. She wasn't ready to become a sous-chef, but her meals were definitely improving. Erika realized that she was changing Lucy's life, just as Lucy was changing hers. In finding common ground, they were also learning from one another. *There could be worse things*, Erika thought.

Fortunately, Tom kept the dinner conversation going because Erika wasn't much help. She half listened as she observed Lucy interacting with the others at the table. She loved watching Lucy with people. She was so good at it, always engaged, listening carefully, drawing others out, generous in her responses. Lucy was a genuinely good woman. *I am very lucky to have her,* thought Erika. *Maybe Papi is right.*

While Erika helped Lucy clean up the kitchen, they finally had time alone.

"You were so quiet tonight," said Lucy, giving her a kiss on the cheek, then trailing her fingertips down it. "Is everything all right?"

Erika nodded. "Yes, fine. I'm thinking."

Lucy gave her a worried look. "Do you want to share your thoughts?"

"No. Not yet." Erika grinned. "But don't worry. That's what philosophers do. We think."

The worried look persisted. "As long as you don't think yourself into hiding from me again."

Erika put down the dish towel and pulled Lucy into a hug. "No, I'm not going to hide. And I'm not moving back to Waterville. I'm staying right here with you."

"I'm so glad," said Lucy, resting her head on Erika's shoulder.

Erika sniffed near Lucy's ear. "I detect Chanel No. Five. Shall I try to discover where you want to be kissed?"

"Not now. We have a minor present and a guest."

"They're in the other room," said Erika and nipped her ear.

Lucy gently pushed her away. "You're so bad." She expertly snapped the end of the dish towel in Erika's direction. "Settle down, there. I'll take care of you later!"

"You know I'll hold you to that."

"I know you will."

30

The after party had drifted from the Irish pub in Webhanet to Liz's deck in Hobbs. After two successive nights of sold-out performances and a stunning review in the *New York Times* by a vacationing arts reporter, the cast and crew had every reason to celebrate. The beer and the wine were flowing, and Liz had just opened a new bottle of single-malt scotch. Erika saw that Tom was already pink-cheeked and heartier than usual. She gave him a nudge with her elbow and wagged her head toward the screen porch.

"Thomas, you might want to leave off the scotch," she said as she opened the door. "Aren't you filling in for Lucy in the morning?"

"I am," he confirmed. "But don't worry. I'm pacing myself."

Erika scrutinized him. His eyes were glassy, but he wasn't obviously inebriated. "I'm glad you're back in time to help Lucy during this concert. To my surprise, it's thrown her for a loop. She was jet setting all over the world and sleeping in a new city every night when she was an opera star."

"That was almost twenty years ago," said Tom. "None of us has the energy we had back then."

"She said she would return after putting Emily to bed. There's no sign of her, so I must assume she's too tired to party further."

"Singing that performance was pretty taxing. I'm surprised Maggie's still going."

"She slept in this morning. Lucy had a nine o'clock counseling session."

"Yes, she's working too hard. Hopefully, I can take some of those duties off her plate."

Erika eyed him. She still wasn't used to this generous iteration of Tom Simmons, so different from the man she knew years ago. "Let's sit down. I want to talk to you about something."

They sat across from one another on the wicker love seats.

"What's up?" he asked, crossing his legs with his ankle on the opposite knee.

"Can you give me a brief overview regarding marriage in the Episcopal church?"

He showed no surprise other than to raise one bushy brow. "Depending on the parish, banns are announced stating the intention of the parties to marry."

"How long does that take?"

"Three weeks. But the couple counseling can take longer."

"And what does that entail?"

"The celebrant or another qualified priest meets with the couple to see how compatible they are in key areas such as communication, shared responsibilities, children, sex."

"Sex?" repeated Erika with surprise. She sat back and studied Tom.

"That's important in a marriage, of course."

"Of course," Erika agreed.

"And what if one of the parties is a priest?"

Tom massaged his beard. "It's really the same, except it's customary to notify the bishop. He or she may want to meet with the priest."

"I see," said Erika. "So, if this priest were to marry in, say, October, it would be wise to start the process soon."

Tom leaned forward so he could look directly into her eyes. "Yes, Erika, if you're going to marry Lucy, you'd better ask her *now*."

Erika was surprised her intentions were so obvious to everyone, but, of course, they were. "I want everything carefully planned beforehand. I don't want her to worry about a thing. She already has more than enough to worry about. I've picked the venue for the reception, The Cliff Manor in Webhanet. I've contacted the musicians—"

"Erika, don't you think Lucy might want to be involved in some of these decisions?"

"Of course, I shall discuss them with her eventually, but some things are already decided. We're going to Acadia with Liz and Maggie for our honeymoon."

"You're taking your friends on your honeymoon?"

"More like they're taking us. They celebrate their anniversary in Acadia every year. We've already reserved side-by-side cottages on the ocean."

"Don't you want a little privacy?" Tom wiggled his eyebrows suggestively.

"It's not as if I'm going to deflower the bride on the wedding night," said Erika. "Seriously, we're going up for the week. They're coming on the weekend. We'll have plenty of privacy."

"You don't want to do something fancier? A river cruise in Europe, maybe?"

"Lucy traveled to all the great cities of Europe when she was an opera singer. She's been talking about this camping trip since I've known her."

"Then it sounds like the perfect Maine honeymoon. I'm jealous. I wish I could go too. I've always wanted to see Acadia."

"There's nothing stopping you, Tom."

"Think they still have cabins available?"

"No, you have to reserve for the holiday weekend well in advance. Plus, you'll have to cover for Lucy while she's on her honeymoon. That's your job. Remember?"

"Right."

Liz came in with the bottle of scotch and offered to refill Tom's glass.

"Tom…" said Erika with a firm look. "You have the 10:30 service in the morning. Don't forget."

He sighed and sat back in his chair. He thanked Liz but passed on the scotch. "I should be getting back soon."

"Are you sure you're all right to drive?" asked Liz.

"I can drive him home," volunteered Erika. "Someone can bring me back tomorrow for my car."

Erika went to look for her bag. When she returned, she went to say good bye to her hosts. Liz gave her a bone-crushing hug, and Erika knew she was feeling no pain. Maggie looked exhausted but triumphant.

"You should go to bed, love," Erika advised.

"I will, but I can't leave Liz with all these people. Are you going?"

"Yes, I'm driving Tom home. He's responsible for all the worship services tomorrow, so he needs to sleep it off beforehand."

Erika took Tom's keys out of his hand and climbed into the driver's seat. It was a Subaru, and the instrumentation was unfamiliar. Erika took a moment to look it over before starting the car.

"Thanks for playing taxi driver," Tom said, reclining the passenger seat.

"You're welcome," said Erika, "and I'll thank you to keep what I told you tonight in confidence. It's a surprise."

"You have my word," said Tom, closing his eyes.

"Don't fall asleep. My days of helping inebriated men into the house are long over."

Tom chuckled. "I'm not really drunk."

Erika walked with Tom to his apartment. She watched him open the door and handed him his car keys. Then she headed down the hall to the rector's quarters. She smiled when she found the door unlocked, which always pleased her, even though Lucy had given her a key.

The light was on over the stove. Erika went into the bedroom, where Lucy lay curled up on her side, still clad in her lace bra and panties. She was sound asleep.

Erika gently rolled her over on her back. "Come, love. Sit up. I'll help you into your nightgown."

Lucy opened her eyes and tried to focus. "Oh, sweetheart, I'm sorry. I meant to lie down for fifteen minutes to see if I could get a second wind. My alarm never rang."

Erika picked up Lucy's phone and saw the ringer was still set to silent. "It doesn't matter now. The party's over. Come on. Sit up."

When Lucy reached out her hands to cup her face, Erika's eyes instantly went to the red fingernails. While Erika had her in a sitting position, she reached around and unhooked her bra. Before she helped her into her nightgown, she gave each breast an appreciative kiss.

"Lie down, lovely Lucy. Panties off."

"I don't know if I can make love. I'm sooooo tired."

"Never mind. We'll have time in the morning."

Erika drew the covers up over Lucy and shut the light. "Sleep now. I'll be in bed in a moment." She tossed Lucy's underwear in the hamper and took her sleeping Tee and shorts out of the drawer Lucy had set aside for her. After brushing her teeth, she lay down beside Lucy. She kissed the nape of her neck.

"I have a surprise for you tomorrow," she whispered to the sleeping woman. "I hope you like it."

Lucy didn't stir. Erika kissed her again and fell asleep breathing the sweet scent of Lucy's hair.

***

Erika thought of how Lucy had awakened her. Her red fingernails gently raked down her arm; her warm lips kissed her breasts. Erika had never favored morning sex until she met Lucy, whose morning smile was like a brilliant sunrise.

As she cleaned her mother's engagement ring with an old toothbrush, Erika remembered Lucy's fingers inside her. In only a few months, Lucy had learned every nuance of Erika's body. As a singer, Lucy's sense of timing and rhythm were impeccable, and she applied them to great advantage in the bedroom. She might claim to be a neophyte at sex with women, but she was a quick study.

Erika held the ring under the light. Her mother had hardly worn it. She'd replaced it with a gold band once she'd married Stefan. The sapphire was still brilliant, a natural stone, deep blue in color. Erika knew she should have taken it to a jeweler to have it cleaned professionally, but now, it was too late. She had been so busy planning everything else, she hadn't thought of it until now. A little dish detergent worked wonders. The stone glistened like new.

Erika dropped the ring into a whiskey glass and placed it on the rim of the sink. She switched on the garbage disposal to feed the peels from the cucumber salad she'd made for her father. When her phone rang, she turned to look for it. A moment later, she heard something crunching in the disposal mechanism.

No! Fumbling, she threw the switch. For a long moment she stared into the sink, trying to look past the pointy rubber fingers into the dark hole. As much as she might be tempted to put her hand into the disposal, she knew it was dangerously unsafe.

She found her cell phone on the kitchen table and scanned her favorites for Liz's number. Her hands were trembling so much she couldn't tap the right spot on the screen. Finally, the call went through and Liz answered with her doctor's voice.

"Elizabeth Stolz."

"Liz! I need you to come right away."

"Are you all right?" Liz asked anxiously.

"Yes, I'm fine. But I dropped my mother's ring into the garbage disposal."

"I'll be right there. I just picked up Maggie from church. Do you have tools?"

"Yes, I have the toolbox you put together for me."

"Okay. Don't worry. I'll be there in a few minutes."

Erika sat down at the kitchen table. She put her face in her hands and cried.

She wiped her eyes with the back of her hand when she heard Liz's truck pulling into the extra parking space next to her garage. Moments later, two pairs of feet were running up the stairs.

Maggie, dressed in her Sunday best, gave her a sympathetic look.

"What happened?" asked Liz.

"I was cleaning my mother's engagement ring. I put it in a whiskey glass. I must have knocked it into the garbage disposal. I don't remember doing it, but I put some scraps in, and now I can't find the glass or the ring."

"Let's see what's going on," said Liz, opening the door to the sink cabinet. She used the flashlight on her phone to illuminate the space below. "Jesus. That thing is an antique!" Gingerly, she got to her knees to survey the situation. She pulled the electric plug to the disposal. "Where are your tools?"

"In the basement."

Liz left to get them. Maggie patted Erika's arm. "Don't worry. Liz will get it out," she said confidently.

"I was such a fool," said Erika. "I should have brought the ring to the jeweler!"

"We all do stupid things. It will be okay."

"Thank you for coming right away. I'm sure you have other things to do today."

Maggie's hazel eyes engaged hers. "There's nothing more important than helping a friend. That's what we're here for."

Liz came back, lugging the heavy toolbox. She searched through the tools until she found a pair of rachet pliers. She asked Maggie to hold a flashlight over her shoulder and tried to open the nut under the disposal. Erika could see the muscles in her arms and shoulder strain as she tried to unscrew it. "Fuck! It's seized!" Liz threw the pliers into the toolbox. "I need some penetrating lubricant. The hardware store should have it. I'll be right back."

Erika heard her feet pounding down the porch stairs. A moment later, the truck roared down the road.

"Sit down," said Maggie. "It will be a few minutes."

Erika took a seat. Maggie massaged her shoulders. "Relax. Worrying isn't going to change anything."

"I know. You are both so good to come at a moment's notice." The tears came again.

"Stop. You know Liz loves you and would do anything for you."

Erika nodded.

"Why was the ring off your finger anyway?"

Erika swallowed hard. "I was cleaning it. I was going to give it to Lucy tonight at the cast party."

"Your mother's engagement ring? Are going to propose? Why didn't you tell us?"

"It was a surprise. She enlisted all of you in her scheme to make her grand announcement. Turnabout is fair play."

"I don't know about that, but congratulations!" Maggie hugged Erika's shoulders.

"Thank you, dear," said Erika, patting Maggie's arm.

The truck roared back into the empty parking space. Liz's rapid steps came up the stairs. She knelt in front of the open cabinet and sprayed the aerosol on the seized joint. She sat on her heels while she waited for the penetrating oil to work. "Keep your fingers crossed this thing doesn't break off. If it does I'm going to have to replace the whole fucking unit. It wasn't my plan to spend the rest of the day doing plumbing." She checked her watch. Erika smiled at the fact that her surgeon-plumber wore a gold Cartier. Liz grimaced as she tried again to loosen the plug. "Goddamn! It's moving. Give me a bowl to catch the contents."

Erika jumped up and gave her a steel mixing bowl. Liz reached in and unscrewed the plug and everything in the disposal oozed into the bowl. Liz brought it to the kitchen table. She pulled something out of the bag from the hardware store—long forceps on a carded package. She tore it open and dug around in the muck in the bowl. As Liz gingerly picked out fragments of glass and arranged them on a plate, Erika realized she was observing Liz at a kind of surgery. Finally, the forceps brought up a mangled piece of gold. Erika's hand flew to her mouth.

"Paper towel," ordered Liz, inspecting the gold in the light from the window. Maggie pulled a piece off the roll near the sink. Liz placed the gold fragments on the towel. She ran some water in the bowl. A moment later, the forceps brought up the sapphire. Liz inspected it in the light. "There's no damage to the stone, but the ring is obviously shot." She laid the sapphire on the towel. "I know someone who might be able to do something with the pieces, but not today. It's Sunday."

"Erika was going to propose today. Now, there's no ring." Maggie raised her hand and looked at her own diamond ring.

"Don't even think it," warned Liz. Maggie instantly dropped her hand to her side.

"This is a disaster!" said Erika.

"Not yet," Liz said, a smile forming on her face. "I have an idea."

"That was my mother's engagement ring. My father especially gave it to me for this purpose!" said Erika, throwing up her hands.

"But it's not the only heirloom ring in the world," said Liz.

"What do you mean?"

"Come home with us and I'll show you. You need to get your car anyway." Liz picked up the sapphire and the mangled pieces of gold and carefully wrapped them up in the paper towel. "Put this in a safe place, and I mean, *safe*."

While Liz replaced the plug in the garbage disposal, Erika carefully wrapped the fragments in plastic wrap and put them in the drawer with her jewelry. On the way to Liz's house, Erika sat in the backseat of the truck, gazing out the window and feeling miserable.

"Come in," said Liz. I want to show you something."

They went inside, and Liz ran up the two flights of stairs to their bedroom. A few minutes later, she returned with a black, velvet-covered ring box. It was faded and dusty. Liz rubbed it against the sleeve of her T-shirt.

"This ring belonged to my grandmother. When my grandparents emigrated in the 1920s, they had nothing. When they married, their rings were gold wire. My grandmother was the superintendent of the apartment building they bought as an investment. The income from the building kept the design business going through the depression. She shoveled coal and cleaned the stairs on her hands and knees. When my grandfather became a success, a self-made millionaire, he bought her a diamond ring to show his appreciation. My grandmother was a simple woman and never wore it. It's a nice stone. My grandfather knew people in the jewelry business. They don't find first-grade diamonds of this size anymore." Liz opened the faded velvet-covered box.

"My God!" Maggie exclaimed. "It's huge!"

"I can't take this," protested Erika. "It must be worth a fortune!"

"I'm sure it is, but because it's my grandmother's, I'd never sell it." She picked up Erika's hand and put the box in her palm.

"I couldn't possibly—"

"Yes, you can, and you will," said Liz looking intently into Erika's eyes. "Take it."

"I'll just borrow it until I can get the other ring fixed."

"No, you won't. I want you to give this ring to Lucy. If you were marrying any other woman, I wouldn't give it to you, but because it's Lucy, it's yours to give her. My grandmother would be happy to know it went to a good home." Liz's eyes were glistening, but she blinked hard and looked away.

"Thank you," said Erika in a whisper. "You have no idea how much this means to me."

"Oh, I think I do," said Liz, gazing at Maggie, who nodded. "And Carats by the Bay can probably make something beautiful with that stone from your mother's ring. They're the best jeweler in town."

***

Erika dressed carefully in a shimmering grey silk dress she'd bought especially for this occasion. Lucy would be all dressed up for the show. She didn't want to look shabby next to her.

Erika took special care with her hair and her makeup. She looked at herself in the full-length mirror behind the bedroom door and hoped Lucy would approve.

She wore flats to drive but had thrown her heels behind her seat. She headed to the rectory to pick up Emily. She'd texted that she was on the way. By the time Erika arrived, the girl was waiting on the concrete landing at the back door. She looked beautiful, a taller and younger version of her mother. When she was fully grown, she would be just as stunning.

Emily climbed into the passenger seat. "Thanks for coming for me," she said.

"Of course, I would come for you. Haven't I these past two nights?"

"I still appreciate it."

"You're welcome," said Erika, nodding in approval.

"You look really nice," said Emily.

"So do you."

Erika navigated the congestion on Route 1. She glanced at the dashboard clock and hoped they would make it in time. They had guaranteed seats, so that wasn't a problem, but she wanted to make sure Lucy saw them when the show started.

"There's something I have to tell you, Emily," said Erika while they were stopped at a light. "I love your mother."

"I know," said Emily.

"I'm going to ask her to marry me."

"I hoped you would."

"Tonight."

Emily nodded. "Good."

"That will make me your stepmother. Is that all right with you?"

"Will it make Professor Bultmann my step-grandfather?"

Erika thought for a moment. "Yes, I suppose it will."

"Then it's all right."

Erika laughed and remembered the old mathematical adage, "there are many valid ways to prove a theorem."

They walked from the VIP parking lot into the theatre. The old building was a landmark that went back to the 1930s. It was an essential feature of the Webhanet landscape with its flags on the roof, carefully manicured lawn, and trimmed hedges.

Their seats were in the third row, not the front, because the acoustics were better a little further back. Liz and Tom were already in their seats. Liz was wearing an elegant, long dress. In another era that never would have shocked Erika. Liz's designer mother had brought her up to move easily among the social elite of New York City and Westchester County. It had served Liz well when she was chief of surgery at Yale. Erika knew Liz hated to dress up, but, when called upon, she could always look the part.

Tom was wearing a tuxedo and black tie. Erika leaned over to whisper in his ear. "You're looking quite dapper tonight, Dr. Simmons."

"Thank you, Professor Bultmann, so are you. I hear it will be a very special occasion." The bastard winked. Erika was startled at first, but she winked back.

"Not a word!"

"No, never!"

Erika looked up and saw her father entering the row. "How did he get here?"

"I brought him," said Liz.

"You told him?"

"Of course. I knew he wouldn't want to miss this."

The house lights dimmed. Tony Roselli came on stage and walked to the microphone in the corner.

"Good evening, ladies and gentleman. I want to welcome you to our Labor Day Gala to benefit the Playhouse and the Hobbs Women's Shelter. We have two exceptional talents tonight, Maggie Fitzgerald, of Broadway fame and Lucille Bartlett, formerly a principal soprano of the Metropolitan Opera.

"Both of these beautiful ladies are cornerstones of our community here in Southern Maine. Professor Fitzgerald is emeritus at the University of New England as well as NYU. She teaches at York Community College and coaches the drama club at Hobbs High. She's also on the board of the Playhouse and the State Theater. Reverend Bartlett, known to her congregation as Mother Lucy, is the rector at St. Margaret's by the Sea Parish in Hobbs. Both of these grandes dames of the theater have generously given of their time to benefit the Playhouse and the shelter. There will be a collection during intermission. Please give generously. And now, without further ado, the Webhanet Playhouse Labor Day Gala!"

The theater went black. Then a spotlight shone on center stage. Maggie and Lucy, glamorous in long gowns, their rhinestone necklaces glittering, entered from opposite ends of the stage to thunderous applause. They joined hands under the spotlight and took a little bow. Erika had seen this moment repeated now for the third time, but her heart still swelled with pride. As the applause continued, the ladies bowed, embraced, and bowed again. Then the orchestra began to play, "Ohio."

Emily reached out and took Erika's hand. "My mom is beautiful, isn't she?"

"Yes, she is," said Erika, smiling.

The numbers went by. Erika was glad someone was videotaping this last performance because she wanted to remember it years from now. Lucy and Maggie were perfect—every word, every note, every gesture. Erika reminded herself that they were professionals who had reached the highest ranks of their craft. They might be stars of the past, but they were no less disciplined and talented than in their prime.

Maggie was at her entertaining best. Looking down the row, she saw how proud Liz was, sitting on the edge of her seat whenever Maggie sang. Lucy's arias from operetta and solos from Broadway shows gave Erika shivers. She wondered if the audience had even an inkling of how special this performance was.

The applause and encores seemed to go on forever. At the final curtain call, bouquets were delivered to the stars. Lucy pulled out a red rose and threw it in Erika's direction. Emily caught it. She handed it to Erika. "It was for you," she said. Then Lucy threw another one. This time Erika caught it.

"This one's for you," she said, handing it to Emily.

It took a long time for the theater to clear. The cast party was being held in the room below the theater. There was no hope of getting near the main stairs until the crowd dissipated. Meanwhile, Tom kept Stefan entertained. Emily was asking Erika questions about the music she'd heard on stage, about Broadway, and the musicals she'd seen. Liz was browsing the internet on her phone.

Finally, the doors opened behind the stage and the stagehands came out to strike the sets. Liz looked up. "We can go down now." She led them down the rear stairs behind the stage, taking Stefan's arm to help him navigate the narrow steps.

The music was loud. The orchestra had re-established itself downstairs, where there was a small practice theater. Waiters moved through the crowd delivering champagne. This was a cast party in the grand old tradition.

Tony was still playing MC. He called Maggie and Lucy to the stage. The orchestra launched into "All that Jazz" from *Chicago*. Maggie belted out the number. Then Lucy joined in.

Erika led Emily to the buffet to help her get food and filled a plate for her father. The orchestra played numbers from the show and the stars came to the stage in turn. They started taking requests. Lucy sang "Climb Every Mountain" from *The Sound of Music*. Maggie sang her signature theme from *Les Miserables*: "I Dreamed a Dream."

The musicians stopped for a break, and Erika was grateful. Her ears were ringing. She watched her father placidly chewing the food she'd selected for him.

"Something unfortunate happened today," she said.

"I know. Elizabeth told me."

"Are you angry?"

"No, I know you will take care of it."

"Are you disappointed I won't use Mutti's ring?"

Stefan shook his head. "It's a thing, not really important. You know better."

"Liz gave me her grandmother's ring."

"That is love too." Stefan bit into a tea sandwich.

Tony approached the microphone. "May I have your attention, please!" Erika's heart pounded. She'd asked him to find the most opportune moment, and now it had arrived. "I have an important announcement to make."

Erika looked at the crowd. All of the arts people of Hobbs and Webhanet were there. The Webhanet and Hobbs police force who directed traffic for the shows were invited, along with the volunteer ushers and ticket takers, all of the cast and crew, the board and patrons of the Playhouse. She'd have quite an audience.

"Your attention, please!" Tony said more insistently.

The crowd finally settled down.

"Lucy, will you come out on stage, please?" Lucy came out to a standing ovation. Tony's eyes searched the crowd. "Erika, we corralled her for you. You'd better come up here. Quick!"

Erika's heart was thumping in her chest. Somehow, she got to her feet and propelled herself toward the stage. She climbed the stairs. She hated being under spotlights, but there she was.

Tony's baritone was magnified through the microphone. "Everybody pay close attention now. I think Erika has something important to say." He walked across the stage and gave Erika the microphone.

Lucy's eyes were wide. Erika approached her, carrying the microphone.

"Lucy, you were magnificent tonight. I loved watching you on stage. You sang so beautifully."

There was an enthusiastic round of applause.

Erika licked her lips and took a deep breath. She could do this. Although she wasn't a natural actress, she could pull it off. She felt the little velvet box snug in her hand.

Lucy looked puzzled and curious, but she stood attentively, waiting to see what would happen next. Maggie came on stage and put her arm around her. Out of the corner of her eye, Erika saw Liz and Emily coming up the stairs to the stage. They stood beside Tony.

"Lucy..." As always, when Erika spoke into a microphone, the sound of her magnified voice startled her. "Lucy, I'd get down on my knees, but they don't cooperate anymore, so I hope you don't mind if I stand."

Now, Lucy looked anxious. Maggie gripped her tighter.

"Lucy Bartlett, you are a very special woman. You light up the lives of so many, but especially mine. You have illuminated some of my darkest days. I want your radiant light in my life forever. I love you with all my heart, and I would be honored if you would marry me."

There. It was out.

Lucy's hands flew up to cover her eyes.

Erika handed off the microphone to Tony. "Oh, Lucy, please don't cry." Erika's voice was strong enough to carry through the room.

There was a collective. "Awww."

Maggie gave Lucy a little nudge forward.

"Please say, yes," Erika urged, opening the ring box and offering it to Lucy. "Please?"

Lucy fell into her arms. "Yes," she said. "Yes!"

The crowd gave them a standing ovation as Erika slipped the ring on Lucy's finger.

Then people were clapping Erika's shoulders and shaking her hand. Lucy had been pulled away. A knot of women had gathered around her to offer congratulations and admire the ring. Lucy was laughing and blushing.

Across the room, Erika caught her attention. The green eyes smiled first. Then Lucy's lips curved into a perfect smile so radiant the whole room seemed to blaze with brilliant light.

About the Author

Elena Graf has published three historical novels set in Germany during the Weimar Republic and the Nazi era. *Lies of Omission*, the third book in the Passing Rites Series, won a Golden Crown Literary Society award for best historical fiction as well as a Rainbow Award. *Acts of Contrition* was also the recipient of a Rainbow Award. *High October*, the previous book in the Hobbs Series, was her first contemporary romance.

The author pursued a Ph.D. but ended up in the "accidental profession" of publishing, where she worked for almost four decades. She lives with her wife in coastal Maine.

If you liked this book and would like more stories about the people of Hobbs, Maine, write to Elena at elena.m.graf@gmail.com.

Also by Elena Graf

OCCASIONS OF SIN

For seven centuries, the German convent of Obberoth has been hiding the nuns' secrets—forbidden passions, scandalous manuscripts locked away, a ruined medical career, perhaps even a murder. In 1931, aristocratic physician, Margarethe von Stahle, is determined to lift the veil of secrecy surrounding her head nurse, Sister Augustine, only to find herself embroiled in multiple conflicts that threaten to unravel her orderly life.

LIES OF OMISSION

In 1938, the Nazis are imposing their doctrine of "racial hygiene" on hospitals and universities, forcing professors to teach false science and doctors to collaborate in a program to eliminate the mentally ill and handicapped. Margarethe von Stahle is desperately trying to find a way to practice ethical medicine. She has always avoided politics, but now she must decide whether to remain on the sidelines or act on her convictions.

ACTS OF CONTRITION

World War II has finally come to an end and Berlin has fallen. Nearly everything Margarethe von Stahle has sworn to protect has been lost. After being brutally abused by occupying Russian soldiers, Margarethe must rely on the kindness of her friends to survive. Fortunately, the American Army has brought her former protégée, Sarah Weber, back to Berlin. As Margarethe confronts painful events that occurred during the war, she must learn both to forgive and be forgiven.

HIGH OCTOBER

Liz Stolz and Maggie Fitzgerald were college roommates until Maggie confessed to her parents that she'd fallen in love with a woman. Maggie gave up her dream of becoming an actress and married her high school boyfriend. Liz became a famous breast surgeon. Maggie is performing in a summer stock production near the Maine town where Liz is now a general practitioner. When Maggie breaks her leg in a stage accident, she lands in Dr. Stolz's office. Is forty years too long to wait for the one you love?